Child's Play

CLARE NONHEBEL launched her novel-writing
career by becoming the joint winner of the first Betty
Trask Award for *Cold Showers* in 1984. Since then she
has written three highly praised novels, *The Partisan*,
Incentives and *Child's Play*. Her latest novel, *Eldred Jones*,
Lulubelle and the Most High is equally brilliant (Lion,
1998). Her recent non-fiction work, *Don't Ask Me to
Believe* (Lion, 1998), is an exploration of religious
experience.

Born in 1953, Clare was educated in London
and Salisbury. She graduated in French Studies from
Warwick University and has worked in social work,
public relations and journalism. She lives in London
with her husband Robin, a history teacher.

Also by Clare Nonhebel

FICTION
Cold Showers

The Partisan

Incentives

Eldred Jones, Lulubelle and the Most High

NON-FICTION
Healed and Souled
(by Ashuli: co-written with Joseph Stefanazzi)

Don't Ask Me to Believe

CLARE NONHEBEL

Child's Play

A LION BOOK

This book is a work of fiction and the story is
entirely a creation of the imagination. No parallel
between any events or persons is intended.

First published in 1991 by
Barrie & Jenkins Ltd,
Random Century House,
20 Vauxhall Bridge Road,
London SW1V 2SA

Published by
Lion Publishing plc
Sandy Lane West, Oxford, England
ISBN 0 7459 3811 6

First edition 1991
This paperback edition 1998
10 9 8 7 6 5 4 3 2 1 0

A catalogue record for this book is available
from the British Library

Printed and bound in Great Britain by
Caledonian International Book Manufacturing, Glasgow

Chapter One

Mrs Grenville was not racially prejudiced. She had, as she was fond of telling people at dinner parties, spent part of her childhood in the West Indies. 'Ah, Jamaica!' she would sigh expressively, somewhere between the smoked salmon and the dessert, implying that while the rest of the company might be grounded in dark, drizzly England on an unseasonal May night, her soul was aflame in the tropics.

To tell the truth, her impressions of Jamaica, even at the time, had not been very clear; she had been an unobservant child and now, as an unimaginative adult, she could not force colourful memories to rise to the surface. Faced with direct questions about the exact nature of the charm of Jamaica, she became vague. It was difficult to put into words, she sighed. Something in the *atmosphere*. Impossible to explain to anyone who had never actually *experienced* it.

This ruse usually left her with the aura of a woman of infinite horizons, without narrowing the questioner's focus to potentially tricky foreground details. She had only had one really nasty moment when a dinner guest, silent up to that point, had suddenly said, 'I spent nine months there myself in Sixty-four,' and began interrogating her about climate, politics, ecology, economics, national characteristics and culture.

Mrs Grenville had escaped with her reputation only by dabbing her eyes discreetly with her table napkin and murmuring, 'How it pains me still to remember!' Still, it had been a confrontation she did not wish to have repeated.

It was essential to Vera Grenville to sound authentic when she spoke about her time in Jamaica, for this was her only claim to anything exotic and her life now was so shamefully mundane. George was little help either. He was normally so reticent about his job at the Home Office that in the first few years of their marriage Vera had told all her acquaintances, in strict confidence, that George's work was 'terribly hush-hush'.

On the one occasion that someone had insisted on drawing George out on the subject of his work, however, it had become painfully obvious that what George did in the daytime was no more exciting than what George did in the evenings and at weekends. Vera had been mortified to overhear one of the ladies remark to her neighbour, in a piercing undertone, that George's job was 'not so much hush-hush as yawn-yawn, wouldn't you say, darling?'

Vera Grenville could imagine the same lady's comment if it were to become known that her own recollections of life in a tropical paradise were limited to a clear memory of her black nanny (who imitated Vera's mother so assiduously that she became hardly distinguishable from the expatriate Home Counties matrons who were her neighbours) making her wear white gloves whenever she was taken out to tea.

So when the Household Help agency had phoned to enquire whether the Grenvilles would consider a Jamaican woman as their next cook-housekeeper, Mrs Grenville saw an ideal opportunity to refresh her fund of West Indies stories.

'I should be only too delighted,' she had cooed into the receiver. 'You see, I am not racially prejudiced. I was brought up in Jamaica myself and I am quite accustomed to black servants. We took them for granted there.'

Really, it was providential. New acquaintances might even suppose, romantically, that the housekeeper was an old retainer slavishly devoted to the Grenville family, who had insisted on following little Vera to England and . . . no, that wouldn't work, of course. An old retainer would, realistically, be in her eighties by now. The Household Help agency provided a range of unsuitable people, but not eighty-year-olds.

Mrs Grenville hesitated for a moment when the agency lady

told her that the prospective housekeeper was only twenty-one, unmarried, and had a four-year-old daughter. On second thoughts, though, Vera decided that the child would be a bonus. It would only contribute to the exotic ambience of the Grenville household and the liberal reputation of Mrs Grenville herself to have a West Indian child living there as well as a West Indian housekeeper. And it was not as though Mrs Grenville would have to see much of them. They would have their own room, in the other wing, and Sonia's work would confine her mainly to the kitchen.

As for eating food prepared by black hands and having a sing-song voice answering the phone – well, Mrs Grenville was just an expert at taking that kind of thing in her stride, and her husband, following her example, would learn to have the same high-minded indifference to it. And the child might prove quite useful at running small errands.

It was not because they were racially prejudiced, then, that the Grenvilles now stood on the gravel outside the front door of their imposing house and waited for Barnes, the gardener-handyman, to stow Sonia's small stock of possessions in the boot of the Volvo.

How could racial prejudice be the motive for dismissal when Sonia had, disappointingly, turned out to be hardly more steeped in Jamaican culture than Mrs Grenville herself? Raised in Birmingham, Ilford and Luton by a series of English foster parents, Sonia retained only the sketchiest memories of Jamaican 'white sands, hot streets, and trees that scratched your legs when you climbed them to see the sea'. She had failed dismally in providing her employer with promising material for dinner party conversation.

A reliable worker, Mrs Grenville had assured the agency when they phoned to check on the arrangement after the one-month trial period of Sonia's employment at the Sussex house. Yes, a quiet, unobtrusive personality. Yes, a competent cook, a thorough cleaner, an efficient organizer of linen cupboards and preparer of guest rooms. Willing, yes. Efficient, certainly. And – an unexpected bonus – creative, clever with her hands, a deft flower-arranger and an imaginative designer of cakes for all kinds of special occasions.

Why sack such a treasure? The agency would be sure to ask, and Mrs Grenville would have to come up with a plausible explanation or they might not send her a replacement. Future employees might not wish to risk taking a post with a woman who had dismissed her last housekeeper at a few hours' notice, with no reference and no time allowed to make arrangements for alternative accommodation.

Mrs Grenville did not want to gain a bad reputation. This was partly why she was allowing Barnes to help with the luggage and letting George drive Sonia and Lois to the station. No one should say she had just thrown them out. Loss of job was loss of home, in this case, and she did not want to be accused of making a mother and child homeless.

What reason should she give? Anything except the truth, which was unspeakable, unthinkable even. If the agency had known what Mrs Grenville knew now . . . If Mrs Grenville had only known in the beginning, then none of this would have happened. But how could she have even suspected such a thing? She may have been naive, of course, but how could a decent-living woman with a respectable upbringing (even if some of it had been in the West Indies) have imagined that anyone could be capable of . . . ?

No. She would tell the agency that her willing, efficient employee had, during her six-month period in the Grenville house, unfortunately turned lazy, as so many did. The agency would believe her. There would be no problem. And to write a glowing reference about the good work Sonia had done at first would be dishonest, she would tell them. She simply could not, in all conscience, bring herself to do it. Such practices only encouraged these people.

'Get out of my house!' she wanted to scream as she stood on the steps now, a dumpy, compact figure clad in a grey tweed skirt and jacket with a tie-necked cream silk blouse revealing smooth pearls around a slightly wrinkled neck. Unyieldingly thick ankles ended without warning in a pair of elegant shoes,

4

giving her feet the same note of surprise as her face – its wide-open blue eyes and plucked high-arched eyebrows endowing its owner with a permanently startled look. 'Get out of my house! Get out of my sight and mind!' But of course she said nothing of the sort.

Instead, in a cool voice, she said, 'Where on earth has Barnes got to? He's taking his time.'

'He's fetching their things, dear. Shall I go and hurry him along a bit?'

'No, George, stay here,' she said sharply. The situation was awkward enough without her husband leaving her alone with the silent Sonia and the blank-faced little girl, who covered her eyes with one hand and clutched a small grubby rag doll in the other.

'Here is Barnes now,' George said. He spoke in a slightly hushed voice, as one does after a tragedy. It was the voice he reserved for funerals and other socially embarrassing occasions.

George did not like to be embarrassed. He wished this whole unpleasant episode would be over as soon as possible, so he could go quietly back to work and forget about it. It was essential to get them out of the house immediately, there was no doubt about that, but he wished there had been some other way, especially as Sonia was a competent cook and it was bound to be some time before his wife could secure the services of a replacement. And the child's face bothered him. The whole thing was very tricky.

Everyone turned to watch Barnes, a wiry man in close-fitting faded denims and a check shirt with rolled-up sleeves, as he strode across the gravel carrying a laundry bag, a dust-bin liner tied with string and two Sainsbury carrier bags. A small teddy bear peeped over the top of one but Barnes, looking straight ahead, ignored this indignity. Lois, peeping back through her fingers, kept an eye on it.

Seeing the final bag tossed into the boot of the Volvo, Sonia told Lois, 'Get in the car now,' but the child, still covering her face with one hand, moved over to one of the two deep base-ment areas in front of the house and, leaning over the lower railing, threw her doll down into it. Uncovering her face then, she turned to look at the adults one by one and said, 'I've lost my doll.'

Sonia, already distressed by the day's events, became enraged. 'You haven't lost it!' she cried. 'You've thrown it away! What did you do that for?'

Lois, impassive, still looked from face to face. 'Get it back for me,' she said.

George and his wife exchanged a glance. Really, thought Mrs Grenville, this is the limit.

'How can I go down there and get it back for you?' Sonia demanded. 'There's no steps.'

Lois turned to Barnes. Her hand was halfway up to her face now, but she looked him in the eyes. 'He'll get the ladder and go down there,' she said confidently.

Barnes turned on his heel.

'You may return to your work now, Barnes,' said Mrs Grenville.

George opened the back passenger door of the Volvo. 'Righty oh,' he said, with forced joviality. 'All present and correct. Off we go.'

Lois stared at him. 'I want my dolly back,' she said clearly.

'Get in the car, Lois,' Sonia said. 'It's too late now. You'll have to do without it.'

As the car turned out of the long, tree-hung driveway on to the public road, no one looked back and nobody watched them go.

Mrs Grenville, already in the house with the front door closed, was dialling the number of the Household Help agency. Barnes, in the garden, hacked at the roots of a rose bush past its prime and wrenched it from the ground. The rag doll lay, passive and abandoned, in its basement grave.

A month later, passing the area and forgetting not to look down, Barnes would catch sight of it, soaked, muddy and lichened green, and would think, It's time I got rid of that, but then would leave it there still, trusting the passage of time to do the job for him.

At the station, glad to be busy, and relieved that the awkward situation was nearly banished, George bought tickets, carried the plastic bags, bought chocolate for Lois, gave Sonia an envelope.

Her eyes lit up. 'A reference?' she said.

'Money,' said Grenville. 'Forty pounds. For emergencies.'

'I won't get another job with no reference,' Sonia said. 'Please. Just write a few lines. It would make all the difference.'

'Oh,' murmured George into his moustache. 'Can't be done, you know. My wife's department, domestics. Besides, any prospective employer would ring to check with her first, don't you know. Bound to.'

'What will she tell the agency?' Sonia asked. She had hold of his sleeve, or he would have walked away.

'I don't know,' he said honestly. He knew that Vera would think of something. He hoped she would deal with it without telling him. He preferred not to be involved. He was not involved, damn it. He wished this clinging woman would understand that. He had thought her a sensible girl – fun, and not too sensitive. Now the damn woman turned out to be neurotic like all the rest. George took two steps away.

'Must get back,' he said. 'Best of luck, my dear.'

'Luck with what?' said Sonia. 'Going on the streets? Is that where you and your wife hope I'll end up?'

George was profoundly shocked. He turned his back.

'Well, I'll tell you for nothing,' Sonia said, raising her voice (and thank God there was nobody on the platform, George thought), 'I'll starve before I do that. Me and Lois both.'

George descended the steps, disappearing under the canopy marked Platform 1 and Station Exit. When she saw his bald head re-emerge from the subway, the other side of the rail track, Sonia wept. Lois held on to the belt of her mother's jeans. With her other hand she covered her face.

They heard the noise of the Volvo leaving the car-park. When the noise died away, the small country station was very quiet. Sonia realized she had not asked the time of the next train. Leaving the bags on the platform, she led Lois into the waiting-room. Averting her eyes from the graffiti, she sat down on the bench, pulled the child on to her lap and prepared to wait.

Chapter Two

Lois came to life on the train. Sonia, staring out of the window and seeing only Mrs Grenville in that blood-chilling interview early this morning, took a while to notice the change in the child.

Not only did she take both hands away from her face in order to watch the fast-moving green and brown scenery from her kneeling position on the train seat; she also made audible comments about lambs and sheep and telegraph poles, and when a fellow passenger supplied answers to the questions that Sonia did not even hear, Lois turned and smiled at the woman.

With a shock Sonia realized how long it had been since she had seen Lois smile. She had begun to take it for granted that her daughter was a shy, solemn child whose peephole view of life through fingers parted slightly over her eyes was 'just her way'.

Now she saw Lois drop this mannerism, she was struck by how unnatural it was, and forced herself to remember that Lois had only adopted it fairly recently – shortly after they had moved in with the Grenvilles, in fact.

She reached out a hand to the little girl's head, covered in tiny black pigtails plaited from sections of Lois's firm springy hair, parted in chequerboard patterns while she slept. Lois would never sit still for long enough to endure her mother's creative hands weaving new hairstyles for her, but she slept soundly at nights and never stirred while Sonia parted, combed, twisted and ribboned her hair or moved her head from side to side. She even seemed to find it soothing. If she was restless at nights she would often settle into calm sleep, breathing rhythmically, as soon as Sonia began work on her hair.

'Okay, Lois?' Sonia asked the little girl, and was rewarded with a smile. 'You like the train, huh?'

Lois threw herself back in the seat and looked up at her mother. 'Where is it taking us?' she asked.

'To London. Victoria station.'

'Why are we going there?'

Why indeed? A good question. 'To seek our fortunes,' Sonia said lightly. 'The streets are paved with gold – didn't you know?'

Lois frowned at her. Already, at four years old, she knew that fortune and gold were not designed for them. 'Why really?' she persisted.

'To find somewhere to stay, and some work to do,' Sonia amended. It was silly to tell the child stories; children deserved the truth. About almost everything, anyway.

'When are we going home again?' Lois asked.

'That place isn't home any more,' Sonia told her. 'Home is the next place.'

'Why?'

'We don't always live in the same place, do we? Remember before we went to Sussex we lived on that farm?'

'No.'

'Yes, we did. You remember, Lois. With the goats. And that little boy you used to play with. Christopher. And his granny, Margaret, used to give you sweets.'

'No.'

'Well, what do you remember? Before we lived with the Grenvilles?' Children's memories were different, Sonia reflected. Lois had a knack of recalling details which seemed insignificant to adults, while disregarding their context.

'Don't know.' Lois was puzzled.

'You didn't think we always lived with the Grenvilles, ever since you were born?' When the child didn't answer, Sonia sighed. 'It seemed like that, I suppose. It seemed like that to me at times, as well – as though we'd been there for ever and we always would be.' She hooked an arm round Lois's neck and sank her chin on to the top of her head. Lois looked out of the window.

The woman who had spoken to Lois left the train at the next station, and other people got into the carriage. After this station, the scenery began to change from countryside to sprawling city outreaches: no longer acres of fields with occasional villages but acres of houses with ever-tinier back gardens, ever-diminishing patches of muddy green. Lois slept.

Sonia let her sleep until the train had pulled into Victoria station and the carriage had emptied. Already passengers for the return journey were pushing their way on to the train, scarcely leaving time for the others to alight. For a minute Sonia considered the idea of letting Lois sleep on, letting the train move off, letting themselves be carried endlessly back and forth, postponing the moment of decision.

'Lois! Wake up. This is where we get off.'

Lois stared blankly. The compartment was filling up. Sonia panicked. 'Wake up! Get off the train! We'll get charged for the fare if we stay on.' She tugged Lois by the arm and the child immediately put both hands over her eyes.

'Don't start that!' Sonia shouted, exasperated. 'I need you to carry some of these bags.' Passengers looked at her and looked away. She picked up Lois, who went rigid, and almost threw her off the train. Finding herself on her own in the dark, behind the shutters of her hands, Lois screamed and tottered forwards, close to the gap between platform and train.

A woman grabbed her.

'Thanks!' Sonia gasped, her arms full of carrier bags.

'Very dangerous, letting a young child do that!' the woman proclaimed. 'Totally irresponsible! These young mothers have no idea,' she informed her companion. Both were beyond middle age, with rinsed hair and comfortable shoes, and carried bulging leather handbags.

Sonia gritted her teeth. 'Perhaps you could help me,' she said. 'I've got my hands full,' but the women moved on and selected another carriage.

The secret was not to panic, not to let the words 'I can't cope' even enter her mind. She would cope; there was no other choice. Not coping meant seeing Lois taken away from her and put into care, and without Lois she had no life, no reason to go on coping.

'You know what we're going to do?' Sonia said. 'We're going to go through that gate and hand in these tickets and then we'll sit on the station and have a Coke.'

Lois brightened. The fingers of one hand parted, revealing a small flash of white eye.

'I can't hold your hand,' Sonia said. 'You'll have to follow me. Keep your hands off your face and look where you're going.'

The journey from the train to the ticket gate and through to the kiosk on the station concourse took twenty minutes. Sonia had to keep stopping to put down the bags and change hands, while Lois, still covering her eyes, stumbled along with three fingers hooked into the handle of one of the carrier bags.

Sonia left the bags in a heap, sat Lois on a bench, and bought a paper cup of Coke, with two straws. The two of them drank. Refreshed, Lois sat up straight and began to assess her surroundings, covering her eyes only when somebody glanced in her direction.

'What are we going to do now?' she asked.

'Find somewhere to stay for tonight,' Sonia said. She tried to keep her voice calm, matter-of-fact.

'Are we going to Aunty Sue's?' asked Lois.

'Aunty Sue doesn't live in this country now. She went back to live in Jamaica. I told you.'

'Are we going to live in Jamaica?'

'No.' For a moment she wished it could be as simple as that. If Aunty Sue had been a real relative she might have said, on parting, not only, 'I'll miss you and that precious child,' but, 'Why don't you come home and live with me?' Home.

'Where is our new home now?' Lois was right on cue.

'We haven't found it yet. That's why we have to get moving. The rush hour will start in two hours, so we'll try to get our travelling in before then. Will you sit here with the bags while I find a phone? I'll come back in a few minutes.' But Lois was already clambering off the seat and clutching her hand. It was too much to ask.

From one of the bags Sonia pulled a length of Lois's hair ribbon and used it to tie the two carrier bags into one. She put the dustbin bag over her shoulder. The blue plastic laundry bag sat on the ground, its handle too short to go over her head like a nosebag, its contents too bulky to share the hand that held the dustbin bag.

She dropped the bin bag, picked up the laundry bag, caught hold of the bin bag by the neck and dragged it behind her. Lois held on to the bin bag and followed, tripping over it and pulling on it, adding to the weight.

The phone kiosks were near the station exit. Sonia deposited the bags near a vacant kiosk and passers-by kicked them, tripped and swore as they rushed past. She pushed the bags into the kiosk and leaned across them to reach the dial. Lois clung to her legs.

'Directory enquiries? Household Help agency, please. Yes? Okay. Thank you.' She muttered the number under her breath, pushed more coins into the box, dialled again. 'Hello. Is that the Household Help agency? Can I speak to Barbara? Barbara . . . No, I don't know her surname. She got me my last job, six months ago. She left? Okay. Who can help me? . . . Thank you. Hello? Hello? Yes, can you help me please? I have just left my previous job and I want to find another post as quickly as possible. At the moment I have nowhere to go, so I really need something today. Can you help? Oh no . . . sorry, the money is about to run out . . .'

She replaced the receiver and hailed a passer-by. 'Have you got change for the . . . Excuse me.' People sidestepped her outstretched arm and increased their pace. 'Please,' Sonia said firmly, accosting a tall man. 'I need change for the phone urgently.' Reluctantly he fished in his pockets, handed her one ten-pence coin, waved away the coppers she offered in return and sped on.

Sonia dialled again. 'Household Help agency? I got cut off and I only have ten p now, so if you could pass me to someone quickly . . . Who am I speaking to, please? Tracy. Tracy, my name is Sonia. I had a job through your agency, which I left today, and I need something else really quickly. I only have this one ten p for the phone, so I'm sorry to rush you. If you like I can call at the agency this afternoon, but if you could look something out for me and perhaps fix me an appointment with the people . . .

'Reason for leaving? Reason for leaving was that I was dismissed with no reason given, and now I have nowhere to go, me and my little girl. Yes, I know that makes it more complicated, but I am willing to take anything you can find. Cleaning, nannying, whatever anyone wants, but I need to start very soon.

'No, no reference; that's what I'm saying. Can the agency give me a reference? Previous employers? No, the previous employer was an old lady. She died. Okay, but look. Sonia . . . I'll spell the surname. The money is running out. Would you call me back? Would you take this number and call . . . oh no!' Sonia repeated her performance of accosting strangers. By the third attempt she was desperate, grabbed a teenage girl by the shoulders and demanded, 'Please give me money for the phone!' The girl, alarmed, pulled away from her and ran.

Finally, with twenty pence wrested from an African man who knew very little English, she tried again.

'Tracy? Yes, that's right, the employer's name was Grenville. How did you know that? She's been on the phone to you? Already? The . . . She told you what? Lazy? That's not true! I worked really hard! She told me herself I was a very good . . . Why? Why do you have to take her word for it? I'm your client too. I know she's the one who pays . . . This isn't fair, you know.

'The reason she gave me? She wouldn't give me a reason. No, nothing. She said words like unsuitable and the arrangement not working out, but she wouldn't be definite. I'm telling you, she asked to see me this morning and she threw me out.

No notice, no reference. Yes, maybe you will have to look into this, but please find me another job first. I have nowhere to go.

'I know, without a reference . . . I know the system, but Tracy, put yourself in my place. Write me a reference from the agency, just enough to get me another job . . . Okay, you can't. More than your job's worth, I see.

'Well listen, Tracy, my money's about to run out, I have a four-year-old child and nowhere to sleep tonight; tell me, as a human being, what am I supposed to do? No, I can't hang on; there is two p left in this box. What? Women's refuge? Where? Where is it? Samaritans? Okay. Okay, Tracy, thank you. God bless you, Tracy. Thank you.'

Begging, she thought disgustedly, putting the phone down as she was cut off in mid-word; begging and pleading with some young girl who shouldn't even know about things like homelessness and obviously didn't want to. That's what I've come to, Sonia thought: begging ten-pence coins off strangers, pleading with agency people, dragging round my belongings in dustbin bags. What next?

'Operator, please give me the number of the Samaritans. Thank you. Okay, I got that . . . Hello, Samaritans? Thank you. Can you tell me where to find a women's refuge for myself and my little girl? . . . Sorry? Victoria station is where we are at the moment. Is there somewhere near? Mostly full, except for real emergencies? We have nowhere to stay: is that an emergency? At risk from physical violence in the home – no. There is no home. We were turned out today. No, not by my husband; I don't have a husband. It was a living-in house-keeping job. We were fired this morning, without any notice. No, we don't have any relatives. No, I don't know any friends who could take us in.

'Would you do that for me? That's very kind of you. How long will it take? Okay. God bless you. Thank you very much. I'll phone you back in twenty minutes. Bye now.'

'Sonia,' said Lois. 'Can we have something to eat?'

'Hang on a minute, child. Listen, this lady is going to phone round some refuge places for us to see if anyone will have us to stay – right? We have to wait here twenty minutes and then phone her back. I'm too tired to carry these bags back to that drinks stall, so sit down here. Yes, it's dirty; it doesn't matter. Sit here with me and we'll wait the twenty minutes.'

Lois refused to get her red dress dirty. Sonia sat on the ground beside the phone booth with Lois on her lap and the bags all around them.

Lois soon became bored. 'Is it time for dinner yet?'

'We missed dinner. It's nearly time for tea. Are you very hungry?'

'I want to go to the toilet.'

'No. Not just now. Just wait a few minutes. Think about something else; take your mind off it.'

'I can't!'

'Lois! Listen, Lois, do something very important for me, something that really will help. Yes?'

'What is it?' Lois was interested despite herself. She uncovered her eyes. She looks exhausted; she had no lunch; it's all my fault, Sonia thought.

Aloud she said, 'I want you to pray – right? Pray for us to find a place to stay tonight. Okay?'

'How?'

'Like this. Put your hands together. Close your eyes. Then you say, "God help us." Ready?'

'Why?'

'Just do it, Lois. With me.'

'Why "God help us", Sonia?'

'Because if He doesn't, Lois, we're really stuck because we don't know anybody else.' She began to cry.

Lois removed her hands from her own eyes and placed them over Sonia's, as if to shield her from the public gaze. 'God help us,' she said obediently. 'Are you better now?'

Chapter Three

The news was good – or so it seemed at the time. A woman called Bella, who ran a refuge in Camberwell in south-east London, was prepared to take them in for a few nights. Sonia was to phone her, reversing the charges if necessary.

Sonia decided it was necessary. She had money, but no change. Tiredness was overwhelming her.

'I'll accept the charges, yes,' a brisk voice on the phone informed the operator. 'Sonia Leroy? The Samaritans said you'd be phoning. My name is Bella, and I'm in charge of the refuge. I asked you to phone first because we don't give out our address; we have to be very careful. So I'm going to have to ask you to agree not to let anyone know where it is. Okay?

'Now strictly speaking we don't take women and children who are homeless; if we did we'd be overrun. We're here for victims of domestic violence, but I understand in your case you've been forcibly thrown out of the home. Is that right?'

'Yes, my job . . . where we live . . .' Articulate until now, Sonia found her flow of words had ceased. Were there words to explain what had befallen them? Even Mrs Grenville had not found words to express something so terrible. 'We both know what I am referring to,' she had said. 'I won't demean the reputation of this house by spelling it out.'

'Was your employer violent?' Bella demanded.

'No,' Sonia said. 'Not violent, no.' Aggressive, hostile, threatening, sinister maybe, but no one could describe Mrs Grenville as violent; she was far too well brought up.

'What is your accent?' Bella demanded next. 'West Indian?'

'Yes.' She hadn't known she had an accent.

'Was the dismissal a case of racial prejudice?'

'No.' How much easier it would be to say yes! Why didn't she say it? It would solve everything. No, it would not. It would not explain the fact that Mrs Grenville had taken her on in the first place and employed her – apparently happily – for six months.

'Your employer was not colour prejudiced? You're sure?'

'No. I mean, yes they were prejudiced, but that wasn't the reason.'

'What was the reason?' Bella's voice was incisive. Sonia was sure she meant well, but she sounded uncomfortably like Mrs Grenville at this moment. Probably she was a very kind woman, though, who happened to sound abrupt on the phone. She must be kind, to be running a refuge for unloved women and children.

'The reason . . . she didn't give any reason. She asked to see me this morning and turned on me and told me to get out.'

'She must have said why,' Bella stated.

'She didn't.'

'No reason at all? Just "Get out of my house"?'

'Yes, that's right,' Sonia affirmed, though of course Mrs Grenville had said no such thing. 'I am sure you will agree with me,' was what she had actually said; 'I am sure you will agree with me that the only decent course of action would be for you to remove yourself and your child from my house im-mediately. I am prepared to be discreet about this matter, and you may be assured that no further action will be taken against you as long as you . . .'

'Sexual harassment?' Bella interrupted her recollections.

'What?' Sonia was taken aback.

'Your employer – was it only the woman, or was there a husband?'

'Yes, no . . . a couple,' Sonia stuttered.

'Was there sexual harassment from the husband? Is that why the wife dismissed you? Was there a sexual relationship?'

'No!' Sonia was outraged.

'All right, don't get indignant,' Bella said. 'It wouldn't be the first time, would it?'

'I wouldn't do that!' Sonia said. 'Just because I'm an un-married mother, you have no right to assume . . .' Oh Sonia, keep your big mouth closed, she told herself despairingly. Don't offend this woman!

Bella wasn't offended. She laughed. 'Keep your hair on!' she said. 'I didn't mean it wasn't the first time it had hap-pened to you. I meant it happens all the time – men taking advantage of women in their workplace.'

'Does it?' Maybe she was naive, but this had never occurred to her. She was there to do a job; the employer expected her to work hard, and paid her for it; she herself expected no trouble beyond the inevitable niggles over laying the table in exactly the way the employer required, or the invariable refusals to recognize her right to time off.

Had she been naive? No – no one in her right mind could have suspected George of anything remotely sexual. He had never, in the six months she was there, even managed to re-member her name but referred to her always as 'the house-keeper'; in his mind that was all she was. He might have noticed that periodically his housekeeper changed, but as long as his dinner was on the table George showed no interest in the person who had provided it.

'So there was no trouble of that nature from either employer while you were there?'

'No,' Sonia said.

'Ah.' Bella was puzzled, Sonia could tell that. She persisted, 'So she just told you to go, and refused to give any reason?'

'Yes.' Sonia was glad this conversation was on Bella's phone bill. Lois was fidgeting, twisting Sonia's belt loops round and round like a tourniquet till Sonia's waist was con-stricted. Leaning into the phone booth across the luggage on the ground, she was uncomfortable and wished the call would end and Bella would decide whether or not they qualified as victims and could have a bed for the night.

'You're not just being discreet?' Bella said suddenly. 'I mean, can you talk where you are? No one's preventing you from talking freely? The employers aren't there, are they?'

Sonia felt exasperated. 'I'm on Victoria station,' she said. What kind of world did Bella inhabit? Did she think the Grenvilles held her bound and gagged? Well, maybe they did in a sense. ('I'm warning you,' Mrs Grenville had said, 'that if you fail to respect your part of this agreement, you will find yourself in more trouble than you can possibly get yourself out of . . .')

'Oh yes,' Bella remembered. 'Look, lovey, you can tell me anything, you know. I'm not easily shocked and I've heard most things before. I'm not laying blame, but it does help if I know the circumstances; then we can work out exactly what kind of support you need.'

'Support' sounded alarming. It suggested dependence, which was something Sonia avoided. 'We just need somewhere to stay till I get another job,' she said quickly.

'Mmm.' Bella sounded doubtful. 'Well look, Sonia, come on over now. I can't guarantee how long we can put you up, because obviously we have to give priority to the real emergencies, the victims of battering, rape and so on. But we'll do what we can to help you get yourself back on your feet for the time you're with us.'

'Okay.' Sonia was in no position to bargain. Anyway, it would probably be all right. After years of social-service care Sonia was an expert on avoiding sympathetic counselling and probing questions. (The social worker's, 'Now Sonia, let's sit down and have a chat about how you're getting on in your new foster home,' had always been Sonia's cue to clam up, smile brightly and say nothing other than, 'Everything's fine.') Bella would be no problem, she was sure.

'Do you have money for the fare?' Bella asked. 'Good. Fine. Got something to write the address down? But please remember to throw it away afterwards, and let no one know where you're going.'

Perhaps I should swallow it, Sonia thought irreverently, and then take a cyanide pill to make sure I can't spill the secret under interrogation. She was beginning to suspect Bella of a relish for drama, but that was unfair of her: the precaution was surely justified.

'Now, directions for getting here from Victoria station,' Bella said. She was certainly thorough. Sonia could see that, if you were feeling you couldn't cope, it would be very tempting to lean on Bella.

She was probably solidly built with large shoulders which she encouraged people to cry on. But Sonia would not cry on Bella's shoulder, nor on anyone else's. In her experience the Bellas of the world took on everybody's cares and then suddenly looked for a shoulder to cry on themselves and found no one was strong enough to bear their accumulated weight. Then they got resentful and said, 'I who have helped everybody can find no one to help me.' Sonia had had a foster mother like that once – no, more than once. That was why she never let anyone see her cry, except Lois.

She listened with half an ear to Bella's instructions about regional trains and buses, having already made up her mind to use some of George's parting gift of forty pounds to get a taxi.

'Right,' she said. 'Okay. Right. Thanks, Bella. See you soon.'

Then, because it would not do to arrive too soon, as shrewd Bella would know that trains and buses do not deliver their cargo so quickly, Sonia trailed her baggage and Lois to the station buffet, installed them at and under a table, and bought two mugs of hot chocolate, a ham sandwich and a sticky bun.

Their money would not last long, nor their apparent independence. Tonight they would be inhabitants of a refuge for discarded women and children. Tomorrow they might be the subject of investigations into their history and instructions on how to proceed with their future.

But for now they belonged only to themselves. A pretty young black mother and cute little girl with wiry pigtails sharing a meal at a café table. Eating together and talking. Except that Lois wasn't talking and had hardly eaten a crumb. Too late, Sonia remembered that Lois had wanted the toilet.

'I couldn't hold it any longer,' Lois said. 'It's gone all over this bag.' Her mouth opened in readiness to howl.

'It doesn't matter, Lois,' Sonia said quickly. 'It's not your fault. Come on, help me pick up the bags and we'll go and find the Ladies'. Don't cry, Lois. We're going to clean everything up as good as new. Okay?'

Chapter Four

Sonia need not have worried about arriving at the refuge too promptly. For some reason best known to British Rail, the Ladies' at Victoria station was at the top of a flight of narrow stairs on which people going up and coming down fought to get past each other.

At the top of the stairs was a turnstile which could only be opened by a ten-pence coin and did not accommodate children or luggage, which had to be lifted over it. The cubicles were too small to admit mother and child together, let alone their bags.

The attendant shouted at Sonia that she should not have brought in the bags but paid to leave them in the Left Luggage Office. She shouted at Sonia again when she tried to wash Lois's legs and told her she should pay extra to go to the Shower and Washroom facility.

Sonia was humiliated. 'This place is meant to be for travellers,' she retaliated. 'So why is it made so impossible?'

'This is not Left Luggage or Showers,' said the attendant implacably. 'This is a public convenience.'

'You're joking,' said a fat woman, squeezing painfully through the turnstile. 'Convenient for very agile pygmies, maybe!'

'But it certainly is public,' Sonia said, heartened by the other woman's contribution. She turned on the attendant. 'Would you kindly stop watching us? You never seen a child washed before?'

'This is not the place . . .' the attendant began again, but the fat woman said, 'Oh, leave them alone, can't you? It's hard enough travelling with a child. You come far?' she asked Sonia.

'Sussex,' Sonia told her. She washed Lois as quickly as possible, dabbing her dry with paper towels, and put a clean tracksuit on her. She dried off the carrier bag Lois had soaked, but some of the contents would need to be washed. She didn't dare rinse them out in the washbasin here. Her aim was to get out of the Ladies' before the fat woman disappeared into one of the cubicles and the attendant, sulking now, took advantage of her absence to complain at Sonia again.

On their way down the stairs Lois tripped and Sonia, putting out a hand to save her, dropped one of the bags, which bounced down the steps, spilling its contents.

Women, already aggravated by the climb, the queue, their lack of ten-pence coins and the long delay imposed on an urgent need, either complained, looked away or stepped on the items: clothes, books, photos, a hairbrush, a spare face-cloth. There would be more washing to do now; that meant a launderette, and launderettes meant money.

More problems awaited them at the taxi rank. When they reached the head of the queue, the first driver refused to take them to Camberwell. 'No,' he said briefly. 'Next!'

The next person lost no time in taking up this invitation. He jumped into the cab and it drove off.

Sonia was appalled. Was it because she was black? Surely not. She opened the door of the next cab.

'Did he refuse to take you?' the driver asked her.

'Yes. Why did he do that?'

'Where are you going to?'

'Camberwell.'

'Sorry,' he said. 'Next!'

'Wait a minute,' Sonia said. She held on to the open door of the cab and would not let the next passenger past her. 'This is a taxi, isn't it?'

'It is a taxi, love, but I'm not going to Camberwell. Where to, sir?'

'No,' said Sonia. 'Hold it. Correct me if I'm wrong or anything, but I thought the passenger was meant to choose the destination, and the driver was meant to drive there.' Her

24

anger was rising steadily. I am going to kill somebody soon, she thought, and meant it.

'Look, love, I've got a living to make. It's coming up to rush hour, which is the most important time of the day here for us, and if I'm over in Camberwell I'm not here to pick up the fares, am I? I'm stuck in a traffic jam, earning bugger all.'

'If I wanted to go round the corner,' Sonia shouted, 'I'd walk. But I have to go to Camberwell, which is why I have to take a taxi, because I am dead on my feet and overloaded with luggage and if one more public service refuses to serve me I am going to stick a knife in somebody . . .'

The taxi drove off, door open. The passengers in the queue rushed for the next taxi, the one after and the one after that. Sonia grabbed Lois and one bag, leaving the rest on the pavement. She wrenched open the door of the fourth taxi in the rank, threw Lois on to the seat, pushed the bag in after her, and ran back for the other luggage.

The driver shouted at her. 'Hey you! Wait your turn! What d'you think you're fucking well . . . ?'

Sonia hurled herself through the door of the cab and on to the back seat with Lois, who was dumb with fear. She hauled in the rest of the bags and slammed the door shut.

'It is my turn,' she said firmly. 'Now drive!'

'Okay, okay. Cool down, will you? Where to?'

'Camberwell.'

'Oh no, I'm not going to . . .'

'I am not getting out of this cab,' Sonia said. 'So get on with it.'

He swore and drove off. Sonia was overwhelmingly relieved as they left the station forecourt. She had begun to believe they would spend the rest of their lives at Victoria, never able to leave. Now at last they were moving.

'This is as far as I'll take you,' the driver said after a while. 'You can get a bus from that bus stop over there.'

'This is the place we are going to,' Sonia said, handing him the scrap of paper she had written Bella's secret address on, 'and we are not getting out of this cab until we arrive there.'

The driver glanced at it. 'That's the women's refuge,' he said. 'You don't want to arrive there in a cab. They won't let you in if you arrive like Lady Muck.'

'Muck yourself!' Sonia snapped. 'You can drop us round the corner then. I can't get on a bus with all these bags.'

'This is practically round the corner,' he reasoned. 'A five-minute ride.'

'Then drive for five more minutes,' Sonia said. 'And drive past that very house, so I know where it is, and *then* you can drop us round the corner from it.'

The driver laughed. 'All right, so I'll end up bankrupt! You win. Camberwell it is.'

'At least you won't end up in a women's refuge.'

'No, you got a point there, love. Something to be grateful for anyway.'

'How did you know,' Sonia asked, 'that that address was the refuge? I thought it was meant to be kept secret.'

'Secret? Not to the people who live round there. I got a brother-in-law lives in the next street, that's how I know. The noise from that place is nobody's business.'

'Oh. Is it very noisy?' Sonia's heart sank. The word 'refuge' suggested a haven of peace from a cruel world.

'Noisy? Well, what do you think? Women turn up there in the middle of the night, shouting, screaming, five or six kids crying, then that sets the rest of them off that's there. Then the husband or the lover gets wind of where she is – followed her there most like – and he starts banging on the door to be let in, cursing and swearing, at three o'clock in the morning.

'Then she leans out of the upstairs window, her or a few of the others, and bawls at him to get the eff out of there . . . And the daytime's as bad. If the kids aren't vandalizing the neighbours' gardens and cars, the women are beating each other up. It's a madhouse.'

'I hope you're exaggerating,' Sonia said.

He looked at her in the rear-view mirror. 'I'm telling you, love,' he said more gently. 'If you've got anywhere else you can go . . .'

'We haven't,' said Sonia shortly. 'So keep driving.'

They drove in silence till he said, 'That's the house – that one there with the railings.'

Sonia and Lois peered out of the window. It was quite a small house, Sonia noticed with relief. Not too many families could fit in there. She had begun to imagine a place the size of a warehouse.

The cab turned the corner and stopped. 'Thanks,' Sonia said. 'I didn't mean to make you lose business, bringing us here. I just couldn't face the journey with these bags.'

'That's all right,' he said. 'No, you keep the tip; you'll be needing it. Buy the little girl some sweets.' He got out of the cab and helped Sonia take out the bags. 'Here,' he said, fishing in his pocket and producing a roll of string, 'if you take my advice, you'll tie those bags up securely before you go in. And if you've got money, don't leave it in the bags; keep it on you all the time.'

He shook down the contents of the bags, took a few things out of the carriers and shoved them in the dustbin bag, then tied up the necks of the bags with string. 'Best of luck,' he said, before driving off.

Lois clung to Sonia's hand. 'I don't want to go in that house,' she said.

'Oh, he was only joking,' Sonia told her. 'It's quite a nice place really.'

'He wasn't.'

'No. Well, not joking. Exaggerating. His way of talking is to make everything sound exciting, see? That's why he talked about fights and shouting and everything. When we go in we'll find it quiet enough. You'll see. Come on, Lois! Come and see our new home.'

As the child hung back, she said, 'I'm going, anyway. I'm looking forward to it,' and began walking, dragging the bags. 'I wonder who'll let us in?' she continued, over her shoulder, as Lois still hesitated. 'Probably that nice woman Bella that I talked to on the phone. What do you think she'll look like? I think she'll be really fat – as big as a house.'

'Not as big as a house,' Lois said. 'Or she wouldn't fit.'

'She went in when she was thin,' Sonia said, 'and now she can't get out, so she stays in the house all the time, and visitors have to squeeze in around her. We'll have to hold our breath so we don't take up too much room.'

Lois started giggling. 'Every time she eats she gets bigger and bigger,' she contributed, 'and soon her head will be coming out of the chimney.'

'I think I can see it already,' Sonia said, as they arrived at the gate. 'Look – no, you missed her!'

They were laughing as the door opened.

Chapter Five

The woman who opened the door was massive.

'Yes?' she said.

'I'm Sonia Leroy. I spoke to you on the phone.'

'Not to me, you didn't. That'll be Bella. Come in.'

She stood aside in the hallway and they squeezed past her.

'You brought enough luggage,' she said. 'Most people don't even have time to pack a bag. I arrived here with next to nothing. I been here six weeks,' she volunteered. 'Social services are still working out what to do with us. I got six kids, but I only brought the three. I won't go into bed-and-breakfast; I told the social worker straight. Well, don't stand around. Go in.'

Seven children sat in the kitchen, three stocky, grubby and white-skinned – or greyish – and four thin, Asian, with large solemn eyes. They were all silent. Sonia could not imagine them fighting, as the taxi driver had claimed, or vandalizing anything.

'Have you had your tea?' the woman asked Sonia.

'No.'

'Well, sit the little girl down here. We have to stand; there's not enough chairs for everybody.'

Lois refused to move from Sonia's side.

'What's your name?' the woman asked her.

'Her name's Lois,' Sonia said.

'You let her answer for herself,' the woman said. 'What's the matter? Cat got your tongue? Take your hands away from your face. What you got to hide?'

'She's a bit shy, that's all,' Sonia said. She sat down at the table herself and pulled Lois on to her knee.

They heard the front door open and a thin, harassed-looking woman appeared, accompanied by an Asian woman, even thinner except for a very advanced state of pregnancy.

'Sorry,' said the first. 'There was a queue a mile long. You must be Sonia. I'm Bella. And the little girl . . .?'

'Lois,' Sonia said.

'Hello, Lois. Have you met the others? Mrs Patel, Mrs Riley, Darren, Dean, Daniel – Mrs Riley's children – and Shireen, Riaz, Anita and Pretty, Mrs Patel's children. You'll be sleeping in the lounge, but you can leave your bags in Mrs Riley's room in the daytime, if you want to take them up there now. First door on the left. Bathroom's next to it. Have you eaten? No? Come straight down again then. Only chips, I'm afraid; we've been a bit rushed today, with the court hearing.'

This information was delivered almost without a breath in a toneless voice, as though the speaker could waste neither time nor energy. It was like listening to a computerized message.

Sonia gathered up Lois and some of the bags. No one offered to give her a hand with the rest, so she made two trips. When she returned to the kitchen, Mrs Riley was peering through the handles of one of the carrier bags. 'What you got in here? Clothes?' she said.

'Different things,' Sonia said.

'I can't get clothes for my kids,' she said with a sigh. 'What you got in this one?'

'Just things,' said Sonia, taking it out of her hands.

Upstairs, she tied the bags together with as many knots as she could. The remainder of the money Mr Grenville had given her at the station, and the money she had saved during her six months' employment (had she known that the Grenvilles might turn out unreliable?), she folded and slid into the back pocket of her jeans.

Then she took Lois to the toilet, which was in the bathroom. There was no lock on the door. Privacy was not one of the facilities provided here, she thought. 'Remember we have to thank God,' she told Lois.

'What for?'

'For helping us when we asked. He got us this place to sleep tonight.'

'I want to go home.'

'We can't go home, Lois. We're here now.'

'I don't want to stay here.'

'I know. I don't want to stay longer than we have to either. All right then, what do you say we thank God for getting us in here for now, and we ask Him to get us out as soon as He can? Okay?'

Sitting on the toilet, Lois folded her hands, closed her eyes and said, 'God help us. Again.'

'Amen,' said Sonia. She tipped the bundle of Lois's wet clothes into the washbasin and, in the absence of washing powder, poured in a few drops of shampoo from a bottle on the bathroom shelf. 'Right,' she said, 'we'll go down and eat now.'

'Will that fat woman's head come out of the chimney when she's had her chips?' Lois asked as they went down the stairs.

'Shush!' Sonia cautioned her.

'Is it a secret?' Lois whispered.

'Yes, it's a secret.'

'Here's your chips, Louise,' said Mrs Riley, pushing a small plate towards her across the table. 'The kids ate the rest. We have to go without, Sandra,' she said virtuously. 'Kiddies come first, don't they?'

Sonia was furious. 'Do you want me to go out and get some more?' she asked Bella, who was deep in conversation with Mrs Patel.

Bella looked surprised. 'I thought I'd bought enough for everyone,' she said. 'They can't all be gone, are they, Gina?'

'The kids were hungry,' she said.

'Isn't there anything left for Sonia?' Bella asked.

'I thought she'd eaten already,' Gina Riley asserted. She looked Sonia straight in the eye, and the look was not friendly.

'Oh, have you?' said Bella, relieved. 'That's okay then.'

'No,' said Sonia loudly, as Bella turned back to Mrs Patel,

'actually I haven't had anything to eat, except one bite of sandwich in the station.'

'Oh dear,' Bella said. 'Now, I don't know what we can give you.'

What had happened to the woman? Sonia wondered. She had sounded so decisive on the phone. Then she saw Bella glancing sideways at Gina Riley. She's afraid of annoying her, she thought.

'How much money have you brought with you?' asked Mrs Riley.

'Not much,' Sonia said.

'How much?'

'Now Gina . . .' Bella said.

'I'm just asking,' Gina said, 'why there's any reason for her to expect her food to be provided, if she can afford to get something for herself. We all have to chip in here, you know,' she said, 'out of our benefit or whatever. You are claiming benefit, are you?'

'Sonia doesn't have to answer questions now, Gina,' Bella said, more firmly. 'I am going to sort that out with her tomorrow. Tonight they'll just need a bed, and something to eat.'

The atmosphere was tense. Lois picked up her plate of chips and overturned it. She swept the chips off the table with her hand, jumped off Sonia's lap and stamped them into the floor.

Mrs Riley's hand was faster than Sonia's reactions. She fetched Lois a blow round the head that knocked her to the floor. Lois's screams were of pure terror. She lay on the floor, on the squashed chips, unable to move.

Sonia, in any crisis, went calm and cold. She picked up her chair and held it up to Mrs Riley's face. 'Keep away from her,' she said, very evenly. She put the chair down, picked up the terrified child and carried her, screaming hysterically, into the next room and closed the door.

The sitting room was small and crowded, with a sofa, three armchairs and a table with a television. Sonia sat in one of the chairs with Lois, who had gone completely rigid, half on and half off her lap. She did not know what to do, so she simply held her and listened to her scream.

Mrs Riley opened the door. 'You can't stay in here,' she said. 'The kids want to watch telly.'

'Out,' Sonia said. To her surprise, Mrs Riley went. Bella came in.

'Sorry about this,' she said. 'These things happen. Your little girl is obviously quite disturbed. Have you had a doctor's report?'

'She's not used to being hit,' Sonia said. 'I don't think that's disturbed, do you?'

'Gina's a bit hasty,' Bella admitted. 'Now, we usually use this room in the evenings, you know, or at least Gina and her children do. Mrs Patel stays in her room.'

'Is this the room we'll be sleeping in?' Sonia asked her.

'Well yes, it is.'

'So Lois can't go to bed till Mrs Riley finishes watching telly then?'

'It is a problem, isn't it? But still, in these refuges we have to make do. Sometimes we're much more overcrowded than this. We've had people sleeping in the bath!' She laughed merrily. 'Still, we soldier on!'

'Listen,' said Sonia, talking above Lois's sobbing. 'I am grateful to you for taking us in here, but if you let the people bully each other like this, then it isn't a refuge. And that's what everyone's here for – for refuge.'

'Yes,' Bella said. 'But you're not the only pebble on the beach, lovey. We have to give and take here.'

'Good,' Sonia said. 'Give Mrs Riley the telly, then, for her room, and Lois and I will agree not to go in and watch it. And she can leave us this room, at least after Lois has gone to bed.'

'Well,' said Bella doubtfully, 'I suppose I could suggest that. I'll see what she says.'

'I'm staying here with Lois and not moving,' said Sonia clearly. 'And I want our bags down here, before she ransacks them.'

'This is not a hotel, you know!' Bella exclaimed.

'I just want somewhere to sleep,' Sonia said, 'and not to

have my things stolen. That's all.'

'I'll have a word with her,' she said, 'but I can't promise anything.'

She had hardly gone out when Mrs Patel appeared. 'Can I come in?' she whispered.

'Yes.'

'Is the child all right?'

'Yes, she's calming down now.'

Mrs Patel stretched out a thin hand and stroked Lois's forehead. Lois lay passive and did not flinch. 'The poor child is tired,' Mrs Patel said.

'Yes, she is.'

'If there is trouble about this room,' Mrs Patel said, 'your little girl can sleep in our room. With Anita. It is only a blanket on the floor, but she will be safe.'

'Isn't it safe here, then?' Sonia asked nervously.

'Mrs Riley,' whispered Mrs Patel, almost inaudibly, 'go in the rooms at night. She take whatever she like. But she doesn't come in our room. It is too crowded. When we are all in bed, the door does not open.'

'Oh.'

'If you prefer not to be alone, you can share my blanket.'

Tears came into Sonia's eyes. 'You're a very good woman,' she said.

'No, not good,' said Mrs Patel sadly. 'Very weak. That is not good. Goodness is having courage.'

'I've spoken to Gina,' said Bella, coming in. 'If you let her and the children in to watch TV for an hour, she says, then she'll leave you the rest of the evening.' She did not say this with any conviction.

'No,' Sonia said. 'Lois needs to go to bed now.' This was obvious. Lois was asleep, stretched across Sonia's knees and the chair arms. 'She can either take the telly into her own room, or we'll sleep in with Mrs Patel.'

Bella pursed her lips. 'Mrs Patel has quite enough in her room as it is,' she said. 'However, if you *will* insist, I'll take the telly upstairs. Perhaps you would give me a hand with it.'

Mrs Patel put out her arms to Lois. 'I'll take care of the child.'

'Thanks,' Sonia said.

'You mustn't lean on Mrs Patel,' Bella said, as they struggled up the stairs with the television. 'She's a very troubled woman herself.'

'She's a very nice woman,' Sonia said. Bella shot her a glance, opened her mouth but said nothing.

'There's no room for a telly in here,' said Gina Riley, barring the door.

'I'll take my bags out of your room,' Sonia said. 'Then you'll have more space.'

'Oh, will you?' said Gina threateningly.

'Mum!' yelled one of the boys, from the bathroom. 'There's knickers in this sink!'

'Are they yours?' Gina demanded. 'You're not allowed to do washing here; there's no room to dry it. Go down the launderette if you want to wash.'

'All right,' Sonia said. 'I'll rinse them out.'

'You bloody won't,' Gina said. 'I'm taking them out of that sink this minute.'

As she strode out of the room, Sonia rushed in, grabbed her bags and threw them over the banisters. Bella stood and watched her wordlessly. The last bag bounced off the wall before landing on the floor below. There goes my hairdryer, Sonia thought resignedly. She ran downstairs to retrieve the bags and dragged them into the sitting room, closing the door.

Gina thundered down the stairs, flung open the door and threw the wet washing into Sonia's face. Mrs Patel, holding Lois, shrank back in her chair.

Bella came in behind Gina. 'Stop this,' she said, 'both of you.'

Gina shook her fist in Sonia's face. 'You're going to wish you'd never set foot in this place,' she told her.

'Gina,' Bella said. 'We have to make allowances. We don't know yet what Sonia's been through.'

35

That 'yet' sounded more threatening to Sonia's ears than Gina's menaces. It seemed that Sonia would have no rights to anything of her own here – not even her problems.

Chapter Six

Upstairs, the television stayed on until two a.m. at full volume. Three times during the night Sonia, lying awake, heard Gina tiptoe noisily downstairs. Twice she tried the door, but Sonia had stacked chairs in front of it. The chairs were not heavy enough to prevent the door opening, with Gina's weight behind it, but they made a noise, which alerted Sonia to get up, kneel on the floor and push back with all her strength.

As an added precaution she had laid Lois, in their shared blanket and cushions on the floor, with her head in the window alcove of the room so that if Gina did force her way in, the chairs would topple on Sonia's legs and not Lois's face. Also, she had removed their money from the pocket of her jeans, which she had taken off, and tucked it into one of her socks, which she kept on.

On her third trip downstairs, Gina did not try their door but raided the kitchen. Sonia heard her opening cupboards and the fridge, and heard her muttering, 'Only three slices of bread left. Bloody hell!'

In the absence of sleep, Sonia spent the night praying. She only prayed in emergencies, not wanting to waste the facility. 'Please get us out of here, tomorrow first thing,' she repeated simply.

Lois, surprisingly, slept. She woke only once in the night, to say that she and Sonia had been standing out in the street in the cold, with no clothes on. 'It was only a dream,' Sonia said, and she went back to sleep.

At six o'clock in the morning Sonia went into the kitchen to make tea, and found Bella already there.

'I always get up at this time,' Bella said. 'It's my quiet time.

It saves my sanity.'

'I didn't mean to disturb you. Can I make a cup of tea?'

'Help yourself. Do you eat breakfast? I don't. There should be some bread if you want.'

The bread bin was empty. 'Gina came down in the night,' Sonia said. She didn't want to be blamed for eating the bread.

'Did she come into your room?' Bella asked.

'She tried. Does she go into yours?'

Bella looked guilty. 'There's a lock on the door. I hope you won't fight, you two. It's important not to let tempers flare. These things escalate so quickly in a crowded house.'

'It strikes me,' Sonia said, 'that people go into refuges to escape being bullied. If you've got a resident bully, doesn't that defeat the object?'

'Oh, Gina's had her troubles too, you know,' Bella said quickly. 'A brute of a husband, trouble with the police.'

'A husband who beat her up?' Sonia was incredulous.

'Well, from what she says . . .'

'He must be a sumo wrestler or something,' said Sonia.

Bella, in spite of attempts not to, laughed. 'She is a bit of a problem,' she said, and sighed. 'She should have been moved on somewhere else by now; we're only a crisis centre for the immediate need. But she won't go till she's been guaranteed her own council flat.'

'She'll be here a long time then, won't she?' Sonia said.

'Don't say that!' Bella said from the heart.

Sonia sipped her tea. 'Why do you do this job?' she asked curiously.

'Because I think it's essential. It *is* essential, for those in real need. Mrs Patel, for example. Literally, this place is her lifeline. She would have been beaten to death if she hadn't come here.'

They heard noises of movement upstairs.

'Bella,' said Sonia hurriedly. 'I know you said we would have a chat this morning, but I might have the chance of a job if I go into town and call in personally to the agency that gave me the last one. Is that okay with you?'

'Sure. The last thing I want to do is discourage someone from helping herself if she can. So many can't, you know – have absolutely reached the end of their tether. I could tell you stories that would make your hair stand on end.'

'I'm sure you could,' said Sonia, not wanting to hear them. 'Could I ask you one favour, Bella?'

'If it's money for fares, it would have to be a loan, I'm afraid . . .'

'No, I've got a little. It's just – could I leave our bags in your room, if your door locks?'

Bella seemed anxious. 'I don't know . . . yes, I understand what you're saying, but any sign of special treatment towards you is going to aggravate the situation. I know it's a risk, leaving your things here while you're out . . .'

'It's not a risk,' Sonia said. 'It's a certainty.'

'Yes. All right then, yes. Put them in there now, before she gets up. She usually sleeps quite late. I'll give you a hand with them. Be as quiet as you can.'

She kept the key to her room, Sonia noticed, on a length of tape worn round her neck, under her sweater. She couldn't feel very safe either, in her own house. Tolerance of Gina was obviously not a kindness to anybody, including Bella herself.

I am getting out of here, she swore to herself. Before I become either a witness or a victim of something really nasty. It's like sitting on a time bomb in this place, waiting for Gina to explode.

She and Lois were dressed and out of the house by seven thirty, and joined the commuters on buses into town. They found the agency and went to a café to wait till it opened. Sonia was starving. She ordered a plateful of bacon, egg and sausage, cut some of it up for Lois, and forced herself to eat her share of it slowly. Rain hammered against the café window. Sonia possessed an umbrella. It was securely locked away in Bella's room.

'We better stay here till the rain eases off,' Sonia told Lois, 'or we'll get soaked on our way to the agency and look like a couple of tramps and they won't want to know us.' Not that they will anyway, she added silently.

She knew in her heart the errand would be hopeless, but she had to try so she would know she had tried. She ordered another cup of tea and sipped it slowly, watching raindrops glide down the glass outside, and suddenly felt peaceful.

There was a peculiar kind of relief in knowing that her situation was hopeless: that she had tried her best and could do no more. Since no planning for the future was possible the future seemed to evaporate, leaving her becalmed in the present moment, in which there was no need to do anything except sip tea and watch raindrops. Yes, there was a kind of peace.

'If we were at the Grenvilles' now, I'd be washing up the breakfast dishes,' she said, 'and waiting for Mrs Grenville to come in with a list of chores. A hundred and one chores to do before the clock struck twelve.' She laughed.

'Are we on holiday?' asked Lois.

'You could say that. A sort of holiday, yes.'

'Are we going to die?'

Sonia stared at her. 'Why do you ask that?'

'Because nobody cares about us.'

Sonia's peaceful state of mind deserted her. She pushed her mug of tea away. 'No, of course we're not going to die,' she said sharply. 'I'm going to get another job and look after us. It's not true that nobody cares about us, Lois. I care about you and you care about me. Come on, let's go and get some sense out of this agency.'

The agency was hopeless, as Sonia had known it would be. The girls were friendly, sympathetic, and very busy. They told Sonia 'off the record' that the Grenvilles were difficult clients, that they paid well below the going rate, were hard to please, had upset countless numbers of previous housekeepers, cooks and other domestic helps, and that the agency now sent them only people who were desperate for a job and unlikely to be placed elsewhere.

However, Mrs Grenville was their client and if a client refused to give a reference and claimed that her housekeeper had turned lazy and insolent and refused to work, the agency was obliged to accept her verdict.

'But she didn't tell me that!' Sonia repeated over and over again. 'She never said a word of that to my face – and she couldn't. I was up at half past six every morning, I did everything she asked . . . I know she was hard to please, but she used to give credit where it was due the times I did extra things, like arranging her flowers for her . . . She told me herself she never had anyone so good . . . She told you . . .'

The agency girls agreed with everything. Yes, they had it on record that Mrs Grenville was at last satisfied – no, delighted – with the housekeeper they had sent her this time. She had given them a glowing report when Barbara (who had now left the agency) had called to check, after the month's trial period. But no, they couldn't write a reference on the basis of that. It was not their job to write references. They were not the employer. Mrs Grenville was.

'What seems to have happened, unfortunately,' said the senior assistant finally, 'is that a working relationship which began very well turned sour.'

'No! She was pleased with my work, right up to the last day! I know she was!'

The assistant continued as though she had not spoken. 'So what I will do is to contact Mrs Grenville again now, if you will wait, and try my best to persuade her to give you some kind of a reference in consideration of your good work at first.'

'It wasn't just at first! You're not listening to me!' Sonia pleaded.

The assistant sighed. 'I'm sorry,' she said, 'Ms Leroy, I am trying to be fair. But there has to be *some* reason why she dismissed you, even if it isn't a justifiable one. I can't believe you don't have any kind of idea why it happened. You say she refused to give you a reason . . .'

'She did!'

'All right, I accept that. But you lived with the woman for six months; the relationship must have been deteriorating over that period of time; there must have been some signs of it

41

that you noticed yourself. Either that, or if the change in her attitude happened suddenly . . .'

'It did. It was sudden. There was no warning at all.'

'Then in that case something sudden must have happened to make her change her mind so drastically. I am trying to be sympathetic, and the situation is obviously very painful for you, but are you sincerely telling me that there was no warning, no clue, no reason . . . nothing happened, everything was fine, right up to the last minute?'

Sonia was silent. Lois, who had had her hands over her face ever since they walked through the door of the office, now got down on her hands and knees on the floor and buried her whole head in her arms. Sonia nudged her with her foot. 'Get up!' she hissed. It wasn't going to help if Lois started acting weird.

'I will phone Mrs Grenville,' the assistant said, 'and if we get nowhere with that, I am going to suggest that you go along to the Job Centre and ask them about the procedure for appealing against unfair dismissal. There are tribunals, you know.'

'It wouldn't do any good,' Sonia said. 'She told me if I made a fuss I could only lose.'

'Did she? Well, if that was put in your statement it wouldn't help her – making threats.'

'No, but it's true; they wouldn't listen to me. They'd listen to her. They'd say what you've said: there must be some reason behind it.'

'It is so difficult to prove these cases anyway,' the woman said, 'when it's one person's word against another. And in the end we don't have much control over how our clients treat the staff we send them. We are as careful as we can be and we do check up and so on, but at the end of the day we have to trust them . . . Did the Grenvilles employ anyone else?' she asked suddenly. 'We didn't send them anybody, but wasn't there a gardener or something?'

'Why? What has that got to do with it?' Sonia asked.

'Could he be called in as a witness on your behalf?'

'No,' said Sonia quickly. 'He wouldn't do anything to risk his job. He'd say whatever they wanted him to say.'

'I see. Well, wait here a minute, then, while I have one more try with Mrs Grenville, though I must say that yesterday she sounded adamant . . .'

'No,' Sonia said, standing up. 'Leave it. It won't do any good. It might even make things worse. If you can't recommend me for another job, there's no point . . .'

'We can recommend you,' the woman said, 'but as soon as an employer accepted you he or she would ask for references, and that's as far as it would go.'

'I know.'

'Look, Sonia,' the woman said, as she prepared to leave. 'If you don't mind my saying so, you might do much better anyway to go to the Job Centre. You can explain about the dismissal, and it might not count against you so much in another kind of job. Why don't you try for that?'

'What kind?'

'Factory work, or office clerical work. It is mainly living-in jobs where these personality clashes seem to cause such trouble. You'd be more independent in a day job, and the money might be better as well.'

'I can't leave Lois,' she said.

'There are day nurseries. Some of the bigger companies even have their own crèches.'

'No,' Sonia said. 'I have to look after her myself.' She caught hold of Lois's arm and hauled her to her feet. Lois made a low wailing sound and clamped her hands tightly over her eyes. 'Come on, Lois,' she said.

The woman followed them to the door. 'I am sorry,' she said. 'I wish there was more I could do.'

'Thank you for trying, anyway,' Sonia said. 'You've been very kind.'

'Forgive me for asking,' the woman said diffidently, 'but is there something wrong with the little girl?'

'No,' said Sonia. 'Nothing that a home wouldn't solve. Come on, Lois – move.'

Chapter Seven

The bus was coming as they emerged from the agency, and Sonia ran for it, hauling Lois on behind her. It was only when they had struggled up the stairs and were seated at the front of the top deck that Sonia realized she had not intended returning to Camberwell so early. She had no desire to spend the rest of the day at the refuge, avoiding Gina's malice or answering Bella's well-intentioned questions.

Where else was there to go? The Job Centre? There was no point. She had to have a job where she could keep Lois with her and not let her out of her sight any longer than possible. She could not get that job without a reference from a previous employer. The previous employer, before the Grenvilles, had since died.

Could she forge a reference? Answer a private advert for a housekeeper, take the risk of not going through an agency – which was not necessarily safer, after all – and produce some letters of reference penned by herself? But the employer would check up on them, find the names and addresses were fictitious, fire her on the spot. Again.

Besides, she had her integrity to consider. There were some things she would not do. Not yet, anyway. Who knows what innocent people turn to when they get desperate enough? She hoped she would not have to find out.

'Quick, Lois! We're getting off!'

Lois scrambled off the seat and headed for the stairs. 'Where are we going?'

'I saw a park, over the other side of that high wall there. We'll go for a picnic.'

'Yeah!' Lois applauded. 'A picnic!'

The bus pulled in at the next stop. They jumped off.

'Where is the park?' Lois asked.

'Back there. Let's find a shop first.'

They bought Coke and crisps in a corner mini-mart. 'We have to be careful with the money,' Sonia explained. 'We had a big breakfast, so this is all we can have for lunch. Fetch us a loaf of bread as well, Lois.'

'I don't want bread!' she protested.

'It's to feed the ducks,' Sonia told her.

'What ducks?'

'All good parks have duckponds. This park looked quite big. There were a lot of trees.' She waited at the checkout, fumbling for change. 'Is there a duckpond in that park?' she asked the assistant.

The assistant, a young Pakistani girl, looked uncomprehending.

'Sorry,' Sonia said. 'Don't you speak English?'

'Yes,' she said.

'The park back there,' Sonia repeated. 'Is there . . . are there ducks?'

Receiving another blank stare, Sonia flapped her arms and quacked. 'Ducks,' she said helpfully.

'I don't understand,' said the girl.

'Never mind,' Sonia said. 'Thanks anyway.'

As they came out of the shop, there was a rumble of thunder followed by a few drops of rain.

'I don't believe this,' Sonia groaned. 'Something has got to go right today! Surely!'

The rain became more businesslike. They ran, clutching their purchases. Lois dropped a packet of crisps and they stopped to pick it up.

'Through here!' Sonia gasped, running through the big open gates. 'Let's see if there's somewhere to shelter. Oh, Lord!'

'What are all those white things?' Lois shouted, above the noise of the rain. Droplets of water balanced on the ends of her pigtails.

'Tell you in a minute,' Sonia shouted back. 'Go in that shelter thing over there.'

The 'shelter thing' was a small lodge which looked like a cross between an open-air temple and a bandstand, with a bench seat the length of its curved interior wall, divided up by large pillars. Lois ran up the steps and sat on the base of one of the pillars. Sonia followed more slowly, out of breath. An ear-splitting clap of thunder greeted her arrival.

'Go on, thunder!' Sonia yelled, losing her temper. She flung the loaf of bread down on the tiled floor of the lodge. 'Go on – louder! Enjoy yourself while you're at it, why don't you?'

'Sonia,' said Lois.

'Let's have some lightning as well!' Sonia shrieked. 'And some snow and hail! And the odd hurricane! We can't even have a picnic without something going wrong! We can't even find a park! It has to turn out to be a cemetery! I bought bread to feed the ducks! I might as well have bought bread to feed the corpses! Because that's what we're going to be before too long, if someone doesn't feed us!'

'Sonia,' Lois insisted.

'Shut up!' Sonia roared. 'I'm having a rage. I think I'm entitled, don't you, Lois?'

'Yes,' Lois said, 'but . . .'

Another dramatic explosion of thunder interrupted her. The rain poured in solid sheets.

'Okay, world,' Sonia screamed. 'So you've got it in for us. We've got no job, no home, no references, no prospects . . .'

'No ducks,' supplied Lois.

'No ducks, no bread . . .'

'We have got bread,' said Lois reproachfully. 'A whole loaf.'

'No money,' Sonia amended. 'Don't interrupt me when I'm angry.'

'Are you angry?' Lois enquired.

'Am I angry?' she roared. 'I am mad! Did you hear that, world? Or are you deaf?'

'Sonia,' Lois said.

'Yeah, that's it!' Sonia bawled. 'You have gone deaf, world! Deaf with your own thunder and blind with your lightning and . . . and your senses washed away in your rain! We have nowhere to live, and you don't care, world! Well, let me tell you something!'

'Sonia,' said Lois.

'Let me shout it loud in case you're too deaf to hear!' she shrieked. 'I got a question for you, world! Is this all there is to living? 'Cos if it is you can keep it, and I am in the right place in this cemetery that pretends to be a park. 'Cos you pretend to give me a life, world, and look where you landed me! I am skint!' she bellowed.

'Sonia.'

'I am destitute! I am drowned! I am alone in the world! No one cares about me! The world has gone deaf to joy!'

'Sonia.'

'*What* is it?' she snapped.

'There's a man eating his sandwiches.'

There was. An elderly man in an old-fashioned dark business suit and improbably shiny black shoes with a rolled umbrella at his feet. He was only two bays away on the seat, not even hidden behind a pillar.

'Oh,' Sonia said. She subsided on to the seat, her legs giving way under her.

'How do you do?' he said, regarding her with mild curiosity. Lois covered her eyes.

'I didn't know there was anyone here,' Sonia said lamely.

'No,' he agreed.

'I got a bit angry about . . . things. I didn't mean to disturb your lunch.'

'I would be angry as well,' he said musingly, 'in your situation.' He ate from a greaseproof paper package, neatly folded. His lunch was two rounds of cheese sandwiches, an apple, and some kind of drink in a Thermos. 'Would you care for a sandwich?' he offered.

'Oh no, I couldn't . . .'

'Please. Be my guest.'

'All right then,' she said. 'Would you like some of our crisps?'

He smiled. 'I should be delighted,' he said. He handed Lois a sandwich. Lois, behind her hands, shook her head and backed away. 'Is she shy?' he asked.

'Yes, she is.' Sonia was relieved to hear it called a normal name. 'Don't mind her.'

'All children are shy at first,' he stated. 'And if they aren't, you often wish they were.'

'That's right,' Sonia agreed. She felt calmer after her outburst. She ate the sandwich and opened both bags of crisps, handing one to Lois and the other to the old man, who took one crisp and examined it as though it were a rare delicacy.

'Bit of a disappointment, I imagine,' he said, 'expecting to find a park and then discovering it to be a cemetery.' He had a precise way of speaking, enunciating every word.

'I saw it from the top of the bus,' Sonia explained. 'This patch of green and trees. I thought it would be somewhere to have a picnic.'

'Well, it is,' he asserted. 'I have lunch here every day. A most peaceful place.'

'I suppose so. A bit morbid, though.'

'Not at all. We all have to go some day. I had even chosen a nice little plot for myself – over there, under the yew tree – but unfortunately somebody pipped me to it. A lady had herself buried there the other day, so now I shall have to be immortal.'

Sonia laughed.

'That's better,' he said. 'To hear you laughing. What was it you said? The world has gone deaf to joy?'

'Oh,' Sonia said, embarrassed, 'I was just shooting my mouth off.'

'No, no,' he said. 'It is quite correct. Very true. And very well expressed. Deaf to joy, indeed. That's why I come here.'

'Is it?' Peace was sweeping over her again, or perhaps it was only weariness after the sleepless night and the morning's anxiety.

'My colleagues stay indoors,' he said. 'They either eat their sandwiches in the workshop or the office, or they go to the pub. Indoors all day. Not much of a change, is it?'

'No.'

'And in the company of the same people,' he added. 'It can't be healthy. Where's the pleasure in that? So I come out here, to the cemetery, rain or shine, and have some fresh air and the company of birds – no ducks, I give you that – but pigeons and sparrows and starlings; a robin occasionally. Give them a crumb of bread and there you'll see joy.'

'You still work then?' Sonia asked. 'You're not retired?'

A shadow crossed his face. 'No, I can't think of retiring, somehow. What would be the point of that?'

'What work do you do?' She thought he would be somebody who worked in a bank, with those shoes and that correct diction.

'I am a furniture restorer. Antiques, mainly. Some reproduction furniture, but nothing too recent. I deal in the past, you see,' he said, with a twinkle of blue eyes under the heavy white eyebrows. 'So that's why I'm not afraid to dine in the cemetery.' He brushed the crumbs off his lap and stood up. 'I must return to work. Thank you so much for the crisp. Delicious. I had always wondered what they tasted like.'

Sonia experienced panic on seeing him about to depart. 'It's nice to have met you,' she said.

'And you. I have enjoyed the encounter. Perhaps we shall meet again.' He held out a hand. 'My name is Arnold.'

'Pleased to meet you, Arnold. I'm Sonia.'

'Well, Mrs Sonnier, I look forward . . .'

'No, no!' she laughed. 'Sonia's my Christian name. And I'm not Mrs.' She waited for him to be shocked. 'My little girl's name is Lois.' Lois hid behind the pillar.

'Then we have misunderstood each other,' he said courteously. 'Arnold is my surname. Samuel Arnold. Here is my business card.' He produced one and handed it to her. 'As you see, it has my home address on it as well. I do some private restorative work at home. Perhaps you and your daughter –

Lois – might care to call on me one weekend and have tea? If it's not too far from where you live?'

Tears sprang into her eyes. 'We don't live anywhere at the moment,' she said.

'Dear me,' he said, in consternation. 'That is dreadful. Can no one help?'

A desperate idea came into her mind. 'Listen, Mr Arnold,' she said, grabbing his sleeve, 'you wouldn't consider doing something not strictly honest, would you?'

'Dear me,' he said again. 'Well, it's a long time since I have been invited to be a partner in crime. What would it involve?'

'I need a reference,' she said. 'From an employer. Or else I'll never be able to get another job. The last one sacked me, for no reason, and threw us out and she wouldn't write me one.'

'I see,' he said. He looked interested, not worried. 'And my part would be . . .?'

'If you could write a few lines, saying you had employed me for a couple of months and my work had been entirely satisfactory,' she gabbled. 'It's just that your card looks so professional and you sound so respectable and when the next employer phoned you . . .'

'That I had employed you,' he repeated, puzzled. 'But . . . as a furniture restorer?'

'No, a housekeeper. A living-in housekeeper, cook, whatever you like to call it. If you could write a few lines, "To whom it may concern . . ." That kind of thing . . .'

'Yes?'

'And then say, "Sonia Leroy has been employed by me for the past six months and is a good cook and an efficient housekeeper and works hard and her little girl is no trouble to anybody . . ."' She ended on a sob. Lois stayed behind the pillar.

'My dear girl,' he said with compassion. 'But is it true?'

'No,' she howled, 'it's not true. I'm asking you to tell lies, because if somebody doesn't help me I'll be out on the streets!'

'No,' he said, 'I mean is it true that you are a housekeeper and a good cook and are looking for a job?'

50

'Yes,' she said.

'I think perhaps,' he said, 'we were meant to meet.'

She wiped her nose on the back of her hand, something she would not allow Lois to do. 'Meant?' she repeated.

'My housekeeper retired six months ago,' Samuel Arnold explained. 'The house has got into such a dreadful state that I was ashamed to advertise for another. I thought no one would want to take the post. I have been fending for myself, but I should be so relieved not to have to continue. If you yourself would be interested in the position, it might well be the perfect solution for all of us. What do you think?'

Chapter Eight

'I still can't believe this has happened!' Sonia exulted. They were back on the bus heading for Camberwell and the women's refuge again.

'There's a dog doing a poo on the pavement!' Lois cried excitedly.

'I mean, can you imagine,' Sonia continued, 'that only a few hours ago we had nowhere to live, it was pouring with rain . . . Now we have a new home, a job, everything's fantastic!'

'Are we going home?' asked Lois, her attention diverted from the dog.

'First we're going to the refuge to collect our belongings and then we're going to our new home.'

'Where is our new home?' Lois asked.

'In clover!' Sonia exulted. 'On cloud nine!'

Lois looked confused.

'With Samuel,' Sonia enlightened her. 'The old man.'

'No, I don't want to go there,' Lois said.

'Lois, you'll love it. There's a big garden . . .'

'No, I don't want to,' said Lois firmly.

Sonia was dismayed. 'Why are you saying that? This is our big chance. Our only chance, Lois. We've got to go. There is nowhere else!'

'I don't want to,' Lois insisted.

'You have to!'

'No. I won't!'

'Why? Didn't you like him?'

'No.'

'Lois, he seemed a nice man! Why didn't you like him? What didn't you like? His face? His voice? Answer me, Lois;

this is important.'

Lois put her hands over her face.

'Don't start that with me!' Sonia begged. 'You can't get shy with your own mother, for heaven's sake! Just tell me what you didn't like.'

'His house,' Lois muttered, through her hands, 'and his garden.'

'But you haven't seen . . . Oh Lois, we're not going to live *there*! He doesn't live in the *cemetery*!' She burst out laughing. Lois gave her a furious shove in the ribs. Sonia kept giggling, partly from relief.

Finally, when Lois turned away from her and was staring mutinously out of the window at a crowd of damp people milling round market stalls in a side street, she relented and said, 'He lives in a proper house, Lois, with a garden. No white headstones in it, I promise! It's not too far from Camberwell, so we're going there in another taxi, and he's said he will pay for it. We have to collect his spare key from the neighbour, Mrs Atwood, and let ourselves in. He'll phone Mrs Atwood as soon as he gets back to work and tell her to let us have the key.'

Sonia went through this recital as much to remind herself as to inform Lois – not that she was really afraid of forgetting the details, but she needed to be reminded that it was real.

When they arrived at the refuge, only Mrs Patel and her four children were there, though Gina Riley's three boys were playing in the street outside. Mrs Patel took her time opening the door.

'Were you having a rest?' Sonia asked. 'I saw you looking out of the upstairs window. Sorry to disturb you.'

'No, I was down here with the children,' Mrs Patel said. 'I go upstairs when the doorbell ring so I can see who is there.'

'Are you afraid your husband will turn up? Does he know where you are?'

'No, he doesn't know. But Gina's husband sometimes come here.'

'How does he know where she is?'

'She told him.'

'She told him? Why?'

'She say he must know where she is, in case he want to come and take her home. But he only come to fight.'

'Does she like trouble, or what?' Sonia wondered.

Mrs Patel sighed. 'Yes,' she said. 'I think she like trouble. When there is no trouble, she is bored.'

'Where's Bella?' Sonia asked.

'She go to probation office with Gina.'

Sonia shook her head. 'You're no safer here than at home then. At least at home you only have your husband to avoid; here you have everybody else's to dodge as well. And Gina.'

'That is true,' said Mrs Patel, 'but all the same I am safer here. Would you like cup of tea?'

'Yes please.' Sonia had arrived bubbling over with her good news. Now, after only a few minutes in this place she felt tired. And guilty. What had she done to deserve such unexpected good fortune while poor Mrs Patel had life so hard?

'You sit down,' she said. 'I'll put the kettle on. Do you have sugar?'

'One sugar. No milk. Thank you.' Mrs Patel moved a child off a chair. The little girl giggled and ran upstairs. The others followed her, including Lois.

'What will you do?' Sonia asked. 'If you're not safe any more at home, where will you go?'

'I think baby come soon,' said Mrs Patel. 'The pains are starting, the last few days. So I will go into hospital and the children will stay here. Then we will go home.'

'I thought you said you weren't safe at home?'

'No. At times it is not safe. My husband get very angry when I am pregnant. When baby is born, it is all right. We can go home after baby is born. It was like this with all the children.'

'You mean, every time you're pregnant you have to leave home?'

'Yes.'

Sonia was appalled. 'You have to have every baby on your own, and look after the other children, and then your husband will take you back?'

'Yes.'

'Why do you put up with that?'

Mrs Patel smiled. 'Because I love him.'

'Why do you leave him then?'

'That also,' she said, 'because I love him. He would do something terrible to me if I stayed, and he would never forgive himself.'

Sonia poured water into the cups. There didn't seem to be a teapot. 'How can he forgive himself as it is?' she asked. 'Disowning his wife every time he makes her pregnant?'

'I forgive him,' said Mrs Patel. 'He cannot help it.'

'Why not?' said Sonia belligerently. 'Other people manage to be human beings.'

Mrs Patel smiled again. 'He is very weak. I know about this because I too am very weak.'

'You don't sound weak,' Sonia said. 'Stupid, maybe!' She stirred sugar into Mrs Patel's tea and handed it to her.

'Yes, stupid and weak,' Mrs Patel agreed serenely. 'Otherwise I would not love such a man. I would love a good man.'

'A good man,' Sonia repeated. 'Do you know any?'

Mrs Patel considered this. 'My father was a good man. But too trusting. He trust everybody. He think everybody is his friend. He thought this man was his friend when he chose him for me.'

'Your father chose your husband?'

'Yes.' She laughed. 'English people find this strange.'

'Oh, I don't know,' Sonia said. The tea had a bitter taste. 'It can't work out any worse than girls choosing their own husbands, I'm sure.'

'No,' Mrs Patel agreed. 'You are not married.' This was not said as a question but as a statement.

'No.'

'I am sorry. That is sad for you too.'

'It wouldn't have worked out,' Sonia said. 'He wasn't exactly the fatherly type.'

'Did he love you?' Mrs Patel asked.

55

'For a few weeks he did. Trouble was, I thought it was only me, but it turned out he also loved everybody else. He thought all women were his.'

'Did he leave you because you were having a child?' said Mrs Patel sympathetically.

'No. He didn't see any reason to leave. He had other babies by other women. He quite enjoyed visiting his children. But when I found out he was like that I didn't want him. I told him I wasn't about to join any harem. He wouldn't go away, though. So I did.'

'To a mother and baby home?'

'No. I'd spent a while in a children's home, in between fostering placements, and they said I was really helpful looking after the little ones. So I went back there and asked if I could stay and help until I had the baby. The matron there said okay, but it couldn't be official. Officially I wasn't there; they were meant to be for young children who couldn't be placed in foster homes.'

'Did you like it there?' Mrs Patel enquired.

'Yes, I loved it. That place was the best.'

'You have no mother and father?'

'No.'

'I am the same,' Mrs Patel said. She put a hand over Sonia's on the table. 'We will be friends,' she said.

Sonia felt awkward. 'I'm leaving today. I got a job.'

'Yes. Bella said so. But we can keep in touch.'

'Bella said I was leaving today?' Sonia said, startled.

'She told Gina this morning. Gina thought you had left already because she could not find your luggage.'

'The . . . oh well,' Sonia said lamely. 'Just as well I found somewhere then, wasn't it? Are you all right? Mrs Patel?'

The woman had her eyes closed. Without the expressive dark eyes, the face looked dead – too thin, all bones, with dark patches under and over the lids. 'It is beginning again,' she whispered. 'I think the baby come very soon now.'

Chapter Nine

In the sitting room, every trace of their previous night's occupation had been cleared away, the cushions and blankets gone. Sonia cursed Gina and Bella equally. What was Bella playing at, letting Gina effectively run this place and decide who came and went?

Why did Bella find it necessary to go with Gina to every appointment, leaving a nine-months pregnant woman here alone with her own four children and three of Gina's? And, not least, why did Bella have to be out when Sonia returned to collect her bags, securely locked in Bella's room, the key of which hung round Bella's neck?

She ran upstairs, enlisted Mrs Patel's two eldest children to help her drag a mattress downstairs, and they laid Mrs Patel on it in the sitting room.

'I am going to phone for an ambulance,' Sonia told the children, 'to take your mother to the hospital to have her baby. Will you stay here and look after her till I get back?'

The eldest boy's lip trembled. 'Who will look after us?' he asked.

'Lois and I will stay here until Bella gets back. Then Bella will take care of you until your mother is out of the hospital.' At least I hope she will, Sonia added mentally. 'Lois, you come with me,' she instructed. 'The rest of you stay here. I have to leave the door unlocked because I don't have a key, but don't go out of the house – okay?'

The four of them nodded solemnly. The elder girl took hold of the smallest child's hand.

The phone box at the end of the road was out of order. Sonia began knocking on doors. Lois clung to her, gripping the belt of her jeans. The third door was answered by an elderly man in braces and shirtsleeves. He opened the door a crack and peered at them suspiciously.

'Do you have a phone, please?' Sonia asked. 'There's a woman . . .'

'Phone at the end of the road,' the man grunted, closing the door.

Sonia was ready for him. She pushed the door open again. 'It's broken, and there's an emergency. Please dial nine nine nine straight away.'

'You from that refuge place?'

Did he say refuge? Or refuse? Sonia was not in the mood to give him the benefit of the doubt.

'No, we're not refuse,' she snapped. 'There is a human being about to give birth. Use the phone!'

'I don't have no phone.'

She could see it, over his shoulder, on the wall in the narrow hallway. She gave the door a sudden forcible shove, and pushed her way past him.

'You can't do that!' he spluttered. 'It's breaking and entering. I'll call the police.'

'Ambulance,' said Sonia into the phone. 'Hello? Yes, a lady has gone into labour . . .'

'You darkies think you can come over here,' the man continued, 'taking our jobs, using our National Health Service, having Gawd knows how many babies . . .'

'You got that address? Ten minutes? Thank you,' Sonia continued. 'And thank *you*,' she told the man.

'I'm not putting up with this,' he said.

Sonia turned to leave. He stopped her.

'You women walking out on your husbands,' he said. 'You should go back to your homes where you belong. And back to your own country.'

'Excuse me,' said Sonia with dignity, detaching her arm from his grasp. She reached the door.

'If she's having a baby,' he resumed, 'she ought to go back to her husband.'

'Goodbye and thank you,' Sonia said.

'So why don't she?' he persisted, catching hold of her arm again. 'Why don't she go back to her . . .'

Sonia's patience deserted her. She wheeled round, grabbed the man by his braces and said into his face, 'Because . . . her . . . husband . . . is . . . just . . . like . . . *you*!'

He was startled. 'There's no call for that,' he said. 'That's offensive!'

Sonia and Lois ran back to the house. Mrs Patel was breathing with difficulty, her eyes dilated and her lips a purplish colour. Sonia's courage failed her. She's not strong enough to go through another labour, she thought. What if she dies? She looked at the four children and saw that this thought had occurred to them too. They were crying. She knelt down and put her arms round the nearest two.

'The ambulance is coming,' she said.

Lois crouched down by Mrs Patel's head. 'God help us, all over again,' she said.

Mrs Patel smiled faintly. 'Yes,' she acknowledged.

'You'll need some things to take to the hospital,' Sonia said.

'There is a bag ready,' Mrs Patel said. 'Anita will show you.'

Anita took Sonia by the hand and led her upstairs.

'This one,' she said, picking up a Tesco carrier bag. The room was crowded, even with the mattresses stacked one on top of the other.

Sonia checked the bag. 'A towel?' she suggested.

Anita took one from the windowsill. It was not clean. Sonia had one in her dustbin bag, but it was in Bella's room. She tried the handle of Bella's door, to make sure, but it was securely locked. The dirty towel would have to do. Maybe the hospital would lend her a clean one.

Anita reached into the corner, behind the mattresses, and pulled out a small doll which she put into the bag too. She looked at Sonia hesitantly.

'That's nice,' Sonia approved. 'She can keep your mum company.' She looked at her watch and found it was nearly five thirty. Where had the time gone? They had waited quite a while in the cemetery, after Samuel had gone, till the rain stopped; then they had had to wait quite a time for a bus, and the journey itself was long, but somehow she had not thought it was later than four o'clock. She had hoped to arrive at Samuel's in time to prepare his evening meal: get things off to a good start.

The ambulance, Bella and Gina arrived at the same time.

'Where are my kids?' Gina hollered.

The ambulance men lifted Mrs Patel on to a stretcher. She gasped and bit her lip. Anita held on to her hand and had to be gently detached. 'You'll see your mum later, love,' the man said. Sonia handed the Tesco bag into the ambulance after them.

'These are her things.'

'You coming with her, love?' the man asked.

'No, I can't. Can I phone the hospital later, to find out how she's getting on?'

'Sure. King's College Hospital. You'll find the number in the book.' He slammed the door shut, and the ambulance drew off.

'Oh Sonia,' Bella said, 'what a good thing you were here.'

'Where are my bloody kids?' Gina roared.

'Where you left them, I expect,' Sonia said.

'What are you still doing here anyway?' Gina demanded. 'I thought you'd gone.'

'I can't think who told you that,' said Sonia evenly, looking at Bella. Bella turned away and picked up Mrs Patel's smallest child. 'But as it happens I am just leaving,' she continued.

'Gina,' said Bella, 'why don't you go and look for your boys? They can't have gone far. I'll put the kettle on and make us a cup of tea.' She was obviously exhausted. 'What a day,' she told Sonia as Gina went out yelling the children's names.

'May I have the key to your room?' Sonia requested. 'To collect my things.'

'Are you really leaving? Don't feel you have to. I only told Gina you'd gone, to stop her looking for your belongings.'

'Yes, I am really going. Thanks for putting us up last night.'

'Do you have somewhere to go? Somewhere proper, I mean?'

'Yes, thank you.'

'The agency can't have found you a job that quickly?'

Sonia gave her a wide smile. 'We've been very lucky,' she said. 'Shall I take the key, or do you want to come up?'

Bella put down the child and went up the stairs ahead of her, followed by Mrs Patel's four children and Lois. 'I don't know how I'm going to look after all these,' she said. 'You can stay a few more days if you want to, Sonia. Get yourself sorted out before you move on.'

'We'll be fine, thanks.' Sonia retrieved the bundle of bags. She felt sorry for Bella but resisted feeling she owed her anything, having received no food during her time at the refuge and having had to fight last night to keep Gina from stealing their few belongings. All she wanted was to leave before Gina returned.

Taking the bags with her, Sonia went in search of a phone box that worked. Lois dragged her feet. 'I want to stay and play with Anita,' she said.

Sonia turned to answer her and was struck by how weary the child was. 'Look,' she said, 'we've been on the go all day and you only had crisps for lunch. Do you want to go in the corner shop and get something to eat?'

'You come too.'

'I've got these bags. You take this fifty p and pick what you want, okay?'

'No, you come with me.'

'I can't, Lois . . . oh all right.'

The shop was tiny. Sonia hauled in the bags. The shop-keeper stared at her. 'I'm sorry,' Sonia apologized. 'She wouldn't come in on her own. Find what you want, Lois, and be quick.'

'You taking that lot to the launderette?' the shopkeeper asked. He was a tall Asian, very dark skinned, with a mous-tache.

'No, we're moving homes. Do you know where there's another phone round here? The one outside isn't working.'

'Is it for a local call?' the man enquired. 'If it's a local call you can use the phone here.'

'Thanks. I don't know the number, though. I want a mini-cab firm.'

He produced a card from under the counter. 'You phone this number. My brother-in-law.'

'Thanks. Where's the phone?'

'In the storeroom at the back. On the wall. I'll show you. Leave the bags here; never mind.'

He showed her the phone, leaning too close. 'I do this favour for you because you are a nice girl,' he said.

She picked up the phone and turned her back on him. Lois came and joined her. 'I want a banana,' she said.

'Good. Take a banana.'

'I can't. They're stuck together.'

'Hello? Can I have a minicab please? I'm in . . .'

The shopkeeper took the phone from her hand. 'Riaz? Ah!' There followed a stream of talk in a language Sonia could not begin to decipher. Finally he stopped and said to her, 'Where do you want him to take you?'

Sonia fished out Samuel's card. 'Herne Hill.'

'Herne Hill,' the man reported into the phone. Another stream of talk. 'Okay,' he said finally. 'He'll take you. He will be here in one minute.'

'One minute? That's quicker than an ambulance!'

'He lives upstairs,' the man explained. 'That will be thirty p for the call, please.'

'Local calls are ten p,' said Sonia. 'And you can't get more local than upstairs. You could have shouted for nothing.'

'Shouting upstairs is no way to do business,' the man said. 'Business is done on the phone. And ten p is only for very short local calls.'

'It was a short call. You're the one who turned it into a long conversation,' Sonia pointed out.

'It is important to keep on good terms with family,' said the

62

man reprovingly.

'I want a banana,' said Lois.

Sonia picked up two bunches. 'Have I got time to drop these down the road?'

'Oh, yes,' the shopkeeper assured her. 'He has to put a clean shirt on. He will wait for you, anyway.'

'I'll take these then. Lois, you have this one, and wait here for me. No, I mean it this time. Don't come. I'll be one minute.' She paid the man twenty p short of what he asked for and he grinned and said, 'Okay, okay. I give you a discount.'

She ran out of the shop and down the road. Gina was approaching from the opposite direction, hitting her three sons in turn. Sonia made it to the door ahead of her. The Patel boy opened it.

'Do you like bananas?' Sonia asked.

His eyes brightened. 'Yes.'

'Have these, and make sure your sisters get one each before Gina gets here. Be quick.'

He took the bananas and sprinted up the stairs, calling the other children to follow him. Sonia felt satisfied that the bananas were in safe hands.

'What are you back here for?' Gina challenged.

'I'm not. I'm leaving.' Sonia squeezed past her on the path.

'Lend us sixty p for some chips, will you?' Gina said.

'Sure.' She fumbled in her jeans pocket and brought out a ten-pound note. 'Have some chicken with it.'

'Great!' Gina's normally sullen expression vanished. She smiled. 'Come back and visit us some time,' she called after Sonia.

The minicab driver was waiting outside the shop. Lois sat on the counter eating her banana. Sonia felt hungry and realized she hadn't kept one for herself, but she was anxious to leave now. They piled the bags into the boot of the car and drove off. The shopkeeper waved. Sonia was reminded of their exit from the Grenvilles' the day before. Perhaps this occurred to Lois too, for she said, 'I want my doll back.'

'I'll get you another doll,' Sonia said.

'I want mine.'

'It will be yours too. You'll get used to it. We'll find one with a nice face.'

'I want *my* doll.'

'Come here, Lois. I'll give you a cuddle.'

The child slid across the seat and laid her head on Sonia's knees. She was asleep within seconds.

Sonia was dropping off to sleep herself when the minicab drew up outside a corner house covered with creeper and enclosed by a tall hedge.

'Wake up, ladies,' called the driver. 'Here is your new home!'

It was May and the evenings were drawing out, so although the sky was heavy with rainclouds there was enough light to see every detail of the house clearly. Even in daylight it seemed a dark house. There was a stillness about it that suggested a place long uninhabited.

The front garden was large, setting the house back quite far from the road, and as Sonia pushed open the gate in the hedge and walked up the path she tried not to remember late-night horror films in which innocent victims blithely arrived at spooky mansions with dark windows and ivy-shrouded façades. She had always wondered at their stupidity in entering these forbidding places instead of briskly instructing the driver to turn round and go straight home. Now she wondered at her own stupidity.

Meeting an old man in a cemetery! Agreeing to go and live with him! Even taking a defenceless small child! Arriving at dusk at a gloomy old house, hedged round and hidden from view, with no one to hear their cries for help until it was too late. What was the woman thinking of? Hadn't she seen the movies? Hadn't she read the script?

'Come along!' said the minicab driver cheerily. He was following her with the rest of the bags. Lois tagged along sleepily behind him.

'I have to go next door for the key,' Sonia said. 'Could you wait for me?' What if it was a joke? If he hadn't meant it? They

'We got held up,' Sonia said. 'I didn't call at your neighbour's – is that all right? You said she would be expecting us.'

'No, I arrived home early and let her know I was here,' Samuel said. 'She kindly helped me make up the beds for you. Come and see your room.' He shouldered the bundle of bags without apparent difficulty and led the way upstairs. They were wide stairs, carpeted in dark red, beginning with three steps to the left before a small square landing which turned right into a straight flight, then right again round a fat wooden balustrade, ending up in the centre of a curved landing with doors to left and right.

The stairway was light, with a long window above the straight part of the flight; there were stained glass tulips in the window, and a wide, high ledge in front of it. How do I dust that ledge and clean that window? Sonia wondered. Not to mention polishing all those fiddly banister things.

Samuel opened a door ahead of them, on the right. 'This will be your room,' he said, 'if it suits you. It is the largest, though sometimes a little noisy from the traffic.'

It was the front bedroom, square and spacious, bow-windowed with heavy lined brocade curtains, a fitted moss green carpet, an enormous dark wooden wardrobe – also bow fronted – raised off the ground on feet like claws (and how do I get the Hoover under that? Sonia mused), a large chest of drawers, two single beds with wooden headboards, made up with sheets, blanket and an eiderdown each and divided by a tall wooden bedside cabinet.

A lacquered dressing table with triple mirror and padded stool stood in the window bay, and the corner was taken up by a fitted washbasin and a heated towel rail containing two pink towels, with a small pink rug on the floor. Between the washbasin and the chest of drawers was a small white-painted fireplace edged with dark red tiles. Pictures hung on the walls, one of them a framed tapestry of a bird of paradise, the others watercolours of harbour scenes.

'Wow!' said Sonia, awestruck. 'Is this for us?'

'Is it all right?' Samuel asked. 'Miss Prynne, my previous

housekeeper, preferred the smaller room; she found this one rather cold, but I thought perhaps the two of you would be glad of the extra space.'

'But this is the master bedroom!' Sonia exclaimed. 'Don't you use this room yourself?'

'No, I prefer the back room. I can look out and see the garden in the mornings. Shall I leave you to settle in, or would you like to see the rest of the house?'

'See the rest of the house,' said Sonia promptly.

'And the garden,' Lois contributed.

Samuel smiled. 'You like gardens, do you?'

'Yes, but not with white things in,' Lois answered. She had, Sonia noticed, actually forgotten to keep her hands over her face in the excitement of looking around their new room.

Sonia laughed, seeing Samuel look puzzled. 'She doesn't like gardens with tombstones in,' she explained. 'She thought you lived in the cemetery.' Lois shot her a furious glance and immediately covered her eyes with both hands.

'This garden has no tombstones, I promise you, Lois,' Samuel said. 'It has a birdbath, though. Have you seen a birdbath before?'

Lois, still masked, shook her head from side to side – no.

'The sparrows come and bathe in it every morning,' Samuel informed her. 'If they find it has gone dry they are very disappointed, so we have to remember to keep it full of water. Would you like that job?'

Lois hesitated, then the small pigtailed head nodded yes.

'Good,' Samuel said. 'I shall remunerate you accordingly.' As both Sonia and Lois looked equally puzzled by this statement, he translated, 'Pocket money. As long as the job is well done,' at which Lois lowered her hands and smiled happily.

Samuel opened other doors. The room next to theirs at the front of the house was a smaller bedroom with one bed covered in a green satin quilt, and with similar wooden furniture though smaller in scale: the wardrobe was merely large, rather than massive, and the dressing table had only one mirror, not three. One wall held a bookcase, dark wood, with carved edges to the shelves which held, Sonia noticed, a small library of murder mysteries. This room also had its own wash-basin.

Doors set into the curved wall of the landing revealed cupboards: an airing cupboard with slatted shelves above the hot water tank, a linen cupboard next to it stacked with sheets and towels and spare blankets, the space underneath it filled with an assortment of cleaning materials meticulously arranged – bottles and tins of polish and scourer stacked on a rack, with dusters, cloths, a chamois leather and shoe cleaning kit hung on hooks. Sonia was impressed.

'That's very neat,' she said. Becoming businesslike, she turned to Samuel and said, 'You're going to have to tell me which polish to use for what. All that lovely wooden furniture. You don't use spray polish on that, do you?'

'No,' he acknowledged. 'It can build up a layer of silicones and hide the bloom on the wood. But much of the furniture is French polished; it only needs a wipe with a dry duster. The polishing I do myself, with beeswax, occasionally.'

'You do it yourself?'

'Yes. It's a bit of an art, using beeswax, and of course I do it all the time at work, or teach the apprentices how to. It has to be used very sparingly and worked in well. I have a daily help in the house, but she didn't seem to get the hang of it quite, so I do it myself.'

'You have a daily help?' Sonia's heart sank. He's not going to pay us, she thought. It's just going to be board and keep. He already pays somebody to do the cleaning.

'Not daily,' he amended. 'Twice a week. She cleans the floors and the windows on the inside – a window cleaner comes once a month to do the outsides – and the fireplace and grate in the sitting room and riddles out the boiler in the kitchen. Oh, and packs up the bed linen and my clothes to send to the laundry.'

'Laundry?' said Sonia faintly. 'You don't have a washing machine, then?'

'I have kept meaning to buy one,' said Samuel, 'ever since

69

they were first brought out. The twin-tub machines seemed rather a chore, and then the automatic machines became so automatic I wasn't sure I would be able to understand them. Are they difficult to use, do you think?'

'Easy as blinking,' said Sonia. 'And I bet it would work out cheaper than sending everything to a laundry.'

'Excellent,' said Samuel. 'We shall purchase one as soon as possible. Unless,' he said anxiously, 'you would find it too much work to do the washing at home? I could do it at week-ends, of course . . .'

'Listen!' said Sonia in amazement. 'You're getting a house-keeper, not entertaining a guest! I can do the washing. And the cleaning. You don't need to pay other people. We're here to work.'

'Oh,' he said. 'I wasn't sure what was expected. I am out of touch, you see. My cousin Gertrude assured me that house-keeper-cooks these days don't like to do anything beyond shopping and cooking and generally organizing the running of the house. Also that they want one hundred and fifty pounds a week and one and a half days off and a colour television in their room.' He said this in a rush, embarrassed and awk-ward. Sonia felt immensely relieved. He's as nervous as I am, she thought.

'Of course,' Samuel added, 'I am willing to do whatever is fair. I don't know what is customary nowadays. Miss Prynne was with me for thirty years, you see – probably rather more.'

'And did Miss Prynne have an army of servants and a hundred and fifty pounds a week and a telly in her room?' Sonia teased.

'No, no. In fact, when Gertrude told me . . . I realized I must have been underpaying Miss Prynne quite dreadfully for years. And she didn't take a regular day off, just let me know when she was going to visit her sister in Coventry and took a week or so then. This was her home, you see. Still, I should have been more thoughtful, put things on a proper profes-sional basis, checked the current rates of salary and so forth. She never said anything. I paid her train fares whenever she went away, and something for her expenses on holiday. But evidently I must have been cheating her, for some years.' He looked so distressed that Sonia put a hand on his arm.

'We'll sit down and work something out that suits all of us,' she said soothingly. 'No problem. Let's see the rest of the house now, shall we?'

'I want to see the cellar,' said Lois.

'What do you want to see the cellar for?' Sonia laughed. 'You hated the cellar at the last house. She wouldn't go in it,' she told Samuel. 'I had to go down to hang out the washing there when it was raining outside, and she wouldn't walk past the boiler; she thought it would eat her!'

'No, I didn't!' Lois shouted. She hit Sonia on the thigh.

'Stop that,' Sonia said. 'Behave yourself.'

'There are no cellars in this house, Lois,' Samuel said. 'The house would have been built after that time when most family houses included a basement. This one was built with no out-houses either. I added a coalhouse myself, and a shed, and there is an air-raid shelter still here from the war years – above ground, not an underground one.'

'You weren't here then, though – during the war,' Sonia said. 'When did you come to this house?'

'I was here during the war,' he assured her. 'At least, I was not living here; I was sent abroad, but I owned the house.'

Sonia tried to figure out how old he must be but didn't like to ask such a personal question. She'd find out, or work it out, she decided. She was good at discovering details people did not always want to divulge. She had found out quite a few things about the Grenvilles during her time there.

Samuel opened more doors. 'Bathroom,' he said, 'and lava-tory next door.' Both were small and old-fashioned, with cracked linoleum floors and black and white tiles on the walls. The bath was of white enamel stained yellow by limescale and, like the wardrobe in the big bedroom, raised off the ground by claws. The washbasin was large and square with clumsy taps which had long since lost their shine and become green with age, though not quite as green as the mirror on the side wall. But the room was light, with a frosted window covered with green plastic curtains.

'You like green,' Sonia observed. 'Green and red.'

He looked surprised. 'Yes,' he said. 'I suppose I must do. It's a long time since this house was furnished or decorated. I no longer notice what is in it.'

He can't have noticed the toilet, Sonia thought – or lavatory, as he called it. Not only was it dangerously cracked, right up the bowl from stained base to square wooden lid, but it was filthy. It smelt. And the iron tank high on the wall was so badly rusted it looked as though it might fall at any moment.

'Is this the only toilet?' Sonia asked. If there was another one, she resolved, she would not allow Lois to come in here.

He was taken aback. 'Um . . . there is an outside one,' he said, 'attached to the house but not reached from the house; the door is in the garden.'

'I'm just asking,' Sonia explained, 'because this one looks unsafe.'

'Unsafe?' He was alarmed.

'The tank,' Sonia pointed out. 'It's almost come off the wall there at the top. And this pan could crack in half at any minute.'

'Good grief,' he said. 'You are absolutely right. I must call the plumber in to attend to it. I shall telephone him tomorrow.'

Call the undertaker to bury it, more like, Sonia thought privately, but she did not say this aloud either, feeling that she had been outspoken enough and not wanting to push her luck.

Samuel, however, beamed. 'You see,' he said triumphantly, 'you have started housekeeping already. That is precisely what this house needs – someone to take it in hand and put things right. Now, this is the spare room,' he announced, 'only, as you can see, there wouldn't be very much room for a guest to spend the night.'

The room was stacked with furniture – literally stacked, from floor to ceiling. Sonia gasped.

'My storeroom,' Samuel said.

'However does anybody get in to clean this?' asked Sonia in trepidation.

'Oh, nobody does,' he assured her. 'These pieces are in quite a dirty and shabby state when I bring them here, and they stay like that until I renovate them. My workshop is in the garden. I am just showing you this so you know your way round the place, but there's no need to clean in here – and no possibility!'

'Are these all private commissions, then?' Sonia asked. 'You said you did private work at home. Doesn't it take years, at this rate, for people to get their furniture back?'

'These are not commissions,' Samuel said. 'These are my own purchases. You could call them investments. I go to auctions periodically if I hear of an interesting one, a sale of stately home contents or some such event. Some of the items are in such a shocking state that the antique dealers won't touch them; it would cost them too much to renovate. Some of these pieces here were not even in the sale; I found them in back rooms or outhouses and asked if I could have them.'

Sonia was fascinated. 'Are they valuable?'

'When they are finished they will be, yes,' he said.

'How long would it take you to do something up, something like that, for instance?' she asked, pointing to a round-seated wooden chair that was no more than a frame with a dislocated arm and missing spokes in the back.

'Ah that,' Samuel mused. 'That's a lovely piece, potentially so, at least. As soon as I bring a piece back here I take it first to my workshop and check it for mildew and rot and routinely treat it for woodworm, so that these hazards are not brought into the house. Then . . .'

'I want to see the garden,' said Lois firmly, becoming bored. 'And the cellar.'

'There's no cellar. And don't be rude,' Sonia said.

'No, no, of course,' Samuel said. 'I am the one who is rude, keeping you standing talking. We must have some supper, too.' He closed the door to the room and headed for the stairs.

'Is this your room, this door here?' Sonia could not resist

asking. If their room and the old housekeeper's room were so splendid, Samuel's own room must be like a palace.

'Yes, yes.' He opened the door to show her. The room felt chilly and looked surprisingly bare, although there was plenty of furniture in it. A small window with faded brown velvet curtains shed light on the thin carpet covering the green lino floor, a high bed with an eiderdown that had seen better days, a tall narrow wardrobe, a bureau with a sloping front, and a plain chest of drawers with round handles topped with a square swing mirror and two leather-backed brushes and a comb.

A shaving brush, razor and block of shaving soap, toothbrush and toothpaste and a bath sponge stood on a glass shelf above the green washbasin in the corner, and on the narrow mantelpiece above the small fireplace there was a wooden carriage clock with a brass handle, two carved bears and a couple of brownish photographs in inlaid wooden frames.

It was the room of an elderly bachelor, and bleak. Looking at it Sonia stopped worrying about whether she would be a success in this badly needed new job and thought instead, He needs us too. Not just a housekeeper, someone to cook and clean, but us – Lois and Sonia. We're going to be good for him. It was an entirely new thought.

Chapter Eleven

At Lois's insistence they went out of the front door and toured both the front and the back gardens, taking in the coal shed, the air-raid shelter (empty except for a bench seat and a number of cobwebs), Samuel's workshop (tidy, with tools ranged neatly along the walls, but also full of cobwebs), the birdbath, the big acacia tree, the bonfire, the compost heap, the little apple trees stretched out along a wire trellis and the grass footpaths between the deep flower beds.

It was a beautiful garden – beautiful to look at and perfect for a child to play in. Lois was delighted. She peeped through her fingers at everything Samuel pointed out to her and took her hands away from her face completely two or three times. Sonia was suddenly so tired she could hardly keep her eyes open. She trailed behind Lois and Samuel, unable to take in what he was saying.

Finally, when Samuel was about to fetch a small watering can in order to demonstrate to Lois how to fill the birdbath every morning, Sonia said, 'It's getting late. I think Lois should have something to eat and go to bed,' and Samuel quickly agreed and showed them back to the house.

They went in through the kitchen door, set behind the side gate which separated the back and front gardens. 'I usually eat in the kitchen,' said Samuel.

'Would you like me to cook something?' Sonia asked.

'No, it's all ready,' he said. 'I prepared a snack supper. I hope that suits you?'

'Great,' Sonia said with feeling.

'I bought crisps,' Samuel said proudly. 'And there is bread and ham and cheese . . .'

Sonia was staring at the kitchen, aghast. It was like step-ping into a time warp. The whole room, from floor to high ceil-ing, was yellow with age-old grease and smoke. The floor, clearly visible through remnants of ancient lino, was stone. The cooker bore the scars of a thousand spills and was stained dark brown and black, the oven door so encrusted with dirt it did not seem possible it would open. The sink was a square trough, originally white but now stained and chipped beyond any recognizable colour. The cupboard below the sink had no door and its one shelf sagged with damp.

'Dear Lord!' said Sonia under her breath.

'Is something the matter?' asked Samuel.

She looked at him. He looked back with innocent mild anxiety. She looked at the thick pipe leading across the ceiling, at the barrage of water pipes above the sink, the flue leading to the old boiler. All were greasy, black, festooned with cobwebs. Several pipes had leaked and left green and brown stains down the wall.

Samuel followed her gaze. The sink taps were also green, speckled with mould. The larder door, which Sonia now opened, revealed one shelf containing a couple of tins and a box of eggs and five shelves containing dust, spiders and mil-dew. She turned back to Samuel.

'Is this why you couldn't advertise for a housekeeper?' she said.

'I did say the house had got into a dreadful state,' he said humbly. 'Living here, I suppose I hadn't realized. Then when Miss Prynne left . . .'

'Six months ago, you said?'

'Yes.'

'This kitchen,' Sonia said, 'hasn't been cleaned in years. Possibly centuries!'

'It is extremely dirty,' said Samuel wonderingly.

'And you employ a cleaning lady?' Sonia said.

'Only to do the general rough work,' Samuel said. 'Not to keep the whole house clean. Just the boiler and windows and floors.'

'Not this floor,' Sonia said.

Samuel looked at it. 'No,' he admitted. 'Though perhaps it is quite hard to clean. The linoleum is rather cracked.'

Sonia bit her lip before she was tempted to retort that its owner was severely cracked if he had failed to notice that the people he paid to clean his house had let it sink into this squalor. She must keep her cool. It was a job, at least. They had a roof over their heads. She would get this dump cleaned up eventually. It was only dirt. They had a home.

Samuel watched her. He became nervous. 'I have let matters slide,' he said. 'What can I do to improve things?'

Sonia struggled with her feelings and got them under control. 'There's no problem,' she said finally. 'I can start work tomorrow. The supper looks very nice.'

He was relieved. 'I'll go and wash my hands,' he said.

Sonia was too tired to worry about cleanliness. By comparison with this place she was clean. She sat down at the table and waited for him to return. Lois tried to climb on to her lap.

'No, sit on a chair, Lois. Here, next to me.'

'No,' Lois whined.

'Don't give me any trouble,' said Sonia wearily. 'Eat something and then it's bedtime. I had no sleep last night.'

Samuel returned. Sonia thought he looked tired as well. He must be about seventy, she reflected, and still commuting to work every day. They began to eat. Lois refused to sit on a chair but stood by Sonia, leaning against her and eating small scraps of ham from her plate.

'Do you want to put her to bed and finish your supper afterwards?' Samuel said.

'I don't think she'd sleep in a strange place unless I stayed with her,' said Sonia. 'I'll wash up first and get everything straight and then take her up.'

'Couldn't that wait till tomorrow?' he said.

'Yes, if you don't mind. But we should have a talk, shouldn't we, about the housekeeping arrangements?'

'Shall we postpone that until tomorrow too?' he asked. 'You

look rather tired, if I may say so without offence.'

She laughed. 'I spent last night on guard duty. Someone at the refuge was trying to get into our room. Sleep would be very welcome. What time do you have to be up in the morning, Sam . . . ah, Mr Arnold?'

'I rise at six thirty,' he said, 'because I am no good at rushing in the mornings and I like to take a walk in the garden before breakfast. I don't leave for work until seven forty. There is a bus which stops across the road at seven forty-five.'

'So breakfast at about seven, or is that too early?' Sonia enquired.

He considered. 'It is probably a quarter past seven,' he said, 'by the time I sit down.'

'Right. And what do you like to eat for breakfast?'

'Oh, just tea and toast, you know. There is no need for you to get up,' he said. 'I can easily prepare my own . . .' He caught her eye and laughed. Sonia pointed at herself. 'Housekeeper,' she said. 'Remember? And two sandwiches and an apple for your packed lunch, yes? With a flask of tea or coffee?'

'Coffee,' he affirmed. 'Two and a half teaspoonsful of sugar are sufficient for the flask. And please, when you are shopping, buy whatever you and the child normally have. Cornflakes or whatever it is that children like for breakfast. And for suppers, whatever you like. I eat anything. I will leave you some money for shopping tomorrow. I am afraid there is very little food in the house.'

Lois was asleep on her feet, her head nodding. Sonia shook her awake. 'Say good night,' she instructed.

''Night,' said Lois dreamily, too weary for shyness.

'Goodnight Lois,' Samuel said. 'Sleep tight. Good night Sonia.'

'Goodnight Samu . . . Mr Arnold.'

'I much prefer Samuel,' he said. 'After all, you are going to be family, aren't you?'

On impulse, Sonia leaned over his chair and kissed the top of his head. 'Family,' she said. She had always thought that word had a nice ring to it.

Lois lay like a log on the bed as Sonia struggled to undress her. Her pyjamas were in one of the bags, but the string tying the bags was now tightly knotted. Sonia left Lois in vest and pants, covered her up, then remembered she had not taken the child to the toilet; she would have to wake her. Lois refused to be wakened. Sonia debated whether to risk a wet bed and decided not to, not the first night. It would make a bad impression.

'Wake up, Lois,' she insisted. She pulled Lois to her feet and the child complained, whining in her sleep. Sonia forced her to walk along the landing, sat her on the toilet, shaking her when her eyes kept closing. 'Stay awake! You have to wee before you can go to bed!' Finally the child complied, and instantly fell asleep. Sonia tried to carry her but was too tired. She shook Lois awake again. 'You have to walk!'

The child started retching. Sonia felt guilty but persisted. 'You'll be all right when you're in bed. Just walk!'

'Feel sick!' Lois moaned.

'You're just tired. Walk to the bed now.'

By the time they got there Sonia was too exhausted to lift Lois on to the bed. She fell on to her own bed and realized she should have gone to the toilet herself. Then sleep hit her.

She thought she woke up in the night, but it was light and Samuel was standing over Lois saying, 'You'll feel better now,' and stroking her head. She wanted to tell him to leave her alone, that Lois didn't like that, she hated strangers, but she found she was unable to open her mouth. Lois was sitting up in bed, wearing a pink towel for some reason, and seemed quite calm. In the morning, Sonia would work out what this dream could have meant.

Chapter Twelve

Something had gone wrong. Sonia knew it as soon as she woke up. Something had happened to Lois, and now someone was trying to murder her, was painfully constricting her around the waist and stomach.

She forced her eyes open. Lois was gone. A pink towel was draped across her open bed. Sonia jumped off the bed, the pain in her stomach making her double up and groan. Her watch said ten past eleven; it must have stopped.

'Lois!' she shouted, but Lois had been kidnapped. The dream last night had not been a dream. Samuel had lured them into his house, having heard Sonia shouting in the cemetery about how desperate they were, and now he had enticed Lois away from her for his own sinister ends.

'Lois!' she yelled again, but the house was quiet, as quiet as death. She flung herself along the corridor and pushed Samuel's door open. The room was empty, the bed neatly made. He hadn't even been to bed the night before! He had come in and drugged Lois – and then drugged Sonia herself, maybe. She never slept heavily like that. She looked at the clock on Samuel's mantelpiece. It also said ten past eleven.

If only she could wake up properly, think clearly! Her stomach hurt so much. She must have slept in her jeans. Her hazy brain told her she needed to go to the toilet, so she went. The pain eased.

She ran downstairs, still shouting Lois's name. The downstairs rooms were empty: the rooms they had not seen last night. She had a brief impression of a sitting room with solid armchairs in front of an open fire, and a dining room with a large table like a great slab cut from a tree, seamless and polished like a conker, but what struck her most was that both these rooms were empty – empty of Lois.

There was no one in the kitchen either. Last night's dishes stood waiting on the wooden draining board beside the stained sink. Nobody lived in this house! That was why it was so filthy! It had been deserted for years, all this old furniture left standing about. Samuel was front man for a gang, luring children into the uninhabited house . . .

'Shut up, Sonia!' she told herself fiercely. She was being ridiculous, paranoid. 'Lois!' she shouted again.

For some reason she ran back up the stairs to their bedroom. The curtains were open; she had been too tired to draw them last night. Had he drugged them at suppertime, then? Put something in the food, or the Coke? Lois had eaten and drunk little. She had felt sick. Sonia had not listened to her complaints.

She looked out of the window, over the front garden, up and down the street. Traffic passed, cars and buses. The next door neighbour – that must be Mrs Atwood – walked in at her front gate, carrying a bag of shopping, casting a glance up at Samuel's house. Sonia quickly drew back from the window.

She returned to Samuel's room, looked out of his window. Here she could not see the street; the garden was well screened by the apple trees and a garage at the back, high fences at the sides. She was turning away from the window, deciding to phone the police, when she saw something move in one of the flower beds – a small brown figure in white vest and pants with a halo of white sunlight outlining the halo of black hair.

Sonia wrestled with the window catch, pushed the window open and bawled, 'Lois!'

Lois looked up and waved.

Sonia felt faint from sheer relief. 'What are you doing there?' she croaked.

'I'm in the flower bed,' said Lois. 'I filled up the birdbath this morning, and a bird came and had a bath in it!'

'Come up here,' Sonia said. 'This minute.'

'All right,' said Lois cheerfully. She wriggled her way out of

81

the flower bed, between a white and a pink bush, and scampered across the lawn, barefooted.

'You mustn't go off like that without telling me,' Sonia said, meeting her at the top of the stairs and leading her by the hand into their bedroom. 'I thought you'd been kidnapped!'

Lois regarded her with large eyes. 'By the gardener?' she asked.

'No, by . . . never mind. You're okay. Why is that towel on the bed?'

'I was sick,' said Lois proudly. 'In the night.'

So she hadn't dreamt it. 'Did Samuel come in?'

'Yes, he did.'

'Why didn't you wake me up? Or why didn't he?'

'You were asleep,' said Lois.

'But I remember seeing him. I must have woken up for a minute.'

'Yes, you said, "Leave me alone,"' Lois recalled. 'And then you went fast asleep.'

'I didn't say leave me alone,' Sonia corrected. 'I was telling him to leave you alone because you don't like strangers to touch you.'

'No, you said "Leave *me* alone,"' said Lois firmly. 'And then you . . .'

'What must he have thought of me?' exclaimed Sonia. 'What a bad mother! I never sleep heavily like that. I wake up if you even sigh in your sleep, normally. Did I snore?'

Lois shook her head. Only one pigtail remained; the rest of her hair stood out in a soft fuzz. 'Nuh-huh. You didn't snore.'

'And I slept all this time?' Sonia was incredulous. 'Till eleven o'clock? I meant to get up at seven and make Samuel his breakfast, and his sandwiches. He must have had to do it himself.'

'No,' said Lois. 'I helped him. And I filled the birdbath. Come and look.'

'In a minute. We've got to get dressed. I've wasted half the day.' She sat on the bed. 'I can't wake up!' she wailed. 'I was going to do so much work!'

'Samuel said two things to tell you,' Lois remembered. 'Don't do any work today.'

'He didn't say that.'

'Yes, he did,' Lois confirmed. ' "Tell your mummy no work today. She needs to *sleep*!" ' She leaped on the bed beside Sonia.

'What was the other thing he said?'

Lois furrowed her brow. 'I don't know.'

'You're too young to remember messages,' Sonia said. 'He should have woken me up, or left me a note.'

'He left you a note,' said Lois, jumping energetically. 'On the kitchen table.'

'Don't jump on the bed; you'll break it. Come on, we'll go and read this note.'

'Put my clothes on!' Lois demanded.

Sonia started wrenching off the string that tied the bags. 'I'll have to iron these clothes,' she said. 'Look how creased they've got.' She found Lois a T-shirt and a pair of dungarees. 'I should give you a bath first, but the bath needs a good clean. I am so tired!' she exclaimed, sitting back on her heels. 'Why in heaven's name am I so tired?'

'You haven't had any breakfast,' Lois said.

'Did you have breakfast with Samuel?'

Lois nodded. 'We had toast and tea. Samuel had tea and I had Coke.'

'Coke for breakfast?' Sonia laughed. 'Listen, Lois, you are not to go running about after Samuel, okay? We're here to work. You don't ask him to get your breakfast; you ask me.'

'You were asleep!'

'I know. I overslept, I know. And listen, don't go running around with no clothes on like this. You wake me up and you ask me to get you dressed. Right?'

'I woke up like this,' said Lois, in defence. 'You didn't put any pyjamas on me.'

'I know. Look, here are your pyjamas, in this bag. Put them on your bed for tonight. Are there any hangers in that big wardrobe?'

Lois ran to look. 'There are lots, but they're right up high.'

'Okay, I'll reach them.' She stood up and groaned.

Lois shook her head impatiently. 'Samuel said don't work today,' she reminded Sonia. 'You have to go and have breakfast.'

'Yes, you're right. He can't really have said don't work though, Lois. I can't take a day off before I've even started.'

Lois sighed and raised her eyes. 'He *did* say. And he wrote it down in a note.'

The note was on the kitchen table, in an envelope with twenty pounds in it. 'Dear Sonia,' it said, in immaculate copperplate handwriting, 'Forgive me for not waking you but I thought you needed to sleep. Please do not start cleaning today, but take the day easy and Recover your Strength after your recent Ordeal.'

'Will you listen to that?' Sonia marvelled. 'How's that for a nice man?' And I suspected him of being part of a vice ring, kidnapping children, she reflected guiltily.

'I am leaving you Twenty Pounds,' the note continued, 'for any immediate Shopping you may need to do. Be sure to have a proper lunch. Do not prepare anything for Supper, as, if convenient to you and Lois, I will bring home Fried Chicken from our local Take-Away Shop at about six thirty. Yours, Samuel Arnold. PS: Lois was unwell during the night, but appears well and chirpy this morning. If you should wish to ring the Doctor, however, the Telephone number is in the Address File by the phone, under D.'

'Lois,' said Sonia. 'We've got a day off. What do you want to do?'

'Go in the garden,' said Lois promptly, 'and show you the birdbath. I filled it up myself.'

'So you told me. I'm coming to see it now. Then I'm going to have a coffee. This is the life, eh Lois?'

that. But she tried, and she believed it was because she kept trying that Mrs Grenville trusted her. Bit by bit Mrs Grenville became less careful about making the right impression, and let slip a few items of truth.

Mrs Grenville's privileged upbringing, in the West Indies, Paris and then England, had shielded her from financial poverty but from not much else. Her parents were cold and loveless, her father selfishly preoccupied with pursuing a career and cultivating useful contacts and her mother concerned with presenting an enviable image to the world, collecting people with famous names and holding famous parties, dressed in clothes by famous designers.

To Sonia it seemed that the child Mrs Grenville had been was not so very different from the child Sonia had been. What both had in common was that they had been surplus to requirements. Rich or poor, they had not been wanted.

Sonia shook herself to banish these thoughts. Here she was on the first day of a new job – and a day off, at that – and all she could do was sit letting her coffee go cold and dwelling on the past. Surely there were better things to dwell on than memories of Mrs Grenville! The past was gone, thank God, and here she was in a fine big empty house with no employer breathing down her neck. The only things she had to do were to glance out of the window to check on Lois, who was skipping round and round the big tree on the lawn, and put the kettle on again.

It was lunchtime before she remembered Mrs Patel and went to phone the hospital. The nurse on duty on the maternity ward informed her that Mrs Patel had had her baby this morning, after a long and difficult labour – a girl, six pounds, healthy – and that Mrs Patel herself was all right but had been sleeping since the birth and had been found to be severely anaemic. She would be in hospital till her condition stabilized.

'Can she have visitors?' Sonia asked, but was secretly relieved when the nurse said, 'Yes, but you'd do better to wait a day or two. She will probably be less drowsy when she's had more iron.' Sonia, still feeling drowsy herself, was not sorry to postpone a trip to the hospital. She hoped the children would be all right with Bella and Gina, but did not want to risk phoning them to find out. For one thing they might want her to go back and help, and for another she did not want them to ask her where she was living.

I'm not being unfriendly, she excused herself. It's just that I can't go handing out Samuel's address and letting people pop in and visit. It's not my house.

Having convinced herself she had no right to invite people she didn't like into her employer's house, Sonia proceeded to treat the house as though it were her own. A house yielded a wealth of valuable clues about an employer, Sonia had found, and she liked to be one step ahead.

Samuel's furniture, lovingly polished, spoke of patience and care for natural woods; his bedroom spoke of a disregard for luxury, but it was always the small details that revealed most about the occupants of a house.

In the sitting room, for instance, a book and a bag of peppermint humbugs placed on a side table indicated which chair Samuel normally sat in, and examination of the book itself revealed that it was borrowed from a local library, was not due to be returned for thirteen more days, and was a travel book on the Philippines written in 1968.

In the dining room, when she could divert her attention from that gleaming glossy tree trunk of a table (she had never seen anything like it, all one piece of wood, no joins, with great whorls and stripes in the grain) Sonia discovered more clues to her employer and his former household. The candlesticks, which looked dingy, like old stained metal, were silver, hallmarked on the base, and simply had not been cleaned. Or not cleaned properly. Streaks of Silvo caked the crevices.

The cabinet in the dining room, with its canopied three-sided top cupboard supported by wooden pillars on a wide surface with two drawers and two large cupboards underneath, contained bottles of drink – Irish malt whiskey, gin, sherry, brandy, Benedictine, and tonic and bitter lemon.

The rest of the cupboard space contained glasses, some

plain, some with delicate gold patterns around the rim, some cut crystal, and a couple of sherry decanters and water jugs. They were uniformly dusty and several contained dead flies.

In the drawers were a couple of packets of white candles and an assortment of table linen – heavy damask tablecloths, fine white linen cloths edged and inset with lace, matching napkins, a few embroidered tray cloths and small tablecloths that made Sonia gasp with admiration. They were exquisite but badly creased, yellowed where they had been folded, and they smelt musty. Sonia shook them out and laid them on the table one after the other. With careful washing, the yellow would probably come out. A collector would give a fortune for these. She folded them up and put them back in the drawers.

'What are you doing?' asked Lois, coming in search of her.

'I'm seeing what work will need to be done here,' Sonia told her.

'Are you exploring?' Lois asked.

Sonia looked at her and laughed. 'I'm leaving it to you to explore the garden,' she said. 'How are you getting on?'

'I found an animal,' Lois said. 'I've brought it to show you.'

'Ugh!' exclaimed Sonia. 'A snail! Don't put it down on that table, Lois!'

'Why?'

'Because they leave slimy trails. Look at this beautiful polished table.' She led Lois out of the room, noticing as she did that there was a key in the lock. She took the key, locked the door from the outside, and put the key in her pocket.

'Why did you do that?' asked Lois, sharp-eyed.

'I think this room had better stay locked in the daytime, Lois,' said Sonia apologetically. 'It's not that I don't trust you to be careful, but the things in there are very fragile – very easy to damage without meaning to. We won't need to go in there, except to clean. There are lots of other rooms.'

'I want to go in there!' Lois protested. 'I want to see the things.'

'Okay, you will. But only with me. It's better than at the Grenvilles',' she added, forestalling Lois's next protest. 'Mrs

Grenville didn't let you in any of the rooms, did she? Except our bedroom and the kitchen.'

'And the cellar,' said Lois.

'Yes, but you only went in the cellar with me, and you didn't like it then.'

'No, I didn't only . . .'

'Lois, stop arguing with me over everything! Take that snail back into the garden . . . why? Because I say so. Because he doesn't like the feel of carpet on his tummy; he likes to be crawling on grass, okay? And I'll tell you what I'm going to do. I'm going to bring you a picnic lunch in the garden. You go and get ready.'

The child ran out of the door, happily. Sonia went upstairs to Samuel's room. Just one more exploration before she made them some lunch. She didn't ask herself why she was doing this. It was something she always did, at the first available chance, in a new house. It was a kind of security; her hoard of knowledge of people's secrets was her insurance policy. Against what? Not against dismissal, evidently, since this had not worked with the Grenvilles; perhaps against feeling powerless. After all, if an employer could demand references, collect information about her, why should she not do the same?

There was always a locked drawer somewhere, and Samuel's was in the bureau in his bedroom. And to every locked drawer there was a hidden key, normally not very ingeniously hidden. It took very little ingenuity to find Samuel's key. It was not even really hidden, only placed in the tiny (unlocked) drawer between the compartments inside the desk part of the bureau. A small brass key, it fitted neatly and easily into the lock of the drawer underneath.

Having found the key so easily, Sonia hesitated. The locked drawer was itself the key, she had always thought, the key to what the person really treasured. What people kept under lock and key was what they most valued. Mrs Grenville had kept jewellery in a safe above the bed – a safe whose combination Sonia had discovered quite easily.

Mr Grenville stored the deeds of the house, plentiful cash and his shares certificates in a second safe, and bank statements, bill receipts, and other certificates and documents of ownership in locked drawers in his desk. The opening mechanism of his safe was a bit more complicated, but Sonia had soon mastered it, and the keys to the drawers were located, not long after her arrival, in a decorative Oriental spice jar on his study bookshelf.

Sonia could have quoted the Grenvilles' income, investments and capital reserves to within the nearest hundred pounds, while copies of correspondence (kept in a lockable file; key in the left-hand drawer of the hall table) gave details of credit card expenditure, household bills and salaries and agency fees for previous staff.

Now she was about to embark on a similar programme of research into Samuel Arnold.

Chapter Fourteen

Lois was sitting on the grass making patterns with flower heads.

'You mustn't pick the flowers,' Sonia told her, coming out of the house with a tray bearing the remnants of last night's supper.

'Why?'

'Because they're not yours. You don't take things that don't belong to you.'

'Who belongs to flowers?' Lois asked.

'These flowers belong to Samuel.'

'Why?'

'Because they grow in his garden, which belongs to his house. He's the only one who's allowed to pick them.'

Lois thought about it. 'You pick flowers,' she observed.

'I picked flowers at the Grenvilles' house,' Sonia corrected, 'because Mrs Grenville liked me doing flower arrangements for her house.'

'Do flower arrangements here,' Lois suggested.

Sonia laughed. 'I'm going to have my hands full doing cobweb arrangements. This house will get flowers when I've cleaned it. And that's going to take me some time.'

Lois picked up the flower heads, scattered them joyfully across the lawn and gave Sonia a wide smile. 'I'm doing a flower arrangement for Samuel's garden,' she said.

Sonia giggled. 'Oh well,' she said, 'I don't suppose he'll notice a few missing. You want ham or cheese in your sandwich, Lois?'

'Crisps.'

'Samuel put the crisps in the fridge last night, so they're not exactly crisp any more,' Sonia said.

'What are they if they're not crisps any more?'

Sonia considered. 'They're soggies,' she said solemnly.

'No, they're not!' Lois shouted. 'You liar!'

'Don't call me a liar. I'm telling you. I'll get them and you'll see.' She went into the house and returned with the bowl of crisps. She showed Lois. 'They bend. They're real live soggies all right. These are not crisps.' She threw one at her. 'You try.'

Lois threw it back. 'Soggies!' she roared.

Sonia flipped more crisps at her, laughing. Lois grabbed a handful from the bowl and flung them into Sonia's face. Sonia threw more. Lois crawled around the lawn picking up crisps and stuffed them down the front of Sonia's jeans. Sonia screamed. She caught hold of Lois, rolled her on the grass and pushed crisps down the back of her neck. They were both screaming with laughter, hardly able to breathe.

'Cooee!' said a voice. 'Cooee! Everything all right?'

Sonia looked up and saw a blue-rinsed permed head bobbing above the fence: Mrs Atwood, the neighbour she had seen returning from shopping. Either the woman had grown six feet tall or else she was perched on something in order to see over the fence.

Sonia stood up. Lois, taking advantage of the distraction, inserted crisps down the back of Sonia's jeans as she turned to face Mrs Atwood. 'Stop that now, Lois,' said Sonia, in her grown-up voice.

'Good morning,' she said. 'I hope you don't think I'm intruding.'

Sonia wondered how the woman could balance on whatever she was balancing on, peer over the top of someone else's fence to see what they were doing, and then hope they didn't think she was intruding. She stared at her.

'I rang Mr Arnold's front doorbell,' the neighbour explained, 'but you can't have heard me. So I thought you might be in the garden.'

'We are,' Sonia said. 'Stop that, Lois,' she hissed.

'Mr Arnold told me you were coming,' Mrs Atwood went

on, 'to be his housekeeper.'

'Yes.'

'You'll find a lot of work to do,' said Mrs Atwood. 'These houses are deceptively big, and all those high ceilings, and of course poor Mr Arnold hasn't had any help for such a long time. I expect you'll be kept very busy.'

'I'm sure we will,' said Sonia evenly. If the woman was saying that poor Mr Arnold's new housekeeper should not be wasting time throwing crisps around his garden, she would have to come right out and say it. Sonia was not going to respond to subtleties.

'But you're not busy just now, are you?' suggested Mrs Atwood. 'Are you having lunch?'

'Yes.' Why else, Sonia thought, would there be a tray of food in the middle of the lawn? To feed the birds?

'Perhaps I could pop round?' Mrs Atwood said. 'If it's convenient?'

'For lunch?'

'No, no,' said the woman, becoming flustered. 'For a little chat. I can tell you some of the things you'll be wanting to know about the neighbourhood.'

'Oh.' Sonia digested this. 'What kind of things?' she asked. She didn't want to encourage the woman in case she turned out to be like a neighbour of her third foster parents', who called round two or three times a day to relay gossip about who was having affairs with the milkman and who was in trouble with rent arrears.

The blue perm bobbed agitatedly. 'All kinds of things,' she said, 'such as which day the dustmen call and which shops to go to, and so on.'

'Oh, thank you,' Sonia said with feigned courtesy, 'but Mr Arnold has already told me that.' She must remember to ask Samuel about the dustmen tonight.

'Oh my dear,' Mrs Atwood laughed. 'What do men know about such things? He does his shopping at the nearest shops, which are also, of course, the most expensive, and I don't care what that butcher says, his meat is *not* fresh.

'I go to Brixton or Camberwell every Monday and I can give you a lift in my car and show you the best things to buy as well. You have to be so careful, don't you? Some of these pre-pared foods are not food at all, and you pay through the nose for . . . what? Additives and a lot of cardboard. And by card-board I mean the food; that's before you look at the packaging they charge you for!'

She laughed gaily, obviously pleased with the originality of this remark. The laugh was a mistake, for she began to wobble dangerously; the next moment the blue head disappeared abruptly and there was a gasp and muttered exclamations.

Sonia ran. Afterwards, she felt ashamed of herself, but at the time it was an unthinking reaction to pick up the tray and run into the house as fast as she could, with Lois following at her heels.

'Why are we running away?' Lois asked.

Sonia closed the kitchen door behind them. 'We'll have lunch indoors,' she said. 'Go and wash your hands.'

They ate at the kitchen table.

'You said we could have a picnic in the garden,' said Lois reproachfully.

'This is an indoor picnic,' Sonia said.

'Can we go back in the garden now and throw crisps?'

'No, because we have to go out and buy bread and milk.'

'When we come back can we?'

'We'll see,' Sonia said evasively.

Lois wiped her mouth with the back of her hand. 'I've finished.'

'Good. Go upstairs to the toilet and then we'll be off.'

'You have to come with me.'

'Please,' Sonia prompted.

'Please.'

'Yes, I'd better come with you in case that rusty old tank falls on your head.'

It was only when they were going out of the front door that Sonia realized she did not have a key. Damn, she thought; Samuel must have forgotten they didn't collect it yesterday from that Mrs Atwood.

For a moment she considered leaving the house unlocked, but it was unthinkable with such precious furniture in it. She resigned herself to facing Mrs Atwood again and walked up the neighbour's front path. As soon as Mrs Atwood answered the doorbell, Sonia said rapidly, 'Mr Arnold said I should collect the key from you.'

'Oh yes,' she said. She took it from the hook by the front door and handed it over. 'You will bring it straight back, won't you?'

'Bring it back?' Sonia repeated.

'Yes. I always keep a key for Mr Arnold.'

'Doesn't he have his own key?'

Mrs Atwood gave a small sigh and smiled. 'Of course he has his own key,' she said with pronounced patience, 'but he leaves a key with me in case there are workmen or the meter reader to be let in, or in case he ever locks himself out.'

'Yes, but he has a housekeeper now,' Sonia said. 'I can let people in. But I forgot to ask him for the door key. We were meant to collect it from you yesterday, but as it happened he was home when we got here.'

'Well, I'm sure he will give you a key when he sees fit,' said Mrs Atwood. 'But until I hear from him that there is to be some alternative arrangement, I will hold on to my key. I'll lend it to you for now, but perhaps you would be kind enough to drop it through my letterbox on your way back from where you're going . . . Will you be out long?'

Sonia gritted her teeth. 'No,' she said. She put the key in her pocket.

'Off to the shops?' Mrs Atwood asked.

'For a few things,' Sonia said, afraid of being whisked off on a shopping and advice trip.

'Mr Arnold won't like a lot of foreign food,' Mrs Atwood said. 'Just so that you know.'

'I am buying bread and milk,' said Sonia with dignity.

'Oh. Well, I'm telling you for future reference, because I don't know what you usually eat, where you come from, but he won't like that kind of food.'

'Where we come from?' Sonia queried. She tried to keep her voice steady, feeling anger rising.

'The West Indies, or Africa, whichever it is,' Mrs Atwood explained. 'Which is it?'

Sonia took a deep breath. 'Sussex,' she said, giving their most recent address and smiling her brightest, most innocent smile.

'Oh, you're second generation immigrant, are you?' Mrs Atwood said. 'What were your parents?'

Sonia was strongly tempted to say, 'Monkeys,' but she was afraid Mrs Atwood might believe her. Instead she smiled again, said, 'Thanks for the key,' and made for the gate, pushing Lois ahead of her. Lois had kept her eyes covered during the whole of this interview.

'The shops are the other way,' Mrs Atwood called after them as they turned left out of the gate. 'That is, unless you're going to Camberwell.'

Sonia turned and went the other way. Mrs Atwood waved. Sonia spent the walk to the shops plotting ways of sneaking back into Samuel's house without being seen by Mrs Atwood and having the key reclaimed.

The local parade of shops included a small supermarket which stocked, as well as the bread and milk they wanted, Lois's favourite brand of chocolate biscuits. Sonia paid for them with Samuel's money.

'Can I have an ice cream?' Lois asked.

'Yes, all right.'

'We don't sell ice cream here,' said the cashier, overhearing her. 'Two doors down there's a sweet shop. What a lovely little girl,' she added, smiling at Sonia.

'Thank you,' Sonia said.

'What's your name, darling?' the girl asked Lois. Lois shot a swift look at Sonia and covered her face with her hands. The girl laughed. 'Are you playing hide and seek?'

'Tell the lady your name,' Sonia chided her. When Lois refused to yield, she told the cashier herself.

'Lois!' the girl said. 'That's a nice name. My name's Candy. You going to give me a smile, Lois?'

Lois peeped through her fingers.

'Here,' said the girl. 'I've got a sweetie for you.' She took an opened pack of boiled sweets from under the counter and gave Lois a red one. One hand parted from Lois's face, cautiously, and took the sweet.

'That's better,' Candy approved. 'Next time you won't be shy with me, will you? Bye bye now.'

Sonia smiled at her. 'Goodbye,' she said. We'll go in that shop again, she decided, even if it is a bit expensive. It's worth it to see a friendly face.

They bought Lois a pink ice lolly in the sweet shop, which was crowded with children in navy-blue uniforms, just out of school. 'Is it that late already?' Sonia marvelled. 'Where has the time gone today?'

They walked back slowly, Lois stopping every now and again to suck the drips from the lolly which plopped on to her dungarees, leaving pink stains.

At the corner of their block, Sonia turned left down a side street. 'We're going home a different way,' she told Lois.

'Why?' said Lois inevitably.

'Just to explore,' Sonia lied. They turned right and right again, coming up past the houses that adjoined the back of Samuel's garden. There was no side gate in the high garden fence, but where the garden ended there was a garage with a short driveway, blocked off by double gates. Sonia pushed them, without much hope, and they gave way. She opened them just enough to squeeze through. Another fence separated the garage from Samuel's garden, but there was a gap in it, with three shallow steps leading up to a narrow path behind the screen of small apple trees. The garage must belong to Samuel as well.

'Be very quiet,' Sonia whispered to Lois, tiptoeing up the path and hoping Mrs Atwood was not looking out of her upstairs back window.

'Why?' Lois whispered back, letting her lolly drip all over

her hand and wind a sticky trail down her wrist.

'Because we're Red Indians, like in the Westerns on telly,' Sonia told her. 'We move very quietly so nobody hears us coming.' She caught Lois's hand as it moved up to her mouth. 'No war cries,' she hissed. She crouched down, clutching the bag of bread and milk and biscuits to her chest, and slunk up the garden. Lois followed, crawling. Her ice lolly got covered in bits of grass. 'Oh no!' she said.

'Ssh!' Sonia cautioned. They ran to the kitchen door, which Sonia had forgotten to lock anyway. So burglars could have got in, she thought, if they'd known about that garage entrance.

She wished she had known herself, then she wouldn't have had to call on Mrs Atwood. Never mind, at least it had been an opportunity to relieve the woman of her key. Who knows, otherwise Mrs Atwood might have let herself into Samuel's house on some pretext, at an unexpected time, unannounced. Sonia was not going to give that key back if she could help it.

Samuel Arnold might have been used to letting neighbours and cleaning ladies have the run of his house, but that time was past now. Sonia and Lois had moved in. The others would have to move out.

To console Lois for having to stay in the house, Sonia continued the game of Red Indians. She unpacked a few of her belongings and made Lois up with streaks of pink lipstick and purple eyeshadow and blobs of white face cream. 'Warpaint,' she said, 'to frighten off other natives.'

Lois was delighted. While Sonia finished unpacking, she hid under the beds, crawled on her tummy around the room, stalked her mother's every movement and leaped on her now and again, uttering bloodcurdling whoops.

Sonia gave her the hairbrush. 'Tomahawk,' she said. 'For scalping cattle rustlers and white settlers.' She wondered if she should have made this last remark, but Lois was too young to suspect her of being racist, and besides, what was cowboys and Indians all about if not racism? I must be a hypocrite, thought Sonia resignedly.

'Where does a Red Indian live?' Lois wanted to know.

'In the Wild West. In a tepee – a tent.'

'Where's my tent?'

'I'll make you one tomorrow,' Sonia promised. 'In the garden. You can be a proper Red Indian and live out of doors. I'll tell Samuel you won't need your bed or this bedroom.'

'Yeah!' Lois applauded. She danced around the room brandishing the hairbrush and hollering vociferously.

Sonia thought with grim satisfaction that no one who saw Lois now would make silly comments about her strange habits and extreme shyness. Sonia had been right: there had never been anything really wrong with the child. And even if there had been, sometimes the best way was just to turn a blind eye. Then the problem, whatever it was – not that there was one, in Lois's case – would simply go away. Sonia felt confident that it had gone away now.

Chapter Fifteen

She began work on Samuel that evening. By the time he came home, with a box of fried chicken and chips under his arm, Sonia had finished the unpacking, cleaned the bath, had a bath and washed her hair, given Lois a bath and removed all the traces of her Red Indian warpaint, and washed their dirty clothes with shampoo, hanging them to dry on an ancient clothes horse she found (and dusted) in the cupboard under the stairs. She had also found and tried out the vacuum cleaner, which was elderly and ineffective.

'We went out to the shops for bread and milk, and I found I didn't have a door key,' she began.

'How foolish of me to forget,' said Samuel. 'I have a spare key upstairs, the one that belonged to Miss Prynne. I will get it for you.'

When he had fetched it Sonia said, as he was handing it to her, 'Mrs Atwood gave me her key; she won't be needing it now we're here, but I better have Miss Prynne's key as well, just in case I lose one.'

Samuel's eyebrows met across his forehead. 'You could still leave Mrs Atwood a key,' he pointed out. 'She has always kept one for me, and I am sure she wouldn't mind.'

'No need,' said Sonia blithely. 'I'll keep the spare one in a safe place. I never lock myself out.'

'It is up to you, of course,' Samuel acknowledged.

Sonia brought plates. 'How was your day at work?' she asked.

Samuel looked surprised. 'Um ... very good,' he said. 'Much as usual.'

'What do you like to drink with your meal, Samuel?'

'Just a glass of water. I'll fetch . . . oh, thank you. There is Coca-Cola in the fridge if Lois likes it.'

'She drank it this afternoon. It was a warm day,' Sonia added defensively, in case Samuel would begin to think Lois was expensive to run.

Samuel beamed at Lois. 'Did you enjoy playing in the garden?'

Lois, who had had her hands over her eyes ever since Samuel entered the house, nodded blindly.

'Splendid,' Samuel said. 'She was all right, after last night then?' he asked Sonia.

'Oh, fine,' Sonia said.

'I was afraid I had given her something for her supper that had upset her stomach,' Samuel explained. 'I am rather unused to children nowadays.'

Sonia picked on the 'nowadays' like a hawk pouncing on a sparrow. 'Did you have children of your own, then?'

'No, no,' he said. 'I never married. But I had some experience of my sister's children, when they were young. They are grown up now, of course, with families of their own.'

'And do you . . .?' Sonia was about to continue with her investigation, but Samuel held up a hand apologetically and interrupted her. 'I usually say grace before meals,' he said. 'Would you mind?'

Sonia stared. 'No,' she said. She had never met anyone who prayed before they ate, especially not over Kentucky Fried Chicken.

Samuel bent his white head, joined his hands and said respectfully, 'Lord, bless the food we receive from your hands and may it bring us health and life. Amen.'

'Amen!' said Lois enthusiastically. Samuel laughed and patted her on the head. They began to eat.

'Have you settled in?' Samuel asked. 'Managed to find everything you wanted?'

For one second, in the face of his clear blue gaze, Sonia quailed. For all his childlikeness, his expression could suddenly turn shrewd. She felt uncomfortable, dipped her eyes and attacked her chicken portion with knife and fork, giving her attention to its dissection.

'Eat it in your fingers,' Samuel advised. 'I always do.' Lois had not waited for this invitation and was gnawing ferociously, her head tipped at an angle almost level with the table.

'Yes, we're unpacked,' Sonia said, 'and ready to start tomorrow. I couldn't get your Hoover to work. I emptied the bag but it wouldn't suck up the dirt. It just glides over the surface.'

'My daily help keeps leaving me messages saying I need a new one,' Samuel confessed. 'I am afraid I haven't made time for these things.'

'There's no point just going out and buying one, anyway,' said Sonia firmly. 'You need to know what you're doing, to get the right kind for the house.'

'Exactly as I suspected!' agreed Samuel. 'We shall obtain Gertrude's advice.'

'There's no need to ask your daily help!' Sonia said. 'I can choose . . .'

'No, no,' said Samuel. 'Gertrude is not the daily help, but my cousin. She frequently travels up from her home in Sussex by train, does some shopping in town and comes to visit me. She is a very practical person and full of good advice.'

'Don't bother your cousin,' said Sonia quickly. 'I can easily . . .'

'She was delighted to be asked to help,' Samuel confided. 'Between ourselves, I believe she may be somewhat lonely. Her husband is retired and has his own interests, and Gertrude was never one for making friends.'

'You've asked her already? To help choose a new Hoover?' Sonia was seething. Who was the housekeeper around here?

'Not about the vacuum cleaner,' Samuel said. 'But I was reflecting, on my way to work this morning, about your quite justified observation on the lavatory pan and tank – if you will forgive me for mentioning such things at a mealtime – and it occurred to me that there may well be other items in this house that have outlived their usefulness. So when I arrived at work I telephoned the plumber first and then I telephoned Gertrude. She will visit us on Saturday.' He said this with an air of pride and triumph, looking to Sonia for approval of his thoughtfulness.

'Great,' she said grudgingly. At least he had remembered to call the plumber. At least he had taken her comment on the unsafe toilet seriously. He needed to get used to the fact that she was the housekeeper now, that was all. It wouldn't take long. She would soon deal with cousin Gertrude and Mrs Cleaning Lady. Mrs Neighbour Atwood was already history.

When they had finished eating, Samuel said an after-meal grace and stood up to clear the dishes. Sonia put a restraining hand on his arm, and he gave her a schoolboy grin. 'I keep forgetting,' he admitted. 'But mayn't I do something to help?'

'Yes,' she said. 'Tell me whether you'd like a coffee, and how you take it.'

'Thank you,' he said. 'That would be very nice. Milk and one sugar, please.'

'Lois, you go upstairs and get into your pyjamas and clean your teeth,' said Sonia.

'Not yet,' Lois said.

'Now,' said her mother firmly. 'Samuel and I are going to talk business.'

Samuel looked slightly startled, and then said, 'Oh – housekeeping arrangements and so on. Yes, of course.'

'You come with me,' Lois bargained, peeping through her fingers at Sonia.

'No. You're going to have to get used to this house, so start now. You don't need me to go everywhere with you.'

Lois pouted and remained rooted to the spot.

'Go,' Sonia said.

Lois sneaked another look and decided Sonia meant business. She went, only saying plaintively, 'The toilet will fall on my head.'

'We'll risk it,' said Sonia, unmoved, 'just this once.'

'Bring the coffee into the sitting room,' Samuel said. 'Much more comfortable. I shall light the fire; the evenings are still chilly, I find, and the front rooms of the house are cold.'

Sonia followed him in with the coffees. 'Show me how you start a fire,' she said. 'I've never lived in a place with real open fireplaces.'

He knelt back on his heels in front of the grate and gave her a lesson in setting firelighters on a nest of small pieces of smokeless coal and neatly rolled twists of newspaper, topping them with larger coals as the flames grew. With bellows, he blew steadily on the flame from beneath the fuel, sending sparks shooting up the chimney.

Sonia took the bellows out of his hands. 'Let me have a go.' Secretly it worried her to see him using them; wouldn't that kind of exertion put a strain on the heart, at his age?

'What's that?' Lois asked. Sonia, stooped over the fire, didn't turn round. It was Samuel who answered, 'It's a coal fire; don't come too close, Lois. There can be sparks. I will put the fireguard on once it gets going properly.'

'What's Sonia doing?'

'Sonia is using the bellows to blow air into the fire, to help the flame along,' Samuel told her. 'That will do nicely, Sonia. Don't become breathless.'

'I am out of breath!' she admitted, laughing. 'I can see why central heating was invented!' Turning round, she saw Lois standing there naked.

Sonia sprang towards her, grabbed her arm and turned her round, wrenching her shoulder. Lois yelped. 'Get up those stairs,' said Sonia between clenched teeth. She pushed Lois ahead of her and, when they reached the bedroom, gave her a resounding slap on the bottom. 'Ow!' Lois howled.

'You'll get hurt much more than this if you don't do as I say,' Sonia threatened her. 'I told you not to go downstairs with nothing on – didn't I tell you that this morning?'

'I forgot!' Lois sobbed.

'That's why I'm giving you something to make you not forget,' Sonia said. She slapped her again, hard. 'Now get your pyjamas on.'

Lois's mouth was open in a big soundless O. Shock deprived her of breath. When the howl came it was earsplitting and tragic. Samuel, in the sitting room, shuddered to hear it.

Sonia clapped her hand over Lois's mouth. 'Listen to me,' she said, quietly and intensely, forcing Lois to look at her. 'You've got to do what I tell you, Lois, and don't make a fuss or a noise, or we are going to be out of here, and it will be your fault. Now calm down.'

She held her in a firm grip till the child, whether through calm or through fear, stopped struggling and made no noise. 'That's better,' Sonia said. 'Now, do you want to be allowed to come downstairs and sit by the fire for a while before you go to bed?'

Lois nodded mutely, tears in her eyes and blocking her throat.

'Then come here, give me a hug,' Sonia instructed, 'and when we get downstairs sit quietly and don't bother anyone. Is it a deal?'

Lois nodded again. She allowed Sonia to hug her, take her hand and lead her downstairs. With her free hand she covered her eyes as soon as they entered the sitting room. She sat where Sonia put her, on a low stool to one side of the fire, and put both hands over her face. Samuel watched her, and his expression was grave.

'She has to learn to do what she's told,' Sonia explained. 'I'm quite strict with her, so she won't be a nuisance. I locked the dining room door – is that okay? I didn't want her going in by herself, with that lovely table and everything in there. Shall I leave the key somewhere safe, so you know where it is?'

Samuel shifted his gaze to Sonia's face. 'Whatever you think best,' he said. He looked suddenly old – older than Sonia had suspected. Perhaps he was even more than seventy.

She wondered if there was a birth certificate somewhere.

'Here's the key, then,' she said. 'I put it in my pocket. Where would be a good place to hide it?'

'I will show you,' he said, standing up. Sonia followed him

into the hall and watched him place the key on top of the grandfather clock. 'Is that safe enough, would you say?' Samuel enquired.

'Perfect,' Sonia approved. They returned to the sitting room. 'I made a list,' she said, 'of questions to ask you.' She looked at him doubtfully. They were all essential questions, or had seemed so when she wrote them down, but Samuel looked so tired. He had said he was not used to children. Perhaps he would prefer just to be left alone to read his library book on the Philippines and drink his coffee. But he waved a hand. 'Please,' he said. 'Anything you need to know.'

'Apart from working hours and salary,' said Sonia nervously, clearing her throat, 'I need to know things like which day the dustmen call, and the daily help, and how the milkman gets paid. Also what you like and don't like to eat and how you like your shirts ironed – hung on hangers or folded.'

'I see,' Samuel said. 'Well now, let us deal with the matter of salary first, shall we? Then we shall know where we stand. Perhaps you could give me some idea of what is a suitable sum?'

Sonia was embarrassed. 'It's for you to say,' she said. 'You're the employer.'

'Ah yes,' he said, as though he had forgotten this for a moment. 'But it is such a long time, as I told you, since I employed anybody that I am quite out of touch. You would have a better idea, I am sure, perhaps based on the salary paid by your previous employer?'

'I got ripped off,' Sonia said bluntly, 'but then the best jobs don't go to unmarried black women with a child, so I expected it. Mind, she was desperate too because no one would work for her. I ended up doing as much as a team of people. It was very long hours, and an enormous house. If she'd doubled the salary, she still would have been underpaying me. It's not the same here. You don't do a lot of dinner parties and entertaining, do you?'

'None at all,' Samuel said. 'And I certainly would not wish to overwork you. You must tell me at once if you find the work too much to manage. And I do insist that you and Lois eat proper food during the day. You are much too thin, my dear, if you will forgive my indelicacy in remarking on it.'

'Yes, well, that's another thing to be taken into account,' Sonia said. 'Whether the food for me and Lois is provided or whether it comes out of the salary. That would make a difference, you see. Some employers offer free meals and board for the housekeeper but the child's food is extra.'

'Truly? How shocking!' said Samuel severely. 'Well, here your food is to be provided, for both of you, and you must have whatever you like. As for my likes and dislikes, my dear, and how I like my shirts folded, there is really no need to be anxious about such things. I am not difficult to please and, to be absolutely honest, I probably should not notice if you gave me bread and cheese every evening and ironed my shirts in pleats.'

Sonia smiled. 'I won't do that,' she said. 'And the lady next door kindly warned me not to give you any nasty West Indian food.'

Samuel's eyebrows rose. 'That was kindness indeed,' he said solemnly. 'The poor old fellow must be protected from foreign food, at all costs.'

Sonia frowned, unsure of whether he was making fun of her or of Mrs Atwood.

'What a pity she did not warn me of the dangers earlier,' Samuel sighed, 'when I was out East during the war. As it is, I am left with a shameful taste for spicy foods and hot curries. And as you can see, it has been the ruin of my health. I am really only twenty-five years old, you know.'

Sonia burst out laughing, and he chuckled wickedly. 'Don't tell the good lady next door,' he said, 'but I do very much enjoy trying new food. Do you cook West Indian meals?'

'I can,' she said. 'I did a few recipes for Mrs Grenville, because she said she used to live in Jamaica, but I don't think she really liked them. I didn't learn them in Jamaica; I was only seven when I left, but we met this lady called Aunty Sue at one place we lived – she wasn't a relative or anything, but that's what everyone called her – and she taught me how to cook a few things, but mostly I cook English food, or French, or whatever anyone wants. Mrs Grenville sent me on a course, one day a week, to learn the fancy stuff but I can do traditional cooking or . . . well, anything.'

'Perhaps we could invite this friend of yours,' Samuel suggested, 'for a West Indian meal here, if you could cook it. You mustn't lose touch with your friends, so please invite guests when you wish.'

'Aunty Sue went back to Jamaica to live,' said Sonia dully, 'and we haven't got any friends. Only a lady we met at the refuge – Mrs Patel – but we don't really know her.' As Samuel opened his mouth to ask further questions, she said, 'So – dustmen. What day do they call here?'

It was one thing for her to pry into his secrets and entice information out of him, and quite something else for him to get her talking about herself like this. Not that she had said anything revealing, but it was a dangerous habit to get into. Neither Samuel Arnold nor anybody else was going to get the chance to investigate Sonia and Lois. There was far too much at risk.

Chapter Sixteen

Because Samuel was accommodating, it didn't take long to come to an arrangement. Before their cups of coffee were drained, he and Sonia had established that he would pay her fifty pounds a week, clear, with board and lodging for herself and Lois provided free. 'Including all the essentials apart from food, like soap and toothpaste,' Sonia said, 'but not clothes or personal things or sweets for Lois.'

Samuel objected to this. 'If you are to be family,' he said, 'then treats for children are part of the household budget. Children need such things. I would not wish this family to be . . . what was it now that you said? Deaf to joy? Joy is an essential item, not a luxury.'

Sonia frowned at him. 'I buy Lois's treats,' she said. 'I'm her mother.'

Samuel gave her a steady look. 'Yes,' he said. 'Of course. I didn't mean to intrude.'

The only point of difficulty, surprisingly, turned out to be the twice-weekly cleaning lady. Here Samuel was obstinate. In vain Sonia argued that this service was now unnecessary, that expense would be saved by asking her to leave, that the woman was highly incompetent as the house was unarguably dirty and neglected, that the woman would have no trouble in finding another job since people were desperate for domestic help, however slapdash, and that it was only a kindness to let her go to a place that was less challenging to her limited capacity for work.

Samuel listened to these arguments, but his response was the same to every strategy: Mrs Baker had been here a long time; Miss Prynne had found her invaluable for doing the heavy work that Miss Prynne found too much; the woman liked the job and was used to it and, as she lived only down the road, found it handy to pop in here for the odd hour that suited her, when not needed by her confused and incontinent elderly mother.

Sonia had not expected this response. It was easy enough to prove that it was not in Samuel's interests to keep Mrs Baker on, but Samuel was apparently not employing her for the service she supplied. He freely admitted her work was not very good, and that quite possibly she was not turning up for it at all, or at least not for anything like the number of hours for which she charged.

He was, however, insistent on paying Mrs Baker for spending as much or as little time in his house as she wished, whether or not the state of the house showed any signs of improvement in cleanliness.

Finally Sonia understood that they were arguing from completely different viewpoints. She was saying the house did not need the woman. He was saying the woman needed the house. The budget would certainly be lightened by losing Mrs Baker, but Mrs Baker's life would not be lightened by losing the salary.

'She could work somewhere else,' Sonia insisted.

'She may not be very attractive to another employer,' Samuel said gently. 'She cannot keep to fixed hours. Her mother becomes very restless at times, even aggressive, and Mrs Baker can't leave her. The neighbour will sit with the mother occasionally, but only when she is asleep.'

Sonia shrugged. 'She has a full-time job already, then, with her mother. Maybe she just can't handle another one. She's obviously hardly ever coming here.'

'I believe she is coming here,' Samuel said, 'quite often. But, as you say, not doing the work.'

'What *is* she doing then?' Sonia demanded indignantly. How could the woman let herself in with her own key and snoop around Samuel's house and take his money and not do a stroke of the work for which he was paying her? It was criminal, surely.

'I believe I know,' Samuel said. 'I took a day off work, a few months ago, after Miss Prynne had left, and as it was not one of Mrs Baker's official days I did not think to tell her that I would be at home. I spent most of the morning in my shed, and I saw Mrs Baker come in – there is a back way through the garden when the garage gates are open, and I must have left them unlocked.

'I didn't want to disturb her at her work, so it was lunchtime by the time I returned to the house. I assumed she had left. But I found her in the sitting room, still with her coat and hat on and her bag in her hand, just as she had arrived, sitting by the fireplace. The grate had not been cleared, and there was no sign of anything else having been done, as far as I could tell. I am not very observant, so of course she may have done something, but it looked very much to me as though Mrs Baker had been sitting there like that ever since she arrived.'

'Doing what?' Sonia asked incredulously.

'Having a bit of peace, I supposed.'

'What happened then?' Sonia asked him.

'I went out again. She hadn't noticed me. I spent a couple of hours in the library and the park – remind me, my dear, now I mention it, to show you where the park is and to introduce you and Lois to the library, which is an excellent one – and by the time I returned Mrs Baker had left. I never mentioned it to her.'

'Oh,' said Sonia reflectively. 'So she has your key and you're paying her so she can come here and have a bit of peace whenever she feels the need?'

'I suppose that is what it comes down to,' said Samuel.

'But what about when Miss Prynne was here?' Sonia asked. 'Surely she made Mrs Baker get on with her work?'

'Oh, probably not,' Samuel said. 'Miss Prynne herself became very elderly and shortsighted and also, regretfully, almost as confused as Mrs Baker's mother. Mrs Baker was good to Miss Prynne, made her cups of tea and gave her her lunch on occasions when she had forgotten or could not manage it by herself. Miss Prynne welcomed her company. They both seemed to enjoy their chats.'

Sonia shook her head from side to side, in disbelief. 'So Miss Prynne wasn't doing any housework either?'

'Very little,' Samuel admitted.

'Did you get your supper cooked?'

'We usually had a boiled egg,' Samuel said. 'Either Miss Prynne would cook it or else I would.'

'How long did this go on?'

Samuel thought about it. 'A couple of years possibly.'

'A couple of *years*!' Sonia was aghast. There was a silence. 'I can believe there is a couple of years' grime in this house,' she said finally. 'Apart from the furniture being polished beautifully.'

'I did my best,' Samuel said, 'but I am afraid, in the event, it was not very good. This is why I telephoned Gertrude today. Seeing you here, with a child, I realized that this house must be virtually uninhabitable, and without doubt insanitary. If you will give it a little time, I am fully determined to put things to rights. I only need good advice on how to go about it.'

'Samuel,' Sonia said. 'Look. I can see what you've been saying, about Miss Prynne and Mrs Baker and everything. I can see you've been very kind, and I'm in no position to criticize, because in a way you've done the same for us. I mean, you've taken us on without knowing us and without knowing if we're going to do any useful work or just sponge off you . . .'

He put up a hand to interrupt her at this point, but she continued.

'. . . sponge off you, and by that I don't mean those other women were bad, but the fact is you paid them to look after you and as it turned out you had to look after them, while they had cups of tea and chats and turned your house into a pigsty. A pigsty,' she repeated firmly, as he seemed about to object to her choice of words. 'So what I'm telling you is this: you are a good and generous person and I'm very, very grateful you took us in like you did, but this place is not a charity home for unemployable people nobody wants.'

'My dear girl,' Samuel said, distressed, 'I do assure you . . .'

'No, I'm assuring you,' Sonia said. 'I came here because I wanted a job. If I wanted to be rescued I'd have gone to the social services or stayed in the women's refuge. We're here to work. I've had all I ever want of charity homes. I am a capable housekeeper, like I told you in the cemetery, and this is a lovely house. Okay, it's a pigsty right now, but it could be really nice, with this beautiful furniture you've collected, and these big rooms and the curly bits round the ceiling, and the banisters and that. I'm going to clean up this place, Samuel, till you don't recognize it, and nobody's going to stop me.'

He spread his hands. 'If you are sure you want to take it on,' he said, 'I am certainly not going to stop you. My house does need taking care of, I agree.'

'And you do too,' Sonia said.

'And I do too,' he repeated, very softly.

'But if I am going to do it,' Sonia continued, 'properly, I can't run a rescue home for anyone else. It's taken me all this time to get on my own feet and look after Lois, and now I could enjoy looking after you and getting the house straight, but I'm not taking on any passengers, Samuel. I couldn't cope with that, and I know it.'

He nodded. 'So?'

'So no well-meaning neighbours popping their noses in and out of the house and over the fence, telling me what to do and letting themselves into the house with their own key. Mrs Atwood's key stays with me. Okay?'

He nodded again. 'I see your point.'

'No Mrs Baker coming round here to escape from life and telling me her sorrows over cups of tea. If she doesn't want to work, I do.'

There was a much longer pause this time, but finally Samuel said, 'I will call on her on Saturday morning and thank her for her services and tell her there is no longer a need for them.'

Sonia heaved an enormous sigh of relief.

'Is there anything else?' Samuel asked humbly.

'No,' Sonia said, hesitating.

Samuel gave her his gimlet gaze. 'Is there?'

'Cousin Gertrude,' Sonia said after a pause. 'I don't want her choosing my Hoover. Or anything else.'

'Oh my dear,' said Samuel, 'how very insensitive of me. I would not have suggested such a thing, you know. I was only proposing that Gertrude – who has the advantage of always saying exactly what she believes, and extremely bluntly – should point out to me what I should do in order to provide a proper home for you while you're here. I may be offering you conditions that no one should be expected to live in, and I thought that if delicacy prevented you from telling me so, Gertrude would not hesitate . . .'

'But it hasn't, has it?' Sonia interrupted. 'I haven't been too delicate to tell you.'

Samuel began to laugh. 'No,' he agreed. 'You are very well able to speak up for yourself. I shall not worry about you.'

'But can I speak up to Gertrude?' Sonia teased. 'You make her sound like an old battleaxe.'

His eyes twinkled. 'A not inappropriate description,' he admitted, 'though in literal terms it is her husband who is the battleaxe – a retired general. He insists on being addressed by his full title still, except by the family, whom he ignores. Gertrude herself can be rather overbearing, I grant you, but it is only her manner. She has a heart of gold. We have always had a soft spot for each other.'

'She must be all right then,' Sonia said. 'I suppose.'

'You will take the risk of meeting her, then, on Saturday?' Samuel said. 'If I promise to disregard her advice and take yours?'

'Now you make me sound like the battleaxe!' Sonia objected. Suddenly suspicious, she added, 'She doesn't have a key to this house as well, does she?'

Samuel's mouth twitched. 'I am afraid to confess that she does,' he said. 'But I shall relieve her of her command on Saturday. There is my promise.'

'I don't mean to be difficult,' Sonia said. 'I'm sorry.'

'You are not difficult in the least,' Samuel said. 'I find it refreshing when you are honest.'

Sonia shot him a covert look. Was he suggesting she had been less than honest on some occasions so far? She made no answer.

'This has been a very useful opportunity,' Samuel said, 'to become better acquainted with one another. Now, I shall shortly be retiring to bed, and Lois, I can see, is almost asleep, but before we go tell me frankly – is there anything else you wish to ask? Or to tell me?'

For a moment, she thought of telling him everything. He was kind and forgiving. He had employed, out of pity, useless unscrupulous people who took advantage of him. He said prayers when he ate. He liked travel books and unusual food and plain speaking. His gaze was clear, his speech forthright and the key to his locked drawer easily accessible. He might understand.

'There is just one thing,' she said.

'Yes?' he said. He leaned forward in his chair, hands clasped between his knees. 'What is it?'

'I know you said whatever I did would be all right,' Sonia said, 'but there are always limits, aren't there? So tell me honestly, what kind of things can you simply not stand to eat?'

Chapter Seventeen

Sonia congratulated herself on getting it right the next morning: up at a quarter to seven; Lois dressed and Samuel's breakfast on the table at a quarter past; Samuel's sandwiches ready for him to take when he left for work at seven-forty.

Lois accompanied him round the garden before breakfast, and together they carefully refilled the birdbath and stood back to watch a couple of sparrows fly in to avail themselves of the facilities.

Sonia watched them, puzzled. Lois showed no signs of shyness with Samuel, chattering happily and taking hold of his hand every now and again. It was only when they came into the house that the child covered her eyes and would not answer when he spoke to her.

When Samuel said goodbye to them and left for work, Lois followed him out of the kitchen door and the side gate into the front garden, again with her eyes uncovered and her voice operative. 'Where is your cellar, Samuel?' she asked clearly.

'There's no cellar in this house, Lois,' he reminded her.

'Don't hold Samuel up,' Sonia told Lois. 'You'll make him miss his bus.'

'But where is it?' Lois demanded anxiously.

'Here it is,' Samuel said, pointing to the old air-raid shelter. 'This is the nearest thing to a cellar that I have. It's above the ground, that's all.'

'What do you do in there?' Lois asked.

'Lois, let Samuel go,' Sonia warned.

'I don't use it at all,' Samuel told Lois. 'Would you like to make it into your house? Where no one else can come in, unless they knock first?'

Lois was happy. She danced back into the kitchen. 'I've got a house!' she shouted.

'I heard,' Sonia said. 'We'd both better get to work. You can clean your house and I'll clean this one.' She wished she had the child's energy. No one would think, to look at Lois, that she had been sick again in the night – painfully sick, and shaking so much that the bed shook with her. Now she was jumping about, eager to start playing in her new house; it was Sonia who felt drained. I'll be all right once I get going, she told herself; it's probably just the thought of how much needs doing.

'Okay, let's get the day started,' she said to Lois. 'Go to the toilet while I finish the washing up, and we'll go shopping in Brixton.' She didn't want to risk Camberwell, which was nearer, in case they bumped into Bella or Gina Riley.

'Are we going on a bus?' Lois enquired hopefully.

'Yes.'

'Can we go upstairs on the bus?'

'On the way there, but not coming back because we'll have a lot of shopping to carry. Pass me that envelope from the kitchen table, Lois; it's the housekeeping money.'

'Can we leave by the back way?' Lois asked, when she came downstairs again.

Sonia was tempted. It would mean safety from Mrs Atwood. 'No, we better not,' she said regretfully. 'That garage gate ought to be locked, otherwise anybody could break in.'

'Who?' Lois asked.

'Burglars,' Sonia said. Or Mrs Baker, she added silently. She had a flash of guilt. Samuel would find it hard giving her her notice on Saturday. And possibly harder still to ward off Mrs Atwood. She dismissed the thoughts. She'd had life hard too; it was her turn to call the tune. She wondered if it was her fault Samuel had been tired last night, or whether he always went to bed so early. 'Come on, Lois,' she said briskly. There really wasn't time to stand around thinking. They had work to do.

On their way to lock the garage gates, Sonia made Lois play

Red Indians again. They sneaked down the garden, Lois concentrating on moving stealthily and Sonia casting furtive glances up at Mrs Atwood's windows. They locked the gates and made their way back again. Lois demanded Red Indian warpaint, like yesterday. 'Later,' Sonia promised her.

'Why?'

'Red Indians don't wear their warpaint when they go shopping,' said Sonia, and Lois was satisfied with this explanation.

Mrs Atwood emerged from her front door and called to them as they reached the kerb, ready to cross the road to the bus-stop. 'Coo-ee!'

Sonia pretended she hadn't heard. The traffic lights were green. She prayed for them to change.

'Coo-ee!'

The lights turned to amber. Mrs Atwood was almost at her gate. Red. 'Run,' Sonia told Lois, grabbing her hand and pulling her, at a trot, across the road. They reached the bus-stop. Mrs Atwood waved at them. Lois stared at her and tugged Sonia's arm. 'Sonia!'

'Lois, look this way and then you can tell me when the bus is coming,' Sonia said. As if in answer to her most cowardly prayers, a bus was already approaching. 'Does this bus go to Brixton?' she asked a woman in the queue.

'Not this one, love, unless you change at the bottom of the hill. The other one goes direct.'

'We'll get this one and change,' Sonia told Lois. 'Hop on. No, not upstairs, Lois. We have to get off again in a few minutes.'

Lois scrambled on to a window seat and stared at Mrs Atwood, still standing across the road. 'Why are we running away from that lady?' she enquired, wide-eyed.

'She's another kind of Red Indian,' Sonia explained. 'From a rival tribe. She'll scalp us with her tomahawk if we go near her. Stop waving at her, Lois.'

They changed buses at the bottom of the hill. 'There's a park,' Lois observed. 'Can we go in there?'

'Another day.'

'Why?'

'Stop saying "Why?" to everything, Lois! It gets on my nerves!'

'Why?'

'You're doing it again!'

'Why can't we go to the park today?'

'It's not our day off. Today we have to work. We had our day off yesterday, remember?'

In Brixton, all the women with shopping bags got off the bus. Sonia followed them, not wanting to ask directions, and ended up in the market. By the time she had bought fruit and vegetables (there was a good selection of exotic produce; she would make Samuel a Caribbean dish for tonight's supper) she was already finding the bags heavy. When they reached the supermarket she put them into one trolley and used another for the groceries.

'I want to ride on the trolley!' Lois pleaded.

'No, I need you to push one of them. If you're a good girl I'll buy you some sweets when we get to the checkout – right?'

Lois tugged at Sonia's belt. 'I don't like it in here,' she whispered.

'You like shopping usually,' said Sonia, surprised. 'What's the matter?'

'Everyone's got black faces,' Lois said.

Sonia burst out laughing. 'You're right,' she said. 'There are mostly black people here. Including you.'

'No,' Lois said.

'Look in the mirror, angel,' Sonia advised. 'I know you're used to white people around you, but you surely are not white!'

'Yes I am,' said Lois with certainty.

Sonia bent down in front of her. 'What colour is my face?'

'I don't know,' Lois said.

'Yes you do. Black or white?'

Lois pursed her mouth. 'Don't know.'

'Well then, it can't be so very important, can it?' Sonia reasoned. 'It doesn't matter if people's skin is black or white.'

'But what am I?' Lois asked.

'You're beautiful,' Sonia told her. 'No, leave those biscuits, Lois. We've got chocolate biscuits at home.'

Home. It was good to be able to say that word again. Good to have housekeeping money in her pocket, to pay for goods at a supermarket checkout, to carry bags of shopping and not bags of their possessions; it was good to catch a bus *home*.

Sonia's happiness lasted until they reached Herne Hill. As they crossed the road, there was Mrs Atwood in her front garden. Had she been watching out for their return?

'You've been shopping in Brixton,' she accused, as soon as they were in earshot, looking at the supermarket name on the carrier bags. 'I did offer to take you in my car on Monday.'

'We couldn't leave it till Monday,' Sonia said. 'There was no food in the house.'

'Well, next week then,' said Mrs Atwood sternly. 'I'll knock on your door at nine o'clock.'

'That's okay, thank you,' said Sonia, moving with difficulty up the garden path as Lois blocked the way ahead of her, standing stock still with her hands over her face. 'Lois likes going on the bus, don't you, Lois?'

'It's much better by car,' Mrs Atwood stated. 'You wouldn't have to carry all those heavy bags.'

Sonia tried, and failed, to make the bags appear weightless. She prodded Lois with her foot to move her on.

'You never dropped my key back,' said Mrs Atwood.

Sonia ignored her.

'I'll call in for it later,' Mrs Atwood promised. 'Or do you want to let me have it now?'

Sonia wished she had taken the key to the kitchen door. Now she had to take the front door key out of her pocket, in full view of Mrs Atwood, in order to let themselves in. She decided to brazen it out. Honesty was sometimes a more successful tactic than diplomacy.

'No,' she said. 'I'll keep it, thanks all the same. You won't be needing it any more, and we do.' She pushed Lois over the doorstep and hurriedly closed the door behind them.

A few seconds later the doorbell rang. Sonia considered ignoring it, but really it was better to get the battle over with, even if it spelt the start of full-scale war.

She opened the door a crack. 'Hello again,' she said.

'Mr Arnold has always given me a key,' said Mrs Atwood.

'It isn't necessary any more,' Sonia retaliated.

'Mr Arnold hasn't said anything to me to the contrary,' Mrs Atwood insisted.

'He said it to me,' Sonia said. 'We discussed the matter last night. I'm to keep the key.'

'I'll have to have a word with him myself,' Mrs Atwood said.

'All right,' Sonia agreed. She half closed the door.

'I'll take you shopping on Monday then,' said Mrs Atwood.

'What?' said Sonia incredulously.

'I'll call for you and take you to Brixton.'

'No,' Sonia said, 'thank you.'

'You don't want the trouble of taking a child on the bus. The car is much easier, when I'm going anyway.'

'She likes the bus,' Sonia repeated.

'I can go on another day, if Monday doesn't suit you.'

Sonia decided the best policy (since Samuel probably would not approve of her being too rude to his nearest neighbour) was to keep repeating the same answer, in the hope that its meaning would eventually make an impression on the woman's mind. 'We'll go on the bus, thanks,' she said, trying to keep her voice calm.

'I wouldn't charge you petrol.'

Sonia took a deep breath. 'We like going on the bus. Thank you.'

'What day would you be going? I could meet you there and bring you back. You could go there on the bus and come back with me.'

Sonia became curious. 'Why do you want us to go with you?' she enquired.

Mrs Atwood flushed. 'I'm trying to do you a good turn,' she said.

'But we have refused your offer,' Sonia pointed out, 'and you keep on asking us. Is there some other reason?'

Mrs Atwood stared at her for a moment. 'You're very rude and ungrateful,' she said.

'Then I won't waste another minute of your time,' said Sonia coolly. She could feel her legs shaking. What have I done to invite this? she asked herself. She closed the door and flung herself down on the bottom stair. The grandfather clock informed her that it was half past ten. The doorbell rang again. Sonia hesitated, took a deep breath and went to answer it.

Mrs Atwood said gruffly, not looking at her, 'I find Brixton a bit rough. It's best for shopping, but there's trouble sometimes. White people have had their cars turned over, on their way home.'

Light dawned. 'You want us to go with you in your car because we're black? You'd feel safe from trouble if you had black people with you?'

'Sort of,' muttered Mrs Atwood.

'Because we're sort of black?' Sonia said, raising her eyebrows. Mrs Atwood flushed again. Sonia felt sorry for teasing her. 'Okay,' she relented.

Mrs Atwood looked at her. 'You'll come?' she said. The relief in her voice was obvious.

'Yes, we'll come with you. Why didn't you say you were frightened to go shopping there on your own? We would have said yes straight away.'

Mrs Atwood struggled with several answers and finally said stiffly, 'Pride, I suppose.'

Sonia admired her honesty, slow though it had been to hatch out. 'I suppose it was pride making me say no,' she said, not to be outdone. 'I thought we were being patronized.'

'No,' said Mrs Atwood. In a rush she added, 'Would you like to come in for a coffee?'

Sonia nearly accepted, but said, 'Some other time. I've got to start cleaning.'

'I see. Monday morning then, nine o'clock?'

'Okay. Thank you, Mrs Atwood.'

'Molly,' she said. 'And you?'

'Sonia.'

'And your little girl?'

'Lois.'

'If you ever want me to keep an eye on her,' Molly Atwood offered, 'so you can get on with your work, or babysit while you go out for an evening, just let me know.'

'Thanks,' Sonia said, 'but she won't go to strangers, and I never go out in the evenings. Thanks all the same. Bye now.' Closing the door, she puffed out her cheeks and blew a sigh of relief. 'That was close,' she murmured.

'Did she scalp you?' asked Lois, peeping round the door of the sitting room where she had been hiding.

'Not quite,' said Sonia, laughing. 'Just a few grazes. Carry this bag to the kitchen for me, Lois. I'm going to unpack the shopping and have a coffee before we start work.'

'You can have a chocolate biscuit if you like,' Lois said.

'How kind of you,' said Sonia gravely. 'Is that a way of telling me that you want one?'

'No,' Lois said. 'I want two.'

Chapter Eighteen

'You've been in that air-raid shelter for ages, Lois. Come out and have some fresh air now. It's a lovely day.'

'You can't come in here! This is my cellar!'

'Come on, Lois. You're breathing dust in there. We'll give it a clean out another day. Look how filthy it is.'

'It's my cellar! You have to knock or you can't come in. Samuel said so.'

'Okay, okay, I'm knocking on the door – listen. Now can I come in?'

'No, go away.'

'Oh, that's not very nice, Lois!'

'You're the wrong kind of Red Indian,' Lois explained. 'You'll get escaped if you come in.'

'Scalped?'

'Yes, scalped.'

'Lois, if you come out of that cellar I'll make you a tepee in the garden, like I promised. Is it a deal?'

There was a silence. The door opened. 'Okay,' said Lois graciously. She put down the short length of hosepipe she was carrying, and came out.

Sonia looked past her into the air-raid shelter. 'What were you doing with that?' she asked.

'It's a snake,' Lois explained.

'Well, you certainly better come out then. You don't want to be shut in a dusty cellar with a snake.'

Sonia enjoyed making up games for Lois. She inverted the clothes horse she had found the previous day and over it she draped a blanket. Clothes pegs secured the blanket to the frame and held the tent opening closed at the back.

She made Lois up as a Red Indian again, using fluorescent poster paints. Lois's toys were unpacked now, and awaited her in a neat pile at the bottom of the huge wardrobe in their room. They would never have enough clothes between them to fill all that space. Lois selected a teddy bear to share her tepee.

'I lost my doll,' she recalled sorrowfully.

'You threw it away,' Sonia corrected her. 'But I'll get you another one, I promise.'

'I want mine.'

'Listen! Look in the garden and see if any of your bird friends have left you a feather. Indian squaws wear feathers on their heads. Take this hairband with you and tuck the feather into it if you find one.'

I must get on with my work, Sonia thought. It would be easy, with no employer in the house, to spend the whole day playing with Lois. She felt mean sending her away or trying to find her games to play on her own, but what could she do? She was paid to keep house, not to play with her small daughter, much as she would have liked to.

Sonia wanted to give Lois the kind of carefree childhood she had never had herself. Being passed from one foster family to the next caused all sorts of anxieties about tomorrow, making it impossible to relax and enjoy today. Lois was going to have a proper childhood. Sonia wouldn't have minded having one with her, but it was too late. She was twenty-two now, grown up, and had to work at cleaning the house, not playing Red Indians with Lois.

Fortunately Lois was good. After initial protests she usually understood that Sonia had to leave her to play alone. When they had been at the farm, the old granny had kept an eye on toddler Lois, along with her own little grandson, while Sonia carried out the chores she had been employed to do in the house – and many more she had not been employed to do, on the farm. Like feeding the pigs.

When the old lady died and her nephew took over the farm and Sonia and Lois had to move on, the one bright spot, for

Sonia, was that the Grenvilles did not keep pigs. Or at least only human ones, she thought grimly.

She poured more scouring cream into Samuel's washbasin and scrubbed it viciously. She had decided to start by cleaning the rooms he used most – his bedroom and the sitting room. She would leave the Hoovering, even though the carpets were filthy. Using that Hoover was a waste of effort, and she needed to save her energy to make a real impression on this house.

She gave the taps a final polish and began to put clean sheets on Samuel's bed. Out of the window she could see Lois crawling round the garden on her tummy, her yellow and green painted face intensely serious. She was wearing the headband and, in the absence of feathers, had tucked leaves and sticks into it.

Sonia went into their room, took out the fluorescent paints again and began painting faces and masks on sheets of thick paper. She made holes in the top of the paper, threaded ribbon through them, and ran downstairs to show Lois.

'What are they?' Lois asked.

'Totems,' Sonia said. 'We'll hang them on the tree, to frighten enemy tribes of Red Indians away.'

'Like that lady next door?' Lois asked, in her most piercing voice.

Sonia giggled. 'Ssh! She'll hear you.'

'You be the other Red Indian tribe,' Lois suggested, 'and be scared away.'

'I've got to go and work,' Sonia reminded her.

Lois pouted. 'Just for a minute.'

'Okay. One minute.' It was more fun than changing sheets, anyway. She crept up behind the tree and pretended to be scared of the fluttering masks. She had made them grotesque, with sticking-out tongues and black and white staring eyes. She was quite pleased with the effect. The paint was luminous and would glow in the dark. She would let Lois come out and see them tonight. Or maybe not. They might look too realistic and give the child nightmares.

Lois lurked in the tepee and rushed out to ambush her.

'You're scolloped!' she cried, pulling Sonia's hair as she knelt on the grass.

'Scalped . . . ow, stop it, Lois; that hurts!'

'I'm going to eat you now,' said Lois cheerfully. 'What's for dinner?'

'It's not nearly dinner time yet,' Sonia said. But it was. 'Look at me, wasting all this time!' she reproached herself. 'I'll finish Samuel's bedroom, then I'll get us something for lunch,' she promised Lois, but Lois was hungry now and would not wait.

Sonia took her a picnic in the tent and went back to changing sheets, deciding to get something later for herself but knowing she wouldn't. 'I insist you and Lois eat proper food during the day. You are much too thin, my dear, if you will forgive my indelicacy in remarking on it.' She heard Samuel's voice suddenly as clearly as if he were standing behind her. It made her jump. 'All right,' she said aloud. 'You're probably right.'

She went downstairs, ate bread and cheese and an apple, sitting on the kitchen doorstep at the side of the house. The windows of the air-raid shelter, she noticed, were so black that you couldn't see in. Lois would like that. She was always looking for places to hide away.

Funny, how Lois had been with Samuel this morning. Was she always like that with strangers, then? Confident on her own with them, but shy when Sonia was there too? Impossible to know, really. The child used to follow the gardener around, occasionally, at the Grenvilles' house; she hadn't seemed shy with him, though she always hid her face from Mrs Grenville – or was that only when Sonia was around too?

She was not going to think about the Grenvilles: hadn't she already decided to put them right out of her mind? That chapter was closed. Neither would she worry over Lois; there was no need. The child was perfectly normal. All children had their funny little ways. She hoped Lois wouldn't be sick again tonight. Samuel might think they ought to call the doctor. She didn't want nosy doctors looking at her child. If Lois was sick,

Sonia could look after her herself, better than anybody. But Lois was all right. Of course she was. There was nothing wrong with Lois.

'I want some Coke,' said Lois, finding her.

'In the fridge.'

'Come and do it for me, Sonia.'

'No, you have a try at pouring it yourself.'

'Why?'

'I want you to learn to do things for yourself.'

The child went to the fridge. 'I can't open it.'

'Pull harder. See? You can do it when you really try.'

'I can't get the top off the bottle.'

'No, you probably can't. It's a new one. Bring it here.'

'Sonia, come and play with me.'

'No, I have to work, Lois; you know that.'

'Just for a minute.'

'It never is a minute, that's the trouble. Last time was an hour. I must get on with things.'

'I want you to play Red Indians with me.'

'Come and play in the sitting room, then, while I do the dusting.'

'No, I want to stay in the garden,' Lois objected.

'Well, you can't have both. I have to be in the sitting room. Don't grizzle, Lois. Are you tired? Shall I put you upstairs for a rest, in bed?'

'*Nooo!*'

Perhaps the child was not well. She looked tired, and it wasn't like her to cry for no reason. Sonia compromised.

'Bring down one of your books and I'll sit down for five minutes with you and read you a story. Then you can look at the pictures while I clean the room. Yes?'

'Okay.'

Sonia wondered what it would be like to take Mrs Atwood up on her offer to mind Lois for a few hours, so she could concentrate on her work uninterrupted. It might be worth a try. Lois might take to her; you never knew which people Lois would trust and which she wouldn't.

What was Sonia thinking of, even to consider it? It was not Lois's preferences that were the problem, but Lois herself. What if someone found out about her? There was too much at risk. Her child could be taken away from her.

There was nothing wrong with Lois. Sonia knew it. It was just that not everyone saw things the same way. Mrs Atwood would not understand and neither, for all his kindness, would Samuel.

For the moment they were safe. No one would be allowed to come into the house unannounced. Samuel would take cousin Gertrude's key away from her this weekend. Sonia would continue to do as she had always done and keep an eye on Lois herself. If Lois showed signs of doing anything terrible while she was with Samuel, Sonia's instincts would tell her when to rush in and rescue her.

As long as they were careful, nothing would go wrong, not this time.

Chapter Nineteen

Sonia had Friday all planned. A superficial cleaning of the kitchen (it would have to wait till later for a thorough clean) followed by a baking session: home-made cakes for Gertrude's visit on Saturday. Then a brief visit to Mrs Patel in hospital before returning home to prepare supper and wash up the baking tins.

So it was annoying, as well as worrying, that Lois was sick again in the night and showed no signs of wanting to get up on Friday morning.

'Where's my birdbath attendant?' Samuel greeted Sonia when she came downstairs to make his toast.

'Still in bed.'

He looked concerned. 'Was she ill again in the night?'

'A bit,' Sonia said. 'I hope we didn't disturb you?'

'I heard some noise. I wasn't sure whether to come in. You may always call me, you know, if one of you is not well. Would you like me to telephone the doctor before I leave for work?'

'No, don't worry,' Sonia said. 'I expect she'll feel better later on.'

'That's three nights running, isn't it?' Samuel asked tentatively. 'That she has been unwell?'

'Yes, but she's fine in the daytimes. Probably she's just unsettled with all the moving. She'll be all right.'

Samuel stood pondering. 'You know her best, of course,' he said. 'Is it like her to be tired and want to stay in bed in the mornings?'

'No,' Sonia admitted.

Samuel saw fear and worry on her face. 'The doctor is a nice chap,' he said. 'I have known him personally for a number of years, and he is said to be good with children. Of course it is your decision.'

'She hates strangers,' Sonia said wretchedly. 'If she is ill, it might make her more upset.'

'Would it help if I stayed at home today?'

Her eyes lit up with relief, then her expression became guarded. 'No,' she said. 'It's better if I deal with it myself.'

He refrained from questioning her further. 'If you decide later on to call him,' he said, 'the number is in the book. I believe he is in the surgery until twelve and begins his house calls after that, so it's best to ring before twelve if you can. Dr Carroll is the one I usually consult, but the other partners are equally efficient, I believe.'

As soon as Samuel had left for work, Sonia ran upstairs and took another look at Lois. She was listless and when she opened her eyes they looked unfocused.

'You might feel better if you had some breakfast,' Sonia suggested, but Lois shook her head and tears came into her eyes. Her forehead was hot.

'Lois,' said Sonia gently, 'you're not very well, are you? Listen, honey, what if I call the doctor? He'll come and have a look at you and give you some medicine to make you feel better.'

Lois bit her lip. The tears brimmed over her eyelids and rolled down her hot face. Sonia felt cruel.

'He's a nice man,' she said, but her voice shook. 'Samuel said so. He's Samuel's friend. Will you let him see you, Lois? I promise it will be all right.' She was crying as well. 'I promise. Okay?'

'Okay,' Lois whispered.

Sonia went to the phone, found 'Dr Carroll and partners' listed in Samuel's old-fashioned copperplate handwriting in the address book, and began to dial the number. Then she replaced the receiver. I can't do it, she thought. What if it's not something simple? If, instead of writing out a prescription for a bottle of medicine for a child's upset stomach, he says, 'This child is disturbed. I am taking her away for psychiatric tests?'

Then what? Then the psychiatrist would say, 'This is not a normal disturbance. We will have to look into this further.' Or even, 'This is beyond my field of expertise.' And, surely, they would investigate the mother as well. 'Two of them in that state! Mother and daughter. Well, it's only to be expected the child should turn out like that, if the mother . . . Yes, far better to separate them. The child's interests must come first; avoid further damage . . .'

She was letting her imagination run away with her. The doctor would not be suspicious and perceptive. He knew nothing about them; why should he look for anything sinister? Doctors were busy people. The child had a stomach upset, that was all. She was unsettled by moving house; it was only natural. Sonia banished the small voice inside her that said, 'But what happened to cause the move was not natural – not natural at all.'

She closed the address book. She would nip out to the local chemist later and buy a bottle of milk of magnesia. In the meantime, Lois would probably be fine after a good long lie-in, and Sonia would refrain from worrying and get on with her work. Didn't people say that time healed everything?

She sprayed oven cleaner liberally over the inside of the filthy oven and left it to soak in while she scoured the cooker top and poured boiling water on it to soften the grease. She was glad it was back-aching, grimy work. It was like a penance.

I should never have had Lois, she told herself. A woman like me should never have children. This is a judgement on me.

She forced herself to stop thinking, to get on with the work. Too restless for the patient task of baking cakes, she began scrubbing the walls. She broke two fingernails in the process and got dirty grease in a scratch on her hand, which stung. This gave her a grim satisfaction.

When the doorbell rang, she was startled. 'Oh, Mrs Atwood.' Sonia was aware of being covered with grime, her hair hanging down at one side of her face. She tucked it hastily behind her ear and wrapped her hands in the towel she was holding.

'I'm going up to the local shops,' Mrs Atwood said. 'Is there anything I can get for you while I'm there?'

'Oh, yes please,' Sonia said, 'if you wouldn't mind. A loaf of white bread and a bottle of milk of magnesia. Hold on and I'll fetch you the money.'

Mrs Atwood stepped over the front doorstep and into the hall. 'Would Lois like a walk to the shops with me?' she enquired, as Sonia returned from the kitchen with the money.

'She's not well this morning,' Sonia said reluctantly.

'I am sorry to hear that. Have you called the doctor?'

'No, she'll be okay. Just a stomach upset. Children get these things.'

'Is she running a temperature?'

'No.' Sonia crossed her fingers behind her back.

'Oh well, that's something,' said Mrs Atwood. 'If you want to call the doctor, though, I can phone him for you. I go to Dr Lightbourne.'

'Thanks, but I've got the number of Mr Arnold's doctor here.'

'You don't want Dr Carroll!' exclaimed Mrs Atwood. 'The man drinks.'

There, thought Sonia, relieved. I was right not to call him in. Lois is better without him. 'We don't need a doctor anyway,' she said aloud. 'She'll be better by this afternoon or this evening.'

'Right. Well, if there's anything I can do to help, don't hesitate to call me. Shall I leave my telephone number, in case you don't want to leave the house to ring my doorbell?'

'No. No, please don't worry. Just the shopping would be a great help: save me going out. Thank you very much, Mrs Atwood.'

'Molly.'

'Molly. Thank you.' Sonia closed the door. The woman was kind and well-meaning, no doubt, but exhausting. A fusser. Children didn't need fussing when they were ill, just a bit of peace.

She went upstairs and looked in at Lois, hunched up

miserably under the blankets. Lois heard her come in and rolled over.

'Still feeling sick?' Sonia asked her. Lois nodded. 'The bucket's right here by the bed, if you need it,' Sonia said. She did what Samuel had done the other night, when she had thought she was dreaming, and draped the pink towel over the sheet.

'I'm not going to be sick; I just *feel* sick,' Lois said.

'All right. That was Mrs Atwood at the door. She's going to the shops to get some medicine for you. I decided we don't need to bother the doctor; he's very busy. You'll feel better when you've had this medicine.'

Lois nodded and rolled over again, away from her. Sonia felt dismissed. 'Shout for me if you want anything,' she said. 'Or bang on the floor.' She was not sure if she would hear Lois shout, in this house. The walls and floors were solid. 'Would you rather come down in the kitchen? It's warmer down there and you can watch me work. I could carry the mattress down for you.'

Lois mumbled something.

'What was that?' Sonia asked.

'No,' Lois said.

'Okay, then. Call if you want me.' She sounded like Mrs Atwood, she thought. Fussing.

By the time Mrs Atwood rang the doorbell again, Sonia was even hotter and grimier than the first time, but no visible impression had been made on the kitchen wall.

'You need something heavy duty, like sugar soap,' Mrs Atwood advised. She had declined to hand over the purchases on the doorstep, saying, 'Let me sort this bag out in the kitchen; I can't see what's yours and what's mine here,' so Sonia had no option but to let her come in. 'Of course, the whole place needs redecorating really. Mr Arnold had the hall, the lounge and the dining room done a few years ago, and his own bedroom and the big front one, so they're not in too bad condition, but Miss Prynne didn't want him to touch the kitchen or her room.'

'Why not?' Sonia asked. 'You'd think she would jump at it.'

'She didn't like to be disturbed,' said Molly Atwood. 'She was in enough of a nervous state as it was, having workmen in the house, but she wouldn't let them go anywhere near her territory. She shut herself in the kitchen all the time they were here – wouldn't even let them in to get water; they had to go through the dining room and use the garden tap, and she wouldn't let them make themselves tea. I used to pass them trays of tea over the fence.

'They were nice chaps, too. It wouldn't have hurt her to make them a cup of tea, would it? But then, she was old and set in her ways, I suppose, and her nerves weren't good at the best of times. How Mr Arnold put up with her I don't know.'

'Where did she go when she retired?' Sonia asked. 'To her sister in Coventry?'

'Good Lord, no,' Molly said. 'Her sister couldn't have coped. The woman was gaga, and quite nasty with it on occasions. No, she went into a nursing home finally. Should have gone years ago but she always fought the idea and Mr Arnold wouldn't have her talked into it. By the time she left she was past knowing where she was. Mr Arnold was dreadfully upset, though.'

'Maybe he could see himself ending up like that,' Sonia ventured. She didn't want to encourage the woman to gossip, and she wasn't going to let Molly distract her from her work, but the opportunity of collecting information was too good to miss. Sonia had so little, so far. 'After all,' she said casually, 'he is getting on in years himself. Over the retirement age, I suppose.'

Mrs Atwood laughed. 'Well over!' she said. 'But he won't think of retiring, says he'd rather die at work, and he probably will. He's marvellous for his age.'

Sonia waited, but Molly did not elaborate. 'About seventy, is he?' Sonia hazarded.

'Seventy?' Molly said, raising her eyebrows. 'He'll be eighty-five this year.'

Sonia's mouth fell open. 'You're joking,' she said.

Molly was delighted to have caused a sensation. She sat down at the kitchen table.

'I must get on with my work,' said Sonia hastily. 'Don't let me keep you from yours.'

Molly put packages on the table. 'Bread, milk of magnesia,' she said, 'and a couple of things I bought for Lois; I hope you don't mind.'

Sonia did mind. 'She won't always take presents from strangers,' she said.

Molly didn't seem offended. 'They're only little things. Not to worry if she doesn't like them. Here – it's a doll I happened to see in the sweet shop, and a box of fruit jelly sweets; I thought they would be light. I wouldn't give her chocolate, not when she's got an upset stomach, but she might fancy one or two of these.'

The doll was a black doll, with a red dress and matching knickers. 'I hope it's all right,' said Molly anxiously, watching Sonia's face. 'I thought it was rather cute.'

It was cute. Sonia could not possibly take offence, as she was secure in the knowledge that Lois would hate it. 'I'll take it up to her later,' Sonia said. 'When I've finished this cleaning.' Mrs Atwood took the hint and left.

As soon as she had gone, Sonia ran up the stairs. 'Mrs Atwood brought you some presents,' she said, 'but I don't think you're going to like them, Lois. Still, never mind; it was a kind thought, wasn't it? You'll have to remember to thank her.'

'What are they?' said Lois, sitting up and looking at Sonia with interest.

'Here, some sweets – but you'd better not have them while your tummy's sick. And a doll.'

Lois held out her hands for the presents and examined them intently, turning the doll round and round and upside down. She beamed. 'My new doll,' she said.

'I was going to get you one,' said Sonia jealously, 'as soon as I had the chance. I didn't think you'd like this one, anyway, as it's black. You said in the supermarket that you didn't like black skin.'

'It isn't black,' Lois said.

'It is! Look at her face and legs! This is a black doll, Lois. Mrs Atwood got it for you because you're black yourself.'

'No, I'm not,' said Lois. 'I'm clean. And this doll is clean like me.'

Sonia stared at her. 'Where do you get this from? Who's been telling you black is dirty? Lois? Answer me!'

'I want to be on my own,' said Lois.

'Lois,' Sonia said, 'do you want to go out in the garden? It's a nice warm day again.'

'No, I'm sick,' Lois said.

'You might feel better for a bit of fresh air, don't you think so? Look, here are the Indian masks and the tepee; I brought them in last night before Samuel came home, in case it rained. Shall I put them up again for you?'

'No,' Lois said.

'No *thank you*,' Sonia said, but Lois turned her head away. She opened the box of sweets and started rearranging them, picking out the different colours. 'Red, yellow, three, five, blue,' she said under her breath. Sonia left her to it. Perhaps she just needed peace. It would do her no harm to have a day in bed if she wanted one. It wasn't until she was downstairs that she remembered the milk of magnesia. She decided not to go back with it. Lois had made her feel definitely unwelcome at the moment.

Giving up on the kitchen walls, which were being equally unresponsive to her ministrations, Sonia took out the baking tins and mixing bowls and set to work on the cakes for Gertrude's visit.

Chapter Twenty

Sonia met Samuel at the door. 'You never told me you were nearly eighty-five,' she said accusingly. 'Look at you, working all these hours! No wonder you're so tired.' She took his umbrella from him and placed it in the stand.

He smiled at her. 'I always look a bit tired by the weekend, I shouldn't wonder. How is Lois?'

'As right as rain except that she won't get up. She's been in bed all day, playing. Mrs Atwood brought her a doll.'

'Shall I go up and see her?' Samuel asked.

'Wouldn't you like a cup of tea first? I made a pot, in case.'

'That would be welcome,' he admitted. He sniffed. 'What a delicious smell. Have you been baking?'

'Yes. For tomorrow.'

'Tomorrow?'

'Your cousin Gertrude's visit,' she reminded him.

He looked amazed. 'How very kind of you to make cakes specially. She will be pleased. We usually just make ourselves a sandwich. My word, you have been busy,' he added, coming into the kitchen and seeing neat rows of buns and scones cooling on a rack on the table. 'They look very tempting.'

She laughed at him. 'Help yourself. There's a fruit cake in the oven.'

'May I really?' He took a scone and Sonia handed him the butter dish and a knife. 'Will you have one with me?' he asked.

She had missed lunch, forgotten about it altogether, since Lois had not wanted anything to eat. She helped herself to a bun.

Samuel ate with appreciation, dabbing up crumbs from the table with his thumb. 'It's a long time since I came home to freshly baked cakes,' he said with deep satisfaction.

Sonia smiled her wide smile at him, a sudden gleam of white teeth, reminding him of Lois when she forgot her shyness. 'Did your mother used to bake cakes when you were a kid?'

'No,' he said, 'or not that I remember. There was a cook and a kitchen maid, I believe. I went away to boarding school when I was seven.'

'Seven?' said Sonia. 'That's young. Did you like it?' She was not so much collecting information now as trying to prolong the moment. When he had finished his tea he would go up-stairs to see Lois. Sonia had been on her own all day, with only the company of disturbing thoughts, and it was pleasant sitting here now with Samuel. He brought with him an air of peace.

'No, I am afraid I did not enjoy it much,' he confessed.

'Were you homesick?'

'Yes, very homesick.' He stirred sugar into his tea and sipped it reflectively. 'So the oven works, does it?' he asked, changing the subject.

'The oven is fine. One of the top burners is out of order and the grill only works on one side, but the oven was okay once I'd cleaned it three times.'

'Ah,' he said. 'Perhaps a new cooker is called for, would you say?'

'It depends,' said Sonia awkwardly, 'on what you can afford. The plumber is coming tomorrow, remember. He might say you need a new loo.'

'I had forgotten the plumber's visit,' Samuel said. 'What a good thing you reminded me. I shall have to make a point of waiting in for him.'

'I can do that if you want,' Sonia said. 'You were going to see Mrs Baker tomorrow, weren't you?'

'Mrs Baker? Oh, Mrs Baker, the cleaning lady. Yes.' He went silent, then said, 'I'll pop up and see how Lois is, if that's all right with you?'

'Sure,' she said. The sigh was almost imperceptible. 'I'll get on with icing these buns.'

'Shall I take one up for Lois?' he suggested. 'With a drink?'

'You can try. She's been refusing to eat. Here, I'll pour a cup of milk; she better not have Coke.'

After ten minutes, Sonia went and stood at the foot of the stairs. She could hear Samuel and Lois laughing. She went back to icing the buns. After a further ten minutes Samuel came downstairs. 'Lois has decided to get up,' he told Sonia, 'and come and give me a hand in my workshop.'

'Oh good,' Sonia said. She went upstairs. 'Feeling better now?' she asked Lois.

Lois was eating a bun and putting her dungarees on back to front, both at the same time.

'Let me help,' Sonia said.

'No, I can do it,' Lois insisted. She got tangled up in the straps and dropped a handful of crumbs on the carpet. Sonia looked at her. 'Okay,' said Lois, giving in gracefully. Sonia peeled the dungarees off her, turned her round and inserted her into them again. 'This bib part goes at the front,' Sonia told her. 'Just so's you know when you're getting dressed by yourself. I must do your hair, Lois; it's coming loose.'

'Not now,' Lois said. 'I have to help Samuel make something in his shed.'

'What is he making?'

'I don't know. He said it was a surprise.'

'Okay, you're done now. Go and find out. Want your warpaint on?'

'I'm too busy to be a Red Indian today,' said Lois, running out of the room. She slid down the stairs on her stomach, kicking her legs.

'There's nothing much wrong with you, is there?' said Sonia, and laughed.

Sonia cooked fish and rice, with sweet potatoes which Lois loved, in case she didn't feel like eating anything else. Lois hadn't eaten any of Mrs Atwood's sweets, Sonia noticed when she went up to tidy the bed and sweep up the crumbs, but had treated them as toys, arranging them in rows on the bed. Sonia put them back in the box.

The doll was at the bottom of the bed. Its mouth, which had

a round hole accommodating a miniature feeding bottle, was empty except for one of Lois's pink ribbons emerging from it. Most of the pink ribbon was inside the doll. Sonia hunted for the bottle, found it under the bed, pulled out the ribbon and replaced the bottle in the doll's mouth. She propped the doll on the pillow ready for Lois when she went to bed.

When supper was nearly ready, she went to find Samuel and Lois. They were in the workshop, Samuel applying sandpaper to a small piece of wood and Lois sitting on a low stool watching him intently. In her hand was a tiny wooden doll. Samuel was working on a second one.

'Look!' Lois shouted, showing Sonia.

'Isn't that lovely?' said Sonia admiringly.

'Jelly-baby dolls,' Samuel said. 'I used to make them for my nephews and nieces.'

'They do look like jelly babies,' Sonia said. 'Do you paint them or leave them like this?'

'I usually varnish them,' Samuel said. 'But paint would be better, then they could have faces. I don't have any paint, though, unfortunately.'

'Lois has lots of paints,' Sonia said. 'You want me to paint them, Lois?'

Lois nodded emphatically.

Sonia went to fetch the paints. On the way through the kitchen she turned off the flame under the pan. There was no hurry for supper. They were all full of cake and scones.

It was nice in the workshop, she thought, she and Samuel working away. Lois seemed contented too. Samuel tested the smoothness of the second doll with his thumb and handed it over to Lois. 'I need another one now,' Lois said.

'Lois!' Sonia rebuked her.

'I do,' she insisted.

'What for? Don't be greedy. You've got two. Three, with the doll Mrs Atwood gave you today.'

'I need one more.'

'Why?'

Lois pointed at the one Sonia was painting. 'That one is

Mrs Grenville,' she said. 'And this one is going to be you. I need one more.'

'Who's the third one going to be?'

'I've forgotten his name.'

'Mr Grenville? What do you want Grenville dolls for, anyway, Lois? I thought we were going to forget the Grenvilles. Why not have a Samuel doll instead?'

'Because Samuel is here,' said Lois, with devastating logic.

'Well, so am I here,' Sonia pointed out.

'No,' Lois said. 'This doll is for when you were black.'

Sonia looked at Samuel and they both laughed. 'I give up,' Sonia said.

'I will make one more,' said Samuel. 'What colour is this one to be, Lois? Black or white?'

'White,' Lois said. 'This one is going to be me.'

Sonia painted two dolls with pink faces and red cheeks, one doll in a yellow dress and one in a brown suit. When Samuel handed her the third, he had added little spikes to the head, like Lois's pigtails. Lois shrieked. 'That one is me!' she said. She examined the three dolls. 'I need another one now,' she said.

'Oh no, you don't,' said Sonia. 'Samuel has done quite enough. Have you said thank you?'

'Thank you, Samuel,' said Lois. 'I need a house for them to live in.'

'Lois!' said Sonia warningly.

'Maybe tomorrow,' Samuel promised, standing up and replacing the chisels carefully in a rack on the wall.

'I'll make you a house for them,' said Sonia. 'All we need is a couple of cardboard boxes. We'll do it together, Lois.'

'Will it have a cellar?' Lois asked.

'I said a house, not Buckingham Palace,' Sonia told her. 'Samuel, are these made of different kinds of wood? They're different colours.'

'Yes,' he said. 'I thought it would give them variety.'

'Oh, I shouldn't have painted them!' she exclaimed.

'The wood grain shows through the paint,' he said. 'They

still look different from one another.'

'What kind of wood are they?' Sonia asked.

'The lightest one is Swedish pine, that one is beech, and the third is rosewood.'

'Can you tell just by looking at the colours?'

'Yes, partly by the colour, though wood is often stained different shades, of course. Mainly by the grain and texture of the wood. That chair over there is oak, for example, and the stool Lois is sitting on is also oak, but as you can see they are quite different colours. But take a good look at the grain – excuse me a moment, Lois – and you will see the resemblance.'

Sonia was fascinated. 'That big table in the dining room – is that oak too?'

He was delighted. 'Very well observed,' he complimented her. 'A much older and bigger tree, of course, with proportionate variations in the grain, but oak, yes.'

'And that table in the hall – the very dark one, almost black?'

'Mahogany. A beautiful wood, very hard. It can last for centuries. Increasingly rare and expensive, unfortunately. It's more common to find mahogany veneers on furniture made of cheaper woods. And it's sometimes combined with other woods used as inlays – mahogany with a rosewood inlay, for example. Or ivory, in the past.'

'What are you going to do with that oak chair, Samuel?' Sonia asked. 'Make a new seat out of wood?'

'No, really it should be canework,' Samuel said, 'though upholstery can look well, too, on that design of chair. When I've finished repairing and polishing the frame I shall pass it on to an upholsterer.'

'Can't you do that yourself? Is it difficult?'

'Not so very difficult, I believe, but it's not my trade. A different skill. I was trained as a cabinet maker, you see. Too old to learn new tricks now.'

'I've always wanted to learn upholstery,' Sonia confided.

'Excellent!' Samuel exclaimed. 'We shall go into partnership.'

144

She laughed.

'Seriously,' Samuel said. 'The schools in this area offer all kinds of evening classes. Why don't you sign up for a course? Most of them begin in September, I believe, but enrolment may be much earlier, perhaps about now, May or June. Shall I make enquiries at the library?'

'Oh,' Sonia said, taken aback by his enthusiasm. 'No, don't bother.'

'Why not?' he said. 'It would be nice for you to learn something you've always wanted to do, and it would give you an evening out, a change of scene. You don't want to sit at home every night at your age.'

'I don't mind,' she said. 'I don't go out really.'

'Precisely,' Samuel said. 'It would be an opportunity. I shall obtain a prospectus for you tomorrow.'

Sonia felt trapped. He's talking as though we're going to be here for years, she thought. I can't go signing up for things for September; we might not be here. We could get thrown out at a moment's notice, like last time, if Lois . . .

What was the point in making any long-term plans? Sonia felt suddenly weary. 'Let's go and have supper,' she said, smudging the paint on the last doll, giving the miniature Lois one eye bigger than the other.

Lois ate as much supper as Sonia would allow her. 'You go easy,' her mother warned, as she helped herself to more sweet potato. 'I don't want you being sick again tonight. It's becoming a habit.'

'I won't.' She refused to go to bed, though, when Samuel went up at half past nine. Sonia had made her leave Samuel alone for the evening. He sat in the sitting room, with a small fire, reading his library book. 'Don't go in there this evening,' Sonia warned Lois. 'It's Friday night and he's had a long week at work. Samuel is a very old gentleman and he needs his peace. You can talk to him tomorrow.'

Samuel didn't object to being rescued from Lois. He admitted to Sonia, when she took in his coffee, that he did feel slightly tired.

'Can't you afford to retire?' she asked. She wondered if she had asked for too high a salary, but really it was quite reasonable for the job; she didn't want to undersell herself. Apart from anything else, it would look bad when she applied for the next job.

'I can afford it,' he said, 'but I don't care to retire. What would I do all day?'

'You'd probably work twice as hard in your workshop,' Sonia said, leaving him to his coffee.

Sonia sat in the kitchen, making a dolls' house for Lois out of an apple box divided with cardboard.

'What do you think?' she asked Samuel when he brought his coffee cup out to the kitchen before going to bed.

If she had expected him to be polite she was disappointed. He shook his head. 'Fall to bits in seconds,' he said.

Piqued, she turned to Lois, who was playing under the table with a pile of eggboxes which had been inside the apple box in the larder, along with about a hundred paper bags. Miss Prynne had obviously been a hoarder.

Lois was usually easy to please. 'Your new dolls' house, Lois,' Sonia said, showing her. 'We can cover it in some of that sticky-backed shelf-liner. What do you think?'

'No, that's no good,' Lois said.

Sonia was annoyed. 'You're only saying that because Samuel did. What's wrong with it?'

'It hasn't got a cellar,' Lois said.

'It's time you went to bed,' Sonia told her.

When Samuel had gone to bed, she relented and let Lois stay up with her. They sat on the floor in the sitting room and alternately watched the black and white television and the red embers of the fire. Sonia hooked an arm around Lois and the child snuggled up to her. 'How's your tummy now?' Sonia asked.

'Fine,' said Lois sleepily.

I was right, Sonia told herself. A day's peace and no fuss was all she needed.

There was nothing wrong with Lois.

Chapter Twenty-One

Lois wanted to sleep in Sonia's bed, so Sonia tucked her in then sat up braiding Lois's hair. As always, the little girl found this soothing; her breathing soon became rhythmic and peaceful. Please God, don't let her get sick tonight, Sonia prayed. She got into the bed beside Lois, gently shifting her over to make space, and lay trying to sleep, dismissing her worries about tomorrow.

She didn't know why she felt apprehensive about Gertrude's visit. The woman was only her employer's cousin, not the Avenging Angel with a flaming sword arriving in clouds of fury to protect Samuel's interests. Anyway, what was there to hide? Sonia and Lois, so far, had done Samuel nothing but good. True, there was not much to show for it except a clean cooker and a batch of home-made cakes, but neither was there any evidence to the contrary.

Why did Sonia feel guilty and fearful, then? She decided it was ridiculous. She had made cakes for Gertrude's tea and that was her job as housekeeper accomplished. She would leave Gertrude and Samuel to each other's company, carrying in the tray of tea when the time came, and if Gertrude chose to tell Samuel not to let these interlopers take advantage of him by complaining about a perfectly good Hoover and an adequate toilet, then it wouldn't be the end of the world, even if Samuel did take her advice.

No, that wasn't the problem. Sonia sighed and moved restlessly. Gertrude was somehow a threat to them; she could feel it in her bones. Samuel, innocent and trusting, had taken them into his home without a moment's doubt. It was not that he was stupid; Sonia knew he could be shrewd. It was clear to

Sonia, for instance, when he did not approve of the way she treated Lois or spoke about Mrs Baker or Mrs Atwood, but his only reaction was a slight air of sadness. He tried to understand her point of view and didn't condemn her for not sharing his own. But Gertrude . . . Gertrude sounded tough.

This was ridiculous, Sonia told herself. She hadn't met the woman. And even if Gertrude did sweep into the house like the Day of Judgement personified, what could she find to judge? Sonia and Lois had been here less than three days. Gertrude knew nothing about their background, nor would she find out, for Sonia was expert at telling people nothing. If Gertrude was indeed tough she might have her suspicions but what could suspicion do, without a focus?

Okay, so they were not blameless but the blame was – surely – indetectable. After all, no one could have been more suspicious and less trusting than Mr and Mrs Grenville. During the short six months of the Leroys' employment, the Grenvilles had watched Sonia and Lois like hawks.

Mrs Grenville kept inventories of every item in the house, from the silver cutlery to the number of sugar lumps left in the bowl, so great was her fear of 'the servants' relieving her of any of her possessions.

And Mr Grenville – George – was so close he would not discuss anything financial or any family matters in front of the housekeeper, and did not even discuss business in front of his wife, sending her out of the room if he wanted to make a phone call concerning his work. In fact, to George so many matters were 'confidential' that he rarely spoke about anything whatsoever with members of his household, except possibly the weather and his opinions on the incompetence of politicians.

So they were not an easy couple to swindle: confiding in no one, continually on their guard and regarding even their closest friends as potential enemies. Yet Sonia had gained the confidence of the wife, at least, if not the husband, even while she collected information about their most private and intimate lives – information which had, in the event, proved quite useless as an insurance against accusations.

Neither the Grenvilles' most paranoid fears nor Sonia's diligently acquired stock of privileged information had prepared any of them to deal with what had happened. It was simply too bad to be imagined, too indefensible to be defended, too painful to recall now, when sleep was needed and not these tormenting memories.

She had not meant to start going over it again; she was merely trying to reassure herself that what the Grenvilles could not foresee happening would not now be detected by Gertrude either. Sonia was the one with the advantages; she knew what there was to hide and how important it was to hide it. Even if Gertrude turned out to be the human equivalent of a bloodhound, she could sniff and search every corner of Sonia and Lois's present lives and find nothing wrong, because she simply would not know – could not imagine, even in her most excessive suspicions – what it was that she was looking for.

Let Gertrude come! Sonia would lose no more sleep over groundless fears. She turned over and willed herself into sleep and achieved a night of weary repetitive dreams in which she was perpetually opening the door to Gertrude and horrible things happened.

Lois awoke early, wanting to go into Samuel's workshop to see if her dolls' paint was dry. Sonia got up with her and dressed them both in jeans, warning Lois not to make any noise and wake Samuel as they tiptoed down the stairs. She had forgotten to ask Samuel what time he would like his breakfast at the weekend.

'This is our first weekend here,' Sonia told Lois when they reached the kitchen.

'What do we do at weekends here?' Lois asked.

'I don't know,' Sonia admitted. 'Samuel will have his own arrangements. We'll have to fit in. I forgot to ask if he wants a big lunch today or an evening meal. I bought a leg of lamb for tomorrow. That must be all right, mustn't it? Sunday roast dinner?'

'Sonia, can I have my dolls?'

'Oh yes, I forgot.' She unhooked the workshop key from the back of the larder door and went to fetch the dolls.

Lois followed her in and sat down on the stool in the workshop. 'I have to do some more work on them,' she said importantly.

'What work? They're finished.'

'No, I have to rub them with that scratchy paper, like Samuel did.'

'Not now, Lois! You'll scratch the paint off. You have to sand them down before they're painted, and Samuel already did that.'

'I have to do it as well. He showed me how.'

'No, Lois, it would be cruel. Look at their little faces. How would you like your face sanded down with that gritty paper?'

'I wouldn't,' said Lois emphatically.

'Bring your dolls in for breakfast. Then I'm going to iron us a couple of pretty dresses. Today we have to look nice because Samuel's cousin Gertrude is coming to visit.'

'I have to fill the birdbath.'

'Okay, fill the birdbath and come indoors when you've finished.'

'I can't do it on my own.'

'Well, you'll have to learn. Let's see how much of it you can do on your own.'

It wasn't much: the garden tap was stiff and the watering can heavy. Samuel was patient, Sonia thought, to go through this routine with Lois so early in the morning. As she thought of him, she heard him draw back the curtains in his room. She looked up and he smiled and waved at them.

'The birdbath is full, Lois,' she said. 'It doesn't need more water in it.'

'I have to do it every day. The birds have a drink in it, so it has to be fresh.'

'They can't be that fussy, Lois, if they have a bath in it first.'

'We have to do it like this; Samuel said,' Lois told her.

'Oh well, if Samuel said so, how can I argue?' said Sonia sarcastically. She tipped the birdbath's contents on to the lawn. 'Now fill it up with fresh,' she said.

'I can't reach.'

'Try,' Sonia encouraged.

Lois tipped water into the birdbath, over her feet and down her jeans. 'Oh!' she cried.

'Very good,' Sonia said. 'Next time hold the handle of the watering can with a tight grip – like this. But that wasn't bad. Some of the water went in. You go upstairs and take off your wet things and I'll pour a bit more in, so the birds can wash their wings as well as their faces.'

'I've got Mrs Grenville wet too,' Lois said, rescuing the doll from the grass. The paint had run slightly.

'Listen, Lois,' said Sonia, crouching down beside her. 'I want you to promise me something.'

'What is it?' She was pulling her sodden jeans away from her knees.

'Listen to me – really listen. I don't want you talking about the Grenvilles any more. Okay?'

'Why?' said Lois absently, stamping her feet and watching her plimsolls squelch.

'Because,' said Sonia slowly, thinking up a good reason, 'because Samuel will think we're not happy living with him if we keep talking about the last people we lived with. So find another name for your doll, will you, Lois?'

'Okay,' Lois said. 'What is her other name?'

'Whose other name?'

'Mrs Grenville,' Lois said.

'I just told you not to say that, Lois! You don't listen to me!'

'I do! I'm just asking! Her *other* name!'

'It's Vera. You can call her Vera but not Mrs Grenville. Is it a deal?' She held out her hand and Lois slapped it in agreement. 'Deal,' she assented.

Lois began to peel off her wet clothes.

'Not here,' Sonia said. 'Upstairs.'

'I'm wet,' Lois pointed out, continuing to undress.

'Stop that!' said Sonia. 'What do I keep telling you? Do you want a smack?' She drew back her hand warningly.

'Good morning,' said Samuel, appearing in the kitchen doorway.

'I filled the birdbath!' Lois told him. 'But now I'm all wet.'

Sonia said, 'I'll get breakfast. Lois, come inside and I'll find you dry clothes,' and tugged the child by the hand, making it look as gentle as she could, while gripping Lois's fingers to show her she meant business. Lois looked sideways at Samuel and followed her mother.

Now he'll think I'm always beating my child, Sonia swore, and he might even tell Gertrude. Oh, what does it matter what people think of me? I can do what I like.

Except that it did matter, of course. Sonia knew she was a good mother, within her limits, and that Lois forgave her and bore no grudges when those limits were reached, but she needed other people to know it too. If Samuel could like her, perhaps he would even stand up for them both, when and if the axe did fall? If not for both of them, then at least for Lois?

Samuel, though, would have his limits too, as everyone did. Sonia knew that what she and Lois had done would be beyond everyone's limits, really. Beyond the pale, she thought, studying her reflection beside Lois's in the bedroom mirror, and laughed at the pun. 'Two black faces,' she observed to Lois, 'beyond the pale.'

'Not me,' said Lois. 'I'm clean and white.'

Sonia clicked her tongue. 'Who's been telling you these things?' she demanded. 'Who says black is dirty, in front of you?'

'I'm not allowed to tell you,' said Lois.

'Who says you're not allowed to tell me what they said to you?'

'You do,' Lois said. 'You said I wasn't allowed to say the name.'

'Oh, I might have guessed,' said Sonia. 'Mrs I'm-not-racially-prejudiced bloody Grenville.'

Lois turned and swiped her across the face. 'You're not allowed to say the name!' she accused.

'And you're not allowed to hit people, Lois! Whatever next?'

'You hit people.'

'Only you,' Sonia said, 'when you keep taking your clothes off in public. I've told you not to do it. That's two things you're not to do, Lois. Tell me what they are, so I can be sure you remember. One is . . .?'

'Don't hit people.'

'No, not that one. One thing not to *do* is . . .?'

'Take my clothes off.'

'Good. And the other thing not to *say* is . . .? Come on, you remember. What name?'

'I can't say it,' said Lois. 'Shall I whisper it to you?'

Sonia tried not to laugh. 'Okay.'

'Mrs Grenville!' Lois hissed wetly. Sonia exploded into giggles and Lois joined her.

Seeing them coming downstairs laughing, hand in hand, Samuel smiled too.

'I know my new housekeeper will be very cross with me,' he said, 'but I've made the tea. And will you have toast or corn-flakes, Sonia my dear?'

Sonia smiled brilliantly. She thought, with a surge of relief and joy, He does like me.

Chapter Twenty-Two

'Pocket money,' said Samuel, after breakfast. He produced a twenty-pence piece and placed it in front of Lois and handed Sonia an envelope. Both of them looked at him.

'What's this?' Sonia asked. 'You've already given me the housekeeping money for next week.'

'It's your first week's salary,' he said.

She opened it. 'But there's fifty pounds in here,' she said. 'I haven't worked a week yet. We've only been here two full days and the first one was a day off.'

'I can't help that,' said Samuel. 'I have to pay wages on Saturdays. It hinders my accounting procedures to start fiddling about with part-weeks.'

Sonia opened her mouth to protest and decided not to. His eyes twinkled at her approvingly. She laughed. 'I don't mind,' she said.

Lois was staring at the twenty-pence piece. 'I can't have these,' she said.

Samuel and Sonia both laughed. 'She hasn't worked a full week either, filling up the birdbath,' Sonia said. 'Take it, Lois, and say thank you. You worked overtime on filling up the birdbath this morning. And you washed your clothes as well.'

'*No!*' said Lois in exasperation. 'I'm not allowed to have *these*!' She stabbed a finger at the coin on the table.

Sonia was puzzled. 'Why not? Who said?'

Lois grimaced at her. 'I'm not allowed to *say*!' she said conspiratorially.

Sonia shook her head. 'You've lost me. Who said you weren't allowed to have twenty p coins?'

Lois raised her eyes to heaven. 'I can't say the *name*!'

'Mrs Grenville? Mrs Grenville said you weren't allowed to have twenty pences?' said Sonia mystified. 'Why?'

'Because,' said Lois, 'I'm a dirty little thieving black bitch.'

'What?' Sonia shrieked. Samuel clicked his tongue and shook his head. 'Is that what this Mrs Grenville said to you, Lois?' he asked. 'Because you picked up a twenty-pence piece – was that what happened?'

'Yes,' Lois said, relieved to have made herself understood.

'I'll kill her,' said Sonia. 'She had no right to use language like that to a child. Why didn't you tell me about this, Lois, when it happened?'

Lois shrugged and seemed to lose interest. 'Can you make me a cellar today,' she said, 'for my dolls' house?'

'I have to do some ironing first. Samuel, have you anything that needs ironing?'

'No, thank you. The laundry is due to deliver my shirts on Monday. Shall we continue with that arrangement, until we have installed the washing machine?'

'Yes, fine.' So he intended to buy a washing machine; it had not been an empty suggestion. Sonia felt no enthusiasm. She had ceased to believe that they could stay here. It was going too well. Something was about to go wrong. Her intuition was reliable. Let Samuel make plans. None of them would come about. Soon the truth would come out, the truth that nobody wanted Lois and Sonia, nobody could want them, nobody ever had or ever would.

Samuel was taking back the twenty-pence coin and handing Lois a ten and two fives instead. 'Will this be more acceptable?' he asked her.

Lois was thrilled. 'I've got all these now!' she said, collecting them up in her hand. 'Shall we go to the shops?' she invited Samuel.

'Lois!' Sonia rebuked her automatically.

'We shall,' Samuel promised, 'but it is still a little early. Would you like to start work on this dolls' cellar first?'

'Yes.' Lois could be decisive. She fetched the apple-box dolls' house from beside the boiler.

'That reminds me,' Samuel murmured. He took the lid off the boiler and picked up the coal hod, tipping the last few pieces of fuel into the stove. 'I'll just refill this,' he said.

Sonia was stricken. 'I forgot about the boiler, Samuel. What am I meant to do with it?'

'It needs topping up in the mornings,' he said. 'Come with me and I'll show you which is the right fuel in the coalshed. Then this drawer at the bottom pulls out and you tip the ashes into the tin bucket there and leave them to cool before putting them into the dustbin.'

'And what is this boiler for?' Sonia asked. 'I mean, there's an immersion heater for the hot water, isn't there?'

'Only for the hot water for upstairs,' he explained. 'It is rather an old-fashioned system. Gertrude has been telling me for years to have central heating installed. I suppose it is high time I did.'

'It works all right, doesn't it?' Sonia said. She was alarmed at the idea of too many improvements to the house. Especially if they were not to be here very long, she did not want the house full of rubble and teams of workmen. She just wanted some peace, until such time as they had to move on. Really, she thought, she just wanted nothing to happen at all – indefinitely. If time would only stand still, as it appeared to have stood still in this house for the past fifty years or so, then things could not get worse.

'Oh, it will have to go,' said Samuel cheerfully. 'If it goes out it's a devil to relight.' Sonia and Lois followed him to the coalshed and then watched while he gave them a demonstration of filling the boiler and clearing out the ashes, and explained to Sonia how to relight it if it should go out. She listened and tried to pay attention. She felt drained. What was the point in learning these things when they were only going to be here for five minutes?

Samuel and Lois went out to the workshop, taking the rejected dolls' house with them. 'We'll make something a bit sturdier,' Samuel promised.

Sonia cleared away the dishes, washed up, and fetched the

iron and ironing board. She ironed a red dress and a matching hair ribbon for Lois and a yellow dress for herself. Then she changed her mind and ironed a white blouse and plain brown skirt for herself. Gertrude might think she didn't look businesslike enough in the dress – as though Sonia were here to enjoy herself, not to work. Oh, stuff Gertrude!

The phone rang. Sonia answered it, repeating the number on the dial.

'This is Gertrude Gorringer,' said a loud, plummy voice. 'Mr Arnold's cousin. Is that Sonia?'

'Yes,' Sonia said. Mr Arnold's cousin. We're going to have to remember to call him Mr Arnold, not Samuel, in front of her now, Sonia realized, as well as remembering the other things not to say.

'Hello, my dear,' Gertrude said. 'I believe you are expecting me this afternoon?'

'Yes, that's right,' Sonia said. Great, she thought: she's not coming.

'Would it be fearfully inconvenient,' Gertrude said, 'if I were to arrive rather earlier? I came to town, you see, by the early train in order to keep a dental appointment, but the dentist is not at his surgery.'

'Oh,' Sonia said. 'Perhaps he'll turn up, though. Shouldn't you wait?' Panic gripped her. She can't come yet; I'm not ready, she thought.

'No.' Gertrude said. 'His mother died suddenly and he had to go off.' (She pronounced it 'awf'.) 'Dreadfully sad, isn't it?'

'Yes,' Sonia said. 'Dreadfully.'

'So – I do have some shopping to do, as well,' Gertrude said, 'but would it be too much trouble if I arrived with you in time for lunch? Do say if it would be.'

'I'll get Samuel . . . Mr Arnold,' said Sonia. She fled to the workshop. 'Samuel, your cousin's on the phone. Can you talk to her – quick? I think she's in a phone box.'

'Oh, of course,' Samuel said. He rose with alacrity. Sonia stood aside at the kitchen door and let him go ahead of her into the house. Her heart was thumping. This was ridiculous. She must stop this silly vision of Gertrude as The Awful Truth arriving to confront them.

She remembered her final dream before she woke up. She had opened the door, again, and as Gertrude – a tall, spindly figure as thin as Samuel and with the same piercing eyes, but without the kindness – entered the house the whole building collapsed around Sonia's ears, burying her in the rubble.

'Grenville,' said Samuel loudly, from the hall. Sonia froze. She must have misheard. She was becoming paranoid. He must have said something else.

'No, I don't know which part of Sussex,' he said. He spoke clearly on the phone, with more volume than his normal speaking voice. There was no mistaking what he had said. 'I'm not sure, Gertrude,' he said next. 'Would you like me to ask Sonia? Oh yes. Well then, my dear, we shall look forward to seeing you very soon. No, just bring yourself.'

Sonia switched off the iron and slowly folded the ironing board away. Her first reaction was rage. How dare Gertrude check up on her? What right did she have to ask Samuel questions about where Sonia had come from, and how dare Samuel answer her? Then the anger died. What difference did it make? Her instincts were right: Gertrude had a nose for the truth. It was simpler this way, asking questions openly, straight away, with no subterfuge. They might as well get it over with.

'Gertrude wished to know,' said Samuel, entering the kitchen, 'whether it would be too much trouble to give her lunch. I told her she was welcome, but there is no need to make any special effort, Sonia. She will be quite happy with a sandwich.'

'I was going to do salad,' Sonia said.

'Excellent,' he said. 'Is there anything you would like me to fetch from the shops, when I go?'

'No, I've got everything,' Sonia said.

'Ah – and if you wouldn't object to my asking you . . .' he said.

'Yes?' said Sonia sharply.

'. . . whether I might take Lois with me? To spend her pocket money?'

'Oh no, that's all right. If she'll go.' But of course she would go with Samuel, Sonia realized. Lois had not covered her eyes once this morning. She would happily go with Samuel, anywhere. But was it all right? Fear gripped her again. It had seemed all right last time, hadn't it? Lois had liked the gardener, Eddie Barnes. Then look what she did! Samuel smiled at her and returned to his workshop, where Lois awaited him.

Too late. She'd agreed to it now. Sonia felt hopeless. She had decided they would be safe if she stayed in control, watched Lois constantly, kept her close, refused to give anyone any information about them. Now she felt as though everything was already beyond her control and all she could do was watch events unfold, like a bystander.

Even Lois no longer seemed within her control, or even her responsibility. Sonia felt detached. Let Lois fend for herself. Or let someone else cope with her.

If Gertrude was going to prove to be the instrument of truth, let it happen like that. Only, Gertrude would have to cope with the consequences, and she might find she had bitten off rather more than she could chew.

Chapter Twenty-Three

Samuel did not discard Sonia's dolls' house completely. He kept the apple-box foundation but strengthened it, sanded down the rough edges, replaced the jutting staples, and – in accordance with Lois's instructions – added a third storey: the cellar. Lois was happy and Sonia was appeased.

He had not thrown away her flimsy cottage and replaced it with a palace for everyone to admire, but which would take weeks to achieve. He had understood that what Lois wanted, and Sonia was trying to give her, was a simple shelter for her family of dolls, now, not some ambitious project for the future.

Sonia had hastily assembled a structure that would keep Lois happy for the meantime but which would (Samuel was right) fall apart under the slightest pressure. Samuel, without despising the simplicity of her design, had made it safer and ensured that it would last, with occasional repairs, for as long as Lois needed it.

Was it too much to hope that this might be symbolic? That Samuel might help Sonia in her lone effort to secure for Lois a more sheltered childhood than she herself had had? That he would not despise her efforts to provide for Lois but would take steps to ensure that those efforts did not crumble under stress? Could it be that Samuel would strengthen the fabric of their life, not throw it out because it was sub-standard?

If only! But wasn't it already too late for that? Their life was already rotting away, as surely as Lois's doll must by now be rotting in its basement grave at the Grenvilles' house. Samuel, for all his kindness, would not tolerate this corpse in their family history. Sonia was sure of this. Even now, if he were to find some small, dead creature, rotting and mouldy, in Lois's apple-box house, wouldn't he throw the whole structure on the bonfire, despite the work he had put into it himself to make improvements? Of course he would.

Lois was ecstatic over her new three-storey dolls' house. Nothing less than a visit to the shops to spend her pocket money could have persuaded her to leave it, but she couldn't wait to dispose of her wealth. She went off happily holding Samuel's hand, still marvelling that he had given her three 'moneys' in place of the one small coin he had originally offered.

Sonia handed Samuel a note from her salary envelope. 'If they have any of that Fablon stuff in the hardware shop,' she said, 'and it's not too much trouble to get some to cover the dolls' house . . .?'

'Certainly,' Samuel said. 'How very satisfying this is! If only this house could be put to rights so swiftly. But I fear we shall need more than Fablon to cover the cracks.'

He was right. The plumber arrived at ten past eleven. Sonia opened the door fearfully, in case it was Gertrude who had arrived even earlier than announced. Samuel and Lois had left the house at nine. They had been gone for two hours. (Where were they? It couldn't take that long to buy sweets and Fablon. Even if Samuel had several other purchases to make, they should have been back long before now.)

'This place is falling to bits,' was the plumber's verdict, within three minutes of his arrival. 'These pipes in the bathroom are lead and highly dangerous; you'll have to have them replaced, for a start. And when that high-level tank comes down in the toilet – and you're dead lucky it hasn't come down by itself before now – it's going to take half the wall with it. You'll need to have it replastered.'

Sonia's heart sank. This was going to mean a lot of disturbance; there seemed no way round it.

'This your own house?' the plumber asked.

'No, it isn't.'

'Well, you want to tell your landlord . . .'

'No, we're not tenants either. I'm the housekeeper.'

'Oh, are you?' He looked her up and down. 'I'll tell you what, darling, I'll do you a bit of a favour here. That old bath – you don't want to keep it, do you? I mean, it's stained, and the basin is cracked so that'll have to go anyway, so you might as well buy a complete new bathroom suite. Yes?'

'I don't know,' Sonia said. 'I'll have to ask my employer what he wants to do.'

'Well, you tell him, love,' and here the plumber winked, 'that I said the bath is as unsafe as the rest of it – right? And you'd best replace the whole lot with a nice coloured plastic bath with matching basin and toilet with low-level flush.

'Then you let me take this bath away and flog it to some interior designer or someone with big ideas about having an antique-look bathroom, and I'll go halves with you on the cash, and not a word to your boss. Can't say fairer than that, can I?'

'How much would that bath fetch, then?' asked Sonia thoughtfully.

'You'd be surprised. I can't say for sure, obviously; it depends on finding the buyer, but people really want this old stuff, even in that state; they don't mind doing it up a bit themselves.'

'Would it cover the cost of the new suite?'

'It could, yes. Easily.'

'Good,' she said. 'Well, you do that then. I'll go and pick a new bath set and have it delivered here by . . . when can you do the pipes by, and be ready to plumb in the bath and toilet?'

'I've got a free week or ten days, if I leave the lad to finish off the present job. I can start as soon as you like. By the time they deliver the stuff I should be ready. If not, they can leave it in the back garden, anyway; won't come to any harm.'

'Right. Give me a written estimate for your work,' Sonia said, 'and look for a buyer for the bath. Then you can deduct what we owe you from the price you get for the bath and give Mr Arnold the rest.'

He opened his mouth. 'You're not understanding me,' he said. 'This is one of the perks of your job – you and me can go halves on the bath, and your guv'nor can foot the bill for the plumbing and the new suite, and be none the wiser. Now don't say I'm not being generous to you, love, because I could have told you it was rotten and taken it away and flogged it and kept the dosh myself, couldn't I?'

'And I could say that we've decided to keep it, then find another plumber to put in a new suite, and flog the bath to some designer myself,' said Sonia coolly.

'You wouldn't have the contacts,' he said.

'I could advertise.'

'You wouldn't know what price to ask, either.'

'You've just told me,' Sonia said, 'that it would be about the same price as a plastic bathroom suite. Or even more.'

'I wouldn't like to see you get ripped off, love,' he said. 'I doubt very much you'd get what it's worth.'

'No, but I wouldn't have to share the money with you, so I couldn't lose out,' Sonia reasoned.

He glared at her.

'So let's play it straight, shall we?' she said, with a disarming smile. 'You find a buyer and send him round here to have a look at the bath and settle a price. Then we'll go halves with you, like you suggested, and our half will be deducted from Mr Arnold's bill.'

He hesitated then grinned. 'I'd best make my bill nice and high then, hadn't I?'

'Of course I'll compare your estimate with other plumbers' first,' Sonia said.

His face fell. 'You won't find anyone better value than me. Oh, there may be cheaper, but they're cowboys. I'll do a proper job. You won't find them pipes springing leaks for ever after.'

'I hope not,' said Sonia. 'Okay then, you give us a price.'

'Thirsty work, writing estimates,' he said.

'I'll write you an estimate for my tea-making,' Sonia promised. 'Only, look – I'm not being rude, but I don't want you here all morning. There's visitors arriving and I've got work to do, to get things ready.'

He suddenly became businesslike. 'Okay, I won't waste your time, and you don't waste mine. I'll give you a fair estimate for the job, no fiddles, and you can do what you like with your half of the money from the bath – yes, tell your boss if you like and pay me out of it. But in return you promise me I get the job and I can start Monday, no hanging about, while I've got the time free. And I'll bring in a mate who's a plasterer to fix that wall for you, very reasonable, and you'll have enough money left from the sale of the bath to pay him, if that's what's worrying you. My bill ain't going to be that high, if you're worrying about your boss being strapped for cash.'

'That's good news,' Sonia said, leading the way downstairs, 'because I think you better have a look at the pipes in the kitchen as well.'

'Blimey,' the man said, walking into the kitchen. 'This is like something out of the Victoria and Albert museum! You're right about the pipes, love – they're lead as well and way past it. Look at the sink! And the draining board! I haven't seen one of them in years.'

'How much could you get for the sink?' said Sonia hopefully.

'Nobody wants those now, not with them fitted kitchens. It has to be all streamlined.'

'People use them for sink gardens,' said Sonia. 'They're very sought after. I think I might advertise this one and get it replaced.'

'I'll do it,' said the plumber. 'Leave it to me; I can get you a good deal. Blimey, sweetheart, how do you work in a place like this? And that boiler: I bet that's a bugger to light, excuse my language, and you've got to rake it out every day, haven't you?

'Pity your employer's hard up. I could go to town on this place – central heating, new kitchen sink, get some of them self-assembly kitchen units and a carpenter mate to build them in, with a fitted cooker, new fridge, washing machine . . . you need the lot really, don't you? Pity just to replace the old pipes and leave it in this mess, but there you are. People ain't got the cash these days, have they?'

'It's out of the question,' Sonia said, with a deep sigh, filling the kettle. 'It would cost thousands, wouldn't it? No, you'll just have to botch it up: a length of new pipe, that's it. I mean, how much would it come to, the whole job like that? It's for millionaires, isn't it?'

'Oh, I don't know,' said the plumber thoughtfully. 'If you got the rads second-hand – radiators, that is, love – you could knock quite a bit off the price. People are having the old rads taken out, see, either because the original ones are too big and they can't afford the heating bills, or because they want the more compact designs. You can get the older ones quite reasonable now.

'Then the labour for fitting central heating – yes, that would be quite a bit of work, but it would depend on whether you wanted rads in every room or just the main ones. Take the boiler out – that wouldn't take long – and block up the flue. And kitchen units, well, that's up to the individual buyer, of course; you can spend a fortune if you want to, but the cheaper ones are all right. You could do it for . . . let me see . . .'

Samuel returned with Lois to find Sonia and the plumber at the kitchen table, with pages of sums in front of them. 'This lady drives a hard bargain,' the plumber informed Samuel. 'She's got a head for figures. Could save you a lot of money.'

'Indeed?' Samuel said, surprised.

'I'll work this out for you, if you like,' the plumber said, 'and send you something more accurate, then you can have a think about it, all right?'

'Right,' said Samuel.

''Course, you could just replace the pipes and the toilet and muck along, making do,' the plumber conceded, 'and I understand, guv'nor, that you ain't whatsisname, the train robber. What was he called, the one that's living it up in Rio or wherever?'

'Er . . .' Samuel said. He looked completely bemused.

'What about the loo tank?' said Sonia suddenly. 'It's all fancy ironwork. Would someone want to buy that?'

'No, no,' Samuel said. 'It's decrepit.'

'Rusted through,' the plumber agreed, shaking his head sadly.

'Could be welded,' said Sonia. 'From the inside, where it wouldn't show. A designer would love that. I might advertise.'

'I'll have a go,' the plumber said. 'Welding. Want to get it done properly, don't you?'

'No, just cheaply,' said Sonia serenely.

'Right,' he said. 'Right. I'll work this out properly, set it out all official and everything, and talk to a couple of people who might be interested, and in the meantime you do want me to start Monday, don't you? On those pipes.'

'Ah – ' Samuel said.

'Monday's fine,' said Sonia, 'but not before eleven o'clock, because I'll be out shopping. With Mrs Atwood,' she added to Samuel.

'Really? Oh good,' Samuel approved. 'Nice woman, when you get to know her, isn't she?'

'She's okay,' Sonia said grudgingly.

'I'd rather make an early start,' the plumber said. 'Perhaps if I called before you went out, you could leave me to get on with it?'

'Yes,' Samuel said, 'I'm sure that would be . . .'

'No,' Sonia said. 'I'd rather be in the house.'

'Oh, well – up to you of course, my dear,' Samuel assented.

'I'm perfectly trustworthy,' said the plumber indignantly.

Sonia fixed him with a stern eye. 'Eleven o'clock will be fine,' she said.

'All right,' the plumber said. 'You're the boss. Well, I mean . . . no, you are, guv'nor, aren't you? But I mean . . .'

Samuel was trying not to laugh. 'No, I think you were right the first time,' he said. 'You take your orders from Mrs Leroy. Whatever she says.'

He called me 'Mrs', Sonia noticed, and was grateful for the dishonesty. She was the one who had to be in the house with this guy, and although he seemed okay, you could never tell. Men got a bit funny at times if they knew you were a single mother.

When the plumber had gone, Samuel said, 'Do I under-stand that everything is arranged, then, about seeing to the lavatory and the kitchen?'

Sonia launched into an explanation of the state of the piping and plasterwork and the inadvisability of adding new appliances piecemeal rather than taking a whole view of the kitchen, bathroom and heating system. She gained enthu-siasm as she talked, forgetting that she had thought it was not worth starting on anything here; her desire to see a good job well done banished her previous apathy. Even if she and Lois could not be allowed to stay in this house, it would be better off with this work done.

The structure of Samuel's house might be sound, but if the interior did not receive some careful attention soon he would have real problems with it. Leaky pipes, unattended to, could cause damp and mildew; old heaters and stoves could be dangerous. And apart from the threats to the value of the house and the safety of its occupants, the place could only grow increasingly dismal unless some attempts were made now to brighten it up.

Samuel listened and agreed. 'If you are happy with what the man suggested, you go ahead and arrange it,' he said, 'as long as you would not find the responsibility onerous?'

'Are you sure?' Sonia asked. 'You better think about it when you get the estimates. These things don't come cheap.'

'I do not expect them to,' Samuel said. His eyes began to twinkle again. 'However, as I understand it,' he continued, 'you have devised some ingenious arrangement whereby the plumber pays us – out of compassion, no doubt, because I do not possess the income of a bank robber living in Rio.'

Sonia had the grace to look embarrassed. 'I did tell him you didn't have cash to fling around,' she admitted, 'but he would have ripped you off right, left and centre otherwise, Samuel. He wanted me and him to split the proceeds from flogging the bath and then charge you the full rate for the plumbing work.'

Samuel raised his eyebrows. 'He let you in on this plan, did he? He could have told us that the bath was a condemned relic rather than a desirable antique.'

Again Sonia was reminded that he was shrewd. 'And I thought I was defending you from that bloke,' she said. 'I should have let you deal with him yourself: there's no flies on you. I was forgetting you know about the antiques market. I'm the one who'll probably get you ripped off, Samuel; I wouldn't know if the price is right or not.'

'No, let him get on with it,' Samuel said soothingly. 'He probably finds his work a little tedious at times and if he can do a few deals on the side it adds spice. As long as he does a good job for us, then no one loses. And you are quite right, my dear, about looking at the house as a whole and improving it all together. It would be quite foolish to plumb a new lavatory and washing machine into this archaic environment. Like putting new wine into old wineskins, you know.

'No, you plan out the details, if you will, and I shall approve them and foot the bill. I should be very grateful to you, my dear Sonia, for taking the trouble to jolly up my sad old domicile.'

Chapter Twenty-Four

'Shall I make you a coffee, Samuel?' Sonia asked.

'No, thank you. We had one with Mrs Baker.'

'You went to see Mrs Baker? With Lois?'

Samuel looked guilty. 'I thought there would be no harm in taking her with me,' he said. 'Mrs Baker was quite understanding about the job. Here is her door key. There was no ill feeling. I would not have taken Lois, had I thought there might be.'

'No, but . . . did Lois behave herself? Was she all right?'

'Yes, of course. Perfectly.'

'Did she keep her hands over her eyes?' Sonia asked.

'No. Only for a second, when the door opened. Once we were inside the house she was perfectly confident. Mrs Baker was enchanted with her – and Mrs Baker's mother as well. We popped up to see her.'

'You took a four-year-old child to see a senile, bedridden person who is incontinent?' Sonia was angry and didn't bother to hide it. What was the use of her trying to protect Lois and give her a carefree childhood if Samuel was going to expose her to sickroom environments?

'The old lady is prone to a range of human weaknesses,' said Samuel mildly, 'but there is nothing there to threaten a child. She is neither violent nor contagious. Certainly she has her difficult days, when she is not herself, but Mrs Baker would not have invited us up if that were the case today. In herself she is a gentle soul. She and Lois got on very well. Is this the Fablon you had in mind, Sonia, for the dolls' house?'

'Yes, that's fine. Thank you.'

He placed it on the table, along with her change and two

forms, one pink and one white. 'Library membership forms,' he said, indicating them. 'One for you and one for Lois, if you should like to join. I find the selection of books there excellent.'

'I'll think about it.' Sonia knew she sounded surly, but she was not used to letting anyone else decide what was good for Lois. It made her feel insecure, even while it was a relief to share the responsibility.

Single parenthood might not be the ideal role but at least it was a role. Better than being single and unwanted. Lois needed her. Mothering Lois was her purpose in life, for want of any other. If Lois no longer needed to be Sonia's single-minded purpose, then Sonia would have to look for something else, and this idea filled her with fear. Had she not already tried all the 'something elses' and found them lacking?

'Lois,' she said, 'come upstairs with me and change into your pretty dress, ready for Gertrude coming. Samuel, what do we call Gertrude? Mrs what? She did say her name on the phone but I've forgotten.'

'Call her Gertrude,' Samuel said promptly. 'She doesn't go in for formalities. And please don't go to any trouble on her account. She said most specifically not to put yourself out in any way.'

'I'm not putting myself out,' said Sonia grimly. If that Gertrude thought she was going to catch them unprepared, she reflected, then she had another think coming. She and Lois were going to be armed with politeness and armoured with freshly ironed clothes. They might be already condemned before they started, but they would at least go down in style, with dignity.

When Lois had scrambled up the stairs and Sonia was starting to follow her, the doorbell rang. Sonia's heart jumped. When she went to answer it, however, she saw at once that it was not Gertrude, could not be Gertrude, for not only did the woman who stood on the doorstep not resemble the one in Sonia's dream (tall, angular and forbidding), nor resemble Samuel; she resembled nothing Sonia had ever seen before, outside the pantomime.

She was short and extremely wide, with vast bow legs tapering into improbably tiny feet in dainty court shoes with diamanté bows. Her face was large and ruddy, its features amply swathed in wrinkles and folds and with more than the statutory number of chins.

Tiny hands like a baby doll's clutched a large old-fashioned brown leather handbag and a couple of carrier bags, one bearing the name of Hamleys ('Finest Toyshop In The World'), which did little to hide a gargantuan stomach, emphasized by being clad in a skin-tight satin suit in bright kingfisher blue.

This ensemble was crowned with a wide-brimmed straw hat topped with the simulated contents of an entire fruit bowl – cherries, grapes, blackcurrants and the odd strawberry. Sonia would not have been surprised to see a couple of coconuts and a pineapple up there. The woman, she could not help thinking, would not be out of place in a Caribbean carnival. On Samuel's doorstep, she was astonishing.

She had no time to think about who this creature might be, however; as she stood there gaping at the apparition it flung itself at her with a hoarse cry and wrapped itself round her, crushing the sturdy handbag and the Hamleys carrier bag between their two stomachs. 'Aaagh!' Sonia yelled. Instinctively she reached for Samuel's umbrella from the umbrella stand.

'*How wonderful*,' the woman roared, 'to meet you *at last*! My dear, I have been positively on *tenterhooks*!'

'What?' Sonia gasped. Where was Samuel? Perhaps he would know what to do with this overdressed maniac.

'*Samuel!*' the woman yelled, half an inch from Sonia's ear, making her jump again. 'Here you are!'

Here he was. Sonia backed away from the woman and legged it towards the stairs.

'Gertrude, my dear,' said Samuel placidly. 'A pleasure, as always, to see you.'

This is not happening, Sonia thought wildly. This is some practical joke he's cooked up, with some mate who's an old gent who plays pantomime dames. This is not a real woman.

This is not a real cousin. This can't be Gertrude.

'Gertrude,' Samuel said, 'have you met Sonia?'

'We have just met,' Gertrude announced, 'but not properly. Let me have a good look at you, my dear child.'

Sonia sidestepped, but too late to avoid being smothered in another comprehensive embrace. She emerged wild-eyed and shot Samuel a panic-stricken look. His lips twitched and his eyes brimmed with amusement. It's all right for him, Sonia thought; he's used to this . . . this person. Why couldn't he have warned me? Though, to be fair, how would anyone go about describing Gertrude? Even seeing was only half believing.

'And where is your adorable little girl?' Gertrude demanded, beaming.

Hiding under the bed if she has any sense, Sonia wanted to reply, but Lois chose that moment to appear. It was not the child's fault, Sonia was able to reason afterwards, that she appeared clad only in a small pair of pink knickers: she had probably just sneaked out to the landing to catch a glimpse of the owner of the Polaris-missile voice and then had become frozen to the spot and unable to run back to the bedroom and take cover, even in the literal sense of putting on clothes. It was certainly not Lois's fault that the pink knickers had a hole in them.

Sonia understood this afterwards. At the time, all she understood was that at the very moment when they needed to be on their guard, Lois was unprotected and unprotectable.

She therefore pushed Gertrude aside unceremoniously, hurtled up the stairs and lunged at Lois, catching her in a clumsy rugby tackle and dashing with her into the bedroom, where she slammed the door and threw Lois on to the bed, accidentally knocking her head against the headboard. Lois, with the breath knocked out of her windpipe, opened her mouth in a wide soundless scream.

'What have I told you?' Sonia shouted, slapping her hard. 'What have I told you about running around in that state?'

She had always been determined not to hit Lois. She had

never hit Lois before they came here. It was not that she thought hitting a child was the worst thing you could do; it was because she was afraid that once she started hitting out, she might not be able to stop. There seemed to be so many things in life that might make you hit out; the only safe way, Sonia thought, was not to start.

Now she had hit Lois again, and Lois was screaming with fright, and Sonia was more frightened than she had ever been before, because she could see and feel her hand going back and forth, making contact with Lois's head, Lois's arms and chest and legs, but she seemed to have no control over this hand. Like everything else she had tried so hard to control, it had slipped out of her grasp and was dragging her relentlessly towards disaster.

They were both screaming so hard that neither heard Gertrude come in. The first warning Sonia had of her approach was when someone took hold of her hand, surprisingly firmly, and said, 'That's enough.'

She pulled Sonia upright, stood behind her and wrapped both arms around her, pinioning Sonia's arms to her body. Sonia stopped screaming. In the seconds before she stopped, she heard the words, 'You whore!'

It was minutes more before the shock hit her. These were her words, in her voice. These were the words Sonia was screaming at Lois, her child, her little girl, who was four years old.

'Oh God,' Sonia said, in a voice that seemed to come from a long way away, 'what have I done?'

'My dear girl,' said Gertrude. 'Come and sit down over here.' She led her by the hand over to the far bed – Lois's bed. Sonia sat there, stunned. As if she were watching a film, she watched Gertrude, the funny pantomime lady, pick up Lois who was huddled on the bed with her hands over her face and her knees drawn right up under her chin to protect herself.

Gertrude knew what she was doing. Lois did not resist. Gertrude sat down and put Lois on her wide lap, all hunched up as she was, and began to stroke her limbs and talk to her in a soothing voice. Sonia couldn't make out the words. Perhaps there were no words, or at least none that meant anything to her befuddled brain.

When Lois uncurled her legs, threw back her head and screamed, straight into Gertrude's face, Gertrude said, 'Very good girl. That's better. Don't cope with it by yourself.'

Sonia couldn't make sense of this. Why was Lois being a good girl, when she was doing those things she had been told not to do – going to strangers, making a fuss in public, letting people see her without her clothes, screaming her head off? If that had been Mrs Grenville with her instead of Gertrude, Lois would have had her ears boxed, unless Sonia had rescued her quickly enough.

And what did Gertrude mean by, 'Don't cope with it by yourself'? Sonia was the one who had to cope with things, not Lois. Lois was a child. Sonia did the coping for Lois. Sonia was the one who coped all by herself.

Why was Gertrude saying this to a child? Didn't she realize that Lois was only a four-year-old? But then if she, Sonia, realized that Lois was only a child, why had she been yelling at her, 'You whore!'? If Sonia did not understand Gertrude, even less did she understand herself.

Gertrude must know, Sonia thought. Somehow or other Gertrude must have found out that Lois was no ordinary four-year-old, that she could be charming and sweet but also she could be so unchildlike and wicked that nobody would be able to believe it, unless they had seen the things Sonia had seen.

Sonia found herself wishing they had seen. It was too much of a burden to carry on her own. Was it possible that there were other mothers who had to hide their children and cope with this terrible knowledge about them? Did some children get born evil, and have to be protected from acting it out, for their own sakes, for fear that everyone would be afraid and shun them?

Did other mothers sit by like this and listen to people say, 'What a sweet little child!' and hold their breath and pray that no one discovered the truth and turned against the child, frightening her by their sudden change from praise to condemnation? Was there anyone else in the world who had witnessed such terrifying transformations of a cute little child into a perverted monster?

These thoughts passed through Sonia's mind and she watched them pass, as though they were tickertape emerging from a machine; she made no attempt to hold up the process. Let it happen. Let it come out. Better out than in.

When Samuel entered, Sonia wanted to hide. Without realizing what she was doing, she put her hands up to her face, like Lois did – only Lois was not covering her face now but staring intently into Gertrude's eyes. Sonia was the one who would not look anyone in the face.

Samuel sat down beside her and took her hand. She was deeply ashamed. 'I didn't mean to hit her,' she said, 'or to shout at her like that. I don't know what came over me.' Samuel patted her hand and said nothing; it was Gertrude who spoke.

'Samuel tells me,' she said, 'that you have had a quite dreadful time recently.' She looked at Sonia expectantly, but when Sonia did not answer she supplied the information herself. 'Quite appalling,' Gertrude said, 'for that woman to fire you at a moment's notice, with no reason given and no reference.'

Again Sonia did not answer. Samuel continued to pat her hand. He hummed a tune under his breath. Gertrude went on stroking Lois, who was leaning back against her ample chest, perfectly relaxed. Sonia did not know what was going on. People were not behaving in the way that people behaved, in her experience. She didn't know how to react to this.

'Are you taking any steps to deal with the situation?' Gertrude asked. Her tone was sympathetic and interested. This was not an interrogation.

'Deal with what?' Sonia asked.

'The dismissal,' Gertrude said.

'It's done now,' said Sonia, shrugging. 'I can't do anything about it.'

'But it mustn't be left like this!' Gertrude cried, some of her original stridency returning. 'My dear, what a terrible burden to carry around with you! How can you be expected to cope with a new job and bringing up a child on your own, with a dreadful thing like that dogging your steps?'

'I'm putting it out of my mind,' Sonia said. 'It's in the past.' Her voice shook. She sounded completely unconvincing, even to herself.

'No, that won't do,' said Gertrude. 'It needs to be dealt with, once and for all. Otherwise it will just drag on. In the past it may be, but the past has a fearsome habit of clouding the present, and the present usually has quite enough clouds of its own, hasn't it?'

Sonia felt she ought to voice some objection. She was not sure where Gertrude was leading her, so perhaps it was time to point out that she was not going to be led anywhere she did not want to go. 'I prefer to let sleeping dogs lie,' she said firmly, taking refuge in cliché. 'Time is the great healer, people say.'

'People say a lot of bunkum,' said Gertrude. 'Truth is the great healer. Time just rots things down, like compost. Samuel, don't you agree with me?'

Samuel stopped humming and patting Sonia's hand. 'What are you suggesting, Gertrude?' he asked.

'I was about to suggest that we phoned Mrs Grenville,' Gertrude said, taking Sonia's breath away with the sudden-ness of a parachute jump.

Lois sat up and looked at Sonia. 'I didn't say that name,' she said.

'I know,' said Sonia. 'Samuel told her.' She gave Samuel a very unfriendly look.

'I asked him,' said Gertrude. 'When he said your last job was in Sussex, it occurred to me that I might know the people. I live in Sussex, you see.'

Sonia had been right. This woman was going to destroy them. 'But you don't know them,' she said. 'I met their friends. You never came to their house.'

'I don't know them,' Gertrude agreed. 'But Humphrey does – my husband. He has done business with George Grenville on a few occasions.'

'Well, what a small world,' said Sonia dully.

'So you see, I feel responsible,' Gertrude continued.

Sonia gritted her teeth. 'You're not responsible,' she said. 'It's my business. It doesn't concern anyone else.'

Samuel patted her hand again. She felt encouraged. He was on her side. Hadn't he agreed not to take Gertrude's advice, even about the house and the vacuum cleaner, but to listen to Sonia first? Well then, he was certain not to let Gertrude give advice about matters that were even more obviously only Sonia's business.

'Samuel, what do you say?' Gertrude appealed to him. 'Is it better to let the matter rest, do you think? Or do we have some responsibility to sort it out?' She waited, looking at him.

At least she was waiting for his answer, Sonia thought; she was not going to bulldoze him into it. There was quite a long pause, during which Lois slid off Gertrude's lap and came over and climbed on to Sonia's. Samuel let go of Sonia's hand and patted Lois on the head instead. Lois smiled at him.

Sonia thought, it's going to be all right. He's on our side. He won't do anything to upset Lois. He won't let Gertrude interfere with our lives.

Then, to her disbelief, she heard Samuel say, slowly and deliberately, 'My dear, you are right. Far better to sort this out. Shall you telephone the Grenvilles or shall I?'

Chapter Twenty-Five

They decided it should be Samuel who phoned, as Sonia's employer. Sonia felt too listless to be angry with Samuel but when Gertrude went downstairs she tried to make him aware of what he had done. 'You have no business to interfere,' she said. Her voice was expressionless and tired. 'Not you or Gertrude or nobody.'

She registered her error of grammar mechanically. Usually she tried not to make these mistakes in speaking. They gave you away, made you seem inferior, gave people the right to patronize and dismiss the content of what you were saying to them.

Samuel seemed to dismiss it now. He stood up and said, pointing to the newly ironed clothes that Sonia had hung on the outside of the wardrobe, 'Is this the dress for Lois to put on?'

Sonia gave up. 'Yes,' she said. She didn't want to tell him off and there was no point in it; he had done what he thought best. The fact that it was the worst thing he could possibly have done, for Sonia and Lois, was not his fault. He didn't know what he was doing.

She slipped the dress over Lois's head, took a pair of clean white socks out of the drawer and found her red sandals in the bottom of the wardrobe. 'There,' she said. 'You're ready.' Ready for what, she did not want to know.

'I shall leave you to change, yourself,' Samuel told her, 'while I go and telephone.'

'Oh, I won't bother,' said Sonia wearily. 'Gertrude's already seen me like this.' There was a white patch on the knee of her jeans. She must have splashed bleach while she was cleaning the kitchen.

Samuel held out the coathanger holding her yellow dress. The white shirt and brown skirt still hung on the wardrobe door. 'Please,' he said. 'I would like to see you wear this.'

'I was going to wear the skirt and blouse,' she said.

Samuel gave them a passing glance. 'Not as pretty as this,' he pronounced. 'Too prim and proper.'

She smiled, despite herself. 'Housekeepers are meant to look prim and proper,' she said.

'Good Lord, I hope not,' said Samuel in mock alarm. 'What a very lucky escape I have had, in finding one who is pretty.' He smiled at her disarmingly. She accepted the dress from him. She might as well waste a bit more time anyway. She was in no hurry to hear what Mrs Grenville was going to say about them.

So, when Samuel went downstairs and she heard him dialling the number, she sat down at the dressing table and slowly began to unwind her hair from its neat bun and brush it out. Crackling with static electricity it stood out from her face like a dark halo, alive with energy. The yellow dress was a wrap-over style, with one button securing it at the waist.

She left her legs bare, slid her feet into brown and gold sandals with a thong between the toes, and clipped a plain gold bracelet round her forearm, higher than the wrist. The bracelet had been a gift from Lois's father, the only gift he had given her – apart from Lois herself.

Samuel met her at the foot of the stairs. There was no sign of either Gertrude or Lois. 'You look very nice,' he said. She searched his face, but he looked back at her innocently, with a clear blue gaze. She wanted to scream at him to get it over with, to tell her what Mrs Grenville had said. Instead she let him lead her into the garden and offer her a drink.

He had set out four deck chairs on the lawn, together with a low table scarred with damp, its top layer of wood peeling and curling at the edges. 'I offered Gertrude her usual dry sherry,' Samuel said, 'but she was anxious to try Lois's Coke. I believe we have a convert.' He laughed, gesturing towards the three tumblers of Coke. 'But you have whatever you like, my dear. There is cream sherry or dry.'

'I'll have Coke as well,' she said. 'I don't really drink.' So Mrs Grenville can't say that about me, she thought, whatever else she might have said. She fetched herself a glassful from the fridge and returned to the garden. Samuel sat at the table by himself. Gertrude and Lois could be glimpsed behind the screen of apple trees, chatting away. Gertrude seemed to be describing to Lois the life cycle of the apple, from blossom to fruit.

Samuel drew back a chair for Sonia. 'I should get the lunch ready,' she said nervously. She kept wavering between wanting to get the awful scene over, and trying to postpone the moment of truth.

'No hurry,' Samuel said.

She sat and looked at him. He looked at the garden. 'The laburnum is particularly good this year,' he murmured. 'It doesn't normally flower quite so early.' He seemed to be talking to himself.

'Samuel,' Sonia blurted. 'There's something I want to tell you.'

He turned his head and smiled at her. 'Yes?' he said, without curiosity.

'When I first got here,' she said, very fast. 'The first day you were out of the house, at work, I went through the whole house and looked at everything.'

'Yes?' he said again and nodded encouragingly.

'I did that at the last place I worked,' she said, equally rapidly, 'and the one before. I thought you're always at a disadvantage, being a servant. They can ask all about you and you know nothing about them.'

Samuel raised his eyebrows and appeared to give this idea consideration. 'Mmm,' he said. 'Very true.'

'So I thought if you find out as much about them as possible, then you're in a stronger position. So if Mrs Grenville told you that I'd looked in their locked drawers and found out how to open the safe, then that's right – I did. I never took anything, and it wasn't to blackmail them. Nothing like that, Samuel, believe me. It was just . . . kind of . . . an insurance policy. I don't know what for.'

'I see,' Samuel said. He sat in his chair, quite relaxed, and sipped his Coke. He waited for her to continue.

'So when I got here,' said Sonia, even more quickly than before, seeing Gertrude and Lois approaching, 'I found your locked drawer. I knew there was always a locked drawer, you see, in everyone's house, and there's always a key somewhere.'

'In the small drawer in the top of my bureau,' Samuel informed her.

'I know. I found it.'

'Ah,' said Samuel. 'I suppose you would. If you can open safes.' He laughed.

Sonia leaned forward and caught hold of his arm. 'I didn't do it,' she said. 'I got the key ready and put it in the lock and everything, ready to open it, but I couldn't do it. I felt like I was betraying you.'

He looked at her. 'My dear Sonia,' he said.

Gertrude was emerging from the path through the flower bed.

'I wanted you to know I didn't do it,' she said. 'That's all.'

Gertrude pulled up a chair and sat down in it heavily. 'Who would think,' she said, 'that it's only May? What glorious sunshine. Samuel, how do you get your laburnum to flower so freely? Mine is so very stingy.'

'Bonemeal,' said Samuel. 'Four ounces, every autumn, lightly forked in.' He nodded at Sonia. 'Thank you,' he said. 'I will show you, some time, what is in that drawer.' Gertrude glanced at him but didn't ask him what he was talking about. 'And now,' Samuel said, smiling at Lois, 'Lois is going to fetch her dolls' house to show you, Gertrude. You can carry it by yourself, Lois, can't you?'

'Yes,' Lois said. She skipped off, clutching the front of her red dress and flapping it up and down over her face. They watched her go.

'Now Samuel,' said Gertrude. 'How did you fare with Mrs

Grenville?' Sonia caught her breath.

'My dear,' said Samuel, setting his glass down carefully on the table. 'A rather extraordinary conversation, I fear. I simply informed the good lady that I had in my employ a Sonia Leroy and asked whether she would be kind enough to supply me with a reference. Mrs Grenville became rather . . . hysterical, I believe, would not be too strong a word to use.'

'Gracious me!' Gertrude exclaimed.

'Mmm,' Samuel said musingly. 'I endeavoured to calm her and persuade her to tell me exactly what the difficulty might be, and she said that Sonia was unemployable, not because of her housekeeping skills, which were excellent, but because of her character, which was evil. Yes, Gertrude, that was the word Mrs Grenville used. Both Sonia and the child were evil, she said, and she strongly advised against employing Sonia or allowing either the mother or the child inside the house for any reason whatsoever.'

Sonia looked at the long yellow curtains of laburnum flowers, heard the birds singing, took in an impression of the whole garden. It was a peaceful scene. There seemed no need to disturb it with thoughts. What was there to think about, anyway, that had not been thought a thousand times before? It was over; that was all. She had known it would be. The only new thought that entered her head was, We won't be here to see the apples grow on those trees.

From a long way away, she heard Gertrude's voice. 'That would explain it, I suppose,' she said, quite calmly, and Samuel's voice, hardly less calm, answered, 'Well, of course, it would.'

When Gertrude's hand reached out and caught hold of her arm, Sonia did not flinch. In her heart, she felt relieved. At least it was out in the open. They could do what they liked with her, but at least she would never have to go through this moment again.

'My dear Sonia, tell me,' said Gertrude, 'did you have any prior indication that the woman was like this?'

'What?' said Sonia dreamily. She felt as though she had

182

taken some kind of drug that gave her the illusion of being detached from reality. She would sit here in the garden and wait for someone else to decide how to deal with her and with Lois. There was nothing she could do to save them now. Her actions were powerless to affect their lives. She felt elated.

'Did you have any indication that this Mrs Grenville was going peculiar?' Gertrude elucidated.

Sonia's eyes came back into focus. She looked at Gertrude. 'Mrs Grenville? Peculiar?' she said.

'Yes – you know. Off her rocker,' said Gertrude bluntly.

'No,' Sonia said. Was Gertrude offering her an escape route, or what? What was she up to?

'Quite extraordinary, Samuel, isn't it?' Gertrude addressed her cousin.

'Hmm,' said Samuel. 'I suppose it explains her behaviour. There were, you say, Sonia, no signs of her behaving eccentrically? No outbursts of temper or any such thing?'

Sonia looked from Samuel to Gertrude and back again. They were serious. They seriously believed that if Mrs Grenville came out with this statement about her and Lois being evil and not fit to be allowed in anyone's house, there was something wrong with *Mrs Grenville*? She sat and stared at them with her mouth open.

'Rages?' Gertrude prompted. 'Fits of unreasonable fury – that sort of behaviour? Before she dismissed you, I mean?'

Sonia gulped. 'She . . . um . . . there was one time she screamed at the gardener,' she said, 'for parking the car in front of the house.'

Gertrude nodded. 'For parking the car,' she said, 'in front of the house?'

'He was meant to put it round the back,' Sonia explained. 'It was the house car – the one the gardener used to fetch stuff in. Peat for the garden, or lengths of piping and stuff for the house. He was the handyman as well, you see.' She was almost unable to hear what she was saying. The words were coming out of her mouth without her brain being engaged in the process at all, it seemed. 'There were guests at the house that afternoon,' she said. 'They left their cars in the front drive-way.'

Gertrude was looking puzzled. 'You mean, he hadn't left room for the guests to park their cars? Was that why Mrs Grenville was annoyed with him?'

'No,' Sonia said. 'It was because it wasn't the Rolls. There was plenty of room for the cars, but only the Rolls Royce was meant to be parked at the front of the house. Guests weren't meant to see the car Eddie used. It was a Ford Escort estate. Mrs Grenville didn't want her guests to see it. Eddie – the gardener, the handyman – must have forgotten. He parked it out the front.' She finished. It hardly seemed evidence of insanity.

Gertrude burst out laughing. 'You mean the woman flew into a rage because the gardener let her guests see she owned a car that wasn't a Rolls Royce but only a humble Escort?'

'Yes,' Sonia said.

'*Well!*' said Gertrude, in tones of deep satisfaction. 'Doesn't that take the biscuit?' Samuel laughed. 'And what did you do, Sonia,' Gertrude enquired, 'that was *even more* evil than that?' Both she and Samuel giggled.

Sonia's face clouded. They might have decided to treat this as a joke, but the truth was very far from being funny. The joke had gone on long enough.

'Do you mean she didn't tell you?' she asked Samuel.

'My dear,' said Samuel, 'she was spluttering with rage; I could hardly make out a word she was saying. The woman was quite incoherent.'

'Gertrude!' Lois shouted. 'Come and help me. I'm dropping this house!'

'Oh, the poor child, she can't manage!' Gertrude exclaimed. She heaved her bulky form out of the deck chair, with difficulty, and tottered across the lawn on her little high heels.

Sonia's eyes filled with tears. She didn't think she could stand any more of this. She had been sure it was all over, this time. They weren't listening. They hadn't believed it. She felt very alone.

Samuel placed his glass on the table and leaned towards her. 'May I help you?' he said.

'Yes,' Sonia said. 'If you can.'

'What needs to be done,' he asked, 'for the lunch? Would you like me to wash the lettuce?'

Chapter Twenty-Six

The Hamleys carrier bag contained dolls' house furniture. Gertrude, when she had phoned this morning, had evidently asked Samuel what the little girl would like. Lois was delighted. She immediately installed the best table and one chair in the cellar and demanded to know why Gertrude had not bought a boiler, since cellars had to have boilers?

She was satisfied when Sonia gave her one of the segments of an egg-box to make do as a boiler. Lois moved all three of Samuel's wooden dolls into the cellar of the house, showing little interest in furnishing the rest of it. 'You do it,' she said when Sonia pointed out that she had been playing with the house for an hour without even taking the miniature bathroom or bedroom sets out of their bag.

Sonia, who had sneaked a look at the receipt, didn't want Gertrude to think Lois was ungrateful, so when lunch was cleared away she joined Lois on the back lawn and arranged the rest of the furniture in the house for her. It was restful, she found, playing with Lois, and saved her from having to think about anything. She had never had a dolls' house, in her childhood.

Gertrude, looking down at the two dark heads close together, nodded with satisfaction and beamed at Samuel, who smiled back.

Presently, Samuel dropped off to sleep and Gertrude went into the kitchen and began washing up. Sonia caught her at it. 'Hey!' she said. 'You don't do that. You're the guest.'

'Nonsense, my dear; I'm family,' said Gertrude heartily. 'And it always makes a change to wash up in somebody else's kitchen, doesn't it? Quite different from seeing the same old dishes at home.' She had used so much washing-up liquid, Sonia noticed, that suds came up to her elbows and dampened the kingfisher blue jacket, which she had rolled up at the sleeves.

'I bet it makes a change to wash up in this kitchen,' said Sonia grinning.

Gertrude slammed down a plate with unnecessary emphasis and turned to Sonia, waving her hands at her and showering her with froth. '*Get rid* of the whole bang shoot!' she cried. 'Scrap the lot, my dear, and get in a kitchen designer. Look at these walls! You've been scrubbing away at them, haven't you? Well, *don't*! Life is too short, my dear, unless you are trying to knock off a few years' purgatory here on earth. Get a designer in, and the whole place done over, top to bottom.

'There now!' she said, on a gasp. 'I've gone and done it now, haven't I? I promised Samuel I wouldn't bore you with advice. I'm an interfering old cockroach and don't know when to stop, that's my trouble.'

Sonia laughed. 'No, I've been thinking about doing that,' she said. 'I was talking to the plumber about it this morning. But what about Samuel?' She had forgotten to call him Mr Arnold in front of Gertrude, but it didn't seem to matter.

'*Samuel?*' shouted Gertrude. 'What on earth has it got to do with Samuel? My dear, Samuel wouldn't notice if he lived in a cave full of bats. You go ahead and do what you want. You've got to work in the place.'

'No,' Sonia said, trying to imagine Samuel living in a bat-infested cave, 'I meant the expense. It costs a lot to get a whole kitchen done. I know it's better value than replacing things one by one but . . . well, he's a furniture restorer, isn't he? I mean, manual work isn't that well paid, is it?'

Gertrude stared at her for a moment, then threw back her head and roared. 'Manual worker?' she brayed. 'Samuel? My dear girl, the only manual work Samuel does is in his shed at home, doing up the bits of furniture he picks up at auctions. He's a partner in his firm. He's one of the country's leading experts in his field. Lords and ladies send chauffeur-driven cars for him, to bring him to their stately homes and advise them on their priceless antiques. Museums call him in for advice.

'You *don't* think he gets out the sandpaper and does it himself? He has an army of staff and apprentices. That's partly why he does this work at home – to keep his hand in with the techniques. He only does the very fine, expert stuff at work.'

'Oh.' Sonia felt foolish. 'So he's not short of money, then? For improving the house?'

'Rolling in lolly, my dear,' said Gertrude cheerfully. 'It's not for lack of cash that this house has got into the shocking state it is in. Lack of interest, that's all. Lack of time. Lack of incentive. Nobody to brighten it up for. You get it brightened up, my dear. Make it nice. It's about time, isn't it?'

'Yes,' Sonia said. 'I suppose it is.' I might as well go ahead then, she thought. It looks as though we'll be staying. Gertrude is certainly talking as though we are, so I suppose we must be. She found no pleasure in this, only weariness. Sooner or later they would be found out. It should have been today. Now they were back where they had been before – waiting: making plans for a tomorrow that might never come; never knowing when the truth would catch up with them.

She heaved an enormous sigh. Gertrude removed the tea-towel from her hands. 'Go and sit down,' she commanded. 'You're tired.'

'I'm fine,' said Sonia automatically.

'Sit down anyway,' Gertrude told her. 'I want to have a word with you, while Samuel is out of the way. A serious word.'

Sonia's heart started thumping.

'Now listen,' said Gertrude, sitting down at the kitchen table and pulling up a chair so close to Sonia that she was almost sitting on top of her. 'I am very glad that you have come here, my dear. I know it may not be for very long.'

Sonia looked at her wildly. 'Why not?' she said.

'You're young, my dear,' said Gertrude. 'You won't want to be stuck here keeping house for an old man for ever and a day, and there's no reason why you should. I'm not going to say anything that will make you feel obliged to stay.'

Sonia wondered if the woman was mad. 'I want to stay,' she said. She had been feeling frantic about getting chucked out, and here was Gertrude telling her she shouldn't feel obliged to stay. Was this some subtle way of telling her to hand in her notice immediately?

'Of course you want to stay, for now,' said Gertrude. 'It's a job and a chance to get back on your feet after the last nasty experience . . .'

'What nasty experience?' said Sonia sharply.

'Living with that loopy woman,' Gertrude said, 'and getting thrown out on your ear without a by-your-leave. So, my dear, you settle in and make yourself at home here and get the house sorted out just as you like. And when the time comes for you to move on, or you meet a nice young man who is fond of you and Lois, you go, without any regrets.'

'Wait a minute,' said Sonia, annoyed at having her future planned out like this. 'Who says I'm going to . . .'

'What I mean, my dear,' Gertrude continued, 'is that you may feel at the moment that Samuel has saved your bacon, which of course he has, coming along at exactly the right time, by the sound of it – and no one can tell me that was coincidence, my dear, because only Providence is that efficient. So thank God for Samuel, my dear, but thank God for you and Lois too, because I can tell you, you are precisely what he needed.'

'Oh?' said Sonia.

'Precisely,' Gertrude repeated. 'And for the time you are here, you will do him nothing but good, believe me. You have already had an effect. He was like a schoolboy the day he arranged for you to come and live with him. He phoned me up and I haven't heard him sound so happy and excited in years. It's quite transformed the old boy.'

'Oh,' said Sonia again. She hadn't thought of Samuel being excited. He seemed so calm.

'Between you and me,' said Gertrude, leaning even closer

and lowering her voice to only a fairly loud shout, 'he was getting quite miserable and sorry for himself. Miss Prynne, bless her soul, was not the most enlivening company. Her chief interest in life was her arthritis, and that was before she went . . . you know . . . a bit out of touch with what was going on.

'But she was at least another presence in the house, and since she's gone Samuel has been *quite* lonely, my dear, I don't mind telling you. Terrified to retire, and really he should, you know. All this commuting on buses every day takes it out of him more than he realizes. And he will not turn down work. It's my belief he does it to fill in the time, so he doesn't have to sit on his own here and think.'

Sonia nodded. She knew what it was like to keep busy because the alternative was to think. But that was because the things she had to think about were not pleasant. Why was thinking a problem for Samuel? 'I thought people liked to have time to sit and think, when they got older,' she said. 'Think over the past, and that.'

'Depends on the past,' said Gertrude sadly. 'A lot of people get lonely in their old age – nothing unusual about that – but Samuel has been lonely all his life. What I am saying to you now, my dear, is do the best for him while you're here; don't worry about him being bothered by the child; don't slave to death scrubbing walls and floors and so on. It's very good for him having you here.

'So you get out of it what you need, and he will get what he needs, simply by you all living here in one place. But don't look on it as a life sentence, my dear. While it lasts, it will be very good. And when it's time for you to move on, it will be time for Samuel to have a change as well; you can be sure of that.'

'How can I be sure of that?' Sonia asked. She was still trying to work out what Gertrude was actually saying.

'Because God has brought you here, my dear,' said Gertrude, 'and He never gives one person a good thing at the expense of another. He doesn't have to make people pay for each other's good fortune; He has enough to go round for everybody.'

Sonia grimaced. 'You mean, if I decide to pack up and walk out on Samuel it will be good for him? Just because I feel like going?'

Gertrude flung out her arms expressively. 'Only if it is the right thing for you,' she said. 'If it's right for you to do something, then you can be sure the effects won't harm anybody else.'

'That's a very convenient philosophy,' said Sonia.

'Not always convenient, my dear,' Gertrude said. 'It can be the most difficult thing on earth to do what is right for you. But it is the truth.'

Sonia shifted her chair back a bit, as if to claim independence from Gertrude's views. 'So what are you telling me?' she said. 'I'm not with you.'

'Two things,' said Gertrude, ticking them off on small plump fingers. Her plain gold wedding ring, Sonia noticed, had been made for a thinner Gertrude and was so firmly embedded in flesh now that it was a part of her body. To remove it would require surgery of such delicacy that it would be like having an internal organ removed.

Sonia wondered, fleetingly, whether Gertrude would regard this operation to remove the symbol of her marriage as a bereavement, like having her womb removed, or simply the elimination of a painful and wearying complaint, like an ingrowing toenail. She could not hazard a guess at this, having no idea of Gertrude's attitude to her husband.

'First of all,' said Gertrude, 'I'm telling you that you are a godsend to Samuel, as well as Samuel being a godsend to you. And secondly, I'm saying that if you have any plan to stay here for the rest of Samuel's life, I do most sincerely believe that would be quite wrong.'

She does know, Sonia thought with awful certainty. They really did believe Mrs Grenville. Mrs Grenville must have said more than they are letting on. Sonia decided to bluff it out. If that was what Gertrude was hinting at, she must say so plainly. She seemed to be no stranger to plain speaking.

'First you're telling me we're good for Samuel,' Sonia said bluntly, 'and then you're saying it would be bad for everyone if we stayed. Which one is it?'

'*Both*, my dear!' said Gertrude. 'Very good for you all, the present situation – no doubt about it – and you must feel free to enjoy and make the most of it while you're here. But you're at the start of your life; you have many more changes ahead of you yet, and Samuel, old though he is, may not be at the end of his lifetime yet. He may well have a few changes ahead of him too. The Lord knows best. Samuel may be eighty-four. He may even – I hope – retire. But he isn't dead yet, and may not be for quite some years.'

Sonia was shocked. 'That's not a very nice way to speak about your cousin,' she said.

'Samuel would be the first to agree with me,' Gertrude said, 'that everyone has to keep living life right up till the moment they die. People think they can retire from life and settle back and let other people take charge of the rest of their days for them. A number of men of Samuel's age, let me tell you, would think themselves in clover if they got hold of a willing house-keeper like you. They would hang on to you for the rest of their days.'

Sonia looked at her in perplexity and shook her head. 'Then why aren't you hoping I'll stay and look after him for the rest of his days?' she asked.

'Because you have a life to live,' said Gertrude. 'You mustn't let this job be your whole life – nor Samuel, nor Lois, for that matter. You must have a life of your own, a full life. Friends, outside activities, time to discover the world and its possibilities. You are not eighty-four and about to retire. Nor are you four years old and content to while away the days in little activities.'

'I know that,' said Sonia with dignity. 'But in case you're not aware of it, it is a full-time job running a house and bring-ing up a child.'

'It doesn't have to be,' Gertrude said. 'Samuel and Lois's lives aren't yours, and your life – important though you are to them, undoubtedly – is only a small part of theirs. You can't just be an appendage to other people's lives.'

Sonia was seething with indignation. 'Oh, I'm supposed to dump them, am I? Leave Lois alone in the house, and let Samuel come home to find no supper prepared, while I go out discovering the world?'

Gertrude leaned forward and patted her hand. Sonia withdrew it and leaned backwards.

'Of course that's not what I'm saying,' said Gertrude, 'as well you know. But no one – old man or child – needs your twenty-four-hour-a-day devotion. It would be an intolerable burden to them. You have a great deal to give, my dear, but if you reserve it for one or two people you will smother them. You need to have a life of your own, and you need to share it in small doses with a large number of people. Lois will be going to school soon. She'll have friends. Samuel, if he retires, will have to make friends, too, and see more of the people he knows in the neighbourhood. So – what about you?'

'What about me?' said Sonia sullenly.

'How are you going to make friends here? And keep in touch with the friends and family you already have?'

'I don't have friends or family,' Sonia said.

'Rubbish,' said Gertrude. 'Nobody gets to the age of twenty-two without meeting people, do they? Where are the people you've met in the past twenty-two years?'

Sonia looked desperately towards the garden and willed Samuel to wake up, or Lois to come running in demanding something. But both of them were quite happily engaged in sleeping and playing. Sonia was alone with Gertrude and her intrusive questions.

'I've lost touch with them,' Sonia said. Gertrude waited for her to go on. Sonia could see she was not going to let the subject drop until she had extracted Sonia's whole life story from her. Sonia decided to give in gracefully and fob her off with a potted version. She knew a dedicated information-gatherer when she saw one.

'I never knew my father,' Sonia said, ticking people off on

her fingers as Gertrude had ticked off the points she was making. 'And there's no way of tracing him, because I don't know who he is. All my mother's relatives are in Jamaica and I don't know them, because we left when I was seven – right?'

'They might still be happy to hear from you,' Gertrude said. 'Blood is thicker than water. Have you ever written to any of them?'

'I had a few letters from an aunty,' Sonia said. 'But then I moved to some other foster parents and she didn't have the new address.'

'You didn't let her know where you were?'

Sonia shrugged. 'I didn't know how long I'd be there either. There didn't seem any point. By the time she wrote, I might have moved somewhere else.'

'Why foster parents?' Gertrude enquired. 'If you came over to England with your mother?'

'With my mother and her boyfriend,' Sonia corrected. 'They put me in care for a while, till they found somewhere to live. Two years later the social worker told me they'd gone to live in the States. They never came back for me.'

Gertrude's eyes filled with tears. 'Dear God,' she said.

Sonia continued to tick people off on her fingers. 'The first foster parents, Emmie and Jake, lived in Birmingham, but they were only on the short-term fostering register, so when it was found out that my mother wasn't coming to take me back, the social worker said I couldn't stay there; I had to go to foster parents who were on the long-term register.'

'What?' Gertrude exclaimed. 'You couldn't stay with the people you knew?'

'No. They don't do it that way. Short-term fostering and long-term fostering are separate jobs. Emmie wanted to keep me and they said she could apply to do long-term fostering if she wanted, but by the time she was registered it would be too late for her to take me. I had to go somewhere already on the long-term foster register.'

'Mindless bureaucracy!' Gertrude spluttered.

Sonia shrugged again. 'It happens. The next foster parents

I went to, the mother took on more kids than she could cope with and found she couldn't manage. She preferred looking after boys than girls, so I got moved to a children's home. That place was all right. I went back there when I was expecting Lois. Unofficially.

'But the social worker thought I'd be better in a family, so I got sent to another one, in Luton, only that mother had a nervous breakdown. She wanted me to stay anyway, and I wanted to help look after her and the younger kids, but the social services said it wasn't suitable, so I went to another place in Luton, and then I got pregnant, when I was sixteen, and I went to see the matron back at the children's home and she took me in.

'I had to give another address, if anyone asked me. She told me a friend of hers' address and I had to put that down on benefit forms and things. But I had a room in the children's home – it was a spare office – and I helped look after the other children till Lois was eight months old. Then I took housekeeping jobs.'

'How many?' Gertrude asked.

'Six. Before this one. This is the seventh.'

'In four or five years? Seven jobs?'

'Yes.' Sonia was not going to give away information till Gertrude asked for it. Let Gertrude ask her directly if she wanted to know how anyone could get through six jobs in four years.

Gertrude did not ask. She sat staring at Sonia, shaking her head, with tears rolling unashamedly down her pouchy pink cheeks. Then she shook herself abruptly and thumped her hands on the table as though she meant business.

'And friends?' she demanded. 'Did you meet any people in any of those jobs who became friends?'

'No,' Sonia said. 'They were people I worked for, that's all.'

'Not one encounter with anyone who wanted to continue to know you? Nowhere?'

'There was one,' said Sonia. 'Aunty Sue, we called her. A Jamaican lady. She lived near the farm we worked at. She was the only black person for miles, around there. She got lonely at times, she said. She used to ask us to visit, me and Lois, on our days off. But she's gone back home now.'

'To Jamaica? Did she ask you to keep in touch?'

'Yes. Yes, she did. But I kept waiting till I had some good news to write to her, and there was nothing much to tell, really.'

'Friends don't just want to hear the good news,' Gertrude said. 'They want to hear about *you*! Do you have her address?'

'Yes.'

'And the address of your aunt in Jamaica, and your first foster parents? And the foster mother who wanted you to stay when she had the breakdown? And the matron of the children's home? Do you have all those addresses?'

'Yes, I have them, but . . .'

'Do you have writing paper and envelopes and stamps and airmail letter forms?'

'No,' Sonia said. Once again, she had the impression that things were rolling away from her, out of her control. She was good at avoiding interference with her life, but Gertrude had an exceptional talent for it, she had to admit.

'Samuel will have them,' Gertrude said. 'I shall go and raid his bureau immediately, and you must write to these people, straight away. Will you do it?'

'Yes, I suppose I should do that, some time; I have kept meaning to. Maybe I'll do it tomorrow. I'm too tired today.'

'No wonder you're tired!' Gertrude exclaimed. 'Coping with life on your own like this! No, you sit there right now and don't stand up from that chair until these letters are written, every last one. It will be a great weight off your mind when it's done, let me tell you. You'll see, you'll feel much less tired.'

Chapter Twenty-Seven

Gertrude was unbelievably bossy, Sonia concluded. It was no wonder that, as Samuel had said, she had few friends. Who would put up with such an insufferably pushy person, who went round telling – no, commanding – people what to do?

Sonia admired Gertrude's nerve. She quite obviously knew she was risking losing people's friendship, and she risked it and was left friendless as a result. Sonia could not believe that Gertrude did not mind this, because she was not thick-skinned. She was effusive, interested in people, and concerned when they were not happy.

A tough, assertive woman would not have had that calming effect on Lois, Sonia pondered, nor would she have cried when Sonia had spoken – as drily and unemotionally as could be – about an unsettled childhood.

Gertrude was the goods, Sonia decided. For all her theatrical appearance, there was nothing artificial about her. She did not, as so many people did, disguise her interference and pushiness under a veneer of detached objective advice. She was quite blatant about what she felt Sonia should do, and un-repentant in believing herself to be right.

Sonia had met many experts in manipulation, but Gertrude was something else. Without any subtlety, she set out to make Sonia do what she felt Sonia should do, and did not relax till she achieved what she wanted, whether Sonia liked her or hated her as a result.

Sitting at the kitchen table for the entire afternoon, writing letters to people who might have forgotten or might not wish to be reminded that she existed, Sonia discovered that she did not hate Gertrude – even though Gertrude had poached Lois, bribed her with presents, and now had taken her off to the park with Samuel, leaving Sonia alone in the house.

If it wasn't for Gertrude, Sonia knew she would not be writing these letters. She would have gone on wondering, perhaps for the rest of her life, whether the people who had once loved her still did love her or not. She would never have known whether they rejected her, or whether she had rejected them for fear that they might.

It was an enormous risk to take, Sonia felt. If none of them replied, or sent a cold, formal answer, it would be worse. But at least she would know where she stood and who, if any, her friends were. And really, when she thought about it, was it any greater risk than Gertrude had taken with her?

Sonia had power over Gertrude, because Gertrude had given it to her. She had the opportunity to be extremely rude to her, out of earshot of Samuel – and Gertrude, Sonia knew, would think any criticism well-deserved. She knew she was 'an interfering old cockroach', as she had put it. She would not complain to Samuel if Sonia agreed that she was, or even expressed it in more forceful terms.

For love of Samuel, Gertrude would have pretended everything was all right – would have gone for a walk with him to the park, chatted about his flowers and his work, returning to have tea with him in the garden, hiding her hurt.

Also, Gertrude had been a fool where Samuel was concerned, for hadn't she told an unknown and penniless woman whose only character reference was that she was evil, that Samuel was 'rolling in lolly'? Gertrude had not only made herself vulnerable to Sonia's possible malice, but had made Samuel vulnerable to Sonia's possible criminal tendencies.

The woman had really set herself up for some very nasty treatment, Sonia concluded. If anyone came out of this encounter bruised, it was unlikely to be Sonia. Gertrude was asking to be a victim. Sonia was impressed by this, because Gertrude did not have to be a victim of anybody, certainly not of an immigrant unmarried mother who relieved her frustrations by beating hell out of her child.

Sonia had been right in her analysis of Gertrude's nosiness, she now knew – and her determination to get her own way. What she could not have suspected was Gertrude's refusal to trade on her advantages. What Sonia could not understand was why Gertrude placed Sonia in a position of power over her. It was like playing cards with somebody who held all the aces and suggested swapping hands with you.

Didn't Gertrude realize what she had done, then? Sonia was sure that she did. It was very puzzling.

Meanwhile she felt inclined to award Gertrude the victory for which she had laboured so hard this afternoon. By the time Gertrude, Samuel and Lois returned from the park, a small pile of envelopes stood on the kitchen table, neatly addressed and stamped and ready to post.

'Go straight away and post them, before you change your mind!' Gertrude cried, as soon as she saw them. 'Look, Samuel, what my bullying has made Sonia do. She has missed the whole afternoon's sunshine, scribbling away in here. I shan't blame you if you give me no tea, my dear, even though Samuel has whetted my appetite by telling me you have made some delicious cakes.'

Samuel gave Sonia an anxious look. How easy it would be to make this foolish old woman look even more of a fool. 'Cakes?' Sonia would say. 'No, I'm sorry, Gertrude. I didn't make any cakes for tea. Samuel must be mistaken.' How easy. How humiliating for Gertrude. I don't like you, it would inform her. I bitterly resent your steamroller tactics; I've done what you said, since you were so persistent, but I'm going to prove you have no influence over me. I will not give you one inch, one crumb of myself – not even my home-made cakes for tea.

Gertrude had not offered to post the letters. 'You post them,' she said, 'immediately.' Sonia knew if she said carelessly, 'Oh, I'll do it later. Or maybe I'll have second thoughts and not send them after all,' that Gertrude would say nothing, would drink her tea (with or without cake) and leave to catch her train, embracing Sonia perhaps a shade less suffocatingly, and thanking her for a very pleasant day. Gertrude was pushy until she got her own way. If you did not allow her to get her own way, she was shrewd enough to know it was time to stop pushing. All it would take would be one snide remark, disguised as polite unconcern, and Gertrude would back down.

She looked at Samuel, who had 'a soft spot' for Gertrude so he had said, then at Lois, who was holding Gertrude's hand, and finally at Gertrude. For a second she saw Gertrude as herself, and saw herself as Mrs Grenville – queen of her own kitchen and empowered to say anything she liked, knowing that the underling would have to take it, if she did not want to cause an argument which would disrupt the whole household and possibly make her unwelcome there in the future.

Samuel had already taken Gertrude's house key away from her. He had told her not to give Sonia advice about choosing a vacuum cleaner or washing machine. He had not let Gertrude use her advantages over Sonia, as an employer's relative over the employer's servant. He had given authority over his house, his kitchen, to Sonia. If she chose not to do what Gertrude said, and not to serve Gertrude with her own cakes, he would back her up, she felt.

Three people stood waiting to hear what Sonia was going to say, and all three of them would accept it without question. It was strange, this sensation of power. It was heady. She could get used to it, this being allowed to express her opinion, even to being rude and pushy like Gertrude.

Get back those door keys, Sonia had told Samuel, and Samuel had demanded them back – even from his own cousin. Sack Mrs Baker. Tell Mrs Atwood she can't pop in and out of here whenever she feels like it. Don't call the doctor for Lois, unless I say so. Leave it to me to make deals with the plumber to sell your valuable antique bath and replace it with a plastic suite.

Samuel had said yes to Sonia's demands. He had not agreed with them all, but he had accepted her right to decide what she wanted and what she didn't, and accepted that he had no right to force her, although he was the employer and she was the servant. Hadn't she been as pushy as Gertrude? Samuel did not despise Gertrude for being a ludicrously overdressed bossyboots, but had 'a soft spot' for her. Yet if Sonia chose to despise her, that was Sonia's choice; Samuel would not force his preference on her in this matter either.

Picking up the letters from the table, she said briskly, 'Lois, you come up to the postbox with me, and then we'll bring out those cakes and have some tea. Gertrude, would you rather have tea in the house or in the garden?'

The tension evaporated. Samuel and Gertrude's relief was a tangible presence in the kitchen.

'My dear, whatever you prefer,' Gertrude said, wreathed in smiles.

'May I give a hand with anything?' Samuel offered.

'You can put the kettle on,' said Sonia graciously. 'And sit out in the garden. I'll bring the tea there. Like you said, Gertrude, I missed all the sunshine this afternoon, and I surely do need to get myself a suntan!'

Amid laughter, she took Lois by the hand and went off to post the letters to people who had regarded her as family in the past, leaving behind her (she was beginning to dare to hope) two people who might . . . possibly . . . come to regard her as family in the future, in spite of what Mrs Grenville had said, and in spite of the way she really and truly was herself.

For Sonia was certainly evil, and she knew that she had passed it on to Lois. And Samuel and Gertrude were wide-open victims. They made no attempt to protect themselves. But Sonia was beginning to wonder whether that might, in itself, be the best protection.

If they were going to allow her to do her worst, and then not condemn her for it, that was surely an open invitation to Sonia and Lois to do worse than they had ever previously done? Yet somehow it didn't seem to work that way.

Sonia knew she hadn't figured this out yet, but she would soon. She was good at acquiring information. Samuel and Gertrude were different from the other people she had met. They didn't act like them, or think like them. Their minds seemed to work differently. They were shrewd, but they weren't suspicious. They seemed foolish, but they were not all that innocent. Sonia couldn't quite crack the code by which they lived, but she would. She could open quite sophisticated safes. Samuel and Gertrude would pose no problem.

Sonia was going to make it her business to find out exactly what these two old croakers would put up with and what they wouldn't. They had made it their business – despite their apparent acceptance – to find out about her, and Sonia was fairly sure they would not let it rest there, but would go on ferreting into her and Lois's life. Now she was going to do the same with them. They might have her fooled so far. She was not ashamed to admit she did not understand their way of thinking yet, but she would not let it take her long before she did.

Sonia was going to get to the bottom of this.

Chapter Twenty-Eight

'How on earth do you manage to get the fruit distributed so evenly through the cake?' Gertrude demanded. 'My fruit cakes end up with all the fruit at the bottom. Do tell me – am I simply a rotten cook, or is there a secret to it?'

Sonia felt awkward giving cookery tips to a woman three times her age. 'Well . . .' she said.

Gertrude raised her hands in the air. 'I am simply a rotten cook – that's it, isn't it?'

Sonia laughed. 'No, but you might be making the mixture too wet, so it isn't firm enough to hold the fruit. Or do you flour the fruit first?'

'Flour the fruit? No, I don't. Should I?'

'Yes,' Sonia said. 'It stops it from sticking together and sinking. You have to keep the bits of fruit separate.'

'There now!' Gertrude exclaimed. 'How gratifying to learn that, after all these years. The next time I come, I shall bring you a fruit cake and you can tell me whether I have got it right. If I haven't, we shall all have the tummy ache. Samuel, did you grow those delphiniums from seed or from root cuttings? You see, Sonia, how I pick everybody's brains? I am a veritable magpie for information: never go home without picking up something new.'

'Whereabouts in Sussex do you live?' Sonia asked her. If Gertrude's hobby was picking up information, she had picked up quite enough for one day about Sonia; it was Sonia's turn to start on her.

Gertrude did not prove to be much of a challenge. Delighted at Sonia's interest, she poured out a torrent of facts about her village, her garden, her husband Humphrey ('Aptly named, my dear, because he does so often get the hump, poor old boy') and the county flower shows.

Samuel, who surely had heard it before, nodded and listened with every appearance of interest. Sonia found the fare a bit bland. It could have done with more malice, she thought. Surely Gertrude's neighbours couldn't *all* be so uniformly kind and friendly? It wasn't natural.

Sonia's experience of village life, in various jobs keeping house at the back of beyond, was of unmitigated snobbery, gossip and bitchiness, everyone considering themselves a cut above everyone else. But then, Gertrude was probably at the top of the feudal village hierarchy and so above most of the locals' struggles for power and influence. Gertrude already had it.

Humphrey sounded a bit of a pain in the neck, Sonia thought. Gertrude made it clear that she thought so too, though she spoke about him – which Sonia found puzzling – with obvious affection, as though his irritability and pennypinching were somehow his particular claims to being lovable.

'Poor old boy,' said Gertrude. 'He can't help it, can he, Samuel?' Samuel smiled and said nothing. Perhaps, Sonia concluded, Samuel thought Humphrey could very easily help it if he wanted. 'He lost his mother when he was very young,' Gertrude explained, 'and it turned him bitter, I fear. Mind you,' she said, turning to Sonia, 'Samuel lost his at seven and it didn't turn him bitter in the least, did it, my dear?'

Samuel leaned forward and helped himself to a second slice of cake. 'I didn't lose my mother, Gertrude,' he said mildly. 'She lived until I was twenty-three.'

'No,' Gertrude agreed, 'but you were seven when she abandoned you. Poor little boy,' she told Sonia. 'Sent off to boarding school while the wretched woman absconded with the rest of the family.'

Sonia was agog. This was more like it. 'Your mother abandoned you?' she asked Samuel.

Samuel was frowning at Gertrude and clicking his tongue. 'Of course she did not abandon me, Gertrude; it is perfectly ridiculous to suggest such a thing. Absconded, indeed!'

'Don't argue with me, Samuel; you know quite well that is what she did,' said Gertrude roundly. Sonia watched them glaring at one another and hoped they were going to have a row. It was quite exciting. Lois, flat on her stomach in front of her dolls' house, moved two of the little dolls to the second storey and began banging their heads together, as if in imitation of what was happening.

'Why, I clearly remember my parents talking about it, Samuel, when I was a child,' Gertrude continued. 'For a mother to abandon her seven-year-old boy and go off to that dreadful country . . . and to separate twins, as well. That was the worst. Deny it if you will, Samuel!'

Samuel denied it categorically. 'You are talking a great deal of bunkum, Gertrude,' he said. 'There was no question of anybody abandoning me. I was simply sent to continue my education at a decent public school while the rest of the family pursued new opportunities. Now we shall change the subject, if you please.'

Gertrude subsided, but Sonia had no intention of letting them change the subject. This was fascinating. 'What were the new opportunities?' she asked Gertrude, with her wide-eyed, most innocent look.

Gertrude glanced at Samuel, who glowered at her forbiddingly, but the temptation was too much for her to resist. 'Pioneering,' she said in a stage whisper. 'In Canada. All of them went – mother, father, and the other children. Must have needed their heads examining. It was the wilderness in those days, you know, and none of them knew anything about farming except the eldest boy, Claude.'

'Why did they take the other children, Samuel?' Sonia asked him. 'Why not you as well?'

'They didn't take all the others,' said Samuel testily. 'My eldest sister, Elcie, remained in England, and in the school holidays I made my home with her.'

'She only stayed because she was already married, Samuel, and her husband did not wish to go,' Gertrude prompted.

'Neither did I wish to go,' Samuel said. 'It was my own choice to remain in this country.'

'Nonsense!' Gertrude declared. 'You were asked for your opinion, along with the others in the family, and you argued against it, yes – and very sensibly, in my consideration. But instead of discussing it as a family and deciding as a family whether to go or stay, they allowed Claude to go ahead with the arrangements and then informed you that they were going and you had been enrolled in a boarding school.

'Don't think I don't know how they went about it, Samuel, because my father, as your father's first cousin, was consulted for his opinion at the time and advised most strongly against dividing the family, not to mention separating twins.

'It was an extremely shabby thing to do, Samuel, and no amount of arguing will persuade me otherwise. You cannot say you were offered a choice. You had simply expressed an opinion, along with everybody else. You were not asking to be left alone in England while the rest of the family went to Canada.

'It was dreadful of them to arrange it behind your back and tell you when it was too late to change anything. I blame Claude, as you know. He was always insanely jealous of his brothers, and your Mama was far too afraid of offending him.'

Samuel gave an impatient exclamation and got up abruptly from the table, leaving his tea unfinished. He stalked off into his workshop and closed the door. Lois jumped up and ran after him. Sonia called her back.

'Leave Samuel alone, Lois. He wants to be by himself.'

'No, he *doesn't* want to be by himself,' said Lois severely. She hammered on the door of the shed and called his name until he let her in. Sonia was torn between going after Lois to insist she came out of the shed, and staying with Gertrude to hear the rest of the story. She stayed with Gertrude.

'Oh dear,' said Gertrude. 'Now look what I have done. I must go and put things right.'

Sonia detained her. 'Was Samuel a twin, then?' she asked.

'Yes, my dear, he had a twin sister, Joyce. They were very

close. But then, there were only two girls in the family and with Elcie staying in England, Samuel's mother felt she must have a daughter with her for support. Of course in those days it was not considered important for girls to be educated. So Samuel went to boarding school, and Joyce went to Canada. It was hard on both of them, but on Samuel most of all, because he lost his whole family as well as his twin.'

'Did they keep in touch?' Sonia asked.

'Very seldom, I fear,' said Gertrude sadly. 'When Samuel was older and in work – and he left school very young; couldn't stick it – they used to write and ask him to send money, or to obtain things for them that they needed. When his father died, nobody informed Samuel for a long time. Then his mother sent a brief note, enclosing a silver toothpick for Samuel to remember him by.'

Sonia was silent, thinking of the seven-year-old Samuel, perhaps not so very different from the seven-year-old Sonia. The same thought must have occurred to Gertrude, for she said, 'I hope you will forgive me for bullying you into writing to your old friends and family, Sonia, but it is so very hard when one loses contact, isn't it? One wouldn't want it to happen unless one had absolutely no choice.'

'No,' Sonia agreed. 'You're right. And Samuel's family, then – none of them ever came back?'

'A few of his nieces and nephews have been over to visit, some of them quite recently, but no – none of the brothers ever returned here to live, and Joycie died young. She never saw her twin brother again.'

'Couldn't Samuel have gone over there to visit?' Sonia asked. She was beginning to feel upset by this. She had seen Samuel as a rock, calm and confident. Now Gertrude was telling her he was an abandoned child who had been lonely all his life. 'Or when he had enough money, couldn't he have gone over there to live?'

'I suppose he could have done so,' Gertrude said, 'if there had been some indication that he was wanted. But the general view of the brothers – which I do believe they persuaded their parents to share – was that Samuel was a spoilsport, the one who had put the damper on their plans when the idea was first suggested, and that it was just as well he had stayed at home.

'And of course, they did encounter great difficulties there, over the years: it was a hard life and they had been used to a comfortable home with servants. They were quite unprepared for such a life, and although they didn't lack courage and they were willing to learn, it's my guess they found it comforting to have Elcie and Samuel in England – a kind of anchor. To have lost all links with the homeland would have made *them* feel abandoned. They settled in a very isolated spot.'

'Samuel had you, though, didn't he?' Sonia asked. 'His cousin?'

'Well no, my dear, not for a long time. I wasn't born. I am very much younger than Samuel, though to your young eyes we old fogies might look much the same age. But my parents came to regard him as one of their own; in fact, my mother, when she died, left a will dividing everything between the four of us equally – my two brothers and Samuel and me.

'That's partly how Samuel could afford his own house – that and the fact that he always worked all the hours he could. It paid off, of course, not merely financially but in expertise, but I believe his chief reason for working so hard was to stave off loneliness. Now he's still afraid to stop work, or perhaps he doesn't know how to stop; it has become such a habit.'

Gertrude struggled to her feet. 'I must find him and apologize,' she said. 'It really was too tactless of me to harp on the past like that.'

'Does it still upset him so much to think about it?' Sonia asked. She recalled that Gertrude had claimed time did not heal; only the truth could. 'Doesn't he like to face the truth?'

'The truth that they abandoned him?' Gertrude asked. 'Well, he admits that on occasion he *felt* abandoned, but not that he had real reason for thinking so. He would consider that disloyal to his parents. He says they acted from perfectly good motives.'

'But you don't think they did?' Sonia asked.

Gertrude looked cynical. 'Perfectly logical motives,' she said, 'and utterly selfish. They always said Samuel was the selfish and difficult one, who never would fit in with the family's plans. I believe they convinced him that he was, which is why he won't really blame them; in his heart he believes he brought it on himself.'

'And do you think he did bring it on himself?' Sonia asked. It was suddenly important to know. Hadn't she too felt, at seven years old, that a mother must have a good reason for emigrating to 'a better land' with the man she loved, leaving her child to the care or neglect of others? 'I mean, maybe he was a difficult child who would never have fitted in with the family, whatever they did?'

'My dear, he was a child,' said Gertrude, shocked. '*Their* child. Clearly it was their duty to love him as he was. A child does not always conveniently fit in with plans, does it?

'As for Samuel voicing doubts about their making a new life in Canada, he probably only voiced the doubts they all felt, in private. Perhaps they were trying to dismiss their doubts – but they dismissed the child! There is no excuse for that, nor can there be.'

Sonia sighed. Gertrude was very clear on rights and wrongs. In one way it was comforting; in another way worrying. A child is a child. If the child causes difficulties, the responsibility for coping with them lies with the adults. The adults must deal with the problem in the child in order to deal with it in themselves, not dismissing it or turning a blind eye.

That could sound quite threatening, Sonia thought, to people who believed themselves to be well-balanced parents who just happened to have a problem child.

Gertrude was tottering across the lawn. She knocked humbly on the workshop door and was admitted to the company of Samuel and Lois. Sonia supposed she ought to go and join them, but instead she began to clear away the tea things.

Samuel might say that Sonia was family but she was, after all, only the housekeeper – and at times perhaps she found it easier that way.

Chapter Twenty-Nine

According to Samuel, Sunday was a day of rest, but Sonia soon realized that to Samuel 'rest' did not mean sitting down putting his feet up. First of all, he got up early, dressed in his business suit, cleaned his already perfectly shiny black shoes, did his usual tour of the garden (aided by Lois, the apprentice birdbath filler), ate his usual breakfast of toast and marmalade and announced his intention of going to church, shamelessly pressuring them to come with him.

'We don't go to church,' Sonia told him. 'We're not religious.' You couldn't really count the odd prayer for help in a bad situation, she reasoned. Anyone could get desperate. It didn't mean they were holy.

'I want to go with Samuel,' Lois said.

'Don't you want to stay with me?' Sonia appealed to her.

'No,' said Lois.

Sonia was jealous. 'You're going off with Samuel and leaving me on my own – again?'

'You can come too,' said Lois.

'I don't like church services,' Sonia said. 'I get bored.'

Samuel grinned. 'You may not get bored with this one,' he said. 'Deafened, maybe.'

Sonia was intrigued. 'Is it loud?'

Samuel put his head on one side. 'Do you like loud rock music and people jumping up and down?'

'You're joking,' Sonia said. 'You don't go to that kind of church service. Do you?'

'Come and see,' he said, with an expression of wicked glee.

He did. Sonia had expected the neatly dressed old gentleman to be part of a tiny congregation of senior citizens warbling eighteenth-century hymns and muttering prayers full of 'thees' and 'thous'. Instead, she found herself in the middle of an exuberant crowd in a massive hall, all of whom – including Samuel – were singing loud choruses, clapping their hands and – yes, jumping up and down. The West Indian members, who made up about half the congregation, danced.

Sonia stood stock still in the middle of it, stunned. When she had decided she would work out Samuel's way of thinking, she had not expected quite so many inconsistencies.

There he was, eighty-four years old, dressed in an old-style pinstriped business suit, white hair immaculately slicked down, rocking from one foot to the other and singing 'He come from the glorious kingdom' with all the gusto of his Caribbean neighbours. It was Sonia who was paralysed with embarrassment, too English and inhibited to join in.

Lois had no such reservations and entered into the spirit of it, giggling happily. People around her turned and smiled, asked her name and patted her on the head. Lois smiled back, answered questions and lapped up the attention with every appearance of enjoyment. At no point, during the whole service, did she cover her face. Sonia was astonished. She was not only, it seemed, seeing new aspects of Samuel's character every day, but also seeing new sides to Lois. Was this her child? Shy Lois who let nobody look her in the eyes?

Even when the crowd fell silent and listened attentively to the readings from scripture and the sermon, Lois was perfectly at home. She sat quietly, holding Samuel's hand, and did not fidget, whisper to Sonia or demand to go home.

The other children in the church behaved similarly. On the odd occasion when a small toddler ran down the aisles, he or she was simply allowed to run, and was picked up by the nearest adult when the child showed signs of distress or became rowdy.

It was the strangest church Sonia had ever been in, and yet it was in some way familiar. She had a flash of vision of a small white-painted wooden church filled with thin men and ample ladies in floral hats, singing and shouting and holding hands.

It must have been in Jamaica, for nearly all the congregation were black and sun streamed in through the open door and windows.

Sonia had not known she remembered anything about her first seven years in Jamaica. When Mrs Grenville had willed her to recall every possible detail, she had drawn a blank. Yet this morning, listening to the preacher talking about repentance and forgiveness and looking at the rapt faces around her, memories stirred and came to life.

By the end of the service she felt more at home, holding hands with Lois and her neighbour, a white teenage boy with crew-cut hair, wearing paint-splattered dungarees, and singing, 'How lovely on the mountain'.

When Samuel suggested staying for a cup of coffee afterwards, she agreed, and found herself immediately accosted by a large friendly lady with a Trinidad accent, who swept her off to meet a number of West Indian people, who told her, in unison, that she must be sure to come to the Caribbean Society on Wednesday evenings.

'I work in the evenings,' she said, overcome with cowardice. 'And I have to look after my little girl.'

'Bring her with you!' they chorused.

'It's too late for her,' Sonia said.

This was not accepted as an excuse. 'She can go to sleep on your lap when she's tired,' one lady said. 'You will have a lift home. No one goes home on their own on the buses. Late nights don't hurt a child if she's enjoying herself.'

'I have to work,' Sonia repeated lamely.

'What work do you do?' a man asked. He was tall, in his thirties, Sonia guessed, with clear, wide-open eyes and a slow smile.

'I'm a housekeeper,' she said. 'Cook-housekeeper.'

'Your employer makes you work every evening?' the man said. 'That's not right.'

'No, not every . . . but he's an old man. I can't go disturbing him, coming home late at night.' Why were these people so persistent? Couldn't they take the hint, that she didn't want to come? They were as bad as Gertrude, with their interference in her life. Unconsciously, she followed Samuel with her eyes.

'That's him?' the man said quickly. 'You work for him?'

'Yes,' she admitted, cursing herself. They all began to laugh.

'He won't mind!' they said. 'He'll be glad for you to go. He's one of the earliest members of this church.'

The lady who had first appropriated Sonia said, 'Want me to go and ask him for you?' and went before Sonia could refuse. She saw Samuel turn as the woman caught hold of his arm and smile first at her and then, across the room, at Sonia. He nodded and waved at her encouragingly. The woman returned satisfied. 'He says go and have a good time,' she said conclusively, as though that settled everything. 'And either bring the little girl with you or else he will mind her for you.'

This magnanimity was applauded by the whole group, who then began to discuss among themselves which Caribbean Society member would have the privilege of collecting Sonia and Lois on a Wednesday evening.

'Not this week,' said Sonia hastily, playing for time. 'I can't manage this Wednesday. We've only just moved in. We need time to get settled.'

'Okay, next week,' said the tall man graciously. 'You be ready next Wednesday and we will call for you. Do you play any instrument?'

'No, I don't. No.' Sonia was frankly terrified. What was she getting into? 'I'm not really qualified,' she said, 'to come to a Caribbean Society. I've lived in England nearly my whole life. I left Jamaica when I was seven and I don't remember anything about it.'

Since they were still in church (even though they were standing round drinking coffee in it and chatting) she thought she had better not lie, and quickly amended this to, 'Hardly anything, anyway,' but her objection was already being swept aside.

'You can be English and Jamaican,' said the first woman generously. 'Some of us were born here, so you see you have an advantage. Seven years in Paradise!' Everybody laughed at this.

'And we organize group trips to the West Indies, every year,' another man contributed. 'So your easiest and cheapest way of getting home to visit your family is with us.'

Sonia was about to come out with her well-worn phrase, 'I don't have any family', when she recalled that she had just written to her aunt, and to Aunty Sue their non-relative who had been as close to them as any family and who had said to them, on leaving, 'Stay in touch; come and visit; don't make yourselves strangers now.'

A sudden yearning came over her to go back to the West Indies, whether she had any real memories of it or not, and see what the place was like and find out whether she had any affinity with the blood relatives she knew she had there, whether they seemed like strangers or felt like family. A yearning too for sunshine and white smiles and white sands. A fantasy, maybe – an English fantasy culled from travel programmes on TV, rather than any flashback to a culture she had any right to call her own – but still, it would be nice to go and see . . .

'I want to go home,' said Lois, tugging at her hand.

'Okay,' Sonia said. 'Go and tell Samuel we'll see him back at the house.' But Samuel decided to leave too. They said goodbye to the people they had been talking to, and left as a family group.

'Next Wednesday evening,' the tall man reminded Sonia on her way out. 'We'll be there, so you be ready!' He laughed, his eyes crinkling and his teeth showing white. She smiled back. 'All right,' she agreed.

At home, Samuel poured them both a sherry and insisted that she sat down with him to drink it before starting to prepare the lunch. He was delighted with the idea of a roast dinner. 'A proper Sunday lunch,' he said with glee.

Sonia had found an old dog-eared cookery book – presumably Miss Prynne's – in the bottom of a drawer, and had chosen a traditional recipe for Eve's Pudding to follow the roast lamb with rosemary. She asked Samuel if they could eat in the dining room, and he entered willingly into the spirit of celebration once he had assured Sonia there was no obligation to 'do the job properly' and she assured him that she would find it a pleasure.

She demurred when, opening the seventeenth-century court cabinet, he took out crystal glasses and white embroidered linen. 'You don't want to risk that best stuff with Lois,' Sonia told him. 'She's a good girl, but all children can have accidents.'

'So can grown-ups,' Samuel pointed out, 'but what's the use of having these things locked away and never using them?'

'They're antiques,' Sonia protested. 'You can't just use them for dinner.'

'They were created to be used,' said Samuel firmly. 'Not to be shut in a cupboard and revered. Look at this cloth. You see? All those faint stains? Wine and tea, no doubt. It didn't get those by not being used, now did it? A few more won't do any harm.'

'I could probably get those out,' Sonia said, examining them. 'There are good stain removers these days.' She washed the glasses and polished a couple of silver candlesticks, fitting new white candles into them, and ironed the embroidered cloth, in ecstasy at having the use of such beautiful things. She picked a few flower heads from the garden and floated them in a crystal bowl in the centre of the table. Samuel and Lois were equally appreciative of the result.

'A real family dinner table,' Samuel said, and Lois added, in tones of awe, 'A very posh family!'

'But of course,' Sonia said. 'That's what we are.'

They looked around the big table at each other, over the shining silver and cut glass, and for no reason at all began to laugh.

Chapter Thirty

Afterwards, Sonia thought she could have said, 'I knew it.' Hadn't she always been able to trust her instincts? Yet in this case the evidence was so confusing that she would have been able to say, 'I knew it' to quite contradictory conclusions.

She knew and could have told anyone that Samuel was a good man, a kind man, that she and Lois had had a stroke of extraordinary good fortune in meeting him, and that she had recognized this right from the beginning. Equally well she knew, and had always suspected, that there was something very wrong.

So whatever happened she could have said, 'I knew it,' or told herself, 'I told you so.'

What did happen was so unpredictable that she could not believe anyone could have foreseen events taking quite that turn. How could anyone, however good their instincts, imagine such a bizarre outcome to this oddest of family sagas?

Sunday afternoon was entirely unremarkable. Sonia remembered thinking that she would find it no problem if Samuel retired, for it was not difficult having him at home all day. He was content for her to spend her time as she decided, while he gardened and pottered in his shed and chatted to Lois, who followed him like a puppy wherever he went.

Lois used to do the same with Eddie Barnes, the gardener at the Grenvilles', until Sonia called her away, for Eddie was short-tempered and Sonia never trusted him not to inflict his sudden moods on Lois as he sometimes did on Sonia or even on Mrs Grenville. Samuel, however, was placid in temperament and seemed to enjoy Lois's company, or so Sonia thought.

Believing that it was good for both of them to be together, she enjoyed the unaccustomed solitude and spent most of the afternoon in the kitchen, soaking the linen tablecloths and polishing the rest of the silver, with the radio for company.

At tea-time it began to rain and as Samuel retreated to his workshed Sonia brought the tea out there, and the three of them sat companionably sipping and chatting among the half-finished cabinets and broken chairs. When the rain cleared at about five o'clock they went for a walk and Lois delighted in showing Sonia the park, with all the possessiveness of one who had been there before.

In the early evening Samuel had a bath and came downstairs again in a brown plaid dressing gown as thick as an overcoat, belted with a plaited cord that fascinated Lois, who tied elaborate knots in it while Samuel sat in his armchair, half drowsing and half listening to the large wheezy radio in the sitting room, in front of a small fire.

When he finally fell asleep, Lois became bored and came out to Sonia in the kitchen and asked to be made up again in her Red Indian warpaint.

'It's too late,' Sonia said absently, her mind on the old recipes she was reading. 'You'll be going to bed any minute.' But the evening was light and mild, the sky clear after the rain, and Lois, despite her long walk, looked far from sleepy, so Sonia gave in. She did a good job with the make-up, with white shiny streaks and luminous yellow and orange whorls and stripes. 'Lois, you look truly ferocious,' Sonia assured her.

Infected by Lois's enthusiasm and by admiration for her own artistry, Sonia fixed up the tepee again in the garden and strung the totem masks from the acacia tree, where they fluttered in the half-light, the fluorescent paints giving them a weird glow. Sonia and Lois chased each other round the garden, whooping exuberantly, and stalked each other up and down the winding path through the flower beds and the alley behind the strung-out apple trees.

When they returned to the house, Sonia made Samuel a cup of cocoa and put it on a tray with a couple of biscuits and gently shook him awake. 'Have something before you go to bed,' she said. It wasn't good for old people to go too long without food, so she had read. Little and often was best for their health.

So it couldn't have been her fault, what happened. It wasn't because Samuel had overeaten or had eaten too little. There must have been some other reason for the whole senseless, unreasonable episode.

He was tired and admitted it, that evening. He even relaxed his standards far enough to accept Sonia's offer to wind the grandfather clock for him and clean his shoes ready for their Monday morning excursion to work. Sonia carried out both tasks carefully, in accordance with his instructions. Nobody but Samuel himself, he told her, had ever wound that clock. A fine clock was like a well-trained dog, he said, only half jokingly; it only responded to one master.

In fact, when Sonia heard him go downstairs in the night, the first explanation that crossed her mind was that he might have become worried about the clock and gone down to see whether it had stopped.

While she was winding the clock and shining his shoes (as though anything could make them shinier: they were already so spotless that even the cracks in the leather gleamed as brilliantly as the wood of Samuel's precious furniture) Samuel drank half his cocoa and then fell asleep again.

The first indication of trouble Sonia received was when she heard him shouting, 'Cree!' or something that sounded like that, and rushed in to find him cowering in the chair and staring with horrified eyes at the small warpainted Lois.

Lois was offended but not perturbed. 'Why is he shouting at me?' she enquired of Sonia.

'Go away into the kitchen, Lois, and wait for me,' Sonia told her hastily, giving her a shove in that direction. 'Samuel,' Sonia said, standing in front of him and trying to get his eyes to focus on her. 'What happened? What's wrong?'

Beads of sweat shone on his forehead. His eyes were glazed. His hands, clutching his dressing gown cord, were trembling.

Sonia was seriously alarmed. 'Samuel!' she said again, shaking his arm. 'Look at me, will you?'

Slowly his eyes found her face. The pupils, dilated, began to return to normal. 'You know who I am?' Sonia asked.

'Sonia,' he said faintly.

'Yes. That's better. What happened, Samuel? Were you taken ill or something?'

'Cree,' he whispered. 'Here, in this house.'

'Cree?' she said in perplexity. 'Who is Cree? That was Lois you were seeing. Is something wrong?'

A wondering expression came over his face. His vision cleared and he sat up and looked around. 'I don't know what came over me,' he said, in his normal voice.

'Neither do I,' Sonia said. 'You looked scared to death, Samuel. Were you frightened of something?'

'Was I asleep?' he asked. 'Was it a dream?'

'That must have been it,' Sonia said, relieved to be offered a simple explanation. 'Why don't you go to bed? I've cleaned your shoes for the morning. There's nothing else to be done, is there?'

'No,' he said. 'No, nothing. Yes, I shall go to bed. Good night, my dear. Will you be long going up yourself? You look a little tired as well.'

'No, we won't be long. I'll give Lois her bath in the morning, so we don't disturb you tonight. You sleep well, Samuel.'

Sonia herself fell asleep easily that night, for the first time since they had been in the house. Her last waking sensation was a sleepy recognition of mild sexual stirrings, not intrusive and not unpleasant, and a hazy vision of a young man's face, a man with milk-chocolate-dark skin and brown eyes and a wide, friendly smile.

Sonia acknowledged this as a sign that she was settling in, beginning to feel at home in this new place. When she was anxious she always forgot she was a woman. Her body only reminded her of the fact when she was relaxed. The reminder, this time, was tactful enough not to make her feel worried about it becoming a problem, and she was soon fast asleep.

It must have been the noise Samuel made going downstairs that woke her and made her reach for her luminous alarm clock to check the time. It was half past two in the morning. He made quite a lot of noise, which surprised her; in fact, she wondered if she should check that it really was Samuel and not a burglar, till she heard him clear his throat and cough. It was Samuel sure enough.

She intended to stay awake till she heard him return, in case he was unwell and needed help, but the bed was warm and she was tired. It was six o'clock in the morning when she awoke again.

Sonia decided to get up. Lois had been sick again in the night, she saw, as she was getting dressed. As the child was sleeping peacefully now, drawing deep contented breaths, Sonia thought it best to leave her and clean up the mess later on. She tiptoed downstairs and put the kettle on to make herself an early cup of tea, drawing back the kitchen curtains (which were old wartime blackout ones) to let in some light. As she did so, she let out a gasp. The totem masks on the acacia tree were in shreds, and the tepee was destroyed. The blanket looked as though it had been systematically ripped apart; pieces of cloth were scattered all over the garden. The wooden clothes horse which had formed the tent frame was split into tiny pieces. On the ground, beside all this carnage, was the carving knife.

Sonia's first thought was to clear up the mess before Samuel and Lois saw it. She ran out of the back door, grabbing a spare black dustbin bag from the sink drawer, and began stuffing paper and fabric into it as quickly as she could. The remnants of the clothes horse she gathered up and placed in a pile beside the incinerator used for garden rubbish.

There were no footprints except her own in the dew on the grass. The garage gate was firmly bolted and there were no signs of anyone having climbed over it. Sonia walked back across the lawn, shaking her head. Who could have done this? Surely not Mrs Atwood . . .? Had she and Lois been making so much noise, on a sacred suburban Sunday evening, that the neighbour had flown into a mad rage, leapt the fence and set about the child's playthings in a fit of destructive vengeance? Surely not. The idea was ridiculous. Then who . . .?

Samuel, drawing back his bedroom curtains, waved at her from upstairs. She waved back, relieved to have removed most of the evidence before he could be distressed by it.

He met her downstairs. 'You're up early,' he said cheerfully. 'Have I given you my bad habit of inspecting the garden before breakfast?'

'Samuel,' she said uncertainly, 'you didn't hear anything in the night, did you?'

He looked surprised. 'No, my dear.'

'I mean, I heard you go downstairs at about half-past two,' she said. 'It wasn't because you heard noises in the garden was it?'

'No, he said, frowning. 'Why do you ask?'

'Lois left some things she was playing with in the garden,' Sonia told him, 'and they're all torn to shreds this morning.'

'Good gracious!' said Samuel. 'Could it have been a dog, do you think?'

'A dog?' Sonia said.

'Yes, we have once or twice had a dog in the garden,' Samuel said. 'I'm not sure how, because the fences are high and apparently secure, but it has happened on occasions.'

Sonia held out the carving knife. 'It wasn't a dog,' she said.

He stared at it in blank incomprehension. 'Was that in the garden?' he asked.

'Yes.'

'I don't understand,' Samuel said. 'We didn't leave it out there yesterday afternoon . . . no, of course we didn't. We only used the carving knife in the house, didn't we?'

He looked so worried that Sonia put her hand on his arm and said lightly, 'Well, it's a mystery. I expect there's some explanation. You get ready for work, and I'll put your breakfast on.'

He accepted her reassurance gratefully. 'Yes,' he said. 'I had better get ready or I shall be late for work. That wouldn't do, would it? They might fire me, and where would I get another job at my age?' They laughed. Sonia put the carving knife in the sink, ready to wash when she did the breakfast dishes. The blade was jagged from cutting wood when it was only designed for cutting meat. She would have to resharpen it later, with the long honing steel Samuel had used. She knew how to do it.

'By the way, my dear,' Samuel said. 'Thank you for cleaning my shoes last night, but where did you leave them?' He was still in his slippers, Sonia noticed.

'Outside your room,' she told him. 'I brought them up last night when I went up to bed.'

'Oh, I must have overlooked them,' Samuel said. He went upstairs again, but came down looking puzzled. 'They are not there.'

They searched the house, but the shoes were nowhere to be found.

'Could Lois have hidden them, for a joke?' Samuel suggested.

'I don't think she would do that,' Sonia said, 'but I can ask her.' She shook Lois awake. 'Lois? Did you see Samuel's shoes outside his bedroom door?' Lois opened her eyes and shook her head. 'No,' she said. She turned over and went back to sleep. Sonia hoped she was not going to be ill again today. It couldn't be good for a child to keep staying in bed.

'Perhaps I only thought I brought them up,' Sonia told Samuel, 'though I was sure I did. Weren't they there when you got up in the night? Did you notice?'

'No,' he said. 'I didn't.'

'You weren't sick in the night, were you?' Sonia asked anxiously. 'Did I cook something that disagreed with you?'

'Oh, not at all, no,' Samuel said.

'I was worried,' Sonia explained, 'when I heard you go downstairs. I didn't hear you come up again, because I went back to sleep. But Lois was sick in the night again, so I hoped it wasn't that.'

'Was she?' Samuel said. 'Sonia, I do believe it would be best to call the doctor, you know. I know the child seems healthy enough in the daytime, but this keeps happening, doesn't it? There must be something wrong.'

Sonia felt security seeping away from her. Something wrong, indeed. Something very wrong here. She changed the subject quickly. 'So you weren't ill in the night, then?'

'No,' Samuel said. 'No, I wasn't. Do you know, I can't think why I did come downstairs in the night. In fact, I do not remember doing so. Are you sure you heard me?'

'Yes, I did,' Sonia affirmed. 'At half-past two.'

He shook his head. 'Well, if you say so. My dear, these shoes are a mystery. Another mystery. I shall have to wear my brown ones, else I shall miss my bus. No doubt the black ones will turn up in some perfectly obvious place and we shall be kicking ourselves for not looking there.'

Taking the shoe-cleaning bag he returned upstairs to polish his brown shoes. Sonia buttered and marmaladed his toast for him, to save him time, and poured and sugared his cup of tea. He was grateful for these extra attentions. 'It is doubtless a vanity,' he confessed, 'but I do detest arriving late for work. Unpunctuality is a sign of inefficiency, so we were always told as apprentices.'

'You're hardly an apprentice any longer,' Sonia teased him. 'Why don't you work part-time now, Samuel? Or else retire from the firm and do those lords' and ladies' commissions privately?'

'I could do that,' Samuel said. 'Yes, I hadn't thought of doing it that way. Do the commissions privately, yes. Now there's an idea. I shall have to give it some thought.'

'Don't give it some thought,' said Sonia severely, taking a leaf out of Gertrude's book. 'Just give in your notice.'

'Wouldn't you find it a nuisance,' he said humbly, 'having me at home, under your feet all day?'

'Don't be silly!' Sonia exclaimed. 'This is your house! It's you who would have to put up with having us under your feet. It was all right at the weekend, though, wasn't it?'

He gave her a radiant smile. 'The weekend was very nice,' he agreed.

When he had left to catch his bus, Sonia went to call Lois. 'You can't spend another day in bed,' she said firmly. 'There is nothing wrong with you, Lois, and we have a busy day ahead. We're going shopping with Mrs Atwood, and then the plumber is coming. Come on, you'll feel all right once you're up.'

Lois allowed herself to be washed and dressed. 'Where's the Red Indian things?' she asked, as soon as she was downstairs in the kitchen.

'I took them down,' Sonia said. 'The blanket got ruined by the dew, though, and the clothes horse fell to bits.'

'Oh no!' Lois's mouth turned down at the corners.

'We'll make another tepee sometime, a better one. Those things were old; they were no good. Eat your cereal, Lois. Mrs Atwood will be here soon. You like going shopping.'

'I've got a tummy ache,' Lois complained.

'You're just hungry. You'll feel better when you've had your breakfast.' She sat down and began to make out a shopping list, then as Lois dawdled over her breakfast, she got out the ironing board and ironed the tablecloths she had soaked and washed yesterday. Most of them had come up well but one or two still had faint stains on them; she would add stain remover to the shopping list.

Sonia folded the cloths and took them back to the dining room. The door was locked; she had forgotten it would be. They had locked it again after clearing away the lunch yesterday. She took the key down from its ledge on top of the grandfather clock in the hall, and opened the dining room door. There by the French window leading into the garden were Samuel's black shoes, covered in mud.

Chapter Thirty-One

Sonia and Lois were both subdued during the shopping expedition. Molly Atwood chattered happily. No, she had heard no disturbances in the night, she assured Sonia. Were there any signs of a break-in?

There were none. Sonia had checked the windows and doors before they left the house. She had also scraped and cleaned Samuel's shoes. There was no point in confronting him with them. He had said he did not even remember coming downstairs in the night.

Why had he destroyed Lois's toys? Did he know what he had done? Had it, in fact, been him? Or had somebody used his shoes? No, it must have been Samuel, Sonia thought wretchedly. The dining room door had not been forced, nor the outside door, and only Samuel knew where the key was, on top of the grandfather clock.

Could it have been Lois? Or Sonia herself, in her sleep? Sonia considered every possible explanation. Mrs Atwood found her a distracted audience. She asked Sonia several times if she felt all right, and Sonia gave her innocent smile and her blithest 'I'm fine.'

On their return, Mrs Atwood invited them in for coffee. Sonia refused, politely. She must put the shopping away and then get on with some housework, she said. Lois accepted the invitation. Sonia hesitated, then, as Mrs Atwood seemed delighted at the prospect of having Lois for the rest of the morning, agreed to let her go. It might take the child's mind off feeling sick, anyway.

Lois must not get sick now, thought Sonia fervently. If there was something wrong in this house, they must be free to get out, at a moment's notice. Where could she go, with a sick child? They must have an escape route, just in case.

In case of what? Was Samuel going senile? Was he violent – a wolf in sheep's clothing? No, surely Gertrude would have known that. Maybe she did know. Had she been trying to warn Sonia, by telling her not to plan to stay here long?

'Samuel has been lonely all his life,' Gertrude had said. Why? Because of circumstances – abandonment by his family at an early age? Because, by chance or by design, he had never married, had been a lonely bachelor? Or because there was something so intrinsically wrong with him that he had isolated himself from normal company, and was tolerated only by the unobservant and undiscriminating Miss Prynne?

Sonia was uneasy. The arrival of the plumber was a welcome distraction. In spite of having threatened him not to waste her time, she made him tea and sat down with him at the kitchen table to drink it. He was happy to talk, but she could hardly take in anything he said, and eventually he remarked, 'I can take a hint. I'll let you get on with your work, and I'll get on with mine. I'll have to turn the water off for a while – okay?'

As he was working in the kitchen, on the pipes, she took herself upstairs and cleaned the bedrooms. She took the sheets off Lois's bed and put them in the bath. Why did the child keep being sick every night? Was she aware of some tension in the house that Sonia had not noticed?

She put clean sheets on the bed and dusted the furniture and the window sills. She wished she had a vacuum cleaner that worked. Samuel had told her to order what she liked for the house, but how was it to be paid for?

She spent some time on the phone, with the Yellow Pages open on her knee, phoning stores to ask the price of the vacuum cleaner she preferred, the one Mrs Grenville had had. When she found the cheapest supplier, she wrote down the address and the price.

She would tell Samuel tonight, and he could let her know what arrangement he wanted to make about paying for it.

There she went again: assuming they were staying here, planning for future times, when tomorrow they might be gone.

Those two choruses of, 'I knew he was all right' and, 'I knew there was something wrong' kept playing discordantly in her head. How could she trust her instincts, when her instincts kept giving her contradictory messages? Perhaps, though, both messages were right; the contradiction was not in her instincts but in the person.

She took Samuel's black shoes upstairs and put them in his wardrobe. As she did so, she caught sight of his dressing gown hanging there; it had mud all over its hem. She sat back on her heels in front of the wardrobe and took a deep breath. That proved it, then. It was him.

Why, oh why, had he done such a thing? Crept out into the garden at dead of night and slashed Lois's playthings to bits? Was he truly unaware that he had done it? Was he harbouring an unconscious racial hatred? Or a hatred of children?

Did he believe he was happy to have their company, but underneath there was a rage and bitterness at having his peaceful, if lonely, life disrupted? Was he taking out on his new 'family' some resentment he could not let himself feel for the old one?

Should they not have borrowed his blanket (though there were so very many in the cupboard on the landing that surely he could not have resented them using the oldest and tattiest for the purpose)? Was he furious at having things draped on his rare and lovely acacia tree: did that offend his pride as a gardener?

There was no good reason, Sonia decided. The reason for such an action had to be bad. But which of the possible bad reasons was it? And did that reason make it unwise for them to stay here, or unsafe for Lois to be alone in his company?

Was Gertrude in on this, or blissfully unaware of the hidden viciousness in her cousin's character? Was he sick? Mad? Bad? Was it possible he had been none of these things before Sonia and Lois's advent into his life, and they had infected him with their own undoubted evil? Had they been, in this short time, a corrupting influence on an innocent old man, a churchgoer, a benefactor, a man who thanked God every day of his life for every mouthful he ate?

Sonia shuddered. She considered phoning Bella at the women's refuge to ask if they could go back there. Thinking of the refuge reminded her of poor, neglected Mrs Patel, whom she had promised to visit in hospital. She couldn't face anyone else's suffering, not now.

She didn't want to see Mrs Patel, nor to hear Bella tell her how much Mrs Patel's children were pining for their mother. It was unkind and selfish of her, no doubt, but the slightest problem, Sonia felt – even somebody else's – would break her nerve just now, and she had to keep going, keep thinking clearly, for her own and Lois's sake.

Why do things have to go wrong now? she wailed inside her head. Just when we had escaped getting thrown out of here, even in spite of Mrs Grenville's testimony; just when we thought we were safe.

Perhaps it was *because* Mrs Grenville said they were evil that Samuel was keeping them on? Perhaps he felt they could not or would not judge him, in the state he was in, if they were as bad? But what state, exactly, was Samuel in?

Sonia was going round in circles, even literally. She found herself cleaning parts of the rooms that she had already cleaned. She gave up trying to concentrate and went next door to reclaim Lois, bribing her to come home with a whispered promise of going to the park.

'Can we go to the library as well?' Lois asked, when they were on their way down the hill to the park.

'No, you have to be a member to take books out.'

'We can join!' Lois rejoiced. 'Samuel got us some joiners!'

'Some forms for joining,' Sonia corrected her. 'No, we can't, Lois. I looked at them. You have to have someone to give you a reference, saying they've known you for a number of years and your character is perfect. Bloody references for every-thing,' she added, with sudden bitterness. 'Even bloody library books.'

'Bloody library books,' repeated Lois with satisfaction.

'Don't use that word,' said Sonia automatically. 'I know I did, but I oughtn't.'

'Why?' Lois asked.

'Never mind why. You know what I did this morning, Lois? Found a shop to sell us a new vacuum cleaner. And the plumber has gone to order us a bathroom suite. Pink. Isn't that exciting? Why are you clutching your stomach like that, Lois? You want to go home? Okay, we'll go home. You can have a little lie-down, then you'll be all right.'

The plumber had done what he could, until the new suite arrived. He had been busy, finding out about kitchen fitters, getting quotes from another one of his mates. He left Sonia with a mass of confusing information, but promised to 'get her sorted out' with the minimum of inconvenience to everyone – and the maximum profit for himself, no doubt, Sonia thought.

She was glad to have the matter taken out of her hands, and gave him permission to fix up whatever he thought best. Samuel would not mind. He had said he was happy to pay the bills.

When the plumber left, promising to return later in the week when the arrangements had been made, Sonia saw Lois into bed and then rang the hospital. Using Lois as an excuse, she left a message with a nurse on Mrs Patel's ward, explaining that they had intended to visit but could not, as Lois was ill.

The nurse, in return, informed her that Mrs Patel was making progress. No, she said, Mrs Patel's husband had not visited her.

Sonia felt a renewed anxiety. What if the husband did not follow his previous pattern and return to Mrs Patel once the new baby was born? She shrugged off the fear. She had enough to worry about, and anyway it was hard to see how Mrs Patel could be worse off than she already was.

The non-return of the husband could be a blessing, ensuring the non-return of the beatings and the unaccompanied pregnancies. Mrs Patel, asked why she stayed with him, had answered serenely, 'Because I love him.' What kind of woman loved such a man? A woman, perhaps, who could love anyone.

Could Sonia love Samuel, if he turned out to be bad, if the bouts of unheralded violence recurred? Certainly, she wanted to love him. She needed, badly, to love somebody, to count someone as family. Did Gertrude know this too? In making Sonia write to everyone who had ever loved her, even poorly, was she ensuring that Sonia had an escape route, in case Samuel . . . in case Samuel what? Tried to murder them in their beds?

She considered phoning Gertrude. Tell me honestly, she would say, did Samuel murder Miss Prynne? Are we in danger here, Gertrude? Tell me.

Why should Gertrude tell her? Samuel was her family. She wanted to see him well looked after, naturally. She had said how glad she was that Sonia and Lois were here.

Why had Samuel not advertised for a housekeeper? Was it merely the filthy state of the house? Or did his situation not bear investigation by an employment agency, or by anybody? Should she ring the police, tell them about the mud on the shoes and the carving knife on the lawn?

There was a ring at the doorbell. A woman on the doorstep introduced herself as Mrs Baker. 'I just called,' she said, 'to see how you're settling in. Is everything all right?'

Sonia almost asked her in, but old cautions die hard. 'Yes,' she said. 'Everything's fine, thanks.'

'Oh good,' the woman said. She was in her fifties, Sonia judged, though she could have passed for older; her face was tired and lined but her eyes were kind.

'I'm so glad you've come to look after Mr Arnold,' Mrs Baker continued. 'This house needs a good deal of cleaning, and I'm afraid I wasn't a lot of help to him, what with having difficulties of my own. I hope you won't find it too much for you, dear. I could look in now and again if you wanted, and give you a hand. I wouldn't take anything for it.'

'Thanks,' Sonia said. In a rush of confidence, she added,

'Did you like working for Mr Arnold? Did you get on with him?'

'Oh yes,' said Mrs Baker. 'Such a gentleman. But I do understand about him not needing the extra help now that you're here, and I do wish you all the best, dear, you and the little girl. Such a dear little child. My mother and I were very taken with her.'

'Oh, thank you,' said Sonia, always pleased with praise of Lois.

'Is she playing in the garden?' Mrs Baker asked.

'No, she's in bed. She's a bit off colour – not ill.'

'Oh, poor soul. I expect it's the change of home, don't you? Children do take a while to settle in.'

'Yes,' Sonia said. 'I expect so.'

'Well, I'll be getting along,' Mrs Baker said. 'You will give me a call if ever I can be of any help, won't you? We're only five houses down – the one with the red door. Call any time. Come for a coffee one morning, with Lois.'

'Thank you,' Sonia said. 'We'll do that. Thanks. Bye now.'

The woman was nice, she thought regretfully. And Mrs Atwood wasn't bad, when you got to know her and turned a deaf ear to about half of what she said. Then there were the people at the church, and the Caribbean Society, and the possibility of an upholstery class in the autumn; there was the playgroup for Lois that Mrs Atwood had mentioned this morning; there was the library, which they might find a way of joining (perhaps they would not be so very strict about references; perhaps they could forge some and get away with it); there was the park.

There were so many advantages in staying here, Sonia thought. So many reasons why it was perfect. And one reason why it was wrong, that could render all those advantages meaningless.

There was only one question she needed answered. If the answer to it was yes, they would have to leave, however many benefits this place could offer her and Lois.

The question was – was Samuel dangerous?

Chapter Thirty-Two

Sonia sliced the cold roast lamb thinly, cooked carrots and mushrooms and laid them on top, poured gravy over it and topped the lot with mashed potatoes. She added no onion, garlic or spices, feeling that plain food might be best for both Lois's upset stomach and Samuel's upset mind.

She jumped when someone knocked loudly on the back door, and hesitated a moment before opening it.

A boy in brown overalls stood clutching a large box tied with a strap. 'Laundry,' he said. 'You haven't left this week's out for us.'

'I forgot,' Sonia said. 'Leave it for this week.'

'Righto; thought I'd just check,' the boy said.

'Thanks. Do I have to pay you?'

'No, we send in a bill once a month.'

'Okay. Bye.' She would wash Samuel's shirts by hand until they got the washing machine, Sonia decided. And the sheets could be done in the bath. She drew a final pattern on the top of the potato pie and went upstairs to see how Lois was.

Halfway up the stairs, she heard Lois's voice. The child must be talking to herself. Peeping through the crack of the door, she saw Lois, in her pyjamas, crouched on top of the bed playing with the dolls' house, and she hung back for a moment to listen.

'Mrs Grenville is on the telephone,' Lois said. 'Hello-o, this is Mrs Grenville and I am ringing to tell you my order has not been delivered and I am *very* cross with you.'

Sonia smothered a giggle. The voice was not a bad imitation of Mrs Grenville's affronted tones.

'Soni-aa! Soni-aa!' Lois bawled. 'Oh my goodness, where is

that dirty black cook? She should be in the kitchen and she isn't here. I shall have to fire her.'

Sonia gasped. Dirty black cook? So much for Mrs Grenville's freedom from racial prejudice. No wonder Lois kept saying she wasn't black. Sonia gave up eavesdropping and went into the room.

'Hi, Lois. How are you feeling now?'

'Okay. Look, this doll is you. She's upstairs making the beds, and this Mrs Grenville doll can't find her.'

'That doll is me? No, that one is you, Lois. Samuel made her with little pigtails like yours, remember?'

'No, this one is me,' Lois said, holding up the large doll Mrs Atwood had given her.

'Oh, you've agreed to be black now, have you?' Sonia teased her.

'No, this is a white doll,' said Lois firmly.

'And it's you? Why is it so big? It won't fit in the house with the other dolls.'

'That's why I have to go in the cellar. I need steps for this cellar, Sonia.'

'Um ... I know. If I make a cardboard slope and stick matches down it, like rungs, will that do?'

'Yes.'

'But you still won't be able to get down there, Lois. That doll is too big for a dolls' house, and even too big for the cellar.'

'I know. That's all right.'

'You're bigger than the rest of us, then, Lois?' Sonia said. 'Bigger than me and Mrs Grenville and this Samuel doll?'

'Yes, I am,' Lois said. 'That's not Samuel, that one. That's Eddie.'

Sonia picked up the doll and studied it in silence. 'You spent a lot of time with Eddie, Lois, at that last house,' she said after a few minutes. 'Did you like him?'

'Yes,' Lois said, busily arranging furniture. 'Where's the stairs for the cellar, Sonia?'

'Give me a minute. I'll find a bit of cardboard or something.'

In Samuel's workshop she found a triangular wedge of wood. Perfect. She glued rows of matches down the sloping side and took it up to show Lois. Lois took it with hardly a glance and placed it at the entrance to the cellar. She had put a table and chair down there, and still had the egg-box segment for the boiler. 'It needs to have fire in it,' she said.

'Want me to paint you some flames?' Sonia asked.

'Yeh!'

'Please is what you say, Lois.'

'Please.'

'Okay. You won't be able to touch them till the paint's dry – all right?'

'I can't touch them anyway,' Lois pointed out. 'They're hot.'

Sonia laughed. 'Yes, these flames are hot. Look at this red!'

They were both surprised to hear the front door opening. 'It can't be that time already!' Sonia exclaimed. 'Lois, you had no lunch. You better get dressed now and come downstairs and I'll give you some milk and biscuits.'

Sonia went down and took Samuel's coat from him. 'How was your day?'

He gave her an exultant smile. 'I gave in my notice,' he said.

'You didn't!'

'I did. I took your advice. I shall leave the firm in a month from now but remain available for consultancy work.'

'That's great, Samuel! How do you feel about it?'

'Relieved,' he admitted. 'I do believe it had been getting rather too much for me. I shan't be sorry not to have to make that journey every day.'

'We have to celebrate!' Sonia declared. 'Sherry, whisky?'

'Tea!' he said.

'Tea it will be,' Sonia said. She went ahead of him into the kitchen. She was pleased Samuel had taken her advice. People didn't normally ask Sonia's advice, let alone take it.

Samuel pulled a thick envelope out of his pocket. 'I took some money out of the building society,' he told Sonia, 'because it occurred to me that you would need to pay for the vacuum cleaner and the washing machine, and these stores do not seem willing to accept cash on delivery any more, or indeed a cheque without a card, and you would not be allowed to use mine, would you?'

'Oh. Thanks, Samuel. The washing machine as well?'

'Yes, do go ahead and buy it. I thought there would be no need to wait for the kitchen to be done, my dear, because in the meantime we could have the machine plumbed into my workshed. There is already a sink out there, so it would not be too difficult. Otherwise you may have to wait months for it.'

'Oh, great!' Sonia rejoiced. She beamed at him. 'I phoned round today about a vacuum cleaner, Samuel. I know where to get it from. I can go there tomorrow.'

'Make sure you take a taxi,' Samuel told her. 'Take the money for it out of this. Did you find my shoes? Did they turn up, once we had stopped looking for them?'

Sonia turned slowly away from him and concentrated on emptying out the teapot. She had forgotten. Here she was welcoming him home, celebrating his retirement, getting excited over buying a new vacuum, and this was the man who, last night, had crept out into the garden and taken a carving knife to her daughter's toys.

'Yes,' she said. 'I found them. In the dining room.'

'Oh,' he said. 'Was that where you had left them? We didn't think of looking there this morning, did we?'

'Samuel,' Sonia said, 'they were covered in mud. They were by the door leading out into the garden. Your dressing gown is muddy too.'

'My dressing gown?' he said. 'Why on earth would my dressing gown be muddy?'

'I don't know if you don't,' Sonia said. 'All I know is that somebody slashed up Lois's toys with a carving knife in the night, and that I heard you going downstairs at half-past two, and this morning your shoes are muddy and your dressing gown is too.'

He stared at her. His mouth opened. 'I don't understand,' he said. 'Surely . . .'

235

'Samuel!' Lois roared, hurling herself at him. She jumped on to his lap and flung her arms around his neck. 'I've got a fire in my cellar – come and see!'

Over the top of her head, Samuel's eyes met Sonia's. He seemed completely bewildered. Sonia looked at him for a moment and then shrugged. 'I don't understand it either,' she said.

'Come and see!' Lois pleaded, sliding off his lap and tugging at his hand.

He glanced at Sonia, waiting for permission. She shrugged again. Slowly he followed Lois out of the room and upstairs. Sonia went to the larder, took out a cauliflower and reached for the kitchen knife. She examined the blade of it for a second, ran her finger along it to test the sharpness, then plunged it into the cauliflower, dismembered it and gouged out the heart. She set a pan of water on to boil. Supper would not be long.

Chapter Thirty-Three

They all went to bed at about ten o'clock. Samuel phoned Gertrude before he went up, to tell her the good news about his retirement. While he was on the phone, Sonia went into the kitchen and opened the knife drawer. She took out the carving knife and the big kitchen knife she had used for the cauliflower.

Taking off her sweatshirt, she wrapped the knives in it, and walked upstairs in her jeans and T-shirt, waving goodnight to Samuel as she went. She sent Lois into the bathroom and told her to run the bath and while Lois was out of the room she hid the knives, still wrapped in the sweatshirt, at the back of the wardrobe.

Lois wanted to play in the bath and was annoyed when Sonia soaped her briskly, gave her one minute to 'swim' the soap off, and lifted her out.

'You didn't even give me any talc,' she complained, as Sonia handed her her pyjamas.

'We're out of talc.'

'You should have got some more today, in that shop,' Lois told her.

'Don't give me any trouble, Lois. I'm tired tonight. Go and get into bed now, while I have my bath.'

'I want to stay and talk to you,' Lois said.

'No, you go . . . yes, all right. Stay and talk.' It was nonsense, of course, to worry about Lois being in the bedroom on her own with Samuel in the house and Sonia locked in the bathroom. Her nerves were in shreds tonight. In shreds. Like the torn tepee and ripped masks. Like the splintered wood. 'Stay with me and talk,' she told Lois. She was not going to take any chances.

There was no lock on the door of their bedroom, as there had been no lock on their door at the Grenvilles' house, where Sonia had kept a chair-back jammed under the handle because Eddie had made suggestive invitations and his room was in the same wing. She used to push another chair against the door of the wardrobe there, because it used to swing open in the middle of the night, creaking, which made her feel spooked.

'Lois, you can sleep in with me tonight,' Sonia said, but Lois didn't want to.

'I'm sleeping with my dolly,' she said. 'There's no room for you.'

Perhaps that was safer. If Samuel came in to knife them to death, he would go for Sonia first; her bed was nearer the door. It might give Lois time to escape. She shook her head impatiently, as if to shake out the thoughts.

How could she suspect Samuel of such a thing? Her imagination was certainly running wild. They were perfectly safe in this house. Anyway, she had hidden the knives – though not the tools in his shed, chisels and mallets and saws of all sizes.

Go to sleep, she told herself. Before you know it, it will be morning and you'll wonder what the hell you were so worried about last night.

She must have been asleep for only an hour or so when she awoke with a start. 'What's that?' she exclaimed, fumbling for the bedside light.

It was Lois, sitting up in bed, retching.

'Oh, not again!' Sonia said, scrambling out of bed. 'Oh, Lois!'

The child's small face was screwed up with misery. Sonia grabbed the bucket she had left in the room after clearing up last night's mess, and reached Lois just in time. She was very sick.

'Lois, what is the matter with you?' Sonia whispered. She sat on the bed beside the child with her arm round her. Lois was shaking and sweaty. 'Is something wrong?' Sonia asked her. 'Something upsetting you, in this house?'

Lois opened her mouth and let out a loud wail.

'Sssh!' Sonia begged her. 'You'll wake Samuel.'

It was too late. She could hear Samuel moving around in his room. Lois screamed and was sick again.

'I'm going to get the doctor,' Sonia decided. This was no ordinary stomach upset. The child was really ill. She threw on her dressing gown, pulled the chair away from the door, and went out on to the landing.

'Cree!' shouted Samuel. 'Cree!'

'Oh my God!' Sonia gasped, jumping back against the wall. He was there on the landing, wild-haired and wild-eyed, waving his arms at her and shouting. Behind her, in the bedroom, Lois howled and clutched her stomach. Sonia pulled the bedroom door shut. If Samuel was going to knife her, she would get knifed. He was not going anywhere near Lois.

'Samuel,' she said, her voice cracking. 'It's Sonia. I'm not Cree, whoever Cree is. All right?'

He was not looking at her, but through her. She glanced over her shoulder nervously, but there was no one there that she could see. He began groaning like someone in pain, but standing bolt upright and still staring through her. Sonia felt her flesh go cold. The groans became louder, rising into a shout. 'Aaaaah! Cree! Cree!'

His room didn't lock; she couldn't lock him in his room. The dining room door could be locked. Could she get him into the dining room, lock him in, and phone somebody?

He lunged towards her suddenly. 'Get the children out!' he roared. 'Save the children!'

Sonia flattened herself against the bedroom door, her arms spread out across it. He wasn't saving Lois from anybody, she determined, gritting her teeth; least of all from her mother. She could hear Lois wailing, calling, 'Sonia! Mummy!' from within the room.

'Samuel!' she said, in a loud schoolmistressy voice. 'Stop this immediately. You're frightening the child.'

To her relief, he stopped where he was. It could be coincidence, of course; he still didn't seem to be seeing her.

'The child!' he murmured. Then, in another roar, 'Save the child! Cree! Cree!'

'Downstairs, Samuel!' Sonia shouted. 'Go downstairs and save the child! Run!' She lurched towards him, waving her arms. 'Go! Quick!' If Lois heard this, the poor child would think Sonia had gone crazy as well, but it seemed the only way to lure Samuel away from her.

Amazingly, he turned and headed for the stairs. She followed him, holding on to his arm to steady him so he didn't fall, and pushing him forward so he couldn't turn back. It was finely judged. He obviously couldn't see where he was going; twice she thought he would slip out of her grasp and fall headlong down the stairs. Once she was almost tempted to let it happen, when he wheeled round and screamed, 'Fetch the knives!'

Instead, she used his loss of balance to push him backwards down a few more stairs to the little landing in the hall, where they had to turn left to descend the last three steps. 'Over there!' she yelled, pointing him towards the dining room. 'Cree is coming! Run!'

Standing on the landing, she reached over and ran her hand across the ledge on top of the grandfather clock, closing her fingers gratefully round the dining room door key.

Samuel, standing in the hall below her now, looked bemused. She jumped down the last three steps, shouting, 'Run!' and he looked startled, turning this way and that. She was afraid he would suddenly bolt in the wrong direction. His eyes were completely unfocused, frightening.

Her hands shook as she fitted the key into the lock and opened the door. 'In there!' she croaked at him. 'Save the children! Cree's coming!'

'Aaah!' he shouted again. She got behind him and pushed him into the room, slamming the door and locking it again from the outside. She could hear him stumbling around the room, bumping into furniture, groaning and shouting.

'Oh God!' she said under her breath. 'If you help me now I'll start really believing in you – I promise.'

She ran upstairs, pulled Lois out of bed and said, 'Get under the bed, Lois, and don't move.' The child, sick and silent, made no protest. Sonia bundled her under the bed, pulled off a blanket and tucked it around her, and threw another blanket from her own bed across Lois's bed so that it hung down to the floor, screening the child from sight.

'What's happening?' Lois whimpered.

'Samuel's gone mad,' she said bluntly. As Lois opened her mouth, Sonia warned her, 'I'm telling you, Lois, don't make a sound. This is one time you have to do what I say. Promise me.'

The child, with terrified eyes, nodded.

'Stay there,' Sonia told her, 'and you'll be all right. I'm going to get some help.'

'Don't go!' Lois cried.

'Only to the phone,' Sonia promised. 'I'll come straight back to you in one minute. Don't move from there.'

She ran downstairs again. There was no sound from the dining room. She listened at the door. Nothing. He must have calmed down; perhaps he had even fallen asleep. Or knocked himself out against the furniture?

Sonia had picked up the phone and was reaching for the dial when she realized she didn't know who to phone. The address book was open. The first name that caught her eye was Gertrude's. Samuel must have opened the book at her number when he phoned her this evening. She had time to wonder why he didn't know the number by heart; it was like Samuel to double-check something he well knew.

She dialled the number quickly, glancing over her shoulder at the dining room door. It remained closed, and there was no sound from within, nor from Lois upstairs. For a moment, she wondered if she was the one going mad – if she had imagined the whole thing. Then she heard a banging and rattling sound from the dining room. The ringing tone began, at the end of the phone. It rang and rang.

'Hurry up!' Sonia breathed. She willed Gertrude to wake up and answer it. 'Gertrude!' she pleaded, aloud. 'Come on! Help me!'

Just as she was about to give up hope and call the police instead, the ringing tone stopped and a sleepy voice said, 'Yes?' Thank God, Sonia thought, it was Gertrude's voice, not Humphrey's.

'Gertrude?' she choked. 'Is that you?'

'Yes? Who . . .'

'It's Sonia. Gertrude, Samuel has gone mad.'

'What?'

Sonia started crying. She was trying so hard to get the words out quickly that they got stuck.

The voice on the end of the phone woke up. 'What kind of mad?' said Gertrude briskly. Sonia felt relieved.

'He's shouting and running around the house, shouting things like "Save the children" and also he slashed Lois's toys to bits in the garden . . .'

'Oh good Lord,' said Gertrude.

'What am I going to do?' Sonia sobbed. 'Should I call the police or what?'

'Wait a minute, let me think,' Gertrude said. 'Where is he?'

'Locked in the dining room.'

'Where's Lois?'

'Hiding under the bed in our room.'

'You poor child!' said Gertrude, with sympathy.

'Gertrude, has this ever happened before?' Sonia asked.

'No . . . wait a minute!' Gertrude exclaimed, as if suddenly inspired. 'Malaria! It could be.'

'*Malaria!*' Sonia shouted, the tension making her explode. This family was completely cuckoo. Why had she thought Gertrude could help? 'Even I know you don't get bloody malaria in Camberwell! This might be the urban jungle, Gertrude, but it isn't the mosquito-infested swamp, is it?'

'It's a recurring virus,' said Gertrude, quite calmly. (How dare she be calm? She didn't have to cope with this, waiting for Samuel to break down the door of the dining room and burst through it shouting, 'Cree!') 'Samuel contracted it when he was out east, years ago, and he's had attacks at intervals since. Not for some years now, though. But it could be that, Sonia. It makes him delirious. It took six men to hold him down the last time.'

'Well, I'm here on my own with Lois!' Sonia shouted. 'What am I going to do?'

'Send for Dr Carroll,' Gertrude said. 'He saw Samuel through the last attack; he'll know if that's what it is. Don't be put off with any locum services. His private number will be in Samuel's address book; he gave it to him, I know. Do you have that book in front of you?'

'Yes, I do.'

'Good. Well, I'll stay on the phone while you find it. Look under D.'

Sonia began to feel slightly reassured. 'I've found it,' she said.

'Are there two numbers there?'

'Yes.'

'Read them out to me.'

'The first one is seven three three . . .'

'No, it's the other one. How does that one begin?'

'Two nine nine . . .'

'That's the one, Sonia. Ring that number, and say it's an emergency.'

'He won't answer his home phone at night, will he?' Sonia didn't believe this. Doctors did not give out their private numbers to their patients. They employed central answering services to put people off.

'Give it a try, my dear. Let it ring for a while. If not, then ring the surgery number and you'll get the doctor on call. Dr Carroll doesn't give out his home number to everybody, so he'll know it's urgent if it does ring. If he doesn't answer, he may be out on another call.'

'He might be drunk,' Sonia said. 'Mrs Atwood said he drinks.' She was hanging on to the receiver, not wanting to let go of Gertrude. It was wasting time, she knew, but she felt safer with Gertrude's voice on the end of the line.

'Call me back and let me know,' Gertrude said. 'If I don't hear within fifteen minutes I shall call you.' She cut Sonia off.

Sonia waited and listened. There was no sound now from the dining room. The house was deathly quiet; she jumped when the grandfather clock gave a slightly louder tick. Trying to be as quiet as she could, she dialled the doctor's home number, pressing the receiver to her ear as if to muffle the ringing.

It was answered quickly: 'Hello?' The voice was gruff, unfriendly. Well, no wonder; it was twenty to twelve.

'Is that Dr Carroll?'

'Yes. Who's that?'

'Sonia . . . um . . . Mr Samuel Arnold's housekeeper. He's a patient of yours; you gave him your home phone number . . .'

'What's wrong with him?'

'He's gone mad.'

'What do you mean, gone mad?' The voice was cool, unimpressed.

Sonia got angry, because she was afraid he wouldn't take her seriously, that he would hang up and leave her with this unpredictable Samuel whom she did not know. 'His cousin thinks it might be an attack of malaria,' she said, her voice rising. 'He keeps shouting and he's not himself, and last night he took a big knife and slashed my little girl's toys to bits, and she's in the house now, and if you don't get out here, Doctor, I'm going to go mad myself because I don't know what to do!'

There was a brief pause. 'I'm on my way,' he said.

Sonia put the phone down and sank to the floor; her knees gave way beneath her. 'Thank God,' she whispered.

A loud hammering on the front door made her jump to her feet, clutching her dressing gown around her protectively.

'Open this door!' Samuel shouted. 'You cowards! Let me at you!'

Sonia burst into tears. She ran to the dining room door and unlocked it. The outer door was wide open. Why hadn't she thought of that? He had let himself out that way last night, and now he had done it again. She went to shut the door, to

244

shut him out in the garden, but as she came near it she heard the sound of heavy panting breaths and she ran back into the hall, closing the dining room door. Before she had time to lock it, it was wrenched out of her grasp. She screamed and ran up the stairs to the bedroom, standing inside the room with her back against the door.

Gertrude had said it had taken six men to hold him down, the last time. Sonia heard Lois sobbing under the bed. Would it be safer to put her in the wardrobe? But the child would probably panic and scream. It was better to stay with her. She crawled under Lois's bed, pulled the child against her and covered Lois's mouth with her hand.

'Try not to make any noise,' she whispered into her ear. 'It'll be over soon, Lois; the doctor is coming.'

'Is Samuel sick?' Lois sobbed.

'Sssh. Yes. Yes, he's kind of sick. Stay quiet now, Lois.'

'I know you're there!' Samuel roared, bursting into the room. 'You can't fool me with your damned stalking! Come out and face the music, like gentlemen!'

Gentlemen? Sonia thought. Who was he talking to? Did he think he was chasing her and Lois, then, or someone else entirely? Was it all some fantasy?

He had done what she told him before. If she went out, could she calm him down, lead him away from Lois again, get to the door to let the doctor in? She could hear the phone ringing. If she didn't answer it, Gertrude wouldn't know what was happening. Would she call the police, ask them to break the door down?

'Are you in there?' Samuel bellowed. Sonia heard him fling open the door of the wardrobe and sweep its contents on to the floor. She held her breath.

'Aha!' she heard him mutter. 'So that's where you've hidden the weapons, you scoundrels!'

Sonia pulled Lois's head round to face her, put a warning finger against her lips, and crawled out from under the bed. Samuel, knife in hand, was creeping stealthily towards the window alcove. Sonia got there ahead of him, and pulled back the curtains swiftly. If she stood against the window, maybe the doctor would see them when he arrived and would call the police or would break down the door himself and get Lois to safety.

Samuel, jumping at the sudden noise, lunged at the curtain and stuck the knife into it. 'Got you!' he shouted.

Sonia struggled with the handle on the casement window and pushed it open. Samuel wheeled round. His eyes were still completely unfocused. 'Where are you?' he shouted. 'Come out!'

'I'm here!' Sonia shouted. 'I surrender!'

He hesitated for a second. She could tell that he could hear her but he couldn't see her. He was looking at something beyond her. She moved to one side. His eyes didn't follow her.

'Come out, you cowards!' he roared.

Sonia moved round beside him. She felt safer now she knew she was invisible. 'Samuel,' she whispered, 'go very slowly. They're coming out. They're surrendering.'

'Aah!' he said sharply. Was this going to work? Was he suddenly going to wheel round and plunge that knife into her ribs?

'Samuel,' she said again, 'I'm on your side. I'm the relief troop. You've won the battle. Let me finish it off for you. They're surrendering.'

'Never surrender,' said Samuel staunchly.

'It's time now,' Sonia said. 'Put down your weapons. You've won. They won't give us any more trouble.'

He didn't move. Sonia knew she had to finish this quickly; she was too tired to go on. She decided to take the risk of confronting him. If it didn't work, he would see her as the enemy, but that would also finish it. She just wanted the episode finished.

She stood in front of him. 'Look at me, Samuel,' she commanded. The hand holding the knife inched forward, grazing her ribs. She stepped back a pace. 'The enemy has surrendered,' she said, in a sergeant-major voice. 'I command you to put down your weapons.'

A faint light stirred in the desert wastes of his eyes. 'The child?' he murmured. 'Safe?'

'The children are perfectly safe, Samuel,' Sonia said. Her voice came out in a kind of singsong, like a mother crooning a lullaby to an infant. 'You can go back to bed. You give me what you've got in your hand and go back to bed like a good boy.'

He stretched out his hand to her, like somebody in a dream, and let her take the knife from him. Then he turned and walked out of the room, very slowly, very tired. He turned right along the landing, and left into his own room.

Following him, Sonia saw him take off his dressing gown and climb into the high bed. He lay down and closed his eyes. He looked suddenly very young, like a small child.

Sonia returned to their room, picked up the other knife and the toys Samuel had swept out of the wardrobe, and replaced the toys. She wrapped both knives up again in her sweatshirt, moving slowly and deliberately, calming herself down with familiar movements, setting herself to rights before approaching Lois.

Lois, still under the bed, was limp and heavy. Sonia had to drag her out. She offered no resistance but hung like a dead weight when Sonia picked her up, and lay unmoving on the bed when she put her down. Sonia pulled the blanket over her, tidied up the bed.

'It's over now, Lois,' she said. 'Relax. You're quite safe.'

The child looked at her with unseeing eyes, as Samuel had done, and then closed them wearily.

Sonia went out of the room, taking the knives with her, still wrapped in the sweatshirt; she pulled the door shut behind her, took one final look at Samuel in his room, and went downstairs to phone Gertrude.

Chapter Thirty-Four

'He's calmed down. I'm waiting for the doctor to arrive,' Sonia told Gertrude.

'Are you sure you don't want me to come up?'

'No, we'll be fine. Thanks anyway, Gertrude. Listen, can you tell me who Cree is?'

'Cree? Is that a Christian name or a surname?'

'I don't know. It might not even be a person. It's what Samuel kept shouting.'

'Cree, cree,' said Gertrude musingly. 'It doesn't sound like a name, does it? No one I know.'

'Does the word mean anything then?'

'No. Well, "*cri*" is French for cry, but I shouldn't think that has anything to do with it. "*Cri de coeur*", you know.'

'Cree what?' Sonia asked. 'What you just said . . .?'

'*Cri de coeur*. A cry from the heart,' Gertrude said.

'Oh. And, Gertrude, one more thing. Has Samuel ever got violent like this before? With Miss Prynne?'

'Certainly not, my dear. Miss Prynne would have told me, I'm sure. She was not one for suffering anything in silence.'

Sonia shivered. 'And she did just retire? I mean, did you see her leave?'

Gertrude hooted with laughter. 'My dear Sonia, you surely don't think Samuel did her in? No, she's safely ensconced in a nursing home. I have been to visit her – not that she recognized me. I am sorry; I should not have laughed. After the night you have had, I can see it would not be unreasonable to think anything. But I assure you, I am quite puzzled over this. It is so uncharacteristic of Samuel. Utterly foreign to his nature. There must be some cause, if only we knew it.'

'Do you think he's going senile?'

'Could be.' Gertrude sighed. 'Could be. I suppose it can happen to us all. But shouting and brandishing knives? I would have said pigs would fly before Samuel would do any such thing. But there we are. I shall phone you in the morning, Sonia, but if in the meantime there are any further disturbances, please don't hesitate to call me.'

'Okay. Thanks, Gertrude.'

The doctor took his time. Sonia, sitting shivering on the stairs, was beginning to wonder if he had forgotten them and gone back to sleep, when there was a cautious knock on the door.

Dr Carroll was a short, stocky man with purplish red veins on his face, a brusque manner (he shot through the doorway like the SAS storming a building, and stamped his feet on the mat) and rheumy eyes which, however, met Sonia's gaze candidly. Not a man to waste time, she assessed him.

'Where is he?'

'He's upstairs now, in bed. He's calmed down.'

The doctor was already halfway up the stairs. Sonia was afraid that, seeing Samuel peacefully asleep, he might think she had raised a false alarm. 'He was outside the house, hammering on the door, and then he got a knife and was telling us to come out and fight like gentlemen,' she informed the doctor hastily.

He raised his eyebrows. 'Are you alone in the house?'

'No, my little girl's in bed; she's sick. She was terrified.'

'Not surprised,' he grunted. He knew his way to Samuel's room. Sonia caught a glimpse of Samuel lying in bed with his eyes closed before she found the door shut firmly in her face. Evidently she was not part of the consultation between doctor and patient.

Lois was lying on her side, hot and fretful. When Sonia offered her a drink she said she would like one, but when Sonia brought it to her she took one sip and turned her head aside. Her eyes were filled with tears. She pushed Sonia away when she tried to cuddle her.

'Are you still frightened?' Sonia asked.

Lois shook her head.

'Samuel is in bed now,' Sonia told her, 'and the doctor is with him. He won't frighten you any more tonight.'

'I'm not frightened of *Samuel*,' said Lois contemptuously.

'So what were you frightened of, then, Lois?'

'*No!*' Lois said furiously. '*Samuel* was frightened.'

'Oh. Yes, I suppose that was it. He was frightened of something, wasn't he? It wasn't anything to do with us. But what was he frightened of, Lois, do you know?'

Lois shrugged. 'Ask him.'

'Did he ever mention anyone to you called Cree, Lois? Do you remember him saying that name?'

'I feel sick,' Lois said.

'Sit up, then, quick. Here's the bucket.'

Lois retched and shuddered and sweated, but could not throw up. She fell back against the pillow, exhausted. Dr Carroll came in. He took one look at Lois and asked Sonia, 'How long has she been like this?'

'A few nights. She's okay in the daytimes. A bit tired, that's all.'

'You should have called me before,' he said roughly. He walked towards the bed. Lois put her hands over her face and slid out of bed, crouching on the floor.

'She's shy of strangers,' Sonia apologized.

'I'll have to examine her,' the doctor said. 'Has she had any diarrhoea?'

'No, she hasn't. Lois, stand up. Let the doctor look at you.'

Lois remained hunched on the floor, covering her eyes. Sonia caught hold of her shoulder. 'Lois,' she said, 'now that the doctor is here, I want you to let him have a look at you. Do you hear me? Take your hands away and stand up. He wants to look at your tummy, so he can make you better.'

She pulled Lois to her feet. Lois stood there for a moment, peeping through her fingers at Sonia, then suddenly, as if making an instantaneous decision, she uncovered her face, stared straight at the doctor, pulled down her pyjama trousers and pointed at her genitals, sticking her tummy out. In an adult it would have looked provocative. In a four-year-old it looked strangely pathetic.

'Lois!' said Sonia despairingly. It was no good hitting the child; that didn't work. She had done her best with Lois. Now let the doctor deal with it. Sonia burst into tears and ran out of the room.

When she had recovered herself, she washed her face in the bathroom, looked in on Samuel and saw him fast asleep, and returned to the bedroom. Lois was sitting up in bed with the doctor's stethoscope around her neck. She was smiling happily.

'. . . so you haven't got the measles,' the doctor was saying to her, 'or we wouldn't see you for spots. So what do you think it is, eh, Lois? What would make you feel better now?'

'To play with my dolls' house,' Lois said.

'Where is it? Oh yes, this is a fine mansion,' he teased her, picking it up and placing it in front of her on the bed. 'What's this elegant object here?'

'It's a boiler,' Lois said, 'with fire in it.'

'Of course it is,' Dr Carroll said. 'I should have seen that at once. I'll leave you to play then, Lois, and I'll call in and see you tomorrow. I'll just take this stethoscope back, in case someone else needs their chest sounded in the meantime. Night-night.'

'Night,' said Lois absently, busily moving figures around the dolls' house.

Sonia had started crying again, and could not stop. She moved towards Lois but the doctor held her back. 'A word with you,' he said, 'downstairs.'

When they reached the hall, Sonia stopped to hear what he had to say, but he gestured her onwards. 'In the kitchen,' he said.

Walking down the passage he stumbled and almost fell, knocking his shoulder against the wall and just saving himself. Sonia turned to catch him and smelt whisky on his breath. Strong. Nervously she switched on lights in the passage, and both kitchen lights. Surely this night had held enough night-mares already? There couldn't be more – could there?

'Would you like a cup of coffee?' she asked.

'No. I have to make another call.'

Sonia, as always when she felt cornered, attacked. 'In that state?' she said. 'They won't be exactly delighted to see you, will they?'

He glared at her, then relaxed. 'Most of my patients are used to me,' he said. 'This case is a home delivery. The mother has five children already; she knows what to do.'

'Oh, so you're just there to wet the baby's head,' said Sonia sarcastically. 'Aren't you meant to wait till the baby's arrived before you drink the toast?'

He stood and looked at her squarely for a full minute. 'Put the kettle on,' he said. 'I'll have the coffee. Black. I'll use the phone and tell the service to send out a locum till I can get there.'

Do this, do that, Sonia thought aggressively. I'll use the phone. Not 'May I?' But then of course it was not her phone, was it? No one needed to ask her permission in this house. She was only the housekeeper.

Even while she was thinking these thoughts, she knew she was only trying to keep herself angry so that he could not talk to her about Lois. She was trying to discredit him – the irres-ponsible drunk – so she wouldn't have to take seriously any-thing he said. But he wouldn't accept the role, not even though his face was flushed, his nose red and his breath 40 per cent malt.

'Sit down,' Dr Carroll ordered her, returning to the kitchen. She sat, glowering at him and looking as uncooperative as she knew how to.

'First of all,' he said, 'Mr Arnold does not have malaria; there's no fever. I've given him an injection, a sedative, and we'll have to see how he is in the morning. It would appear to have been dementia rather than delirium.'

'What does that mean? Senile?' Sonia asked. It was safer to talk about Samuel than about Lois.

He shrugged. 'It sounds like it. We can take him into hospital for a brain scan, see if there's any pathological reason why he should suddenly behave like that, but he's best left where he is for tonight. Now the little girl . . .'

'Coffee,' said Sonia, jumping up. She busied herself fetching cups from the larder, though there were two clean ones on the draining board.

'That child has been sexually abused,' Dr Carroll said. Sonia dropped a cup.

'She hasn't,' she said, breathless from stooping to retrieve it from the floor. It wasn't broken. 'That's ridiculous.'

There was a pause, during which Sonia washed and dried the cup and refused to look round.

Finally he said, 'You seem very sure.'

'I am.'

'How can you be sure?' he asked. 'A mother can't be with her child the whole time.'

'How can you make stupid suggestions,' Sonia snapped, 'about things you know nothing about?'

'Unfortunately,' he said, 'I know more about the subject than I would like to. It is all too common. Fathers, uncles, teachers, strangers . . . Mothers as well. All have been known to abuse children, and children who are much loved, at that.'

'If you're suggesting,' Sonia spat at him, 'that I would lay a finger on my own daughter and upset her and make her sick and terrified, then you need your head examining!'

He continued to look at her, drumming his fingers on the table. Anxiously, she reviewed what she had said. She hadn't said anything. She mustn't get angry. He might be drunk, but he was quite lucid. She must keep her head.

'And what would it mean if you had?' he asked her. 'That you were a bad mother?'

'Of course it would.' She heard her voice come out quite calmly. There wasn't a problem.

'Would it really?' He sounded interested. 'Or would it mean that you were a person under unusual strain, who had not quite managed to protect the child from your own stress?'

He was pushing her into a corner. This was worse than the truth. How could he think that? Mothers did not submit their children to sexual abuse. Everybody knew only men did that. Didn't they?

She set the coffee down in front of him. 'Drink that,' she said. 'It'll sober you up, maybe.'

He caught hold of her wrist in a grip so hard that she yelped. 'Don't patronize me,' he said.

Temper rose in her again. 'Look at you!' she said. 'Turning up to examine children, drunk. And people let you get away with it, do they? No one complains. Well, I'm complaining, I tell you. You could do more harm than good.'

'Oh, plenty of people complain,' he said wearily. 'I'm on my last warning from the Medical Council. One more serious complaint would finish me. You're in a very strong position, lady.'

She stared at him. Why was he telling her this? He was as bad as Gertrude for handing Sonia all the aces, when she wouldn't have known he had them in his hand.

'But whether or not you are going to do that,' he continued, 'I am going to get this sorted out. Tomorrow you may change your doctor, and welcome; that's your right. But tonight that child is my patient and I am telling you, drunk or sober, I know in my bones that child has been sexually abused, and what's more I know that you know it too. So either you sit down and stop wasting my time, or it's going to be a very long night for both of us, because I'm going to sit here until I hear the truth.'

There was a silence. Sonia sat down. Her hands went up over her face and covered her eyes.

'Well?' he said.

Sonia put down her hands and looked him in the eyes. 'Okay,' she said quietly. 'I'll tell you the truth.'

Chapter Thirty-Five

'It wasn't me,' she said. 'I wouldn't do that. I have hit her once or twice, under stress, but I wouldn't treat her in that way, honest. Do you believe me?'

He gave her a shrewd glance. 'Is there any reason why I shouldn't? Do you normally tell the truth?'

'Not always,' she said. 'But if you're not going to believe me now, there's no point in telling you. I've lied about it to everybody else.'

He nodded. 'Tell me the truth. I'll believe you.'

'Will Lois be taken away from me?'

'I don't know. It depends on what the truth is. I should think it's extremely unlikely,' he said.

She couldn't be sure she had heard him right. 'Unlikely or likely?'

'Unlikely. Unless for some reason you would benefit from the break from responsibility, in which case the separation would be temporary and you and the child would both receive help, for however long those experts judged it necessary.'

She was relieved that he didn't give her blithe reassurances but spelled out the bad news clearly. It was helpful to know the worst that could happen instead of indulging in fearful imaginings.

'Okay,' she said. 'Well, I didn't abuse Lois in that way, and I don't think I ever would, no matter how much stress. You say women do, but I never heard of that happening. But still. Those women that do are probably no worse than me, because I am not good for Lois, in other ways. I am a bad influence.'

He raised his eyebrows but made no comment.

Sonia began twisting her cup round and round on the table,

then stopped herself. She would have to go through with this, she told herself sternly, with no cop-outs, no distracting fidgets, no equivocations. It was time for the truth to be told, hard though it was, and nothing could be allowed to make it easier.

'At the last place we worked,' Sonia began, letting out a deep sigh, 'there was . . .'

He interrupted her. 'We?'

'Lois and me.'

'How did Lois work? She's only . . . what? Five?'

'Four.' She stared at him. Why was he picking fault with what she'd said? She hadn't even started. He ought to be afraid he'd put her off, make her clam up again. 'Lois didn't work, of course,' she said impatiently. 'I was the cook-housekeeper there, like I am here. We lived in the house.'

'Ah,' he said. 'So it was Lois's home, as well as yours, but your job.'

She shook her head despairingly. 'Of course.'

'You think I'm mad,' he said affably, 'but the way we talk about things is quite important, isn't it? You said, "where *we* worked", you see, as though Lois somehow shared your job.'

'Well, she did,' said Sonia, annoyed. 'She shares my life, and the job is part of it.'

'She also has her own life,' Dr Carroll said, 'as well as sharing yours. And she can't, of course, share your job. That's your job, keeping house, keeping the employer happy, isn't it? Not hers. Her job is being a child, playing, being noisy, being a nuisance at times, being protected. Isn't it?'

Sonia went silent. She thought she could see what he was driving at, and she didn't know how to answer it. He waited.

'It's difficult,' she said finally, 'living in somebody else's house. They're the boss. If you don't do the job they want, you're out on the street. That's what happened to us, before we came here. We were just thrown out.'

'Yes,' he said. 'It certainly is difficult. Why do you say you are a bad influence on Lois?'

He was acute enough, she had to admit, even when he had

had too much to drink, which he undoubtedly had. He was taking in all she said. There would be no chance of telling him tomorrow that he had imagined it.

'Because,' Sonia said slowly, 'of sex.'

'She saw you having sex with men?' he suggested.

'No!' she said, repulsed. 'I didn't mean that.'

'What do you mean?'

'You keep interrupting me,' she said fretfully. 'I can't think what I'm trying to say.'

'I won't interrupt any more. Carry on.'

It was harder than she had thought. He had been suggesting things that hadn't happened, as if trying to help her out with putting it into words, but they were the wrong things. What she had to express could not so easily be translated into phrases.

'There was this man there,' she said. She looked at Dr Carroll but he said nothing. Perhaps it was harder without the interruptions, after all. 'He was the gardener and handyman. Eddie Barnes. He had been there longer than us. He was good at his job. They – the couple we . . . I . . . worked for – were always afraid of losing him. It was hard to get good gardeners who were good at maintenance and things around the house as well.'

'Harder than getting good housekeepers?' the doctor asked, breaking his promise not to interrupt her narrative.

'Yes,' she said, relieved that he had. 'They'd lost quite a few of those. Partly because the woman was difficult to work for, but maybe partly because of Eddie as well.' She hesitated, hoping for more help.

'He had an eye for the women?' Dr Carroll asked.

'Yes.'

'Was he pushy? Persuasive?'

Sonia burst into tears again. 'Yes,' she sobbed.

'And you gave in?'

'No-ooo!' she wailed. 'I didn't give in. But I nearly . . . I *wanted* to, do you understand me?'

He grimaced. 'Was that so bad?'

'*Yes!*' she said. 'I didn't *like* him.'

Another pause. The doctor had not reacted, Sonia saw; he couldn't have understood.

'He wasn't a good man,' she said, in further explanation. 'I couldn't like him, or respect him, or nothing.'

'But you wanted to sleep with him?'

'Yes.'

'And that makes you bad? A bad influence on Lois?'

'Of course it does,' she said. 'Children are affected by their parents, aren't they? Not just what the parents do, but what they have in their heart.'

He said nothing. She stared at him helplessly.

'If you don't understand that, then I don't know how to explain to you.'

'I understand,' Dr Carroll said, 'that being young, healthy and probably extremely lonely, you felt sexually attracted to somebody you didn't like. Also that you resisted sleeping with him, this household celebrity whose employers would do anything rather than risk losing him – which is entirely to your credit in my view, and certainly not a bad influence on your child. Quite the opposite, wouldn't you say?'

Sonia was puzzled by this interpretation. 'But you don't know what happened,' she said.

'Tell me what happened then.'

Sonia gulped. 'Lois began chasing after him,' she said. 'She wouldn't leave him alone.'

'So?'

'Look, I don't know how to put this,' Sonia confessed. 'I love Lois, you know? I don't want to make her sound . . .'

'Just say it,' the doctor advised. 'Don't worry about how it sounds.'

'She chased him,' Sonia said. 'She wouldn't leave him alone.'

'You've already said that,' he pointed out.

'Yes, but she was . . . I mean, I know children get attached to people and that. You would expect it to be . . . a father figure or something . . . but this wasn't like that.'

'What was it like?' he asked.

Sonia was sweating. She hoped Lois would forgive her for her disloyalty. I'm sorry, Lois, she said mentally; it's just that I can't cope with it by myself, not any more; it's too much to carry on my own.

'It was like she was in love with him,' she said in a rush. 'Like she was flirting, teasing him. Asking for it. She used to go up to him and unzip his flies. She kept asking him to come down to the cellar with her. She was like . . . not like a child.'

'I see,' he said. He drank his coffee.

'What happens to those kind of children?' Sonia asked. She was trembling. 'What do they do with them – these experts?'

He put down his cup. 'There's nothing wrong with your child,' he said simply.

'Don't tell me that!' said Sonia. 'I know there is. I'm not stupid. Other children don't act like that.'

'Abused children do,' he said. 'Look – let me get this straight. Bear with me for one moment, will you? What you are saying to me is – correct me if I'm not understanding you – that you felt bad in yourself, a bad woman, for wanting a sexual relationship with somebody, even somebody you couldn't respect or like. Yes?'

She nodded. The tears were very close again.

'You felt that, even while you were telling him to get lost, you were saying yes in your mind?'

She nodded again.

'And that somehow Lois was infected by these wicked impulses you had, so that she did in real life what you were only doing in your mind? Running after him, saying all right, yes, take me?'

Sonia choked. A sudden fit of coughing made the tears overflow. The doctor waited till she had finished. He continued. 'It didn't occur to you that it might not be your fault at all but that this man, furiously annoyed that you hadn't fallen in with his every whim, that you hadn't recognized how important he was in the household and how insignificant you were, but had actually had the strength of mind to tell him no, took revenge on you where you were most vulnerable?'

'What?' Sonia said, bemused.

'He punished you,' the doctor elucidated, 'by abusing your child. Hitting you where he knew it would hurt most.'

'No,' Sonia said. 'You don't understand. He didn't abuse her. Well, he might have . . . But she . . .'

'She abused him?' The doctor was shaking his head. He didn't believe her; she could see that.

'You don't think that's possible, do you?' Sonia said.

'No,' he said. 'I don't. Nor do I think there are any evil, wicked children, either naturally born so or because their evil, wicked mothers have been a bad influence. I think there are children whose actions are badly misunderstood and mis-interpreted, but that is entirely an adult misconception. Chil-dren, unfortunately, are the ones who suffer for it. They do not "act bad" until they have actually been taught to believe that they *are* bad. And who teaches them that? Adults. Confused and disturbed adults, generally.'

Sonia was not sure she was following him. 'I'm not saying it was Lois's fault,' she said earnestly. 'I'm saying it was my fault. And, yes, maybe I am confused and disturbed. I'm not saying I have been good for Lois; I told you I wasn't a good in-fluence. I had no mother myself, so I can believe you saying I taught her the wrong ways . . .'

'Whoa, whoa!' he cried. 'No, you're still not understanding me. Let's leave the question of who is to blame, shall we? Maybe everyone is, to some extent. Let's not worry about that for now, but stick to what actually happened. All right?'

'Okay,' she said. She was feeling very tired. 'I can't take in what you're saying,' she said. 'I can't understand you. Can we leave it till the morning?'

'No,' he said. 'You wouldn't sleep, not with this going round in your mind. Let's get it sorted out now, once and for all. Then you can sleep for a month, to make up for the anxiety. Right?'

'All right. But say it in ways I can understand,' she said. 'I didn't have much education. I can't understand these clever statements.'

'That's rubbish,' he said brusquely. 'You're a bright girl. It's not because this is clever that you can't grasp it; it's because it's a different way of looking at things. You've made up your mind that your way of seeing events is the only way. I'm telling you that it isn't. You've got it wrong. You will have to change. Okay?'

His rudeness and arrogance, she thought, were breathtaking.

'You're so sure you've got it right, are you?' she challenged. 'Seeing as you don't know me or Lois and you weren't even there at the time?'

'Yes,' he said. 'I'm sure your vision of a four-year-old vamp, child of an evilly lustful mother, is a complete delusion.'

'Her father was like that too,' Sonia said.

'Oho, was he?' said the doctor jovially. 'Well then, the plot thickens, doesn't it? *Two* evil parents. Obviously the child has bad blood in her, wouldn't you say? Try as she might, she can never hope to turn out anything but bad. The only surprise is she waited until she was all of four years old before attempting to rape an unwilling man, tantalizing him and dragging him into her cellar in order to act out on him her tormented fantasies. Is that it?'

Sonia stared at him sullenly. 'You may think it's funny,' she said. 'You wouldn't if it was your child.'

'I don't think it's funny,' he said, suddenly deadly serious. 'If you want to know, I think it's heartbreaking. It makes me extremely sad and extremely angry. It's ignorance – paganism – of the worst kind.'

Sonia wished the floor would cave in and swallow her into the bowels of the earth. She said nothing.

'So,' he said. 'Are you willing to reject this interpretation and look for another one? Will you accept an alternative?'

She was very ashamed. 'Yes,' she whispered.

'Right,' he said. 'Firstly, do you know what happens when an adult abuses a child?'

She burst into tears again. 'I don't like to think about it,' she said.

'Well, think now,' he said. 'What happens when an adult tells a child what to do? A good child?'

'The child obeys him,' she sobbed.

'Yes. And a bad child refuses – right?'

'Yes, but some things . . .'

'Don't interrupt,' he said sternly. 'I want you to take this one step at a time.'

'All right. Yes. A disobedient child refuses to do what she's told.'

'And what happens then?' he asked. 'What does the adult do, if the child refuses?'

Sonia bit back the tears. It was only prolonging matters, this crying. It was better to get the question and answer session over with, then she could go to bed and cry in privacy.

'The adult . . . um, the adult . . . tells the child off?' she suggested.

'Tells her off, shouts at her, hits her maybe. Or else promises her treats. Is that a possibility? A reward for being a good child and doing what she's told? Or maybe he threatens her. What could this man have threatened Lois with, do you think?'

'I don't know.' This was awful, Sonia thought. It made Lois out to be a helpless victim instead of a strong-minded child who knew how to say no to anything she didn't want to do. 'Lois doesn't normally do things she doesn't want,' she ventured.

'All that means is that the man would have had to use more force,' the doctor said, 'or more tactics. What would have worked for Lois, Sonia? Telling her that her mother would be upset if she didn't do what she was told? That her mother might lose her job and be thrown out of the house?'

'Oh God,' Sonia said. She put her head down on her arms and wept.

He waited.

'But why . . .?' she said finally.

'Why did Lois like him, run after him, unzip his trousers?'

'Yes. Surely, if he abused her, she would be frightened?'

'I don't know the answer to that,' the doctor said slowly. 'I really am not pretending to know all the answers, Sonia. As you say, I wasn't there and I don't know the child. But one thing I do know: the words you were using for her behaviour – what were they? Provocative, teasing, flirting, asking for it – that kind of thing?'

'Yes.'

'Those are adult words. You can't apply them to children. Children do ask for things: for approval, for love most of all, for treats, for adults not to carry out their threats . . . but they don't ask for sex. Not for its own sake. They don't need it. They can't cope with it. And they don't want it. It may look as though they do, but only to adult eyes. In the child's mind, her actions mean something else.'

'What?' Sonia asked. 'What did it mean, then, what Lois did?'

'You could ask her,' he suggested, 'but she might not tell you.'

'Why not? Why didn't she tell me at the time?' The tears would not stay checked. 'Why didn't she tell me,' she sobbed, 'so that I could stop it happening?'

'There could be a number of reasons,' the doctor said. 'It could be because she didn't know the words to tell you about it. It could be because she'd been threatened that something would happen to you, or to her, if she told. It could be that she did tell you – that she was acting it out, in front of your eyes – and you didn't want to listen, or to look, because you thought it meant she was bad.'

'God forgive me,' Sonia whispered.

'I am sure He does,' said Dr Carroll more gently. 'The difficult part is really forgiving yourself. You will have to try, though, for your own sake and for Lois's. And there is, of course, one further explanation of why she didn't tell you.'

'What's that?'

'It was something that happened in *her* life,' he said, 'not yours. It was not your business.'

'Not my business? I'm her mother! I'm there to protect her from things like this, aren't I?'

'Perhaps you did protect her from the worst thing that could have happened to her,' he said.

'What could be worse,' she said bitterly, 'than being abused by that man, without her mother rescuing her? With her mother even believing she was a bad child?'

'What could have been worse for Lois,' he said, very gently now, 'would be letting it happen to you. Don't you think she should be allowed to protect you too? If she wants to? Shouldn't she have that choice?'

'She's too young,' Sonia wept. 'She's only four years old!'

'It was still her life and her choice,' he told her. 'And maybe she was in a stronger position than you, or felt she was. You say you had no mother to care for you. Well, Lois has. She has had four years of being loved. A good, strong child, loved by a good mother. Yes – and you should believe it too, because she obviously does. Let her be generous to you if she wants to. But now you protect her – all right? – by making sure it never happens again.'

'How can I do that?' Sonia asked him. 'I couldn't the first time, could I?'

'No. But the second time you will. Firstly, you tell her – no, you *show* her – that it's all right to say no, even to an adult in authority, even to an employer, even when there's a risk of losing your home. You teach her that by doing it yourself. You take the risk of getting thrown out. It can happen anyway, can't it? Even when you both do go along with whatever you're told to do.'

'It happened because of that, last time,' Sonia said. 'Mrs Grenville didn't give me a reason for dismissing us . . . me. She said we were both evil and that I understood what she meant without her having to put it into distasteful words, and she told us to go. Immediately. I think she must have seen Lois with Eddie. That's what I thought, at the time.'

'Or seen Eddie with Lois,' he suggested. 'And not wanted

you to find out and make a scandal or have police in her house, or lose her gardener and handyman.'

'Yes,' Sonia said. 'What else do I have to do?'

'Stop undervaluing yourself,' he said. 'Stop looking for people to blame. Yes, you were partly responsible. So were the other adults in the house. But to walk around crippled with guilt is only going to teach Lois to do the same. At the moment she isn't. Children do what comes naturally. They have to be taught about guilt and blame. Don't teach her. That means unlearn it yourself. So, you didn't get it right. Next time you will. Meantime, you're already forgiven, by Lois, as long as you don't try to make her agree that she's bad. She knows it's not true, and she'll only resent you for telling her lies.'

Sonia thought about this. 'Yes,' she said. 'I can see that. What else?'

'Let her tell you the truth. Let her tell you what happened to her, from her point of view. Don't gloss over it or tell her she imagined it or it didn't really happen.'

'I wouldn't do that,' said Sonia.

'You already have been,' he said. 'You've been shutting her up by feeling ashamed of her. You've told her she's being immodest when she's trying to show you what happened. Now let her show you, or tell you, in whatever way she wants to. She may have coped well with the actual event, but as she grows up she's going to find out how adults interpret those things, and that could really cause her distress and make her believe there is something wrong with her. So let her unload it on to you now.'

'But do you think she will?' asked Sonia anxiously. 'If I have been shutting her up, perhaps she won't keep trying to tell me.'

'No, perhaps she won't,' he agreed. 'But she doesn't look like a child who gives up easily. I have the distinct impression, Sonia, that if you are willing to hear the truth – and you stop being afraid she'll be taken away, or will take herself away, from you – that she will tell you. Or show you. In her own way. And in her own time.'

'So what shall I do? Ask her, or . . .'

'Do nothing,' he said, 'for now. Go to bed. Go to sleep. I'll call in the morning to see Samuel. As for Lois, she may be over the worst now, but if she's still not well tomorrow then get in touch with my colleague, Dr Lightbourne. He's an excellent doctor and good with children. He won't arrive drunk, I promise you.'

'Thank you,' Sonia said. 'But if you don't mind, I think we'll stick with you.'

Chapter Thirty-Six

Sonia spent most of the night crying. When light began to filter through the thick curtains and the birds began their astonished applause at the daily miracle of dark-into-light, she fell asleep and dreamed – not of Lois or Eddie Barnes or Samuel but of Mrs Patel.

She awoke feeling calm about Lois and about Samuel, as though their crises were over, but with a strong conviction that something was wrong with Mrs Patel. She couldn't remember the details of the dream, and was no longer sure, anyway, of whether dreams and intuitions were reliable after all, but she felt like running out of the house and down to the hospital.

She told herself firmly to stop these fruitless imaginings and get on with the task in hand. Perhaps she was only escaping her own responsibilities by convincing herself that somebody needed her more than her own daughter and her own employer. She must get up straight away, she told herself, and start caring for the sick in this house, leaving Mrs Patel to the adequate care of the hospital.

Lois awoke as soon as Sonia began getting dressed. She woke up talking.

'What are we going to do today?' she enquired, bright-eyed, 'Are we going shopping?'

'How are you feeling today, Lois?' Sonia asked her.

Lois jumped out of bed. 'I want to wear my dungarees.'

'They have to be washed. Your tracksuit is dry, if you want to wear that. Are you feeling okay now, Lois?'

'Yes. I have to go and fill the birdbath, Sonia. Put clothes on me, quick.'

'Please. Take it slowly today, Lois. You were really sick last night. Have an easy day. No, we're not going shopping. We've done the shopping for this week – remember? We went with Mrs Atwood, to Brixton.'

'I want you to buy me a pink ribbon,' Lois explained.

'You already have a pink ribbon. Want to wear it in your hair this morning?'

'No, that's not a pink ribbon; it's a snake, and my doll ate it.'

'Oh, is that what it was? Well, I rescued it, so you can have it in your hair. Here it is, look.'

'No, I don't want a snake on my head! Take it away!'

'Lois! All right, put your tracksuit on and go and fill the birdbath. I'll come down and open the back door for you.'

'No, I can do it.'

'Let me give you a hand, Lois. I don't want you spilling water over that tracksuit; you haven't got much else to wear.'

'I won't.'

She shot off, sliding down the stairs, on her stomach, kicking her feet to give her speed. Sonia left her to it, and went to check on Samuel.

He was very white, with dark patches under his eyes. He was heavily asleep, his breathing hardly audible. Sonia hoped this was only the result of the sedative. She hoped, as well, that Dr Carroll would not forget his promise to call round this morning.

She stayed for a few minutes watching Samuel. One hand was outside the covers, lying limply on the eiderdown, and she lifted it and tucked it under the bedclothes. The hand was cool, but not cold, and his face was cool too. The doctor had said there was no fever.

She should be glad about that, she supposed, but in one way malaria would have been easier to accept. It had a name to it. It was a medically recognized condition. There was no name for the condition in which a sane and contented person rushed round the house in the middle of the night, yelling, 'Cree!' and hammering on doors and windows.

When the doorbell rang she thought it might be the doctor making an early visit, but it was Lois who had opened the side gate and run round into the front garden.

'Why are you ringing the doorbell?' Sonia asked her.

'I can reach it,' she said proudly. 'I stood on the step.'

'I don't want you reaching it. You come in the back door.'

'No, I like the front door,' Lois said. Sonia reflected that when Dr Carroll had told her to make sure Lois was allowed to say no, he couldn't have had much idea of how often Lois could make use of the privilege.

'Well, come in now you're here,' Sonia told her, 'but I'm not answering the front door to you every five minutes, Lois, so get used to using the kitchen door. And you're not to ring the doorbell, because Samuel is sick. I don't want him disturbed with a lot of ringing. Okay?'

'What's wrong with him?' Lois asked.

'What's wrong with him?' Sonia repeated. 'Have you forgotten how he was last night? Yelling at everyone like that?'

'He's not frightened today,' Lois said calmly. 'I'll go and see him.'

'Leave him; he's still asleep. Lois, your shoes are soaked. Let me take them off.'

'No, they're dry,' said Lois, squelching across the hall. 'I'm going to see Samuel.'

If she has the right to say no, don't I have that right as well? Sonia wondered. What would happen if she stopped saying no to Lois and let the child make her own decisions? On this occasion, obviously, Lois would walk around in wet shoes, leave wet footprints over the house, and wake Samuel up. Admittedly, this would not be the end of the world, but still . . .

'Go on, then,' Sonia said. She had one more try at persuading Lois to give up the shoes. 'You can go barefoot if you like,' she said, 'like a Red Indian.'

Lois stopped her four-pawed ascent of the stairs and considered this option. 'Okay,' she said. She pulled off her shoes and sent them tumbling down the stairs. Sonia picked them up and took them to the kitchen, to stand by the boiler and dry.

The toes of the shoes were nearly worn through; they must be too small for the child. She would have to buy her a new pair.

What if Samuel was really ill, and stayed ill for a long time? How would she be paid? Should they stay here, if Samuel went into hospital? How would they live?

She pushed the panic away. One thing at a time. For the moment, she would riddle out the boiler and top it up with fuel. She would lay the table and set out cereal bowls and the packet of cornflakes for herself and Lois. She would call Lois and tell her to come and eat . . .

'Aaaahhh!'

Oh no, Sonia thought. He's started again. She dropped the packet of cornflakes and ran up the stairs, two at a time.

Samuel was sitting up in bed, his eyes open, staring wildly at Lois, who had entered into the spirit of being a Red Indian by not only taking her shoes off but helping herself liberally to the fluorescent paints and streaking her face (and incidentally her clean tracksuit) with green and orange.

'Lois, go out, quick,' Sonia commanded, pushing her, but Lois stood her ground.

'I'm not a real Red Indian, Samuel,' she said. She moved towards him. Samuel cowered against the wall. 'Fetch the knives,' he whimpered.

Sonia threw her arms round him, partly to reassure him and partly to reassure herself that he was not going to leap out of the bed and attack Lois. He felt frail and exhausted; there seemed little likelihood of his becoming violent again, but she was not going to take any chances.

'Go, Lois,' she said again. 'Do what you're told.'

Lois jumped on to the bed. Samuel gasped and wailed, 'Cree! Cree!'

'Now look what you've done!' Sonia snapped at Lois. 'Will you do what I tell you and go away?'

Lois caught hold of Samuel's hand and clasped it in both of

hers. 'I'm not a Red Indian, Samuel,' she said loudly. 'I'm Lois. Look!' She rubbed his hand vigorously against her face and held it up for him to see. 'It comes off on your hand.'

Sonia felt Samuel relax against her. 'Thought you were Cree,' he said.

'No, I'm Lois,' said Lois. Sonia wished somebody would tell her what was going on. Lois slid off the bed. 'I'm going to get you your breakfast,' she announced to Samuel. 'You can have it in bed if you're frightened.'

'No, no,' Samuel said. 'I shall get up. I must go to work.'

Sonia was alarmed all over again, though glad to see him with his eyes open and to hear him talking. 'You will not get up and go to work,' she said, holding him down.

'I shall be late,' he said. 'What is the time?'

'You've retired, Samuel,' Sonia said. 'You retired yesterday, remember?'

'Notice,' he muttered. 'Have to work out my notice.'

'I have phoned them,' Sonia lied, as the first bluff didn't seem to be working. Evidently he was not as confused as he had seemed, if he remembered that he had not worked out his month's notice. 'I phoned them and said you wouldn't be in today. You have to stay in bed, Samuel, because the doctor is coming to visit you this morning. He said you mustn't get up.'

'Oh well,' Samuel said, subsiding. 'Must obey doctor's orders, eh?'

'Certainly,' said Sonia sternly. 'Now rest, and we'll bring you up some breakfast.'

He murmured something as she reached the door.

'What was that you said?' she asked.

A faint smile crossed his lips. 'Long time,' he repeated, 'since I had breakfast in bed.'

'It's one of the perks of retirement,' Sonia said. 'You could find yourself enjoying it.'

'Yes,' he agreed. He lay down awkwardly, his neck bent against the angle of the headboard. She turned back to him, helped him to sit up and arranged the pillows behind him.

'Lean back now,' she instructed. He obeyed, sitting propped up, his white hair awry. She fetched the brush from the top of the chest of drawers and brushed his hair smooth. 'Back in a minute,' she said.

She found Lois pouring cornflakes into a bowl, over the table and on to the floor. 'Well tried,' she said.

'It slipped,' Lois said guiltily.

'It does that at times. When you lean the packet over, you have to be ready to lift it up again as soon as the cornflakes pour. Can you remember that?'

'Yes.'

'Good. Fetch me the dustpan and brush and we'll sweep these up.'

'Where are they?'

'In the cupboard on the landing upstairs.'

The doorbell rang before Lois returned.

'How is he?' asked Dr Carroll, stepping inside the door almost before Sonia had opened it.

'Awake. Tired. About to have breakfast.'

'Good.' He was already striding up the stairs. Not bad for someone who must have a mighty hangover, Sonia thought. 'Hello, Lois,' she heard him greeting her. 'How are you this morning? You look full of beans to me.'

'No, not beans,' Lois replied. 'I'm going to have cornflakes. But I spilt them on the floor.'

'Oh, is that what the dustpan and brush are for? Very good. You go and help your mum sweep up the cornflakes, and I'll see you when I come down.'

'No,' Lois said. 'I have to help you see Samuel. I'm making him better.'

'Good stuff,' said Dr Carroll. 'I'll just have five minutes with him on my own first.'

'No, I have to come in,' Lois insisted.

Sonia listened, amused. Let him get out of that one, him and his 'Teach the child to say no.'

'I shall call you when I need your help,' the doctor said. 'You have your breakfast, and listen out for my call.'

'Okay,' said Lois cheerily. 'I'll be in the kitchen when you want me.'

She sent the dustpan and brush clattering down the stairs and followed them on her tummy. Sonia went back to the kitchen and pretended she hadn't been eavesdropping. Together, they began to sweep up the cornflakes – at least, Sonia swept. Lois paddled in them, scrunching them blissfully with her bare toes.

You're the housekeeper, Dr Carroll had told Sonia last night. Lois only has to be the child.

She hoped he would come downstairs soon, and catch them getting it right.

Chapter Thirty-Seven

Dr Carroll called them both into Samuel's room. 'I want to test his reactions,' he said. 'His physical responses are good: a little slow, but that could be due to the sedative more than anything. Let's test the mental responses now. Ready?' he asked Samuel.

'Yes,' Samuel agreed, looking bemused.

'Do you know who this is?' the doctor asked him, pointing at Sonia.

'That is a member of my family,' said Samuel.

'Hmm,' the doctor said. He pointed at Lois. 'Who is this?'

'I'm Lois,' said Lois immediately.

'Sshh, Lois,' Sonia told her. 'Samuel has to answer.'

'Why?'

'It's a game.'

'Can I play?'

'Yes, you are playing. Just stand there.'

'That is Lois,' Samuel said, smiling at her.

'Is Lois also a member of your family?' the doctor asked.

'Most certainly,' Samuel said.

'Hmm. Now, look at me. What colour is my skin? Black or white?'

Samuel peered at him. 'Red,' he said positively. Sonia stifled a giggle.

Dr Carroll glared at her. 'What colour is Sonia's skin?'

'Brown,' said Samuel.

'And Lois?'

'At present,' said Samuel deliberately, 'she appears to be orange and green. Normally, however, she is white.'

'White?' asked the doctor. 'Are you sure?'

'Oh, absolutely sure,' Samuel said. 'You may ask her yourself.'

Lois nodded. 'White,' she confirmed.

'Ah ... Do you by chance have three or four similar objects?' the doctor asked Sonia. 'Clothes pegs or some such thing? Preferably different colours.'

'I've got something!' shouted Lois. She ran out of the room and returned with the three small dolls from her dolls' house.

'Yes, those will do fine,' said the doctor. 'Thank you, Lois.'

Lois tapped Sonia excitedly. 'I'm good at this game,' she said.

'Yes, you are.' Sonia was uneasy with it. It didn't seem dignified, asking these babyish questions of an old man. Also his answers, which were perfectly logical when you understood the context, were likely to give the doctor the impression that Samuel was more confused than he actually was.

The doctor held up one doll. 'How many dolls are there, Samuel?'

'Three,' Samuel said.

The doctor put the doll down on the bed. 'Okay,' he said, standing up. 'Now, Samuel, how do you feel about a couple of days in hospital? A few very simple tests?'

Samuel was distressed. 'Oh, I shouldn't like that at all,' he said. 'Are you sure it is necessary?'

'It would be wise,' said Dr Carroll, quite gently.

'If you say so,' said Samuel. 'You are the doctor, of course.'

'No, listen,' said Sonia, stepping forward. 'He knows who you are, doesn't he? He knows you're the doctor. And he knows us. He did say we were to be like his family. He's not as confused as all that. There *are* three of those dolls: he made three. And Lois always says she is white. He does know what he's saying. He's just very tired.'

'I'm afraid it is rather more than that,' the doctor said. Samuel looked from the doctor to Sonia and back again.

'Let's try one more test,' Sonia pleaded.

Dr Carroll grimaced. 'If you like.'

Sonia held up the three dolls again, one by one. 'Samuel,' she said, 'listen to me. I've learnt what you told me.' She handed one doll to him, the one made of the lightest coloured wood. She made him hold it and run his thumb across the grain of the wood. 'This doll is made of mahogany,' she said clearly. 'Mahogany – right?'

She handed him the second doll, checking the colour of the wood under the base of the feet, where she had not painted. It was a slightly darker colour than the first. 'This one is made of pine,' she said. 'Pine wood. Got it?'

Finally she gave him the third. 'This one is made of . . . of oak,' she said. 'Only I'm not quite sure about it, Samuel. Tell me if I'm right.'

He held the dolls loosely, without apparent interest, his attention claimed by the sound of a bird cooing from the acacia tree. 'That's a wood pigeon,' he said. 'Lovely sound, isn't it?' He sat and listened, abstracted.

The doctor looked at Sonia. 'Sorry,' he said. 'I'll make arrangements to have him admitted for a few days.'

'I could take care of him,' she pleaded. 'It'll only unsettle him, going into hospital at his age. Isn't he better in his own home?'

'If his mind is wandering,' Dr Carroll said, 'it's best to check straight away whether there is a physical cause. It's too easy to put it down to age, when it might possibly be a problem that can be treated.'

'He's just very tired,' Sonia said, but the doctor was already out of the bedroom and on the landing. As Sonia reached the bedroom door, following him, Samuel suddenly said loudly, 'It was a good try, my dear, but I am afraid you are quite wrong.'

'What?' she said. 'To want to keep you out of hospital, you mean?'

'No.' He held up the dolls. 'This one is the Swedish pine,' he said clearly. 'The others are beech and rosewood. Not oak and mahogany.'

Sonia turned to the doctor in triumph. 'See!'

He steered her towards the stairs. 'Let's have a chat,' he said.

Downstairs, in the hall, he said, 'Last night you told me he was threatening you with knives. Now you don't want me to take him into hospital. Don't you think it would be the wisest thing to do, for everybody's peace of mind?'

'It was scary last night,' Sonia admitted, 'but afterwards, thinking about it, I can see that he wasn't attacking us. He was attacking something, all right. Lois said he was frightened – that she wasn't frightened of him; she was frightened because he was.'

'Yes, but old people do get these irrational terrors when they are going senile,' the doctor said. 'Sometimes we find a tumour or a blood clot on the brain, and even if the patient is too old or it's too difficult to operate, we can sometimes control the problem with drugs. Isn't it worth a try, even if he is a little upset at being admitted to hospital?'

'He seems so tired,' said Sonia wretchedly. 'He gave in his notice at work yesterday. And he's been struggling to look after himself on his own for the last six months. And before that, Miss Prynne . . .'

'I know,' the doctor said. 'I know.'

'Couldn't it just be reaction to all that stress, or something?'

'It could. Very often, when a person has been coping with stress over a long period of time, it is when the stress is relieved that the symptoms occur – shoot to the surface, as it were. But these symptoms are dangerous. You said he was violent. You have a young child in the house.'

'If we could find out what it is that he's afraid of, perhaps the violence would go. He isn't violent in himself, is he? Gertrude, his cousin, said he never was before, and it was out of character.'

'It certainly is out of character,' Dr Carroll mused. 'I've known him a good many years myself, and a more courteous and sensitive person you could not wish to meet.'

Sonia hesitated. 'I know he's all right, in himself,' she said tentatively, 'and I know there's something wrong with him as

277

well – if that makes sense. If we could just find out what it is that's troubling him . . .'

'Quite. That's why I'm suggesting hospitalizing him.'

'No, I don't mean something physical, on the brain,' Sonia persisted. 'I mean something frightening him. This Cree person, or whatever it is. Some very logical reason for being frightened. Not a sickness.'

The doctor, she could see, was doubtful. 'In the meantime,' he said, 'what are you going to do if he starts running round waving knives at you again?'

'I got him to calm down last time,' Sonia pointed out, 'once I realized he wasn't attacking us; he was going for something we couldn't see.'

'It's all very well to establish that his motives weren't aggressive,' said the doctor bluntly, 'but are you going to be concerned with his motives if, looking at something or somebody you can't see, he sticks a knife into Lois?'

Sonia was silent.

'A few days,' said the doctor. 'A few tests. If we don't find anything physically wrong with him, we'll review the possibility of sending him home, perhaps with a private resident nurse.'

'Give me a few days first,' said Sonia impulsively. 'I know it sounds risky, and irresponsible, with Lois – but I keep feeling that he's over the worst.'

The doctor shook his head. 'We'll compromise,' he said. 'It'll take me a little time to arrange his admission, unless I ask for it to be considered an emergency. I'll go ahead and arrange it, but not as an emergency admission. That'll give you one day, possibly two. That will have to be enough, I'm afraid. He is my patient.'

Reluctantly, Sonia gave in. 'Okay,' she said. 'One day, then.'

He paused on the doorstep. 'I wish you luck,' he said, 'with the detective work. I would like to believe that you're right, but I can't take chances.'

'No,' Sonia said. 'I understand that.'

Lois came bumping and sliding down the stairs. 'You ought to give Samuel his breakfast,' she told Sonia reproachfully.

The doctor laughed. 'Perhaps he already has the private nurse,' he said.

Chapter Thirty-Eight

It was strange that Gertrude had not phoned, as promised. Perhaps, Sonia thought, she was a late riser. It was still only nine o'clock in the morning. Samuel had managed to eat some toast and marmalade and drink a glass of milk: Sonia hadn't wanted to give him hot tea in case he spilled it and scalded himself. His hands were still shaky.

She retrieved the knives from their bedroom and put them in the dining room cabinet. The drawers did not lock, but at least she could lock the door. She kept the key in her pocket instead of putting it back on top of the grandfather clock. Although she had told the doctor she was not really worried about further violence, she was taking no risks.

The doorbell rang again as she was washing up the breakfast dishes. It was Mrs Atwood.

'I saw the doctor's car,' she said. 'Is somebody ill?'

The woman might have sharp eyes, Sonia reflected, but she must have deaf ears or else be a heavy sleeper not to have heard the disturbances in the night. Certainly the houses were detached and had thick walls, but surely she must have heard something. Was she pretending ignorance of something she already knew? Sonia decided to test her.

'You mean you saw the doctor's car here last night?' she asked. 'After there was that noise?'

Mrs Atwood looked blank. 'No, just now,' she said. 'I saw him leaving a few minutes ago. What noise in the night?'

'Oh, he called in the night,' Sonia said. 'Mr Arnold wasn't too well, so I thought I'd better get the doctor, to be on the safe side.'

'Oh dear. Is he all right?'

'He's tired. He might go into hospital for a few tests, but basically he seems okay.'

'Nothing serious, then?'

'No. It's his age, I expect,' Sonia said.

'Yes, of course; it's to be expected, isn't it?'

'Thanks so much for coming to ask after him,' said Sonia sweetly.

'Do let me know if I can be of any help, won't you?' Mrs Atwood said, leaning sideways to look at Sonia round the closing door.

'Yes. Thank you, we will.'

When the door was almost shut, she heard Mrs Atwood say, 'What was the noise in the night, then?', but she pushed the door firmly the last half-inch of the way and pretended she hadn't heard.

The next caller was Gertrude.

'Gertrude!' Sonia exclaimed. 'What are you doing here? How did you get here so early?'

'I bribed a minicab driver to drive me all the way,' Gertrude said. 'I thought it might be better than phoning. But if I am not needed, my dear, I shan't stay. I haven't come to get under your feet; just to see if I can be of any help.'

'I'm really glad to see you,' said Sonia. She suffered Gertrude's all-encompassing hug and even returned it.

'Where is Lois? How is she this morning?' Gertrude asked.

'She seems fine.'

'Not too shaken by her fright last night, then?'

'Not at all,' Sonia said. 'She told me she thought it was Samuel who was frightened. She was frightened because he was.'

'I see,' Gertrude said thoughtfully. 'But Sonia, my dear, you still have no idea of why he was frightened? This is so disturbing, Samuel going berserk with knives.' She seemed rather shaky herself, Sonia observed, and her make-up this morning, although applied with her usual liberality, didn't hide her pallor and was very uneven.

'Come and have a cup of coffee,' Sonia suggested.

'That would be welcome. I'll pop up and see how Samuel is, if I may.'

'Go ahead,' Sonia said. She appreciated Gertrude asking permission. She needn't have said, 'if I may'. She was more at home in this house than Sonia was, and certainly more a member of Samuel's family. The fact that she did say it made all the difference. Sonia was genuinely glad and relieved to see her, but even in the present circumstances she would not have wanted Gertrude taking over. She, Sonia, was the house-keeper.

'Good gracious, Lois, you look very fearsome!' Gertrude exclaimed, encountering her on the stairs. 'Are you a monster from outer space?'

'No,' Lois said. 'I'm a Red Indian. But not a real one,' she added.

'Well, I am glad you told me that,' Gertrude said.

'I told Samuel too,' Lois informed her.

'Just as well,' said Gertrude. 'He is terrified of Red Indians.'

'What?' said Sonia, who had been listening to this exchange from the kitchen. 'Gertrude,' she said, detaining her as she made her way up the stairs, 'what did you say? Did you say Samuel was terrified of Red Indians?'

'Yes, my dear. Always has been, since a very young child. And he has never outgrown it, so he once told me. I suppose it must have something to do with his family, when they emi-grated to Canada, living so near the Indian reservation. In the early months they were perpetually afraid of being attacked, so it seemed. The Indians were not always friendly towards white settlers.'

'Why didn't you tell me this before?' Sonia demanded.

Gertrude looked astonished. 'I told you about his family,' she said. 'Only last Saturday.'

'Not about the Red Indians,' Sonia said. 'You didn't tell me they lived near the reservation or that they were afraid of being attacked by Red Indians, or that Samuel was afraid. Why didn't you tell me?'

Gertrude made her way slowly downstairs again, staring at Sonia uncomprehendingly. 'Is there some reason why it should have been relevant?' she asked. 'I don't understand.'

'Samuel took a knife,' Sonia hissed at her, trying to keep her voice down because of Lois, who had scrambled upstairs again but might not be quite out of earshot, 'and slashed those Red Indian things to bits. That was the beginning of him acting mad.'

'What Red Indian things?' Gertrude said, bewildered.

'I *told* you!' Sonia said. 'Lois's tepee in the garden, and the Red Indian masks and things hanging from the tree.'

'Good Lord,' said Gertrude, suddenly sitting down on the stairs. 'No, my dear, you didn't tell me. You simply said he had destroyed Lois's toys.'

They stared at one another. Sonia was the first to voice their thoughts.

'Do you think this has something to do with it?' she asked.

Gertrude hauled herself to her feet. 'I think we should find out,' she said, 'immediately.'

Like a raiding party, they stormed Samuel's bedroom.

'Samuel,' said Sonia without preliminary, 'are you afraid of Red Indians?'

He opened his eyes. 'Yes,' he said. 'Gertrude, my dear. What a pleasant surprise. Is it the weekend already?'

Sonia interrupted their exchange of pleasantries. 'Tell me,' she said, 'why you're afraid of Red Indians, Samuel.'

Lois appeared in the room, bringing her dolls' house. She set it down on the floor and climbed up on Samuel's bed to retrieve her three dolls. She pulled the larger doll out of the basement of the dolls' house and showed it to Gertrude. 'This is me,' she said.

'Yes, dear,' said Gertrude. 'Isn't that lovely?' She was only half listening. Her ears were open for Samuel's answer.

Samuel was not yet fully awake. He struggled to sit up against his pillows. Sonia went to assist him.

'I don't mean to fire questions at you,' she said apologetically. 'It's just that you have seemed afraid a couple of times recently, and when I think back it was when you saw Lois in her Red Indian warpaint, or maybe when you looked out of your window for some reason in the night and saw Lois's toys in the garden and thought they were real Red Indians or something. So, if you wouldn't mind telling me why you're afraid of Red Indians, it might possibly help.'

He was quiet for a while. She wondered if he was in any fit state to understand the question. Then he said, 'Open the drawer, Sonia – the locked one in the bureau. You will find the key . . . but you know where to find the key, don't you?'

'Yes,' she said. Here was further evidence of his memory. He remembered her confession in the garden on Saturday. Either he was having occasional lucid patches, or else he was recovering his mental clarity. Either way, it must be a good thing.

She took the key from the small top drawer inside the bureau and unlocked the bottom drawer. Inside were slim packets of letters bound with rubber bands, each bundle topped with a piece of paper bearing a date. One was 1912, another 1913-14, and a further one 1918. There were no more than fifteen letters altogether.

'Open them,' Samuel instructed. 'Read what you like.'

Gertrude leaned forward, curious. 'Are these from your brothers, Samuel?' she asked. 'Did you keep their letters, all this time?'

'Not from my brothers,' he said. 'From Mother, and Joyce.'

'Arrived safely,' Sonia read aloud. 'Father very exhausted after journey. Long and tiring trek with wagons driven by oxen, to our new homestead forty miles from North Battleford; journey involving fording a number of deep streams and crossing an Indian Reservation.'

'Ah,' said Gertrude.

'These letters are very short,' Sonia said, taking them out of their envelopes and laying them out on the floor, in the chronological order in which they were arranged. 'They're more like telegrams.'

'Surely there were more?' Gertrude asked. 'Over the years?'

'No,' Samuel said. 'That was all.'

'Why is there a gap in the dates?' Sonia enquired. 'There's nothing from Nineteen fifteen to eighteen.'

'My brother Oscar was killed in the First World War,' Samuel explained, 'and my father died during that period as well. The family did not write then. You will see from the first letter of Nineteen eighteen that my mother explains they had been in mourning.'

'Surely Joyce wrote?' Gertrude asked.

'Joyce was only a child,' Samuel reminded her. 'Her first letter to me was written in Nineteen fourteen, when she was nine. Then there was a letter enclosed with Mother's when she resumed her correspondence with me in Nineteen eighteen. Joyce's letter is dated Nineteen seventeen. Mother must have kept it by her till she came to write herself, thinking she would post them both together. They were miles from any post office, you see.'

'Perhaps Joyce wrote you other letters as well, that didn't get posted,' Sonia suggested.

'Yes,' Samuel said. 'Perhaps she did.' He looked grey and tired, slumped against the pillows.

'We're wearing you out,' said Gertrude remorsefully, but he waved a hand at her. 'Don't mind me,' he said. 'I have never shown anyone these. Perhaps it is time I did.'

Sonia was reading the first letter from Samuel's twin sister Joyce. The handwriting was large and childish.

'This doll is Sonia,' Lois said, waving it in Gertrude's face. 'And this one is Mrs Grenville.'

'Very nice, Lois,' Gertrude said absently.

'Shush, Lois,' Sonia said. 'We're discussing something.' She read aloud from Joyce's letter: 'We heard lots of drums in the night and loud shouting. Mr Armitage who helps Basil and Claude on the farm said the Indians scalp white people and torture them. But it turned out to be the Sun Dance festival. It goes on for three days, and nobody eats anything but they dance and smoke the peace pipe. It didn't sound very peaceful to me. The drums beat all night and I was frightened they would come and scalp our family. Claude said I was silly to be frightened.'

Sonia stopped reading. She looked at Samuel. 'You had this letter, and then no more news for three years? You must have thought they had been killed!'

'Yes,' he said. 'I did.'

There was a silence. 'This doll is called Eddie,' Lois said. 'Eddie Barnes is what he is called, this one.' No one answered her.

'That was the beginning?' Gertrude asked. 'Of your fear of Red Indians?'

He nodded very slowly, very tired. 'I used to hear the drums,' he said, 'in the night. I used to wake up every night in a sweat.'

'You heard them?' Gertrude said. 'You mean you dreamt it?'

'No,' Samuel said. 'The noise wasn't in my dreams. It was the noise that woke me up. It was when I was awake that I heard them. The tom-toms, and the shouts. Bloodcurdling yells.'

'How absolutely petrifying,' said Gertrude.

'Yes,' he said.

'This man doll watches this girl doll eating chocolate biscuits,' said Lois.

Sonia was reading Joyce's next letter, the one after the long interval. 'Mother is coming out of her depression since Oscar and Father died,' she read. 'She joined in the celebrations for Christmas. We had a great feast. Old Moose, the Indian, arrived with his family and brought three fish. Bertrand said the fish were high. The Indians enjoyed the Christmas pudding, but we could not set it on fire this year as Claude hid the brandy in case Old Moose drank it.'

'It sounds as though they made friends with the Indians, then,' Gertrude said.

'Oh yes, they did,' Samuel said. 'They became the best of friends. My niece who came over to England a few years ago – you remember, Gertrude – was brought up alongside the

Indians. They were her childhood friends. She spent more time on the reservation than on the farm.'

'So surely you stopped being afraid then?' Sonia asked. 'After you got this letter saying they were all right? I mean, your father and brother weren't killed by the Indians, were they?'

'No, no. Oscar was a soldier in the First World War; he was killed in battle. And Father died of a heart attack. No, I suppose the fears must have become a habit by then. They did recede over the years, but never quite abated. The drums would always recur at times – I suppose, looking back, at times when I was under duress,' Samuel explained.

'Always at night?' Gertrude asked.

'No,' he said. 'Sometimes on the bus on the way home from work. I would have to get off the bus. I would be overcome with terror, and the people around me would look like Red Indians.'

'Oh,' Sonia said. 'Poor Samuel. That's terrible.'

'All these years and you never told anybody?' Gertrude said. 'I mean, you did tell me, Samuel, that you always had a fear of Red Indians, but I thought you meant an irrational fear, the way some people are afraid of snakes, although they may never have seen one except on the television.'

'It was irrational,' Samuel said. 'How could I tell anybody? They would have thought I was loopy!' He laughed shakily.

'Eddie Barnes is afraid of snakes,' Lois said.

'No, they wouldn't have thought you were mad,' Sonia argued. 'Not in the circumstances, Samuel. It wasn't fear of something imaginary, or something that had nothing to do with you. You thought they had killed your family, or tortured them or something. That's a real fear, of something real.'

'The snake nearly killed Eddie,' said Lois conversationally.

'What is in the box, Samuel?' Gertrude asked. 'Are they keepsakes?'

'Mainly photographs,' Samuel said. 'The two photos on the mantelshelf are my parents, of course. The ones in the box are of the family and their houses. Do have a look, if you are interested.'

'If we're interested?' Gertrude questioned. 'After years of keeping so much to yourself, you ask are we interested? My dear Samuel, for the first time I really do begin to wonder whether you have a screw loose!' They laughed, with mutual relief.

Sonia was examining the small hoard of sepia photographs, reading the scrawled inscriptions on the back and handing them over to Gertrude. Lois leaned over Sonia's shoulder.

A group of people in what looked like fancy dress – long dresses and shawls for the women, fur caps for the pipe-smoking men – sat in a wooden cart outside a log cabin. The writing on the back, in blue ink, read, 'Mother, Basil, Claude, Joyce and Norman'.

A picture of the same older woman leaning over the wooden rail of a narrow bridge was inscribed: 'Mother, Lost Horse Creek (Quicksands) – Claude and Basil's third attempt at bridge, after first two swept away by floods'.

Sonia was fascinated. A further photo showed one of the brothers (they all looked alike in the faded brown pictures) in a sled cart pulled by horses, with a second ox-drawn cart standing by. Snow lay thick on the ground and on the roof of the log cabin.

The last photo but one in the box showed the older woman and the younger one standing side by side, obviously having been told to pose for the camera, appearing stiff and self-conscious. 'Mother and Joyce, Canada', the inscription read.

The final picture, very hazy and faded, was the one that held Sonia's attention for the longest time. It showed a small Red Indian man, apparently old but standing very erect, with one of the brothers outside the house.

But it was the writing on the back of this photograph that really made her catch her breath. 'Basil with Old Moose', it said. Underneath the name Old Moose was added, in smaller writing, 'Indian Chief, of the Cree tribe'.

'Cree!' Sonia breathed. 'So *that's* it!'

Chapter Thirty-Nine

Sonia brought a tray of coffee and cake and biscuits up to Samuel's room. Lois had strawberry milkshake.

'What I don't understand, frankly, Samuel,' said Gertrude, 'is why you should have these outbursts now. Naturally one can understand your terror all those years ago, and that it should have gone on repeating itself even when the actual danger was quite over. But never in that time, even when the fears must have been at their very worst, have you gone around shouting and waving knives and thinking you were attacking marauding bands of Cree Indians. Have you? Or is this also something that you have kept from me?'

'No,' Samuel said. 'It has never happened before. I imagine I should not be in a job if it had.'

'In a job!' Sonia exclaimed, clapping her hands to her mouth. 'I forgot to phone to say you wouldn't be in to work, Samuel. I know I said I had, but I meant I was just about to do it. I forgot about it when Gertrude arrived.'

'Would you like me to do it?' Gertrude offered.

'Oh, yes please,' Sonia accepted gratefully. 'It's eleven o'clock; they must be wondering where he is.'

While Gertrude went to phone, Lois helped herself liberally to chocolate fingers.

'Leave some of those for other people,' Sonia chided her. She handed Samuel his coffee and watched him to make sure his grip on the cup was steady. He looked slightly better, with a tinge of colour in his cheeks.

'Chocolate fingers are for children,' Lois said.

'Oh yes?' Sonia queried. 'Don't be so sure. Grown-up people like them as well.'

Lois thrust a chocolate finger into her mouth, and pulled it out again, sucking off the chocolate with a loud noise.

'Lois, stop that!' Sonia said. 'It's disgusting.'

Lois spoke in a deep gruff voice. 'You like that, don't you, little girl?'

'What?' Sonia said.

'I spoke to the younger Mr Wheeldon,' Gertrude said, returning to the room, 'and he said you are not to worry about anything, Samuel. Take your time and get really well. He said you need to be fit and healthy when you return, because they are planning a big retirement party for you.'

Samuel laughed.

'Gertrude, this coffee is yours,' Sonia said. 'Would you like some cake or a biscuit? Lois, stop doing that this minute.'

'I'll have a chocolate finger, with Lois,' Gertrude said. 'I haven't had chocolate fingers for years.'

'You have to suck them like this,' Lois told her, demonstrating.

'Lois!' said Sonia warningly. 'What have I just said?'

Lois did her deep voice again. 'You like doing that, don't you? You come with me and I'll show you something else you'll like too.'

Gertrude crunched her chocolate biscuit noisily. Sonia stopped drawing attention to Lois's bad manners. If anything, Gertrude's seemed worse.

'What were we talking about, before I went to telephone the firm?' Gertrude wondered.

'About why this happened to Samuel now, and not at any other time,' Sonia prompted.

'Yes,' Gertrude recalled. 'Do you have any idea, Samuel?'

Samuel thought, sipping his coffee. His hand was quite steady. 'I believe it may have had something to do with the child,' he said, nodding towards Lois. 'There is something about her that reminds me of Joyce. It was mainly on Joyce's account that I had those fears, you know. I believed the others could take good care of themselves, unless it really came to the worst.'

'Even your mother?' Sonia asked.

Samuel grinned. 'Especially Mother,' he said. 'She was a fearsome woman. She used to gather the Indians in her cabin and force them to listen while she read them lengthy Bible tracts. Several of her letters to me were requests to send her fresh supplies of missionary pamphlets.

'The Cree didn't understand a word of English at first, and even when they did the content was so elaborately phrased and in such old-fashioned language, I doubt they could make head or tail of it. But apparently the Cree raised no objections to sitting in the cabin in snowy weather, by a good fire, being given hot punch at intervals.'

'So you were always worried about Joyce,' Gertrude hazarded, 'and then when Lois came here, she reminded you of Joyce, and that brought back the old fears? Was that it?'

Samuel looked at Lois, and hesitated. 'Not exactly,' he said.

'What, then?' Gertrude pursued.

'Rather more than that,' Samuel said. He stopped.

'Lois,' Sonia said, 'go into the bathroom and give your hands a good wash before you get chocolate over your dolls.'

'I'm busy,' said Lois.

'No more chocolate fingers unless you do,' Sonia threatened. 'And I don't just mean no more today; I mean no more *ever again*!'

Lois, grumbling, got up and went to the bathroom to wash her hands.

'Very thoroughly!' Sonia called after her. 'With soap, or it doesn't count. Okay,' she said to Samuel. 'What is it?'

'I don't know whether I should say,' he said, looking worried.

'Go *on*!' said both Gertrude and Sonia in unison. It was clear that Lois would not be long in coming back into the room.

Samuel cleared his throat. 'I had the distinct impression, on a number of occasions,' he said apologetically, 'that Lois was similarly under attack. Either that she was now, or that she had been.'

'Whatever do you mean, Samuel?' said Gertrude, shocked.

'No, wait a minute,' said Sonia quickly. She could hear Lois running the tap and muttering away to herself in the bathroom. 'Samuel is right. Lois was abused at the last place we lived. That's why we got thrown out. The woman found out what was happening and was afraid I would find out too and make trouble for her.'

'Abused?' said Gertrude.

'Sexually abused,' Sonia elaborated. 'By the gardener. Eddie Barnes.'

'When did you find out?' Samuel asked her.

'I didn't. I suspected, but it seemed too . . . I didn't know if I was imagining things. Lois liked him. A lot. In fact, I thought . . . well, never mind now. It was Dr Carroll, last night, who said he was certain that she had been. He said she would tell me about it in her own time, if only I was ready to let her.'

'Eddie Barnes?' said Gertrude suddenly. 'She's been talking about Eddie Barnes all morning. Why haven't we been listening?'

'Eddie Barnes,' echoed Lois, coming back into the room. She held up her hands to show Sonia. 'Look,' she said. 'I'm white and clean.'

'Lois,' said Sonia, her voice trembling. 'What were you saying earlier, about Eddie Barnes?'

Lois looked blank. Gertrude picked up the doll and handed it to her. 'This is Eddie Barnes, Lois, isn't it? What does this doll do, when he is in his house?'

'Oh yes,' Lois said, remembering. She took the Eddie doll from Gertrude and held it facing the large doll Mrs Atwood had given her. She put both dolls down on the floor, facing each other. 'Not in the house,' she corrected Gertrude. 'In the garden.'

The tension was unbearable. Sonia thought she was going to scream and run out of the room. Gertrude and Samuel stayed calm, outwardly calm at least. It was important – essential – to stay calm, Sonia knew. They must not worry Lois.

'In the garden, then,' Gertrude agreed. Her voice shook almost imperceptibly. Samuel sat very still.

'Like this,' Lois said. She picked up another chocolate finger and sucked it noisily. She held it to the larger doll's mouth and continued making the noises. She held up the Eddie Barnes doll and said, in the gruff voice again, 'Ha ha, you like that don't you, little girl? I know what you like. You come to my cellar and I'll show you.'

Sonia let out a cry. Gertrude reached over and caught hold of her hand. Lois looked around the room, from one face to another. She gathered up her dolls abruptly and left the room.

'Lois, come back!' Sonia cried.

'Let her go, my dear,' Gertrude said. 'That is probably as much as the child can cope with, for one day. If we all carry on as normal, she won't be afraid to tell you more another time.'

As Sonia stayed hunched on the floor, Gertrude stood up and called to Lois, 'I'm going out to have a look round the garden. I want to see whether the birdbath needs filling up today.'

Lois shot out of the front bedroom at top speed. 'It doesn't need filling up,' she said. 'I did it myself.'

'All by yourself?' said Gertrude in tones of amazement. 'How extremely clever of you, Lois. May I see?'

'Yes,' Lois said. 'I'll show you.'

She went down the stairs, holding Gertrude's hand.

Sonia took a deep breath. 'I don't know what to do,' she said.

Samuel said nothing. Looking up, Sonia saw tears rolling down his face.

'Actually,' she said, 'that's not true. I do know what I'm going to do. I'm going to kill him.'

Chapter Forty

'Why don't you go out for a while this afternoon?' Gertrude suggested. 'Have a break, take your mind off everything? I can keep an eye on Lois and Samuel.'

They were sitting at the kitchen table, having a late lunch, just the three of them – Gertrude, Lois and Sonia. Samuel was asleep.

'Oh, I don't know,' Sonia demurred.

'Why not?' Gertrude encouraged her. 'What were you planning to do today, if nothing untoward had happened?'

Sonia could not think of a time when all this had not happened. 'I don't know,' she said.

'Shopping?' Gertrude said.

'No, we went shopping yesterday. Oh yes, I was going to buy a new Hoover and look at washing machines. That was it.' It seemed a long time ago that she had made those plans, yet it couldn't have been. It must have been only yesterday evening, when Samuel brought the money home and gave it to her to buy those things.

'Why don't you do it?' Gertrude said. 'Take a taxi, and go and look at Hoovers and washing machines. Why not?'

'I don't feel up to it,' Sonia admitted.

'No? Well, you know how you feel, better than anybody,' Gertrude conceded. 'I just thought it might do you good to go out for a bit.'

'I could go and see Mrs Patel,' said Sonia suddenly.

'Can I come?' Lois asked.

'Who is Mrs Patel?' Gertrude enquired.

'A woman we met in the refuge. She's in King's College Hospital, just had a baby. She isn't very well. As a matter of fact, I woke up this morning really worried about her.'

'Do go, if you would like to,' Gertrude said.

'Are you sure you wouldn't mind?' Sonia asked her.

'Sure,' said Gertrude positively. 'I shall play with Lois and leave Samuel to sleep the sleep of the just.'

'I want to come with you,' Lois told Sonia, 'and see Anita.'

'Anita won't be there, Lois,' Sonia said. 'Only Mrs Patel.'

'I want to see her baby,' Lois pouted.

'I know. I want you to see her baby as well. You've never seen such a young baby, Lois. But this one time I want you to let me go on my own. Mrs Patel isn't very well. I won't stay very long, but I want to pay her a visit. On my own. Will you let me do that, Lois?'

Lois put her head on one side. 'All right,' she said grudgingly.

Sonia gave her a kiss on top of her spiky pigtailed head. 'That's a very kind girl,' she said. 'You look after Gertrude for me, Lois. Don't let her get into any trouble.' They giggled conspiratorially.

Sonia decided to walk to the hospital. It was not that far and the walk would give her time to think. She did not want to think about Lois, nor about Samuel. She was content to leave them with Gertrude; even to leave them alone in her mind. It was almost a relief to worry about someone else for the afternoon.

The dream about Mrs Patel was coming back to her in snatches, only now she was not so sure that the dream was about Mrs Patel after all. It was about a woman in hospital, certainly, a woman who had just had a baby, a woman who was very tired, very sleepy after her long labour. A woman who was content to let the nurse take the baby away for a while, to the nursery, while she had a well-earned sleep.

And yet, at the back of her mind, even while she slept, the woman knew it was not safe for the child to be taken away from her, even for a minute. Why was that?

Sonia dodged a passer-by, sidestepping at the last minute as she nearly collided with an old man with his dog. The man clicked his tongue at her. 'Sorry,' she said automatically.

Buses passed her – there were always plenty when she had decided to walk instead of waiting for one at the bus-stop. She had not walked this way before. It was nice to be on her own, to get some fresh air. It was nice, too, once in a while, not to have Lois by her side, pulling on her hand, covering her face whenever somebody glanced towards her, continually asking, 'Why?'

For the first time ever she did not feel guilty for not wanting Lois with her. It was such a relief to leave her with somebody else, and an even greater relief to be able to do that, secure in the knowledge that that somebody would not suddenly realize 'the truth' – the entirely untruthful 'truth', Sonia now knew – that Lois was shockingly and incurably bad. A four-year-old scarlet woman with veins chock-full of 'bad blood' inherited inevitably from both her shockingly bad parents.

The idea seemed ridiculous, now she had been told, 'This is ridiculous.' Sonia could not think how she had ever believed it. Perhaps, she thought, it was because I had been taught to believe much the same thing about myself. Maybe even my mother and my father – whoever he was – had been led to think they were incurably bad as well.

Perhaps the foolish idea was a kind of legacy, handed down through generations, waiting for the day when it would be banished by, 'This is ridiculous . . . ignorance of the worst kind . . . paganism.'

Her father. She had not thought about him for years, not since her teenage days when she felt that what kind of person she would grow into must depend on what kind of parents she had had. Yet what influence could he have had on her life, on the way she turned out as an adult? He had not been there to have any effect on her at all.

His sole contribution to her life had been insemination. She might as well have come out of a test tube. It could hardly have been more clinical. Presumably it had made a difference to her mother, but it couldn't have been much of a relationship if he hadn't even stuck around long enough to see the results.

All of a sudden she knew that the woman in the dream was not Mrs Patel, nor herself, but her mother, and that the baby in the nursery was Sonia herself. She could remember it, suddenly, quite clearly. She remembered the man coming in when the nurse went out. She remembered him bending over the crib, bending over her small defenceless body, touching her at first deferentially and then with decision, with cold-blooded fury.

She remembered the thumb digging in below her right collar bone, the fingers closing around her neck, the way her breath seemed to splutter through her nose, her ears, her eyes, looking for a way out.

She remembered her body going limp, remembered him taking his hand away slowly as the shock sank in. In the last moment before his thumb left that very sore patch below the right collar bone, she remembered feeling all the life – all the love – draining out of her through that one small spot and into him, via his thumb.

She knew now that it had happened, that it was no imagination, and that it was this one last part of the incident that had saved him, and her. In that moment, he had regained consciousness of what he was doing and he was able to stop. He had saved himself from retribution and run away, and no one had known he had been there or what he had done, except the baby Sonia and himself.

And she had been saved too, lying there with the sore spot throbbing so much that it had never quite stopped, not all these years since, although sometimes she hardly noticed it. As a child, she used to stroke that area with finger and thumb when she was tired. A succession of foster mothers had scolded her for the habit, because she wore out a threadbare patch there on her clothes.

The incident, until now, had been veiled from her memory. Why should it return to her today, so very clearly? Perhaps because there was some parallel, after all, with Mrs Patel. Perhaps it was learning about Lois's abuse – or hearing confirmation of it, direct from Lois herself – that confirmed what she really knew about her own.

And then again, perhaps it was just one of those days: a day for uncovering things, as Lois was now beginning to uncover her eyes when people looked at her, as if she knew she was no longer veiled by her mother's fear that those people would see her for what she was, and know she was bad.

Reaching the hospital entrance, Sonia put the incident resolutely out of her mind. There was no need to dwell on things. They came to light when it was their time, and after that time they stayed illuminated forever, and could never sneak back to the darkness of the unconscious. She would think about it on some other occasion, when something or someone recalled the memory again. For the moment, she felt it was best to let it lie.

Mrs Patel was near the door of a long ward. Sonia regarded the fact that she was so near the door with misgiving. Wasn't it the patients most at risk who were placed strategically near Sister's office? She was lying on her side, quite still. There was no sign of the baby.

'Mrs Patel?' Sonia called softly. She didn't stir. Sonia became afraid. She left Mrs Patel's side and went in search of the ward sister.

'Yes, she is very tired,' the duty nurse told her. 'She has quite a serious iron deficiency.'

'She's lying very still,' said Sonia.

'I'll come and have a look at her.' The nurse bustled towards the bed. Sonia envied her her courage. 'She's fine,' the nurse gave the verdict. 'Just very sleepy. She's due for another iron injection soon. That usually perks her up a little bit, but she's like this most of the time.'

'What about her husband? Has he been in?'

'Not as far as I know,' the nurse said.

'Where is the baby?' Sonia was nervous of people in authority and she could see that the nurse was waiting for her to go, so she could get back to her paperwork in the office, but she persisted.

'The baby is in the nursery – a very healthy child. No worries about the baby,' the nurse said cheerfully. She turned away. Sonia caught hold of her arm.

'What would happen,' she said, 'if the husband came in and wanted to see the baby?'

The nurse frowned. 'He would see her in the nursery,' she said. 'Or he could bring her in here, to be with his wife.'

'It's only that he's a violent man,' Sonia said. 'He beats his wife when she's pregnant.'

The shutters came down over the nurse's face. 'Details of the patient's background will be in her hospital file,' she intoned, 'but must remain confidential and can't be divulged to anyone else. You're not a relative, are you?'

I'm hardly a blood relative, Sonia fumed silently; Mrs Patel is hardly the same colour as me, is she? Or is that a confidential detail about her background that you can't acknowledge in public either? Aloud she said, 'I'm a friend. I'm worried about the baby.'

'About the baby?' Finally, it seemed, the nurse was beginning to listen. Sonia knew she had been expected to say, 'I'm worried about my friend,' in which case the nurse would have turned away, since grown women were not considered to need protection. Babies were something else. They were 'priority cases'.

Quite right too, Sonia acknowledged. But sometimes the mothers also needed help, when their children were so vulnerable to abuse. Sometimes it was precisely because the mother had nobody to stand up for her that her child was vulnerable in the first place.

'What about the baby?' asked the nurse sharply.

Sonia decided to be blunt. She was only going to get one chance at being listened to, and if the nurse thought she was neurotic, imagining disasters where none existed, that was her free choice; it was none of Sonia's business what the nurse thought of her. It was Sonia's business that she felt – rightly or wrongly – that the baby could be at risk.

'I'm afraid the husband will come in and try to kill the

baby,' she said.

'Have you any reason for thinking this?'

'Only that every other time she's had a baby, he has come back to her – I mean, she has gone back to him, but she has been able to because he's started treating her more affectionately. He has always been pleased with the baby, once it's been born.'

'How do you know this?' asked the nurse in the same sharp tone.

'She told me,' said Sonia.

'But what makes you think that this time is different?'

'This time *is* different,' said Sonia. 'He hasn't been to see her. And she is ill. She can't go home and start coping with everything. She can't look after the other kids, even if he does let them come home. He might have decided this baby is one too many. And he might decide to do something about it.'

The nurse was frowning again. 'Do you have any firm evidence?' she asked. 'Do you know the husband well?'

'No,' Sonia admitted.

'I see. So this is just a . . . a hunch, on your part, is it?'

'I suppose so,' Sonia said. That was it, she thought. She couldn't do any more if she wasn't believed.

'A hunch based on what Mrs Patel told you herself? Nothing else?'

'No. Yes, I mean. That's it.'

'Was she afraid of this happening?' asked the nurse. 'Did she mention anything like this?'

'No, she didn't,' Sonia said.

'Did she say anything . . .?' The nurse seemed perplexed. Sonia felt something had changed. The woman seemed to be trying genuinely to understand now. 'She must have said something to you that made you believe there was a risk? Look, come into the office a minute, will you?'

Sonia went in. She tried to remember what Mrs Patel had said. She screwed up her eyes tightly and tried to visualize Mrs Patel sitting in the kitchen at the women's refuge.

'She said she loved him,' she remembered. 'That he was

violent, and a weak man, but she loved him whatever he did. And sometimes she had to get out of his way – every time she was pregnant – because otherwise he would kill her, and he wouldn't be able to live with himself if he did. And that everything would be all right once the baby was born; they would go home then.'

'Well, we have notified him that the baby has been born,' the nurse said. 'I can't see what else we can do. This is really the social worker's responsibility.'

'The baby is your responsibility, while she's in here,' Sonia said.

'Yes, but the baby's in no danger while she's in the hospital,' said the nurse. 'She's in with the premature babies and there's a nurse on duty in the unit the whole time.'

'It can still happen, if someone is really determined to do it,' Sonia said.

'There's no possibility of a father coming into the hospital and killing the baby on the premises,' the nurse said, smiling slightly to show Sonia she was being ridiculous.

'I have known it happen,' Sonia said.

The smile faded. 'I can't see what else we can do,' the nurse said. 'If someone is really determined, as you say . . . We're not a security unit.'

'Wouldn't the baby be safer in the ward?' said Sonia persuasively. 'Beside the mother? I know she's not well enough to look after it; the nurses would still have to do that. But there are more people around.'

'The nurses are already overstretched,' said the nurse. 'Perhaps in a few days' time, when the consultant does his main round, we could bring the subject up, and at the ward meeting on Friday, and see what can be arranged.'

Sonia sighed. 'Look,' she said, 'I might be wrong and there's no risk, but if there is a risk then you can't postpone it for a few days till it suits the consultant.'

The nurse looked annoyed. 'It's all very well,' she said, 'but hospitals aren't designed to cope with this kind of situation.'

'Neither are babies,' Sonia pointed out.

There was a silence. 'Okay,' the nurse said, 'I'll talk to Sister about bringing the baby into the ward.'

'Good,' Sonia said. 'I'll go and fetch the baby now.'

She went out of the office quickly, before the nurse could say anything else. Fortunately the phone rang just then and claimed the girl's attention. Sonia followed signs to the premature baby unit and found no nurse there. That settles it, she thought. That baby's not staying here.

Mrs Patel's baby was not hard to identify, even without looking at the tag round her wrist. She was the largest in the unit, the only one in an open cot, not an incubator, and without a tube in her nose. Sonia wheeled the cot out of the door and along the corridor to the ward.

'Now hold on,' said the nurse angrily, coming out of the office and catching her. 'I didn't say you could take matters into your own hands. I said I would talk to Sister about it.'

'There was no one in the premature baby unit,' Sonia said. 'I walked in and wheeled the cradle out. Nobody stopped me. It's that easy to get in.'

'You're going to get me into real trouble, doing this,' the nurse said. 'I don't have the authority to let you move the child in here.'

'I'm not trying to get you into trouble,' Sonia said. 'I'm trying to make sure the baby stays out of it.'

The nurse shrugged. 'I'm the one who'll get the blame,' she said.

'You won't get suffocated,' said Sonia brutally, 'so that the air goes out of your lungs and they feel that they're going to burst, and your nose and ears block so you can't breathe even when he lets go of you.'

The nurse's eyes widened with shock.

'Let me put the cot beside Mrs Patel's bed,' said Sonia more gently. 'Please.'

The girl nodded finally. 'All right,' she said.

Chapter Forty-One

Mrs Patel was awake when Sonia went into the ward again.

'Hi,' Sonia said. 'Do you remember me?'

'Hello!' said Mrs Patel. 'Sonia. It's nice of you to come and see me.' She sat up, with difficulty.

'Let me give you a hand,' Sonia said, pulling out the back-rest and laying the pillows against it. 'How are you feeling now?' she asked.

'Not too bad,' said Mrs Patel. 'Very tired, but not too bad. How are you? Move that baby away, by the next bed, and pull out the stool, then you can sit down.'

'It's your baby,' Sonia told her. 'I brought her in from the nursery. They're going to leave her in here now, beside you.'

Mrs Patel's expression changed. 'No, no, no!' she cried. 'Take it away! Immediately!'

'You don't have to look after her,' Sonia explained. 'Not while you're still so tired. The nurses will do everything for her.'

'No, no, you don't understand!' said Mrs Patel. She waved her arm as if trying to push the baby from her. 'My husband is coming. I must leave this baby alone. He was right. I should have listened to what he said.'

'What do you mean?' Sonia asked. She hadn't expected this.

'He said we would not be able to cope with another child, not him and not me. It was too much. Four is enough. We have all we want, a boy and three girls. Perhaps if it was a boy. No, I should have done what he said.'

'Done what?' Sonia said.

'He said have an abortion,' Mrs Patel said. 'And I said no. I should not have said no. A good wife obeys her husband. This is why he has not come to see me, this time. But now I have sent him a message, by my sister-in-law, that I will do as he says.'

'Do what?' Sonia almost shouted. This was terrible.

'I will abort this baby,' said Mrs Patel. 'Like he told me.'

Sonia stared at her. Had the woman lost her senses? 'You can't have an abortion now,' she said. 'The baby has been born. She's here.' She picked her up out of the cot and held her.

The baby's mouth puckered, expecting milk. Sonia was reminded of Lois when she was a few days old.

'What difference does it make?' Mrs Patel said. 'Whether before or after? It is the same thing.'

Sonia clutched the baby closer to her. 'What are you going to do?' She was horror-struck. How could the woman talk like this? Was it post-natal depression? Sonia had heard it could affect people like this.

'I am not going to do anything,' said Mrs Patel. 'My husband will arrange everything. Put the baby back in the nursery. My husband know where to go.'

'No!' Sonia said. 'Listen, Mrs Patel, if you can't cope with another child, have it adopted. There are thousands of couples who can't have children.'

'My husband would not allow it,' said Mrs Patel. 'He would consider it a disgrace.'

Sonia sat down. The baby opened her eyes and stared blankly. Sonia stroked her cheek with one finger.

'We will tell the children the baby died,' Mrs Patel continued. 'Then we will all go home together and make a new life.'

'You've just made a new life,' said Sonia. She held out the baby so Mrs Patel could not avoid seeing it. Mrs Patel turned her head away.

'It was a mistake,' she said.

'So was Lois,' said Sonia, 'and she turned out to be the best thing that ever happened to me. Look at this lovely child.'

'No,' said Mrs Patel.

'What if it doesn't work?' Sonia asked. 'My father tried to kill me, and my mother either didn't know or she turned a blind eye because she thought he'd come back to her if she didn't have the baby – I don't know which. Anyway, he didn't come back, and he couldn't kill me. He had a good try. I had asthma for years, and a pain in my shoulder and another pain in my side for a lot of the time, so I couldn't run when I did games at school.'

Mrs Patel kept her head turned away and did not reply.

'My mother never forgave me for being born,' Sonia said. 'I wasn't ever welcomed into the world. I wouldn't have minded being fostered, if I'd known she'd welcomed me but couldn't cope. I could have been brought up by somebody else and got to know her when I was older, if she wanted.'

'My husband wouldn't allow it,' Mrs Patel repeated.

'You want your children to live with him, in the same house, when he murdered their sister?' Sonia persisted. 'Do you want to live with a man who murdered your child? You think he'll turn into a loving husband and father, when he's done that? What if it was Anita he'd killed? Or Pretty?'

'Don't say that!' said Mrs Patel.

'What's the difference?' Sonia said. 'You said there's no difference between killing an unborn child and a newborn baby. So what's the difference between killing a five-day-old and a five-year-old girl? Except that it takes more force?'

'You should not say these things to me,' said Mrs Patel tearfully.

'Because you're in a weak state?' Sonia asked. 'Because you've just had a baby? This baby? Look at her.' She put the baby on Mrs Patel's lap.

'No,' said Mrs Patel. 'Take it away!'

Sonia left the baby where she was and took her hand. The baby caught hold of Sonia's finger and clenched it in her tiny fist. Sonia withdrew her finger and put Mrs Patel's in its place. The baby gripped it. 'See how strong she is?' Sonia said. 'There's a lot of life in a newborn baby. You have to use real force to kill one.'

Mrs Patel started to cry soundlessly. Sonia felt remorse. She sat on the bed beside her and put an arm round her.

'I am so tired,' Mrs Patel sobbed.

'You are tired,' Sonia said, 'and I think you're depressed as well, which isn't surprising. It's only surprising you've coped so well up to now. But if you go ahead with this, you'll depress yourself so bad you won't come out of it. How could you and the children be well and happy, with this on your conscience? The children might not know what happened to the baby, but they'd know something awful had happened to you. You'd never forgive yourself.'

'I am a wicked woman,' sobbed Mrs Patel. 'I don't know how I could ever think of doing this.' She was cupping her hand round the baby's head and stroking it with her thumb, without realizing what she was doing.

'You're not wicked,' said Sonia, 'but you were about to get used, all right. Look – how can your husband love you and kill your baby? It doesn't happen like that. What he does to your child, he does to you.'

'I know,' she said. 'I know that. I just don't know what to do. I can't look after five children by myself. My sister-in-law would help, but she has three of her own. I have no parents. No brothers and sisters in this country.'

Sonia knew she should offer to help, and knew she couldn't do it. Tiredness seemed to have caught up on her too, since she had come to Samuel's. It might take Samuel a long time to get well. She had a child and a full-time job, and no family either. She didn't feel she could take on any more. She decided to be honest and say so.

'I don't expect help,' said Mrs Patel. 'I know you can't do it. I am not asking you, Sonia.'

'No, but you must ask somebody. Even if the baby is taken into care. Even if all the children are, for a little while. They'll forgive you, if you make sure they know you love them. That's what counts, isn't it?'

'Yes,' said Mrs Patel. 'That is what count, in the end.'

'I wish I could help,' Sonia said.

Mrs Patel patted her hand. 'You have helped,' she said. 'You told me the truth.'

Sonia laughed. 'Big deal!'

'No,' said Mrs Patel. 'The truth is a very small thing, sometimes. A tiny detail. But it make all the difference in the world.'

Sonia looked at her watch. 'I'll have to go. The old man I'm working for is ill, and his cousin will want to get her train home soon. I'll leave you my phone number. Don't give it to Bella, though, will you?'

'Bella is coming in now,' Mrs Patel pointed out, 'with the children.'

Sonia looked up and saw them coming through the door. Riaz and Anita ran ahead and leaned over the baby, making cooing noises and touching her small hands and head delightedly. Mrs Patel looked over their heads at Sonia and smiled. 'They are telling baby she is welcome,' she said.

Sonia greeted Bella briefly and said, 'I have to rush,' before Bella could ask her where she was living and what she was doing. It was not just an excuse; she had been out for longer than she had expected to be. Schoolchildren were fighting at the bus-stop so she walked home, but almost at a run, feeling guilty for abandoning Gertrude.

Gertrude, calm and smiling, was making tea when Sonia let herself in by the kitchen door.

'How was your friend?' she asked.

'All right,' Sonia said. 'A bit tired.'

'You look tired yourself,' Gertrude said. 'Samuel is getting up for tea. Lois is in the garden. No – don't take over, Sonia. You sit down, for once, and be waited on.'

'What time will you have to go for your train?' Sonia asked her.

'It doesn't matter, my dear. Would you like me to stay a night, or would that be one more person to worry about?'

'Wouldn't your husband mind?' asked Sonia. She was surprised to find she didn't resent Gertrude helping. In fact, it was a relief.

'Humphrey minds everything I do, equally,' said Gertrude, 'so it really makes very little difference. It gives me the freedom to do what I like, since he is so certain to be displeased.'

Sonia giggled. 'It would be nice,' she said, 'if you wouldn't mind staying a night. Would Miss Prynne's room be okay?'

'Perfectly,' said Gertrude. 'I did bring my toothbrush, just in case.'

'I'll go and air the bed,' Sonia said. 'It'll be damp otherwise.'

'Don't worry,' said Gertrude. 'It won't be the first damp bed I've slept in. I shall survive!'

'You let me do it properly,' said Sonia firmly. 'You may be the waitress for today, but I'm the housekeeper – right?'

Gertrude laughed. 'Right,' she said. 'By the way, the doctor called again while you were out. Samuel told him he felt much better, and we'd all had a good talk about why that had happened to him, and the doctor said he would postpone the hospital admission and see how things turned out. He'll call again tomorrow, but said do ring him at home tonight if there are any difficulties.'

'Oh good,' Sonia said. 'Do you think he'd be better in hospital, though, Gertrude? I don't have any nursing experience or anything.'

'He'd be happier at home, if you can cope,' said Gertrude decisively. 'Samuel detests hospitals.'

Samuel came downstairs, fully dressed, a little shaky but smiling. 'How pleasant to hear ladies nattering in the kitchen,' he said. 'Very homely.'

'Nattering indeed!' Gertrude scolded him. 'Serious discussions of affairs of state. Go away and sit in the sitting room. The tea is nearly ready.'

'I'll just have a look at the garden,' he said. 'The lawn needs mowing, doesn't it?'

'Then give Sonia Arthur's phone number and she'll arrange it,' said Gertrude. 'You're not thinking of getting the lawn-mower out yourself, are you – now, this afternoon?'

'No, no,' said Samuel soothingly. 'I'll get Arthur.'

Gertrude raised her eyes to the cracked and cobwebby ceiling. 'He was going to do it himself,' she said. 'There's no hope for the man. When will you remember your age, Samuel?'

Samuel winked at Sonia. 'When I have my birthday party in a few months' time,' he said. 'And I warn you, I shall expect a cake.'

'Then you better behave yourself in the meantime,' said Sonia. 'No more fighting Red Indians in the night.'

'You know,' said Samuel thoughtfully, 'I do believe I have seen the last of those Red Indians now.'

Chapter Forty-Two

Samuel took a while to get well. Every time, it seemed, he was ready to go back to work he had another bout of exhaustion. Sonia persuaded him to stay in bed later in the mornings, to have breakfast in bed and then get up slowly, and to have a rest in the afternoons.

Privately, she thought he would feel stronger when he decided not to return to work; it was stubbornness that made him determined to work out the month's notice, but after she had told him once, 'You've already worked twenty years longer than anyone expected you to,' she stopped nagging him. If he wanted to think of himself as not yet retired, let him. Meanwhile, he was learning to take life at a more sedate pace.

May lengthened into June. The blossom fell from the trees, and Arthur was called in more frequently to mow the fast-growing lawns. Buds on the many rose bushes opened into full fragrant blooms, and on fine afternoons Sonia placed Samuel's deck chair near his favourite rose, Peace, with its ample butter-coloured heads tinged with pink scenting the air for yards around.

Sonia bought a Hoover and a washing machine and spent her days cleaning the house methodically, room by room. She hung the washing out on a rotary line behind the espaliers of apple trees, by the garage.

The plumber and the plasterer worked on the bathroom and toilet and made a start on the kitchen. Progress was slow, and they grumbled that Sonia would not let them work between two and four on cool afternoons when Samuel took his rest in the house rather than the garden, but results were gradually beginning to show.

A letter arrived for Sonia from one of her foster mothers, then another from the matron of the children's home. In mid-June, an aerogramme brought news of Aunty Sue in Jamaica, with a renewed invitation to visit any time they could manage to find the money for the fares, and the next day an identical aerogramme, with an identical invitation, arrived from the aunt in Jamaica whom Sonia could hardly remember.

Gertrude, who had taken to spending a night with them once a week, was delighted that Sonia's efforts had borne fruit. It encouraged Gertrude to continue bullying Sonia. She persuaded her to sign up for the upholstery class in September, made her promise to start at the Caribbean Society 'as soon as Samuel is better' and accompanied her to the local primary school to enrol Lois for the coming autumn term.

Lois spent every waking hour in the garden, protesting when she was called in for meals or to go to bed, and was only persuaded to leave it when offered an outing to the park or to play in Mrs Baker's or Mrs Atwood's gardens.

Sonia resisted Mrs Atwood's attempts to introduce Lois to playgroup. 'It's not worth it just for a month or two,' she said. 'She'll be starting school in September.' Her time with Lois at home was running out. She knew she would soon have to let Lois go, and already she was entrusting her more to other people – to Mrs Baker and Mrs Atwood, to Samuel and Gertrude, and once to a lady from the church who invited Lois to come and play with her children for the afternoon.

Lois adapted easily to other company and showed no signs of shyness even when they visited the school and Lois was left to join the infants' class for an hour, to acclimatize her and twelve other solemn four-to-five-year-olds to being at school. She returned full of enthusiasm for being a schoolgirl and was intensely disappointed to be told she had to wait till September.

'Lois is a different child,' Gertrude remarked to Samuel one afternoon in the garden. Samuel had bought her a swing. Arthur had installed it on a patch of turf by the flowering cherry tree, and Lois was swinging back and forth energetically, singing. 'She obviously isn't damaged by what happened to her before. A more self-assured child you couldn't hope to meet. That whole nasty business is gone and forgotten.'

Samuel agreed, but privately he was less confident about Sonia. She worked too hard, he thought, and still had little appetite for food. When she stopped work, she was restless and couldn't relax, although she laughed and smiled and talked much more freely about herself now; she had lost her secretiveness and yielded to persuasion to go for coffee with neighbours.

Samuel had spoken to the chief librarian and made arrangements for Sonia and Lois to join the library. Sonia brought home a selection of books, but her mind never seemed entirely occupied by what she was reading. Often, in the evenings, Samuel would look up from his own book and catch Sonia with hers open on her knee, staring into space. Once he said tentatively, 'You will let the past go now, my dear – that man Barnes?' and she said sadly, 'No, I can't do that.'

It was one evening towards the end of July that it became clear that Lois had not yet let go of the past either. Samuel, feeling tired again, had been persuaded by Sonia to go to bed after supper. 'I won't sleep,' he had protested, and Sonia replied, 'Who said anything about sleeping? Rest in bed and read, and I'll bring you up some cocoa at nine.'

Lois insisted on keeping Samuel company. She hadn't looked at the dolls' house for weeks, preferring to spend her time in the garden on the swing, or laboriously learning to use a skipping rope Sonia had bought her, but tonight she dragged the apple-box house into Samuel's room and played on the floor, chatting away to herself while Samuel read his book and listened to her with half an ear.

When Sonia appeared in the doorway with his cup of cocoa, Samuel pressed one finger to his lips and mouthed, 'Listen!' at her, nodding towards Lois. Sonia handed him the cup and backed out of the room without Lois noticing her, and stood on the landing.

Lois had placed the lady doll – the one she insisted on calling Mrs Grenville – in the sitting room, while the small black doll she called Sonia (though Samuel had intended it to represent Lois) was upstairs in one of the bedrooms. 'Hoovering,' said Lois, making Hoovering noises.

The man doll – Eddie Barnes – was in the cellar, and the big doll was approaching the matchstick steps that led down to it.

'Oh!' Lois exclaimed. 'What are you doing?' She picked up her pink hair ribbon and draped it across the Eddie doll. 'Oh, you poor man!' she said. 'A snake has got into your trousers and it's dragging you by the hand! You will fall into the boiler and be burnt up in the flames!'

Sonia raised both hands to her mouth. Samuel glanced at her and motioned her to be quiet.

'The snake is getting bigger and bigger,' said Lois, 'and stronger and stronger. It's pulled you right across the room, right near the boiler. You're going to be burnt to death!'

She moved the Lois doll across to the Eddie doll, although it was almost too big to fit into the dolls' house at all.

'I will help you,' she said. She took the pink ribbon away from the man doll, lifted up the girl doll's skirt, and pushed the ribbon into the doll's knickers. Sonia let out a strangled sound. Lois then made the doll fall flat on its back.

'Silly girl!' Lois scolded. 'Stand up! How can this snake go into your tummy if you won't stand still?' She pulled the ribbon back and started stuffing it into the Lois doll's mouth, the open rosebud mouth designed to take the small plastic feeding bottle that had been in the box with the doll.

'This will only choke you a bit,' said Lois, 'but you mustn't be sick, or the snake will come out and eat the man again.' She pushed nearly all the ribbon into the doll's mouth. Then she made the Eddie doll walk up the basement steps and go into the garden, and she showed the Mrs Grenville doll standing at the top of the steps.

'Get back to your work, Barnes,' said Lois in a stern voice. She threw the Eddie doll aside, and made the Mrs Grenville doll descend the steps and beat the Lois doll over the head

313

vigorously. 'You little slut!' she roared. Then she put the Mrs Grenville doll back in the sitting room and addressed the Lois doll severely.

'You are a wicked girl,' she said, 'and for your punishment you will have this snake inside you all your life, and it will eat you alive and make you very, very sick.'

'Oh no!' cried Sonia, running forwards and clasping Lois in her arms. 'No, Lois, that's not true! You mustn't think that!'

Lois looked startled. 'It is true!' she said defensively.

'No, no, it's not! You're a good girl, Lois. There are no snakes inside you – honest!'

'There is a snake,' Lois insisted. 'When I look in the mirror, it comes out of my mouth.'

'No, it doesn't! I'll show you, Lois! Come and look in the mirror with me now. There's no snake. I promise.'

'Not *now*,' Lois agreed. 'It comes when I go to sleep.'

'In your dreams,' Sonia said. 'Lois, that's only a dream. Is that why you wake up sick?' She hugged Lois tightly and rocked her to and fro. 'It's only a dream,' she repeated. 'You're a good girl. Mrs Grenville was wrong. It was Eddie's fault.'

'No,' Lois said, pushing her away. 'It wasn't Eddie's fault. The snake was eating him. It had got inside his trousers.'

Sonia stared at her. 'Was that why you used to go looking inside his trousers sometimes? To see if he was safe from the snake?'

Lois nodded.

'And did it . . . did it happen again?' Sonia asked, dreading the answer.

'No,' Lois said. 'Not in the garden. Only in the cellar. But I saved him from the snake. It went into me instead.'

Sonia looked at Samuel. He was shaking. Tears rolled down his face. 'I don't know what to do,' said Sonia.

'I want you to kill the snake,' Lois said.

'Kill the snake?' Sonia asked.

'You'll have to cut me open,' said Lois, 'and take the snake away and kill it dead.'

314

'Oh,' Sonia said. She thought for a moment. 'You know a better way of doing that?' she said.

Lois shook her head.

'You know what snakes are absolutely allergic to?' Sonia asked her.

'No.'

'Coke,' Sonia said. 'In fact, you've drunk so much Coke recently that the snake is probably almost dead already. All we have to do is give it one last lethal dose.'

'No,' Lois said. 'You're just saying that. The snake isn't killed with Coke. It's still there. I've seen it.'

'Not Coke, Sonia,' said Samuel suddenly. 'Lois is right. It isn't quite strong enough for snakes. I've got a remedy, Lois, but you'll have to be very brave. It's very nasty.'

Lois looked relieved. 'Yes,' she said. 'It has to be nasty, or else it won't do any good.'

'What is it?' Sonia asked Samuel.

'I'll show you,' he said. He got out of bed and put on his dressing gown. 'Follow me,' he told them. They followed him downstairs.

Samuel took the key from the top of the grandfather clock in the hall and opened the door of the dining room. 'It's in the court cabinet,' he said. 'I keep it there for special emergencies like this.'

He knelt down and took out a bottle of vintage cognac. He dusted it off and showed Sonia the label. 'This will be strong enough, won't it?' he said.

'It's certainly strong enough to work,' Sonia said, 'but I'm afraid Lois won't manage to swallow it. I know she's very brave, but it will taste really horrible.'

'I will,' Lois said. 'I will swallow it.'

'Of course you will,' Samuel said. 'You'll take one good big gulp and get rid of the snake for ever, won't you?'

Lois looked at him with complete trust. 'Yes,' she said. 'I will.'

Samuel took out one of the finest glasses, a crystal liqueur glass. He poured a small measure of brandy into the bottom of it and held it to Lois's lips. 'Head back,' he commanded, 'and swallow it down in one go.'

Lois did as she was told. She screwed up her eyes in disgust as it reached her throat. 'Haghh!' she gasped.

'There now,' said Samuel. 'Nasty but very effective. Never fails to work.'

'Lois,' Sonia said. 'Is the snake gone now? Has it fizzled away to nothing in your stomach and evaporated into thin air?'

Lois felt her tummy experimentally. 'Yes,' she said.

Sonia let out a great sigh. 'Thank God for that,' she said. She started to cry in great shuddering gasps, rocking from side to side.

'Can I play in the garden now?' Lois asked her.

'Come and have a walk in the garden,' Samuel said, 'just for five minutes. Then you must go to bed.'

Sonia saw them through the dining room window, Samuel in his dressing gown and Lois in her pyjamas, walking hand in hand round the garden, solemnly discussing the progress of growth of the various flowers. She had no doubts about Samuel now. He was good for Lois. If anything ever happened to Sonia, Samuel and Gertrude would make sure that Lois got well looked after, somewhere good.

As for Sonia, there was something she had to do.

Chapter Forty-Three

Lois was very excited. She was going to spend a whole day at school – a whole day, not just an hour or two. It was a special trial day for the new reception class who would start in a week's time, and Lois would stay there till three o'clock in the afternoon, when Molly Atwood would collect her and take her to her house to play until Sonia came home.

'I'll go with you to school in the morning,' Sonia promised, 'but I might not be here when you come home. I'm going out for the day. You'll be okay, won't you?'

'No,' Lois said. 'You can't go out for the day. Who will make Samuel his lunch?'

'I'm leaving Samuel's lunch in the fridge,' Sonia told her. 'He'll have sandwiches with Bob.' Bob was the plumber. 'Okay?'

'Okay,' said Lois graciously.

Samuel was worried. For the past week he had heard Sonia in the kitchen, early in the morning. He recognized the sound of blade against honing steel. Sonia was sharpening and re-sharpening the carving knife.

When she left to take Lois to school that morning, he asked, 'Where are you off to today?' Sonia looked evasive. 'To visit somebody,' she said.

It could have been Mrs Patel, but . . . when she had gone, Samuel went down to the kitchen, stepped over the builders' rubble, and opened the sink drawer. The carving knife was missing. He went to the phone and dialled. When the number was answered, he said simply, 'I believe it may be today.'

Sonia saw Lois safely into her class, waved to her from the door and walked away slowly. Once outside the school gates, she speeded up, almost running to the bus-stop. She had not slept last night. On the bus, she noticed that her hands were shaking, and forced them to stop. She was going to need steady hands today. She was on her way to murder Eddie Barnes.

The knife was wrapped in a towel inside a canvas shopping bag. Sonia kept it turned away from the lady next to her on the bus. The blade was so finely sharpened by now that she was afraid of stabbing someone by mistake.

Her heart was pumping so fast that she felt she could have run all the way to Sussex, just to work off the adrenalin. She was trying to keep herself calm. She would need all her strength for what she was going to do. Eddie was wiry and strong. Sonia's only advantage lay in taking him by surprise.

She knew he took his coffee at eleven every morning, in the cellar, with his newspaper spread out in front of him on the old Formica-topped table. Sonia used to make his coffee for him, when she made Mrs Grenville's, and he would collect it from the kitchen and take it away with him.

Mrs Grenville took her coffee in the sitting room, or 'the drawing room' as she called it. Sonia sometimes stopped work for a coffee herself, but more often than not Mrs Grenville had set her so much work to do that she had to carry on. She used to give Lois a small cup of milk and a biscuit – usually a chocolate finger – to take in the garden.

It must have been then that it happened, Sonia reflected: at eleven o'clock, with Sonia upstairs cleaning the bedrooms while Mrs Grenville sipped coffee downstairs and Lois, tired of eating her elevenses alone and looking for company while Sonia worked, wandered down to the cellar . . .

It was essential that Sonia should arrive at the house just after eleven o'clock then, while Mrs Grenville was safely inside drinking coffee either alone or with friends – or she might be out drinking coffee in someone else's house, possibly. Either way, provided that she had not changed her routine – and she was a creature of routine habits – she would not be around to see Sonia make her way to the back of the house and down the stairs to the basement.

The house was not far from the station. There should be taxis around, to meet the London train, but if not, then the bus would get her there on time, or she could even walk and make it before eleven thirty when Eddie returned to work. If he hadn't gone back to his work by eleven thirty-five Mrs Grenville would always go and check up on him – as she must have done that morning she found him with Lois.

Sonia took a deep breath. She must stay calm. There was still the local train to catch, before she even got to Victoria Station. She had never known a journey seem so long.

At Victoria, she became seized by anxieties, not about the murder but about something possibly happening to stop her. Suppose the ticket machine rejected her money? Or the train had been cancelled today?

When neither of these disasters occurred and she was safely seated by the window and the train was pulling out of the station, she started worrying that there might be a derailment, or even a collision with another train.

She told herself to be quiet, knowing that she was trying to find something easier to worry about than the problem of killing Eddie Barnes. Hadn't she told Mrs Patel it could be surprisingly difficult to kill a newborn baby? Why, even unborn babies sometimes fought so hard to live that they could not be aborted but were delivered alive and had to be left in some out-of-the-way corner of the hospital or clinic till their unformed lungs finally relinquished their last breath.

How could Sonia hope to kill a full-grown man, even with the advantage of surprise? Surprise and rage, Sonia thought. She felt she had enough rage in her to kill somebody twice his size.

The rage was for herself. She harboured no illusions that she was avenging Lois. Lois, as Sonia well knew, did not need avenging. Lois had been happy to help Eddie in what she had perceived as his moments of danger. She had only been worried that, as punishment for making Mrs Grenville angry with Sonia and herself, she would have to keep the snake and no one would be sent to save her from it, as she had saved her friend Eddie.

Admittedly, as she got older, Lois would have to be taught to see things differently. Sonia didn't want her to feel obliged to go investigating men's trousers to make sure they were not being consumed by undisciplined snakes and offering to help them out if they were. But the child was in no present danger and only really needed to learn – according to Dr Carroll – to value her own safety more highly and to leave grown-ups to deal with their own problems, snakes or otherwise.

Lois was happy. It was Sonia who needed this revenge, for herself. All her life, it now seemed, she had tried not to blame anybody for her suffering – neither her absent father nor her mother who had promised to return to collect her and never had, nor even her mother's boyfriend for taking her mother away to the States to start a new life without her.

Sonia had certainly had periods of trying to blame each of them in turn, but never quite managed it. All the evidence seemed to boil down to the simple fact that these people could not cope. They could not cope with their child, not because they had had the wrong kind of child or had a child at the wrong time or couldn't cope with bringing up someone else's child, but because they couldn't cope with themselves.

There were grounds for pity there, but not for blame. How could you blame anyone for not coping with life? Sonia herself couldn't cope with much of it, so she couldn't find it in her heart to blame them.

But Eddie . . . Eddie Barnes had a good job and a home provided for him. No one could say Eddie Barnes couldn't cope with life. What he couldn't cope with was that any woman he wanted should not be instantly available to him. Eddie Barnes had raped a child because the child's mother barred her door against him at night.

It was only justice, then, that Eddie should pay the price, not only for Lois's sufferings but for Sonia's as well – all Sonia's sufferings, for the whole of her life. As Sonia saw it, her struggles to overcome the disadvantages of her upbringing had been rendered futile by Eddie's crime. She had survived motherlessness, homelessness, rootlessness. She had been born black and brought up white and could not now entirely identify with either. She had been uprooted from a familiar island and abandoned in an unfamiliar one. She had established herself in a culture which still did not wholly accept her because of the colour of her skin and because she was an unmarried woman with a child.

She had survived this and made a life for herself and for Lois. She was dependent on no one. She could hold her head up high. Until Eddie Barnes came along. Eddie had tried to treat Sonia as white colonials used to treat black slaves, and Sonia had rebelled, so he had turned on her child.

Sonia bit her lip. There was of course the fact that white children were also abused, white women were also despised and treated as less than human. There had been that girl from the village who had come to the Grenvilles' front door crying, sobbing that Eddie had mixed her drinks at some party and got her so drunk she didn't know what she was doing . . . George Grenville had sent her away. She remembered that girl's face.

In all honesty, Sonia could not interpret Eddie's crime as a racial assault, except in terms of the human race. There would always be people who abused one another, black or white, men and women.

She knew well enough that she could, if she chose, trade on her disadvantages. If she killed or injured Eddie, who would really blame her? A poor woman, abandoned as a child, an immigrant, an unmarried mother, wrongfully dismissed from her menial job, whose defenceless small child had been molested. Her sentence would probably be light; there was no shortage of mitigating circumstances. Public opinion would be on her side.

Sonia shook her head. If she used those tactics, then it would not be Eddie Barnes who undid the good of Sonia's struggle for independence: it would be Sonia herself. She would class herself as someone who could not be expected to

321

use self-control, someone who could not cope with the tough side of life. All her life she had resisted those who would put her down in this way. Was she going to give in now, let people say, 'Poor soul, who could blame her after the life she's had?'

She had to decide which role was hers now: the rejected child, or the responsible adult who knew perfectly well what she was about to do. She couldn't play both.

And what if sufferings had occurred in Eddie's childhood, too, and these came out in court? If a court acquitted Sonia of responsibility in attacking Eddie, might the same people not acquit Eddie of blame in attacking Lois? What if Eddie, who seemed so self-sufficient, turned out to be eligible for deprived child status too? You never knew what lay in a person's history, did you? Sonia would hardly be able to argue that, whatever his past, he had to be held responsible for his crime and then claim she was not responsible for her counter-attack, could she? The argument cut both ways.

Without thinking, she had slid open the zip of the canvas bag and, through the towel, felt the sharpness of the blade of the knife against her thumb.

It was quite likely that if she drew this knife on Eddie it might indeed cut both ways. Sonia faced the thought that Eddie might kill her. She had faced it before and found it worth the risk. Let him punish himself, committing another crime, then perhaps the truth would come to light and he would get the sentence he deserved.

But who would really be punished if Sonia died, apparently heroically avenging her child? Sonia knew the answer to that. Lois. And Lois had been punished enough, including – it had to be admitted – by Sonia.

The train slowed, stopped at a small country station. The only other person in Sonia's carriage, a middle-aged woman with a dog, got out. She was on her own. Alone with a dilemma that only she, in the end, could resolve.

On impulse, as the train gathered speed again, Sonia slammed down the window and hurled the knife out of it, complete with its swathing of towel.

Then she sat down again. That was one option less to consider, anyhow. If Eddie was going to kill her, he could damn well provide his own knife; she was not going to make it easy for him.

Chapter Forty-Four

She still wasn't sure what she was going to do when she got out at the station. It felt strange coming back.

The platforms and the station forecourt were as quiet as they had been on the day Sonia and Lois were left here by George Grenville, to sink or swim in the world. 'Well, we're swimming,' said Sonia defiantly, under her breath.

What was she coming back here for? She had a home, a job, a new family; Lois was happy. Lois. Sonia pictured her sitting now, with solemn face and green-ribboned pigtails, behind her miniature desk in the Portakabin classroom. For a minute Sonia minded, agonizingly, that she would not be the one to collect Lois from her first full trial day at school. If she caught the very next train back to London, she could be at the school gates when Lois came out, instead of Mrs Atwood . . .

No. She had to go through with this. During the past months she had tried, as Samuel and Gertrude had advocated, to put the whole horrible episode behind her, and she couldn't. Unless she confronted Eddie and the Grenvilles, they would continue to haunt her for the rest of her life, and she would have no peace of mind.

If she saw them, confronted them with the truth, then although they could deny it furiously they would know that Sonia knew it was true. Then let them sit in it. Let them live with this tormenting discomfort of mind. Why should Sonia do it? They should not be protected while she suffered for what they had done.

She did not regret throwing away the knife. Once she had brought the matter out into the open their consciences could stab them far more effectively than any knife, causing far more permanent wounds.

They thought they could hide this away in their minds, pretend it hadn't happened, that they were a nice genteel couple with a devoted, efficient gardener and an ex-housekeeper who had, most unfortunately, turned out to be of doubtful character. Well, Sonia was going to show them that things like this could not be kept dark. She would go in there not with a knife but with an almighty great flashlight.

They wouldn't admit anything; Sonia knew them too well to expect that. But they wouldn't forget it either.

Having made up her mind at least about her objective, Sonia showed her ticket to the utterly disinterested railman who stood reading a smudgy copy of the *Sun* at the exit gate and stepped out into the sunshine.

There were no taxis in the station forecourt, only one young man in a dark blue Cortina who regarded her with undisguised interest but made no move to accost her. Obviously not a minicab driver.

As she had plenty of time, and an excess of nervous energy to work off, she decided to walk. Sure enough the familiar streets and lanes had a calming effect on her. It was quiet here after London. Such a lot had happened since leaving the Grenvilles; it seemed years ago now, yet it was only four months.

Turning off the road and walking down the driveway to the Grenvilles' house, she heard birds singing, felt the scrunch of gravel under her feet, and thought, This could have been a peaceful place.

She stepped off the gravel on to the grass, afraid of making too much noise, not wanting to announce her arrival. She glanced over her shoulder before moving into the shelter of the trees and saw the blue Cortina she had noticed at the station swing its nose into the driveway.

For a moment her heart missed a beat, then she relaxed as she saw the car reverse. It must have been using the driveway to turn in. It used to make Mr Grenville mad when people did that.

Only the Rolls was parked at the front of the house. That meant Mr Grenville had gone to work today as usual. It probably meant that Mrs Grenville was at home and had no visitors – though it might mean that Eddie had chauffeured her in the Rolls to some appointment and then returned here, with instructions to pick her up later.

Sonia took a deep breath. There were two possibilities then. Either Mrs Grenville was somewhere in the house or the grounds and so was Eddie, or else Eddie was here alone. She looked at her watch. Nearly coffee time. With any luck, she would have time to make her way to the cellar and conceal herself there before Eddie came back from the kitchen with his mug of coffee and his newspaper and sat down at the table – there opposite the boiler that Lois had feared would eat him.

She could not think of Lois now without trembling. Steadying herself against the handrail as she walked down the cellar steps, she felt as though she was descending into hell.

The cellar was empty. The broken chair Eddie used to sit on to drink his coffee was pushed back from the table, and both were covered in dust. The boiler was unlit. Sonia was surprised at this. Eddie never let the boiler go out. Standards were slipping on the Grenville country estate. On second thoughts she did not find it surprising. Where could anyone go, after abusing a four-year-old child? Only downhill.

Or after standing at the top of these steps watching it happen, as Mrs Grenville had? How could any woman do that? Sonia felt herself trembling again. She had planned to wait in the cellar till Eddie arrived, but she could not stay here another minute.

She took from the canvas bag – the bag that had held the knife – Lois's black doll, her gift from Mrs Atwood, and laid it on the table where Eddie would see it. Let him sit there by himself, where he had been when Lois came in, and let him try to erase the memory of what he had done. If Sonia was there with him, she would only be a distraction. Besides, she had to get out of this place.

She clambered up the steps again and drew a long shaky

breath at finding herself once more out in the sunlight. But she hadn't finished yet. Who was the worst culprit? Eddie, who had thought he wouldn't be seen, no one would know, the child was too young to tell – and possibly too young to remember as she grew up? Or Mrs Grenville, who had stood where Sonia was now standing and looked down on that horrifying scene, and who had blamed Lois for it? 'You slut!' she had screamed, and had boxed Lois's ears, while to Eddie she had only said, 'Get back to your work.'

Sonia clenched her fist around the handle of the now empty canvas bag. She forced herself to move away from the spot. Eddie would surely be here any minute, whistling – would he still whistle? – and carrying his coffee cup. Or was he sitting in the kitchen? Perhaps the new housekeeper let Eddie have his elevenses with her, as Sonia had never done, having summed up Eddie on her first day at work here.

She had given Eddie Barnes one shrewd glance, that first time he came into the kitchen, and had said, before he could kick off his boots and sit down at the table, 'I'm making your coffee. I'll bring it out to you.' Mrs Grenville had been there and she had said nothing, merely looked uncomfortable and busied herself searching through one of the cupboards. Eddie had stood his ground for a few solid minutes, staring her out, and she had met his challenge unflinchingly until he had turned on his heel and gone out.

Every day after that she had left a tray with a mug of coffee and a biscuit on the ledge in the back porch, and he had carried it away down to the cellar which he had made his territory, always leaving the tray.

He never returned the dirty mugs. When she reminded him, he used to say, sneering, 'They're in the cellar, since you're too high and mighty to let me into the kitchen. Come down and fetch them any time you're free, why don't you?'

She used to wait until he had gone out in the car somewhere and then run down the cellar steps and retrieve the mugs, which he had used as ashtrays. Once, he had returned – perhaps to fetch something he had forgotten when he drove off, or perhaps on purpose to catch her out; she didn't know. He had been standing at the top of the steps when she turned to come out, her hands full of grimy coffee mugs, and he had continued to stand there, grinning, not saying a word.

Sonia had not spoken. She had walked steadily up the steps, though quaking inside, and when she reached the top she had turned her shoulder and squeezed her way past him, sideways. She was tensed, ready to throw him off balance if he grabbed hold of her, but he had not touched her, though he had not moved aside either but laughed loudly as she pushed against him to get past. 'There!' he had crowed, when she was free. 'That wasn't so bad, was it? For a start?'

That night she had jammed a chair-back under the handle of her door, and at one o'clock she had heard footsteps in the corridor and had seen the handle move, stealthily at first and then with increasing impatience, up and down. She had crept out of bed and leaned her whole weight against the door. On the other side she could hear Eddie doing the same thing, breathing heavily, but the chair-back had done its job and after a while his footsteps receded down the corridor again.

Neither of these incidents was ever discussed. It had been a silent battle. There was, after all, no injury, no assault, nothing she could complain of to the Grenvilles. Eddie was invariably smiling and polite. The smile was menacing, the politeness contemptuous, and the threat was implicit, never voiced, never translated into action – Sonia saw to that.

She knew, and had known ever since that first moment she had seen him in the kitchen, that he was dangerous; she knew his type – the type that enjoyed threatening women, who made a sport of it. But never for one second had she thought him a danger to Lois. Lois was a child.

She had to move now. Her feet seemed unable to walk away from this spot, but she had to hurry. Eddie must be alone when he faced the evidence of his guilt, and Sonia had to confront Mrs Grenville. If she was at home.

There was no movement behind any of the windows, but that meant nothing. It was a big house. Sonia had a choice of three ways of getting in: through the kitchen, through the front door, or through the side door that led up a stone passageway to the hall. Eddie might be in the kitchen; so might be the new housekeeper, if there was one. If she rang the front doorbell Mrs Grenville would not let her in. The side door was the only choice.

The bottom of the door scraped slightly on the stone. Sonia froze, listening. The house was silent. Her footsteps along the passageway, as quiet as she could make them, still sounded deafening to her frightened ears – for she was frightened. She was out of her territory now, with no right to be here. She was trespassing in her former employer's house. Mrs Grenville would be within her rights to call the police.

Sonia could hear her heart beating and the matching pulse of her blood seemed to fill her ears till she could hear nothing else. She moved out into the hall. She had forgotten how impressive this house was, with its rugs and its hangings and its chandeliers. The Grenvilles were powerful, influential people, secure in the complacency of their wealth. Could anyone win, with people like the Grenvilles as enemies? Could even the truth win?

Sonia turned to run. She was going home. As suddenly as the decision took flesh, Mrs Grenville materialized – there, coming down the stairs. Their eyes met. After the first few seconds, Mrs Grenville's face clouded suspiciously. But in those few instants Sonia saw the spontaneous reaction of the woman who had dismissed her four months ago. Her expression was one of sheer childlike delight.

Chapter Forty-Five

'Sonia!' said Mrs Grenville, making her voice harsh. 'What are you doing here? How did you get in?'

'Where's Eddie?' said Sonia bluntly.

A slow flush spread over Mrs Grenville's face and neck. She came down the stairs towards Sonia. Sonia took a step back, then restrained herself. If she managed not to show fear maybe she would manage not to feel it.

Mrs Grenville stood two steps above Sonia and looked down on her. 'How dare you walk into my house and ask to see Eddie Barnes?' she said haughtily. 'Your private relationships are no concern of mine.'

Sonia moved forward and raised her arm. Only the glint of triumph in Mrs Grenville's eyes stopped her. She would not play into this woman's hands. She looked Mrs Grenville in the eye and said in a level voice, 'Eddie Barnes raped my daughter and you saw it happen.'

'How dare you?' Mrs Grenville repeated but her voice shook and the last word faded into nothing. She tried to look away from Sonia's face but found she could not.

'You called her a slut and you slapped her,' Sonia said. The house was very still, as if holding its breath. Mrs Grenville's face went white.

'It didn't happen like that,' she said.

'There was a witness,' Sonia said. She spoke these words slowly, as if spelling them out.

'There was not,' said Mrs Grenville. 'You're making this up. You're making the whole thing up, you . . .'

'Slut?' Sonia suggested. 'You employed a gardener who couldn't keep his hands off anything in a skirt – even a *four-*

year-old!' she screeched. 'And you call *her* a slut? *A four-year-old?*'

Mrs Grenville took a step back up the stairs, placing herself on a higher level. 'You came here,' she said, raising her voice as well, 'as housekeeper, you and your illegitimate child . . .'

Sonia let out a squawk.

'. . . your illegitimate child,' Mrs Grenville said. 'And my husband and I gave you employment, took you into our household, paid you fair wages, fed you both. Beyond that, we really cannot be held responsible . . .'

'Lois is not an illegitimate child,' Sonia said evenly. 'I am not married, okay, right. But she's a legitimate child – a real one – got it? A child like everyone else's. And you stood and watched her get raped. And you told her it was her fault. And you chucked us out on the street, while Eddie – *Eddie* – you told to get on with his work!'

'What else could I have done?' asked Mrs Grenville. Seeing the answer in Sonia's face, she added, 'I am expecting a visitor at any moment. I don't have to account for myself to you. You have no right to come here and accuse . . .'

As if on cue, the doorbell rang. Mrs Grenville relaxed, moved towards the sound.

'I'm not finished yet,' Sonia said, blocking her. 'You can let your visitor hear this if you want to, Mrs Grenville. You might not be accountable to me, but you are to the law. You were part of a crime against a child, and there was a *legitimate* witness,' she stressed, 'whether you believe it or not.'

Mrs Grenville hesitated. She glanced towards the smaller of her two sitting rooms. 'Go in there,' she said. 'I have to let my visitor in.'

From habit, Sonia obeyed. Mrs Grenville closed the door on her. Sonia cursed herself. The bloody woman would keep her waiting now, while she supped coffee and exchanged pleasantries with her guest in the big sitting room across the hall. Well, she could entertain both her guests at once, and if she found the topic of conversation too nasty for her friend's delicate ears, that was just too . . . The door was locked. Sonia rattled the handle. Mrs Grenville had locked her in.

Sonia decided to climb out of the window and go and find Eddie. It was Eddie she had come here to see. He would have found the doll by now, and would be working out what it meant. He would think of the ugly things first, Sonia knew: he would wonder if he was being blackmailed. But what she wanted from him was uglier still – the truth.

With her fingers on the window catch, Sonia froze. The man from the station was there in the garden, looking in through the window at her from a few yards' distance. He turned away quickly as soon as he found himself noticed. Sonia fled behind a Japanese screen and crouched there, trembling.

Who was he? Police? Were the Grenvilles so influential that no matter what they did they would have the police on their side? Or was he some 'heavy', something far less legal? Had somebody warned Mrs Grenville that Sonia was coming? But who? No one had known.

As she crouched there, ears alert for the slightest sound, her attention was caught by the voices in the hall.

'I do hope you will forgive the short notice, Mrs Grenville, but as I was in the neighbourhood . . . I have been meaning for such ages to call on you. Do forgive . . .'

Gertrude. There was no mistaking that voice. Gertrude was Mrs Grenville's visitor. Of course. That type always stuck together, come hell or high water as they would no doubt say, Sonia thought bitterly. Samuel had suspected what Sonia was up to today; he had phoned Gertrude; Gertrude had phoned Mrs Grenville; between them they had cooked up a plan to catch Sonia here like a rat in a trap with some help from their large-muscled friend patrolling the garden.

'Come into the sitting room, Mrs Gorringer,' Mrs Grenville was saying. 'Will you have some coffee?'

Sonia heard a light tapping on the window. She tucked her head between her knees, covering her face with her hands as Lois did – no, as Lois used to – and prayed that the man would go away, whoever he was. How could Samuel and Gertrude do this to her? What had Mrs Grenville really told Samuel, that time when he phoned to ask her about Sonia? And what had Samuel arranged with her? To give her fair warning if he believed Sonia was about to make life awkward for her and her husband?

'I'll just call the maid,' came Mrs Grenville's voice again, loud and clear, 'to make us some coffee.'

Sonia found she was standing up. She had forgotten that she was not 'the maid'. This place is having a bad effect on me, she thought; the longer I stay here the more I feel like I never went away. I have to get out of here.

She peeped cautiously round the edge of the screen to see if the man in the garden had disappeared, but he was right there, framed in the window, not even pretending not to be watching her. He waved urgently, making sure of attracting her attention. Sonia's mouth set grimly. She strode over to the window. 'What do you want?' she demanded. Mrs Grenville's footsteps receded down the stone corridor, going towards the kitchen in search of 'the maid', whoever she might be.

The man mouthed something.

'Can't hear you,' said Sonia loudly.

He pressed a finger against his lips, warning her to be quiet.

'Sorry,' Sonia said, no more quietly. 'I'm not into this Secret Service stuff. Who the hell are you?'

He gestured at her to open the window. She ignored his signalling. Was he a friend of Eddie's?

He shrugged his shoulders, looked around furtively, then drew out a notepad and scribbled something on it, holding it up to the window for her to see.

'Rory Gorringer,' Sonia read. 'Gertrude's son. Are you locked in?'

She opened the window and climbed out. 'Why didn't you say who you were?' she said irritably.

'I didn't want to be heard,' he said. 'My mother asked me to keep a low profile, wander round the premises a bit, make sure you didn't come to any harm from that gardener bloke.'

'You were at the station,' Sonia accused. 'You were following me.'

'Sort of. I was meeting Gertrude off the next train. Have you seen him yet? Eddie Barnes?'

'No. I've seen Mrs Grenville. She locked me in the room when Gertrude rang the front doorbell.'

'The old cow,' said Rory.

'Listen, if you don't mind me saying so, this isn't really your business,' Sonia said.

'That's exactly what I told my mother,' said Rory. 'Have you ever tried telling Gertrude anything?'

Sonia opened her mouth.

'My advice is don't,' Rory continued, before she could speak. 'She takes no notice. My interference is meant to be twofold: if Mrs G cuts up rough, I'm to use my law degree and quote her a few cases and convictions of similar crimes, and if Barnes cuts up rough I'm to use my weight training to make sure he doesn't do you any damage. Now, I'm sure my mother's quite capable of dealing with Mrs Grenville, in the early coffee-and-gossip stages anyway, so where are we likely to find this Barnes character?'

Sonia opened her mouth again, then decided not to argue. 'In the cellar or in the kitchen,' she said. 'He wasn't in the cellar when I got here. And the boiler's gone out, which is something he never used to let happen.'

Rory pursed his lips. 'Do you think he might have left?'

'Mrs Grenville didn't say so,' said Sonia. 'I asked her where he was.'

'Why would she tell you the truth?' said Rory cheerfully. 'You can't go on what Mrs Grenville says, can you? Not on past form.'

'No.' Sonia stood forlornly. Rory took her by the elbow and moved her along the path a few yards. 'Better stand away from the window, in case she comes searching for you,' he cautioned. 'Come on, let's look around a bit. Case the joint.'

'Won't you get struck off or something for doing this?' Sonia enquired. 'If you're a lawyer?'

He grinned. 'I always fancied myself as a sleuth. Studying law was the nearest I could get to it. Which way's the kitchen?'

'Round the other side,' Sonia said, 'but we'd better go this way or Mrs Grenville might see us from the main sitting room window when she goes back in.'

'Right.'

The kitchen door was ajar. The sound of a radio issued from it. 'The maid' must be a temp from an agency, Sonia reckoned. Mrs Grenville would not have tolerated this volume from a permanent employee, nor from any woman from the village.

Rory tapped Sonia on the arm. 'Wait here,' he mouthed. He walked up to the door and rapped on it boldly. 'Anybody home?' he called.

Sonia saw the door open and shrank back against the wall, hidden by the porch.

'Yes?' said a woman's voice. Not Mrs Grenville's voice. Sonia breathed again.

'Sorry to disturb you,' Rory said. 'Where can I find Eddie Barnes?'

'Who?'

'Eddie Barnes. The gardener. Handyman.'

'Oh, him.' A sniff. 'He's not here.'

'Where might I find him?' Rory persisted.

'Who's asking?' said the woman suspiciously.

'Rory.'

'And who might Rory be?'

Rory took a few steps back from the door, where Sonia could see him, and smiled disarmingly. 'I am,' he said.

A pause. Sonia waited for the rebuff, but the voice, when it came again, sounded warmer. 'He's left. Left here a month or two ago. I don't know exactly. I'm only here temporary-like.'

'Ah. You wouldn't be able to tell me where he might be now, I suppose?' Rory cajoled.

Another sniff. 'Prison, from what they say.'

Sonia caught her breath. Rory looked alert, interested. 'Really?' he said, drawing out the word.

'Look,' the woman said, 'I don't know who you are and it's not for me to say . . .'

'Of course not,' Rory said. 'I quite understand. You have been most helpful. Thank you very much. Of course you mustn't say anything you're not meant to. I wouldn't want to jeopardize your job.'

The sniff came again. 'For what it's worth,' said the sniffer. 'Some job this is!'

'Not much good?' said Rory sympathetically.

'Do this, do that, this goes here, that isn't the way you do this – the woman's a pain in the backside. Never satisfied.'

'I see,' Rory said. 'What did her last servant die of?' He laughed.

'Last load of servants,' the woman corrected. 'There's been a string of temps here. No one stays. *She* says there was a housekeeper here who was bloody perfect. No one can do anything like her precious Sonia did. I don't believe it myself. No one in their right mind would stay here more than a month, at the outside.'

'How long have you been here?' Rory enquired.

'Four weeks.' She gave a short laugh. 'So she won't be seeing much more of me.'

'I don't blame you,' Rory said. 'You never met this Eddie Barnes, then? He left before you got here, I suppose?'

'Thank God he did,' said the woman. 'I must have had a narrow escape there. Never know what you're walking into, in these out-of-the-way places, do you? After this I'm only going to take jobs in town.'

Rory opened his eyes wide. 'What did he do?'

The voice became hushed. 'Raped a girl in the village.'

'No!' Rory said, gratifyingly shocked.

'He did!' the woman said. She sounded thrilled.

'Tell me,' said Rory invitingly.

Another pause. 'Are you a friend of his?'

'No way,' said Rory. 'I was put on to him by a friend of a friend. Business.'

'Oh, well. He won't be doing business with anybody, where

he is. No gardening, at any rate.'

'Prison?' Rory said.

'On remand. Case to be tried next month, from what they say in the village.'

'Well!' Rory exclaimed. He sounded like Gertrude, Sonia thought. 'The case against raping the girl in the village, you mean? Or was there something else he did?'

'That's quite bad enough isn't it?' The woman sounded indignant. 'She was left in a shocking state. She was only a young girl too. Fifteen or sixteen.'

'That is bad,' said Rory soberly. 'And this happened while he was still employed by the Grenvilles, did it?'

'That's right. Mr Grenville was away, seemingly, and the housekeeper had left, and Mrs Grenville says she never heard him – this Barnes bloke – slipping out. It wasn't his night off or anything. He didn't go in the pub that evening, though, so everyone says. Can't remember exactly what I heard now.

'No, that's right,' the woman continued, recollecting herself. 'She was on her way to the pub; that's what it was. Her mum sent her up there with a message for her brothers to come home now before their dad got in from the late shift and gave them a rollicking for being out drinking.

'Anyway, she never got there, poor little sod. Her mum came looking for her and found her in the lane, all of a heap. Half the village heard her screaming and turned out looking for Eddie Barnes. Too late for the girl, of course, but at least they caught him. And by the time the police arrived her brothers and her dad had had such a go at him he was lucky to survive. If you can call it lucky, that is.'

Sonia let out an audible sigh. Rory scraped his feet on the path noisily, hastily. 'Terrible,' he said. 'Terrible. Look, thanks ever so much. I'm sorry to have troubled you for nothing.'

'Not at all.' The woman came right out of the porch. Sonia froze, but she was only looking at Rory. 'You come far?' she enquired, smiling winningly. 'Want a coffee?'

Rory moved off in the opposite direction, away from Sonia. 'Very kind of you,' he said, 'but I have to be going.'

'Sure?' The woman turned to go back, almost bringing herself face to face with Sonia. Rory grabbed her elbow. 'Perhaps a very quick cup,' he said. He steered her into the porch, throwing a swift glance at Sonia over his shoulder. Sonia nodded.

'Won't I get you into trouble with your employer?' Rory said as they disappeared into the kitchen.

'Oh, her,' said the temp. 'She'll be yakking for ages with her visitor. Until they want more coffee, that is.'

Sonia felt a pang of regret for Mrs Grenville's kitchen – Sonia's domain for six months. She doubted that the temps would keep it clean. It was not a bad kitchen, that one. Homely. She sighed. I work for Samuel now, she reminded herself. And his kitchen will be really good, when it's finally done up. And he's certainly easier to work for than Mrs Grenville. Perfect housekeeper, eh? So Mrs Grenville didn't always speak ill of her. And she had been pleased to see her.

Sonia shook herself. What was she thinking? Regretting leaving the Grenvilles? She knew perfectly well Mrs Grenville was only praising her to make the subsequent 'maids' feel uncomfortable. The woman was a tyrant, for God's sake. A criminal, or as near as. Telling a four-year-old child she was to blame for being abused!

But I thought the same, said the voice of Sonia's conscience. I believed it myself. Mrs Grenville's no worse than me. I didn't chuck Lois out, though, Sonia argued with her conscience. I might have believed she was a bad girl, but I never took it out on her, did I?

An unpleasant memory returned, of her hand striking Lois repeatedly, of Gertrude having to hold her back. Gertrude. Sonia felt overwhelmingly tired suddenly. She wanted to go and find Gertrude, fall down at her feet, bury her face in her lap like a small child. She had even suspected Gertrude of plotting with Mrs Grenville to trap her, when Gertrude was only trying to make sure that Sonia came to no harm today – no doubt warned by Samuel, who was a shrewd old gander but also had her interests at heart, she knew now.

How could she have so confused good and bad, she wondered wretchedly, that she had believed Mrs Grenville's judgement of Lois, had doubted the poor child's innocence – her own child – and had had bouts of suspicion about Samuel and Gertrude? Hadn't it been obvious enough that they could be trusted? Even if her own instincts had been so overturned by fear and worry, she should have trusted Lois's. Lois had no hesitation about trusting Samuel and Gertrude. Why hadn't she followed Lois's instincts, if not her own?

But then Lois had trusted Eddie, even when he had . . . Sonia moved, as though in physical pain. She could no longer stand still. This place brought back unbearable memories, or rather – since she had not known what was going on while she was here – memories of the unbearable revelations that Lois, that reliable 'legitimate witness', had made.

Did I really not know? Sonia tormented herself. Did I really never suspect? Was I so afraid of losing the job, my security, that I let Lois run the risk? Did I turn a blind eye?

She ran to the basement area beside the front door, lowered herself under the railing and dropped dangerously into the deep concrete well. There, in the muddiest corner, she found what she was looking for – Lois's abandoned doll, silt-covered and mouldy, its face eaten away by weather and time.

And there, in the dank-smelling area, Mrs Grenville and Gertrude found her when they ran out of the front door, alerted by the sudden screams and howls. Gertrude ran, shouting for Rory. Mrs Grenville stayed, clinging to the railing, staring with agonized eyes as Sonia twisted and turned in the muddy corner, hugging and weeping over the corpse of the rag doll.

Rory fetched the ladder, as Eddie had mutely refused to do a few months before, descended into the area and coaxed her up the ladder in front of him. Mrs Grenville steadied her as she reached the top, shielded her head from the iron railing as she ducked underneath it.

'I'm sorry, Sonia,' she said. 'I'm sorry. I know it wasn't Lois. George said it was best to say nothing, just send you away. I thought Eddie ... if Eddie was dismissed he might come back with a knife or something. If George was away. All of us in our beds, you know. Lois as well.' She burst into tears.

Sonia patted her shoulder vaguely, then pushed her away. 'I know,' she said without interest. She thrust the doll into Mrs Grenville's hands. 'You better bury it,' she said. 'Lois has got a new one.' She walked towards the back of the house.

Gertrude followed her. At the steps of the cellar Sonia hesitated. Tears started to flow again. 'I can't do it!' she wept.

'Do what?' Gertrude asked. 'It's all been done, Sonia. You've done very well, my dear. Come home now, with me.'

'I can't,' Sonia sobbed. 'It's Lois's new doll. I left it down in the cellar for Eddie to find when he had his coffee.'

'Eddie has gone, my dear. Mrs Grenville told me.'

'I know! I know that! I've got to get Lois's doll, but I can't go down there, Gertrude, I can't face it!'

'I'll go,' said Rory, coming up behind them, but Gertrude put out a hand to stop him.

'No,' she said. 'I think Sonia has to do this herself, Rory, or she'll always remain afraid of that place. Come along, Sonia, my dear, we'll go together. Lay the ghosts, once and for all.'

Arm in arm, awkwardly, they sidled down the narrow steps. Sonia was reminded again of having to push her way past Eddie to get out of here. But the bulky form by her side was Gertrude, not Eddie. Eddie was gone. The fire in the furnace was gone too, the grate wide open and bare. Maybe Eddie would be consumed by flames of remorse, or maybe his heart would be cold and barren like this. Either way, it was no longer Sonia's concern.

She picked up the black doll from the table, straightened its pigtails and held it briefly against her chest. Then she accepted Gertrude's arm again and they climbed up the stairs, out of the deserted cellar and into the sunlight.

In silence the three of them walked down the front drive – watched, they knew, by Mrs Grenville concealed behind the curtains of the front sitting room window.

'Back to my house?' Gertrude asked when they reached the

blue Cortina parked in the lane, but Sonia shook her head.

'To the station, please.'

'Sure,' Rory assented.

'You wouldn't like some lunch first?' Gertrude said. 'No?'

'Another time I'd love to see your house,' Sonia said. 'I'll come down on the train and bring Lois, shall I?'

'Do, my dear, do. I shall keep you to that.'

'But now,' Sonia said, 'I have a family to get back to. Thanks for everything, Gertrude. And Rory.'

'My dear, thank *you*. Don't let that old devil Samuel work you too hard, will you?'

They waited with her on the platform where George Grenville had left Sonia and Lois alone in the world. Sitting there flanked by the solid bulk of Rory and Gertrude, holding the small canvas bag containing Lois's black doll and the bars of chocolate Rory had insisted on wresting out of the machine for her, Sonia said, 'Last time I sat here I thought it was the beginning of the end for me and Lois. Now I feel really relieved we got out when we did.'

'I should think so,' said Rory heartily. 'That poor girl in the village could have been you.'

Gertrude shuddered. 'Don't even think it,' she begged.

The rails began to hum and a train nosed its way on to the visible stretch of track, too far away as yet to make any noise. They stood up.

'I might go back and see Mrs Grenville,' said Gertrude. 'I imagine she has few close friends and she'll be an outcast in the village after this. People will associate her with Barnes, as she was his employer.'

'Hardly surprising!' Rory exclaimed. 'She is the one who left Barnes free to rape someone else, by turning a blind eye to what he did to Lois, isn't she? How many friends does the woman deserve to have, Mother?'

'No,' Sonia interrupted him. 'I wish you would go and see her, Gertrude.'

Rory looked from one to the other in amazement. 'I'll never understand women,' he said. 'You were out for that woman's blood a few hours ago – both of you; don't deny it!'

They laughed, slightly sheepishly. The train arrived with so much noise that further conversation was impractical. Sonia hugged them both.

'I'll come and see you at the weekend,' Gertrude promised.

Sonia got into the train and sank into a seat. Gertrude stood with her nose almost pressed to the window pane, waving and blowing kisses, the roses on her hat bobbing enthusiastically. Sonia waved back self-consciously. Her companions in the carriage stared. Rory, hands behind his back, raised an eyebrow at her and she stifled a giggle.

When the train began to pull out of the station, Sonia gave one last wave then did not look back again.

Also by Lion Publishing

Eldred Jones, Lulubelle and the Most High

Clare Nonhebel

'Eldred Jones taught himself to read at the age of five. This would not have qualified him as a child genius, except for three significant facts: Eldred had spent the first five years of his life in an oxygen tent, he had not spoken a single word since birth, and the book he was reading was a medical textbook.'

Winner of the Betty Trask Award and much-acclaimed author of four previous novels, Clare Nonhebel has written an extraordinary tale of three remarkable children. Eldred's parents simply wish he was like ordinary children instead of dabbling in complex mathematics and designing potentially lucrative farm-waste-disposal systems. Lulubelle has outstanding acrobatic skills and wishes her irresponsible mother would behave more like an adult. And Keith just wishes that the surgeons who keep trying to correct his severe physical disabilities would take his opinion seriously.

All three are caught up in a world of adult agendas, and their determination to break free unleashes past evils and buried memories – through which they are intimately linked. This story, with echoes of Roald Dahl and Kate Atkinson, resonates with profound social concerns and is told with a rare eye for the subtle truth about people. It confirms Clare Nonhebel as a writer of great originality, verve and compassion.

ISBN 0 7459 3812 4 (hardback)

With Hearts and Hymns and Voices

Pam Rhodes

'My name is Jan Harding. I'm a Producer at the BBC. I want
to look into the possibility of doing a "Songs of Praise" from
Sandford.' And so a sleepy little Suffolk village springs to life for
a nationwide television broadcast on Palm Sunday. The Outside
Broadcast team moves in and ambitions and emotions in the
village run high, as local people of all ages and talents are drawn
into the television event.

With Hearts and Hymns and Voices is a wonderfully human, fast-
moving story that will make you laugh and cry, as well as give a
fascinating insight into what really goes on behind the scenes of
'Songs of Praise'.

ISBN 0 7459 3701 2 (paperback)

At Home in Mitford

Jan Karon

Mitford is one of those villages you dream of retiring to. It's as pretty as a picture and everyone stops to pass the time of day. But just when the village's loyal rector, Father Tim, is beginning to think he needs a change, life hots up.

A maverick dog the size of a Buick follows him home and won't go away. A hostile boy is thrust into his care. And his attractive new neighbour begins to wear a path to his door, stirring feelings he hasn't felt in years.

Rich with appealing characters, charm and wit, this delightful novel will enchant all, particularly fans of Miss Read and James Herriot.

ISBN 0 7459 3301 7 (paperback)

All Lion books are available from your local
bookshop, or can be ordered direct from Lion
Publishing. For a free catalogue, showing the
complete list of titles available, please contact:

Customer Services Department
Lion Publishing plc
Peter's Way
Sandy Lane West
Oxford OX4 5HG

Tel: (01865) 747550
Fax: (01865) 715152